SAINTS OF BIG HARBOUR

Lynn Coady was nominated for the 1998 Governor
General's Award for her first novel, *Strange Heaven*.
She lives in Vancouver.

ALSO BY LYNN COADY

Strange Heaven
Play the Monster Blind

Lynn Coady

SAINTS OF BIG
HARBOUR

V

VINTAGE

Published by Vintage 2003

2 4 6 8 10 9 7 5 3 1

First published in Great Britain in 2002 by
Jonathan Cape

Vintage
Random House, 20 Vauxhall Bridge Road,
London SW1V 2SA

Random House Australia (Pty) Limited
20 Alfred Street, Milsons Point, Sydney
New South Wales 2061, Australia

Random House New Zealand Limited
18 Poland Road, Glenfield,
Auckland 10, New Zealand

Random House (Pty) Limited
Endulini, 5A Jubilee Road, Parktown 2193,
South Africa

The Random House Group Limited Reg. No. 954009
www.randomhouse.co.uk

A CIP catalogue record for this book
is available from the British Library

ISBN 0 099 44205 1

Papers used by Random House are natural, recyclable
products made from wood grown in sustainable forests.
The manufacturing processes conform to the environ-
mental regulations of the country of origin

Printed and bound in Denmark by
Nørhaven Paperback, Viborg

This book also is for CHARLES

Guy (n.) *(Informal)* A man; a fellow; "a nice guy."

Guys *(Informal)* Persons of either sex.

(British) An effigy of Guy Fawkes paraded through English towns and burned on a bonfire.

A person of odd or grotesque appearance or dress.

A rope, cord or cable that is used to brace or secure something.

v. tr. **guyed, guy-ing, guys**

To ridicule; mock.

To hold firm or steady, to guide.

O that I was where I would be
then should I be where I am not
here I am where I must be
where I would be I cannot
O, diddle-all-the-day,
O, the diddle-all-the-right-fol-day

—FOLK SONG

1982

SKIN

ALL SORTS OF DEALS being made around here. According to Isadore, everything is working out "beautifully" for "everyone," meaning him. You'd think he'd planned on being arrested all along. So he is paroled to my mother for driving the truck not just drunk but without a driver's license or insurance. My mother pays the insurance now that she's got a job in Big Harbour. I drive the truck all around hell and back, chauffeuring the both of them. My mother into town for her job, Isadore into town (once my mother's gone as if she won't know) to the tavern. And what's Isadore's job in this great deal? Babysitting me, apparently. And Louise, who is seventeen and hardly ever around anyway. The judge was delighted, he said. "I'm just delighted at this prospect. What this man needs is the responsibilities of a home and a family. God bless his dear sister for her generosity."

But it was for the truck. She couldn't have taken the job without it.

Here is Isadore's idea of baby-sitting: he wakes up at seven when he smells the bacon I'm frying for breakfast. He staggers out of—whose bedroom? my bedroom—without even brushing his teeth or picking the crumbs out of his eyes and grabs the plate out of my hands just as I'm sitting down. Then he dumps a bottle of corn syrup all over the bacon so it's inedible for anyone except himself, and when I complain, he tells me to make my own. Make my own, like I hadn't just done it. He reeks. To cover up his bed head, he wears a cap that reads, *Wine me, dine me, sixty-nine me!*

"Don't forget to come get me at noon," he says when he's done eating, heading back to bed. So I get to take the truck to school, after dropping my mother off in Big Harbour, but so what.

My lunch hour is spent driving him into town. We stop at the bank first and he gives me money for gas. Isadore always has money these days. When he's not working in the tavern kitchen for Leland, he's getting welfare. When he's not getting welfare, he has his disability pension. This is Isadore's other job, according to the judge. Helping keep the truck gassed up. And paying for some groceries. "Contributing to basic household maintenance," said the judge. But I drop him off at the tavern and God knows when we'll see him again. He never arranges for me to pick him up, but he always ends up back at the house somehow. I get some fast food and then burn it back to school and am always late for first period. My history teacher goes insane every time. I haven't bothered explaining to him about my responsibilities, because I like it to look as though I couldn't give a shit. He always makes a big production about me coming in late, and I kind of enjoy it.

"Ah, Monsieur Boucher graces us with his presence at long last. Applause! Fanfare!" The history teacher is English, from Truro or somewhere, and thinks it's hilarious to call everyone Monsieur this and Mademoiselle that when most of us don't even speak any French. Sometimes when I make my entrance a few of the guys will clap and whistle just to be assholes. It's the only time I ever get any attention. Sometimes I bow.

After school I drive back into Big Harbour to get my mother, which is not so bad because I can hang around the arcade or the mall or somewhere while I wait for it to be five. The irony of this situation is my mother's job. My mother's job is being a housekeeper. She looks after someone else's house and someone else's kids all day while I fry bacon for her alcoholic brother. She works in a big old house, and the kids she looks after are very small and very cute. She loves it. She can't believe her luck, how circumstances came together so perfectly for us—that Isadore would drive into a ditch with his uninsured truck one night and be forced to live with us.

So my life is incredibly boring, driving into town and back. Guys at school think I have it made because I've got a truck, and I get to go into Big Harbour all the time by myself. It is a big joke. It feels like a big joke.

I get up some mornings, my English teacher's lying on the floor. He drinks with Isadore, which is enormously stupid because Isadore has been known to break the limbs of some of the guys he's drunk with. The English teacher doesn't know this, or else he's not concerned. Drunks aren't picky about the company they keep, as long as it's other drunks, people who won't make them feel bad about it. The smell of bacon wakes the English teacher up too, but he bolts to the bathroom instead of going for my plate. He always comes out after about a half hour or so, always smiling, his hair wet and combed back.

"Ah!" he says. "Guy!" Like it's a beautiful day and nothing short of having woken up on my kitchen floor could have made him happier. "How about a lift to school?" So I end up having to chauffeur him around as well. It's a stupid, embarrassing life.

The English teacher has a girl's name—Alison Mason—but he likes to be called Al, for obvious reasons. He is from New York, and everybody says he is a draft dodger and a back-to-the-lander because anyone who would come here from the States always is.

"Are you a draft dodger and a back-to-the-lander?" I ask him one morning when I am pissed off at him for stinking up the truck with his booze fumes and the fact that I am going to have to listen to him talk about *Flowers for Algernon* all third period and the fact that I've just seen him sprawled across the linoleum.

"Back-to-the-lander I would need you to define," replies Alison Mason. "Draft dodger, yes. I answer without hesitation. It was an unjust war."

"I'd love a war," I tell him.

"You wouldn't, Guy."

"Fuckin Hitler!" I yell.

"Well—that was before my time . . ."

"Fuckin Commies!"

"Please don't yell," says Alison. "I had moral objections."

Yes, you strike me as an extremely moral person, I'm thinking. I would one day like to have the balls to say all the great things I think.

But Alison Mason didn't get where he is today by being dense. He sees me smirk at him and grins wide, like a guilty kid. It's a weird expression to see on the face of an English teacher, and I don't like it. He thinks now we are friends.

A lot of the girls at school think Alison Mason is incredibly hot. It's just because he's American. I should take a picture of him some morning at our house.

Girls are insane and for the most part I can't stand the thought of them. The ones at my school anyway. The girls in town are better, obviously. Last year I went to a dance at the vocational school in Big Harbour and it was like going to Disneyland. I didn't know anyone there, except the guys I came with. There was one girl who kept looking at me, and I danced with her three times. She kept yelling in my ear, "You're not from around here, are you? You're not from around here, are you?" because I think saying it made her feel sophisticated but it also made me feel pretty cool, because I realized I could've been from anywhere, instead of just out in the sticks, out in Frog-town. That's what she was thinking too. I could've been from New York for all she knew. Since the music was blasting, she probably never noticed my accent. She went to the bathroom with her gaggle of friends and after that I lost track of her.

They say in a year or so our school is going to be shut down, and we'll all be bussed into Big Harbour every day. I wish it would happen now.

"It only seems fair that I should be able to take the truck out for myself sometimes," I say. We're sitting around the kitchen table like a happy family, it's hilarious. Except me and my mother are playing gin rummy and Louise is nowhere in sight as usual and Isadore is sitting there nursing a bottle of Captain Morgan and looking at my cards and telling me what to do.

"Where would you go?" says my mother.

"I don't know, I'd go to a dance in town or something."

"You have to take me," says Isadore.

"I can't take you to a high school dance!"

"Into town. If he gets to go into town, I get to go into town."

"I'm always taking you into town!"

"That's the deal, *petit*."

"We all have to share, Guy," says my mother, looking down at her cards. "The truck belongs to all of us."

"No it doesn't!" Isadore thunders, appalled. My mother glares up at him. She had to borrow tons in order to pay the insurance. Isadore reaches for his bottle and smiles in a kind, patient sort of way that says, Think what makes you happy. He's younger than my mother but often treats her like a little girl, even if he's the one who can barely feed himself. He heaves himself up from his chair and lumbers towards the couch, leaving me and my mother in peace. I pick up her hand and smell it. I've been doing this since I was a baby and can't shake the habit whenever she's nearby. Vaseline Treatment for Extremely Dry Skin.

I'm going to take Rene Retard Cormier with me. It's pretty ingenious. That way I won't have to go by myself, but I also don't have to worry about everyone in school finding out and trying to scam a ride into Big Harbour with me. Rene Retard is one of those guys who has no friends, so I know he won't be telling anyone. It's not that he's deformed or anything. He just doesn't seem to know how to function around people. He doesn't know the right things to say or do. If you're aware of that, he doesn't bother you, but he can make a certain type of person really pissed off.

Alison Mason is sitting in the living room when I come back from picking up Rene. Isadore informs me that Alison Mason is coming into town with us to kick up his heels on a Friday night. I'm not happy about it. In class today, we just finished *Flowers for Algernon*. I didn't read the book, because we talked about it in class every day, so I always knew what was happening. Apparently, the guy in the book went back to being retarded at the end of it. It's incredibly disappointing, because the whole reason they picked him for the experiment was because he *knew* how retarded he was, and he was *dying* to be normal. And then after he became a genius and went back to being retarded, he knew what it was like to have been smart. So not only is the guy retarded, but he's not even retarded enough not to know exactly what he's missing. I call that a horrible story. The person who wrote that story was a total bastard. And whenever I see Alison Mason, I feel like he's the guy who wrote that book, or at least the closest thing to him. So that's my problem with Alison Mason tonight.

Someone is going to have to ride in the back of the truck, and it's going to have to be Rene, as God knows the drunken adults will have none of it. Rene is too thick to volunteer, so I have to tell him, "Get in the back, Rene." Isadore demands to sit by the window, of course, so Alison Mason's ass is crammed up against mine as Isadore stretches his legs and gets comfortable.

"I didn't know you were friends with Rene Cormier," says Alison Mason in exactly the same voice he uses in the classroom. God knows how Isadore has kept from punching him all this time. "He's not the sort of person I envisaged you with."

Please don't envisage me at all, with anyone, I'm thinking. I drive. This is a moment when I would like to be Rene. Rene has never felt awkward in his life. He wouldn't feel compelled to make chitchat with the English teacher. Of course Isadore has to jump in.

"I woulda visaged him with a girl, first of all," he says. He is always after me about being faggy. "Too bad he wouldn't visage himself that way."

"What do you think I'm going to the fuckin dance for?"

"I figured you takin' your boyfrien' on a date!"

And him spending every night of the week with an English teacher. But I can't say a word.

As we roll into Big Harbour, Isadore yanks off his *sixty-nine me* cap and shakes out his hair, which is quite thick. He wears the hat to tame it down a little. Alison Mason takes a small black comb from the inside of his jacket. God, the two of them. They are going to the same place they go every weekend, where they will see precisely the same faces.

"Thanks very much, Guy," says Alison Mason, climbing out after Isadore.

"You know I hated your book," I tell him.

"My book?"

"That fuckin retard book."

"Oh." He is looking longingly after Isadore, who's shaking his hair again as he saunters through the tavern doors like a fat Clint Eastwood. Then he looks back at me. "You thought it was badly written?"

I can't tell him I didn't actually read it. I didn't want to discuss it with him, I just wanted to insult him and piss him off. "It's just fuckin stupid," I say. I know I sound like an idiot. I sound like Rene. "What happened. The *story.*"

"Oh!" goes Alison, looking more interested. "What was supposed to have happened?"

"He should've just stayed retarded."

"But that's not a story at all, Guy."

"Yah, well life's not supposed to be a story, anyways," I say. I'm not going to win a debate about literature with Alison Mason so I start up the engine and put the truck into reverse, so he'll have to shut the door. Then I hear a thunk, and Rene shouting. I forgot all about him riding in the back.

On the way to the vocational school I make the ridiculous mistake of trying to talk to Rene about the book. I'm all wound up because I know what I said to Alison Mason made no sense. I keep trying to explain myself even though Alison Mason isn't even there anymore.

"I like when the retarded guy goes back to the bakery where they treated him like shit and figures out a way to like . . . do things better, to make more bread or something. He makes them look like idiots. The whole book should've been that way."

"He should've just fuckin ploughed all those guys," goes Rene.

"It wasn't like he got any stronger, he just got smarter."

"He coulda hired someone to do it for him," says Rene.

"Yeah, but he didn't, asshole! I'm talking about what *happened* in the *book!*"

"Everyone hated him anyways," goes Rene. "They hated him when he was stupid, and they hated him when he was smart. So what's the point anyways."

Already Rene is sucking from a bottle of lemon gin, of all things. Somebody told him once that lemon gin was a "panty remover," and he really believes it, like it's been scientifically proven. So he takes lemon gin to all the dances, hoping to meet a girl.

I didn't bring anything to drink because I hate it. I talk and talk and sound like a bigger idiot than usual.

The first person to get me drunk was Isadore, surprise surprise. I was ten or something. I came home after getting into a huge fight with a guy I used to play street hockey with, Darryl something. I used to be best friends with this kid and then got in a huge fight over something stupid and I went home crying. Isadore was there waiting for my mother to get home from work and give him some money. So he sees I'm pissed off and gives me lemonade with vodka in it and for the rest of the afternoon I'm going on and on to Isadore about how much this kid hurt my feelings. I made a real soap opera out of it, I have to admit. Isadore just sat there nodding and drinking and egging me on. So the next day I get up, sick as hell, and Isadore comes over to get still more money from my mother, which she doesn't want to give. Isadore decides to get back at her by telling her how her son's a little faggot who came home crying because he lost his boyfriend. Isadore thinks it's hilarious. He repeats stuff that I said to him in my drunken stupor. "I thought he *carrrred* about *meeeeeee.*" And it didn't end there; he'll bring this story up to this day. I do anything to piss him off and he'll start whining, "I thought he *carrrred* about *meeeee.*" I never hung out with that guy Darryl again. Any other time I would've just forgotten about it and gone to play hockey with him the next day, but because of Isadore, it ended there.

So Rene stands against the wall sneaking sips of lemon gin out of his jacket and playing air guitar, expecting girls are going to start flocking to him any minute. I'm checking out the crowd, trying not to make eye contact with any of the townie boys, and then this familiar voice hollers in my ear, "You're not from around here, are you?"

Her name's Corrine Fortune. We dance five times, including the final ballad, and I get her phone number. Rene is shitting. He drinks all his lemon gin himself and passes out in the back of the truck, later to puke. Of course it's my job to clean it up once Isadore finally notices, even though for all he knows, he could've done it himself. So even though I'm the one sent out with a mop and bucket the next day, I'm singing as I do it, I'm actually singing because I'm thinking I will call up Corrine Fortune and tell her I can come into town to see her, I can take her anywhere she wants to go in the truck. Finally the puke-ridden truck is going to be of some use to me—not just everyone else. I will be able to see her between four and five, when I drive into Big Harbour to pick up my mother, and on the weekends too.

Isadore is pleased with how his evening went as well, because somebody gave him this enormous Canadian flag that they stole from the flagpole at the Legion. He wants to fly it from the roof of our house and keeps trying to convince me to climb up and attach it to the weather vane or something. I tell him I'll do it for ten bucks. When I get up there, it's obvious the thing is far too huge and will probably just flop across the roof and get all tangled rather than flying majestically the way that Isadore wants. But I tie it there anyway, because I want ten bucks, and when I get back on the ground, me and my mother and Isadore all stand in the yard looking up as if to witness the second coming. Louise has even come out of her bedroom to check it out, but takes one look, rolls her eyes, and goes back inside. There's a bit of a breeze and the flag sort of flops to life for a moment, then hangs limp again, as meaningless as can be. But it's good enough for Isadore; he actually salutes. Isadore is quite the patriot.

She is giggly and embarrassed when I call, and there's stupid
music playing in the background, the kind that girls like to listen
to. I tell her to describe her room for me, and she spends an hour
going on about the rows of stuffed animals, books, pictures of her
and all her friends at dances, at the beach, at parties. None of her
family, which I can understand. I'm not planning on putting up a
shrine to Isadore in my room any time soon—one of the few
places I used to be able to get away from him. Now the only place
I can really do that is the truck, when I have it to myself, but it's
Isadore's truck after all, and it always seems to carry his stink. I'm
thinking it would be good to have a picture of Corrine Fortune,
though, so I ask her to bring me one next time I see her in town.
She says she can't meet me between four and five because she
baby-sits after school, so I ask when her free period is. Right after
lunch. I will have to skip history altogether.

Monday, then. Alison Mason doesn't show up for class, so
the principal has to haul ass out of his office, where he is
rumoured to drink and read porn all day long because nobody
ever sees him out of it, and supervise class. Looking none too
pleased, and squinting like he's never seen daylight, he passes
out a work sheet that is supposed to keep us occupied the full
ninety minutes. I feel like writing a letter to Corrine Fortune,
which is stupid, because I'm going to be seeing her in a few
hours. I do it anyway, though.

Dear Corrine,
How you doing? I'm just writing you a letter in class

because I'm bored as fuck. My English teacher didn't show up today, so we are all sitting here doing a work sheet. I've started calling my teacher Algernon, but his real name is Alison, which is not any better. Did you guys study "Flowers for Algernon" in class? Algernon is the name of the mouse in the book. It is too complicated to explain if you haven't read it. Well you must be as bored reading this as I am writing it.

I tear the sheet out of my binder and fold it up and shove it in my pocket. It's not a bad letter, but I don't feel like writing anymore.

The morning lasts a century, until finally it's time for me to head back to the house and pick up Isadore, all dressed up for going to town, wined, dined, and sixty-nined. He has taken a bath at some point, which is a blessing, especially if I end up taking Corrine Fortune for a ride somewhere. He's got a pissed-off type of hangover, though, so we don't talk much. It takes a lot to get Isadore hung over. God knows what he was doing the night before. Most likely the absent Algernon Mason was with him.

The lucky Big Harbour bastards have a mall right beside their school and that's where Corinne and I are supposed to meet, at the pizza place. I'm going to buy her something with the ten bucks I got from the Canadian flag. Through the window, I can see her coming with a gaggle of friends and for a moment think this is going to be a nightmare, but as soon as she sees me she stops, waves, says something to her friends, and they swarm away from her, off toward the arcade.

"You're not from around here, are you?" she says. She thinks it's clever.

"Do all your friends get the same period off?"

"Yah. A lot of them skip."

I ask her if she wants something to eat, but all she wants is a Diet Coke.

"No, get something big. Get a piece of pizza," I say.

"I already ate lunch!"

"We can go to the Dairy Queen and I'll get you a sundae," I say.

"All I want is a Diet Coke."

"Oh, come on." A Diet Coke is nothing. I go up and get it for her anyway, though, and we go for a walk. Pulp trucks keep roaring by and we have to yell at each other to be heard, just like at the dance.

"We have to get together Friday," I tell her.

"What?" she screams.

"*When can we get together Friday?*"

"*I don't know!*"

Three trucks go by, screaming and hollering, one after the other. "I'll just come into town and call you. We can go for a ride."

"You have a car?"

"Truck. You wanna go somewhere now?"

"No. I have to get back to class."

"Why don't you skip? I'm skipping."

"I don't skip," she says, kind of stuck up. "All my friends skip, but I never skip."

"Are you sure you have to baby-sit every day after school?"

"Yah."

"Every single day?"

"Yah."

"Fuck, that *sucks*," I tell her. So much for my plans to see her every day.

Across the street, my mother is wheeling a baby along in a stroller, and holding a bigger child by the hand. Some lady walking in the opposite direction makes them stop so she can get a look at the baby. While the other woman is keeping the baby occupied, my mother bends over to check on the little boy, making sure his jacket is zipped up and all that. Suddenly she picks him up in her arms, just to hug him. She would be pissed to see me out of school.

Corinne gives me her picture just before heading back to class. She's written the date on the back of it, and then it says:

To Guy,
How are you? This is probably the worst picture ever taken of me, but you asked for it! I look like I have a double chin. Well, I guess I should go now!
Your bud,
Corrine F.

PS You're not from around here, are you? Ha ha!

It's actually an amazing picture. She looks better in the picture than she does in real life. I'm going to put it in my wallet and let it just sort of fall open in front of people like Rene and Isadore.

I show it to my mother when I pick her up from work, but I avoid telling her when and where I got it. She doesn't ask any questions, she's just happy to see it, and goes on and on about how pretty Corinne is, how *gorgeous,* and *beautiful.*

"That is exactly the kind of girl I envisaged you with," she tells me.

My whole family walks around using the word "envisaged" now, ever since me and Isadore heard Algernon Mason say it. I do it too. I used it with Corrine Fortune. I told her I had tried to envisage her in her room when she was describing it to me on the phone. And I had.

My mother has a picture too. The people she works for just got a family portrait taken and gave my mother a wallet-size print to carry around with her. She shows it to me when we're stopped at a light. But they just look like any family from anywhere, the kind of picture you see in the window of a camera store or somewhere, but my mother likes looking at the children. The baby is wearing a knitted cap with cat ears, and the boy is in a tartan vest.

"He's a little highlander," says my mother. I don't know what that's supposed to mean. She reaches over to turn down my collar, even though I put it up on purpose, and I can smell her hand cream again. I inhale hard, snorting almost, and she starts laughing at me. It's a nice drive home. It's almost spring outside, and the night is beginning to smell like living things, not just snow.

Algernon Mason is now on some kind of teaching probation for this reason: he came to school Wednesday morning and spent almost twenty minutes trying to open the door of the classroom with his car keys.

We all just stood there in the hall watching him, his Honda key chain dangling in plain view, some weird ukulele-type instrument poking out from underneath his arm, and a file full of marked tests between his teeth. Nobody bothered to tell him he had the wrong keys, because the longer it took for him to figure this out, the less time we would have to spend in class. We're weren't particularly anxious to see the results of the *Flowers for Algernon* test. A couple of the biggest assholes started egging him on, going "Keep trying, sir! Jam it in there, the lock's right sticky." Algernon didn't even notice that the girls were starting to giggle and cluck, and the guys were nearly pissing themselves. Finally he straightened up and took the file out of his mouth, looking blearily around. Of course it was me he focussed in on.

"Guy?" And he held the keys out and walked towards me like he was offering a present.

"They're the wrong keys, sir."

"Wha?"

Frig me if I'd ever heard Algernon Mason use the word "wha."

"Those are your car keys, sir."

Giggles and snorts all around at the stunned look on his face. Down at the keys, up at me. Down at the keys. Up at me. I looked around at some of the faces, and they all tried to catch my eye and smile, like I had planned the whole thing. I was grinning. I couldn't help it.

"Those keys . . . are for *your car*." Like I'm talking to the retarded guy in the book. *"Your. Car."*

"My car?"

"You need your *classroom keys*. Where are the keys to the *classroom*, Algernon?"

Everyone pissed themselves simultaneously. He straightened up at the noise they made and looked around and shoved the keys back into his pocket.

"I seem to have forgotten them," he said, enunciating every word for dear life. "Guy. Would you go to the office and ask for the spare keys?"

"Yes, I will do that," I enunciated back to him. "I'll be back in just . . . one . . . moment."

As I strolled off, someone nudged me. Someone else actually slapped me on the back. The giggles like muttering birds.

When I returned, the classroom was open and Algernon was slouched in his chair with Jimmy Joe Coffin passing back the tests. Algernon plucked a little at his weird ukulele.

"Sorry, Guy," he said. "My other pocket . . ." and plucked a little more.

I took my seat, thinking I'd bring the other keys back later, and Algernon staggered out from behind his desk with his weird ukulele.

"See this?" he said, waving it around. "I got this in Russia. I did research for a while in Leningrad. Regardless, this instrument is called . . ." He held it up. "I forget what it's called. I got it in Georgia."

"I thought you said you got it in Russia!" one of the head assholes shouted.

Algernon just smiled and plucked. All of a sudden, he launched into "Good Night, Irene." He just sat there and sang every verse of the goddamn song, accompanying himself on the weird ukulele.

When it was over, he asked if there were any questions. There weren't.

"Class dismissed."

And he just wandered out the door.

Everyone sat there talking and yukking it up for the rest of the period. They all wanted to talk to me, all the guys who were usually the biggest assholes in class. Suddenly I had potential in their eyes. I could be every bit as much an asshole as they were.

Now it's Friday, and she wants to meet at another dance. Corinne doesn't like to be too far away from her friends at any time, it looks to me. I just need to get her in the truck at some point. Isadore comes with me into town, staring at her picture all the while. I let my wallet fall open on the kitchen table earlier so he would see it, and he picked it up and hasn't put it down since.

So far on the drive into Big Harbour he has told me that Corrine Fortune wears too much eye makeup. That she looks like a slut. That she has a moustache. That she's some kind of rich bitch. That she's playing a joke on me. That she's got no tits to speak of. That she has a double chin. He says all this in a very cheerful, fatherly sort of way. There's a drug store by the bank, and he wants to know if I'd like him to buy me some condoms.

"I already got some."

"He already got some. Well, *mon petit,* I hope you got extra small. You don't want em falling off!"

And he suddenly raises his fist, gives me a charley horse, and wanders off toward the tavern, leaving me doubled over in pain.

I realize it's weird to be going to a dance alone and wonder why I didn't bring Rene. I had this image of me and Corinne Fortune huddled together in a corner the entire night, but as soon as I get to the gym I realize things don't work that way, at least not yet. She has to be on one end of the gym with her own little gang, and I'm supposed to be off somewhere with mine. Every once in a while, we're supposed to come together, dance, then separate again until the next ballad. It's a pile of crap.

I go up to her as soon as she shows up, because I know if I stand around alone for much longer, the townie boys will get me on their radar.

"Hi, Guy! These are my friends!"

"Let's dance."

All of them get a kick out of that. I sound like some sort of thug, but maybe that's good, maybe I seem mysterious. But girls like this laugh at everything. Nothing can be serious. Corrine Fortune laughs also and rolls her eyes.

I keep her on the dance floor for three songs, and then I yell that we should go for a walk or something.

"I can't go!" she hollers back. "My friend is the DJ! He's going to play my favourite song!"

"Well, let's just go and sit in the truck for a while!"

"I don't know when he's going to play it!"

"Ask him!" I yell.

Bad idea. I lose her in the crowd again, just like the first time I ever danced with her. I get so frustrated after twenty minutes or so that I have to go outside and have a smoke. I sit in the truck to do it, otherwise all the guys smoking by the door will wonder who the hell I am and start in. It's nice to sit by myself in the truck, a relief after wading through all the unfamiliar faces, but it's stupid I lost Corinne Fortune again. I don't let myself sit there for long, as much as I'd like to.

Finally I find her huddled in the corner again with one of her friends, who's leaning forward with her head practically between her knees. I try to be nice, and not act all pissed off or anything.

"Did you get to hear your song?" I ask nicely.

"Yah." She stands up and speaks in my ear. "Pam's right sick. I should stay with her."

"I can drive you guys home if you want," although I don't relish cleaning more puke out of the truck.

"No, if she goes home like this, her parents will kill her. She just needs to sit."

"So you're just going to sit?"

"I guess."

So I guess I'm just going to sit as well.

But we can't talk over the music. I just stare straight ahead watching all the strangers dance, while she rubs her friend's back and yells in her ear every once in a while. Finally she turns to me and hollers something.

"What?"

"I said why don't you dance with Tracy?"

"Why don't I dance with you, and Tracy can stay with Pam?"

"Pam's mad at Tracy."

Fuck's sake.

I should have just given up right there but I didn't. I'd been planning how the night was going to go all week, and it killed me to see things getting screwed up. I figured if I just stayed with her long enough, sooner or later we'd be alone in the truck. So I just sat there until midnight, and then I helped her walk her staggering, singing, laughing, crying friend home, who had been mad at Tracy for dancing with some guy and wouldn't stop talking about it, and who, it turned out, lived just around the corner from Corinne Fortune. So there we were standing in front of Corrine Fortune's house and it's going on one o' clock, and her saying how it was time to go in.

I tried to get hold of her, but she was like a fish. She darted forward and gave me a hug, and then darted away before I could get my arms around her. That was Friday night.

Algernon Mason is more or less able to find his way to the couch these days. He spends all his time at our house drinking with Isadore now that he can't teach. When I get up in the morning he's there moaning, once the smell of bacon hits him. My mother doesn't really care for the sight of him first thing, but since she doesn't have to be there during the day, and since he's Isadore's friend, and Isadore contributes to "basic household maintenance," she doesn't say anything. When he comes out to take my breakfast, Isadore likes to torment Algernon. He waves the plate under his nose and Algernon moans some more and tries to bat it away. If Isadore manages to wake Algernon, he'll be pleased, but if he is able to get Algernon bolting to the bathroom with spray coming out from behind his hands, he jumps up and down and applauds himself, pretending to have scored a touchdown.

Then he sits down at the table to dump syrup on my bacon, and he always says the same thing, motioning to the bathroom with his head.

"Glass stomach pussy."

Which means who knows what. They are an odd pair.

Isadore remembers Corinne Fortune and asks me if we had a nice time on the weekend.

"Get your dick wet?"

"Yah," I answer offhand, because there's no other answer to give Isadore. If I said no, I'd be hearing about it to my grave.

He's pleased, and bobs his head up and down. "Told ya she was a slut. Din't I tell ya? You can always tell a slut. Eye makeup."

"Yah," I agree.

"Good boy," he says. It's a very touching moment.

I try to let Corrine Fortune know, as nicely as I can, that I'm pissed off about Friday night. Over the telephone, I say we should do something by ourselves next time.

"Yah," she goes. "But what can we do? There's nothing to do." She's listening to her horrible music, some guy singing with a really, really high voice. It's almost too loud to talk over.

"Let's just go for a drive."

"That's so *boring*," she says.

"Yah, but we can drive somewhere nice and just park."

"We could go get a pizza," she says, like she hasn't heard me.

"Yah, well. Let's do that too."

"But I would want to meet up with my friends at some point."

The music is grating on me, the guy with his voice going higher and higher. "What the hell are you listening to?" I say. She tells me the name of the band, someone I've never heard of.

"Well, no offense," I tell her, "but it sounds really fucking stupid."

"They're from Germany," she says. "It's an import."

"Well, big fuckin tickle."

"I gotta go," she says.

Everyone at school has heard that Algernon Mason is practically living at my house, and they come up to me and ask me about him. I've never been so in demand. I tell them everything they want to know, about his sleeping on the floor, the couch, the moaning, the races to the bathroom. Sometimes I even make things up at Algernon's expense. Everyone in school calls him Algernon now, too.

Sitting at the table in the evenings playing gin rummy with me and my mother and drinking with Isadore, Algernon sometimes forgets himself and starts talking to me like a teacher again. Isadore bragged to him for days about how I was screwing this townie girl raw, that's exactly how he put it, and Algernon chooses the moment when my mother is sitting across the table from me and I've got her hand pressed against my face, to start talking about contraception, and taking responsibility for your actions. I just smirk at him, but my mother likes the sound of his words and starts listening, and nodding. I've seen her look that way in church, whenever the priest is on about something of particular interest to her, like what heaven will be like, or Judgement Day.

"You should listen to your teacher, Guy," she says.

"He's not my teacher anymore," I announce. "He's on probation for trying to open the classroom door with his car keys and playing "Good Night Irene" on a Russian ukulele." This shuts everyone up except for Isadore, who slams his bottle down on the table and laughs so hard he retches.

"I guess he tol' you!" Isadore shouts at Algernon, and he reaches across the table and gives him an enormous shove. Algernon is knocked right out of his chair and sits there blinking on the kitchen floor, like he's just woken up from some great dream and realizes he'll never get back to sleep. The look on his face. Isadore catches my eye and we sit there laughing our asses off for what seems like hours, my mother shaking her head and rolling her eyes. Algernon sits there for a while before moving towards the couch.

I skip history again. Last time I did it, the history teacher waggled his eyebrows at me in the hall later that day, and whenever I do show up in class, he goes on about how touched he is that I even bothered.

Corinne Fortune has to study for most of her free period, but said she'd meet me in front of the school for a little while. I stop at the D.Q. and pick up a Diet Coke for her on the way, because it's the only thing I know she likes. When I get there, she and her friends are on the pavement in front of the school, sitting on their jackets and trying to get tans from the miserly bit of spring sun. I park the truck up on the hill, and walk towards her slowly, expecting at any moment she'll give the word to her friends and they'll take off like a flock of yelled-at birds. But she doesn't. So there I am standing in front of the bunch of them, holding a Diet Coke. At the last moment I take a sip of it, pretending I bought it for myself. They're all smiling up at me with their sunny, girl faces. I don't think I've been in the company of this many girls at once in my life. I should be feeling great.

"Hi Guy," she goes. "Can I have a sip of your Coke?"

"Yah." I hand it down to her. She sucks back the smallest possible amount a person could drink, and hands it back to me.

"Take more than that, for Christ's sake," I blurt.

"No thanks."

They're just all looking up at me, so I ask Corrine, for the hundredth time, if I can take her for a ride somewhere. She looks at her watch.

"I should study." I'm just about to sit down alongside them when she adds that they should all probably be in the library, and the friends start gathering up their jackets.

Pam says, "Thanks for helping me get home the other night," and pokes me on the arm before they go.

I finish the Coke standing there by myself watching the sky cloud over and spring go away, and then I go into the school to find the library. I can't believe the school—it's enormous. It is made practically all of glass, so the cloudy grey light fills the whole place—it's like I'm still outside. The library has glass walls, and I can see her in there, at a table with her friends. They've got books open in front of them, but they don't look like they're studying at all. Pam sees me coming first, and sort of smiles. Pam, I think, must be nice when she's not barfing drunk. I remember her crying the night of the dance because some girl was dancing with some guy she liked. She's not exactly fat, but she's nowhere near thin. Pam is the kind of girl other girls feel relaxed and good about themselves around.

Pam glances at Corrine Fortune and looks at me again, and I sort of nod at Pam. Very gently, she taps Corrine on the arm. Corrine sees me and jumps up. She comes flying through the library door, and we stand in the hall facing each other, alone, at last.

"Hi! What's wrong?" Like there must be some kind of emergency for me to have followed her like this.

"Jesus fuck . . ." I begin. How to Impress Girls, by Guy Boucher. Begin every sentence you can with "Jesus fuck."

"What?" she says.

"You're fucking me around."

"No I'm not!"

"I came to *see* you," I say. *I thought he carrrred about meeee,* whines Isadore in my head. And then I hate her.

"Guy, it's just that," she says, "I like somebody else, actually." She's blushing and looking around because she knows the people in the library can see us. She has to get rid of me as soon as possible. "I just want to be friends."

"Who?"

"He's just a guy from the city."

"What's his name?"

"Oh God, you don't know him."

"Does he have a truck?"

"No."

"Car?"

"No."

"You won't have any fun with him. You won't be able to do anything."

"We can do lots of things . . ."

"I can take you places . . . I know you, I know you like to do things. I can drive you around."

"We don't have anything in common."

"I've got a truck."

She grins suddenly, and I realize it's because of the word "truck." It's become a joke for her. Me, and the word "truck." How many times I use it.

I walk all over town until I'm pretty sure I've missed my second afternoon period as well, which was chemistry. I don't know why they don't bus us into Big Harbour. There are no more than a hundred or so kids in my own school. It makes more sense. They have a football field here, and an indoor pool. I watched a swimming lesson through the glass walls.

Me and my mother could get an apartment in town, but I know she wouldn't want to leave the house in Isadore's hands. They both grew up in that house. Left to him it would collapse in a month, reeking of booze, cigarettes, the products of Algernon

Mason's glass stomach, and Isadore's own personal stink. Just like the truck. If we moved into Big Harbour, we wouldn't need the truck. We wouldn't need Isadore.

I'm in the middle of thinking this when my mother comes running down the street, carrying the pudgy kid she baby-sits, and hollering to beat hell. I didn't even realize I was shuffling right past the house where she works, kicking an old, rotten chestnut, taking my time. The baby sucks on his fist and goggles at me, and my mother wants to know what in God's name I'm doing out of school. Behind her, the other little kid is approaching, and he's pulling by a string some kind of duck on wheels.

For some reason, the duck causes me to freak out. I go, What the fuck does she care what I'm doing out of school, she doesn't care about anything but her goddamn job, she doesn't care about me or anything that I might be doing.

My mother gets that Algernon Mason look, like someone has just pushed her out of her chair and onto the floor. "Guy . . ." she says.

And what do you know, I am screaming at my mother, the baby looking puzzled and the kid with the duck actually laughing, probably because I am jumping up and down and waving my arms. I tell her she's a bad mother and she doesn't care about me. Isadore in my brain says, *I thought he carrrred about meeee.* All she cares about is her job. She cares more about her fat alcoholic brother than she does about me. She cares more about her fat alcoholic brother's truck than she does about me. I know that I am throwing a tantrum. I know people are looking at me as they drive by in their cars, but what does it matter?

I'm not from around here, am I? I let myself scream and yell. I let spit fly out of my mouth, and I know I have my mother's complete attention, and knowing that, I don't want to stop. I am on the verge of throwing myself to the sidewalk and kicking my legs in the air. She keeps reaching her free hand towards my face and then pulling it away again. I let her do it a few more times, I even slap it away a couple of times. I'm thinking: *She* wants to touch *me*. *She* wants to touch *me*. When I'm finally satisfied, when I finally believe it, I stop yelling and I yank her hand towards my face and she almost falls forward, baby and all. But she gets her balance and we stand like that. The kid with the duck down by my feet, trying to untie my shoelace. Vaseline Treatment for Extremely Dry Skin.

SPRING

ThE CORINNE
FORTUNE STORY

ONE FAT MORNING a fat fat got out of fat and looked out the fat. The fat was in the sky and all around the world was fat. Her fat mother called for her to come downstairs and have fat because she didn't want to be late for fat. Fat she went down the stairs, fat, fat, fat. Her fat father asked her why she always had to be so fat fucking late for fat fucking breakfast every fat fucking day. Except he only said fucking the one fat time, but it echoed fatly in her fat fucking head. She was lazy, fat, and disrespectful, fat, in his opinion, fat. Where the fat disrespect came from was beyond fat her.

Her father needed sympathy and support because he was a man without a job and he hadn't had a drink in a big fat twenty-five years. Pam hadn't even known he was such an alcoholic until he lost his job and kept going on and on about how he wanted nothing more than to curl up on the couch with a big fat bottle of Captain Morgan. He had been ten years away from a retirement package.

Pam's mother would take her for drives every evening after dinner. Just driving around in the night. And her mother would talk about the old days before Pam was born, and how hard they were, and that was how Pam learned about the way her father used to drink. He was a big fat alcoholic and nobody had ever bothered to tell her until now.

So breakfast was a nightmare. Mr. Cormorant would sit at the table fully dressed with exactly nowhere to go but the Liquor Commission, nothing to do but drink. It was like he was waiting for it to be time. Nobody seemed to be aware of this except Pam. A big fat fortune-teller was she, a big pink magic eight ball.

"Wipe the fat out of your eyes."

Pam rubs her fat face. The yellow tinge to everything, like urine-scented fog, lifts, lightens somewhat.

"There's still some in there," persists her mother.

"Fat?" says Pam.

"What?" says her mother. "Sleep. In your eyes. You're not even awake!"

"You might clean yourself up a little before you come to the table," says her father, thin, dapper, in a white dress shirt buttoned at the cuffs. It took around a month before he stopped bothering with the tie, how long will it take with the dress shirts, wonders Pam. He is only going to get egg on them. He drains his coffee, managerial. It's been his demeanour for twenty years.

"But I was late."

"Whose fault is fat?"

"I didn't sleep well."

"And again I ask: Whose fault is that? Do you think you're going to be able to stay up till all hours and walk around with sleep in your eyes in the real world?"

He never used to be like this. He would be gone by now, in the car and off to the mill. Not a word about the real world. The world used to be just the world, neither real nor unreal. He trusted the world, before this—family, car, job. He trusted everything. Now he doesn't trust anything. He looks at Pam with suspicion, like she's hiding booze under all that fat, tempting him with it. Wanting him to fall off the wagon. She is in league with the rest of the world, the real world, dying for him to drink.

Two blobby yellow eyes stare up at Pam and her father. Facts shrouded in egg. Pam's fried egg tells her she is fat, just like it does every morning. But Mr. Cormorant's egg has something new to say to everyone. His says that he is a drunk. Without having even touched a drop, as yet, at seven-thirty on a Monday morning. Drunk is the opposite of employed, Pam sees.

"Don't be smart!" snaps her father.

"I didn't say anything," Pamela protests.

"But I could see you being smart." He folds his napkin and puts it on his plate. He looks around for his job.

Pam Cormorant and Corrine Fortune are best friends and always have been. Even in nursery school, no one was allowed to try and be their friend. Other people could play with them, but had to keep their distance. Many were not good at this. Once, when they were scrambling to their seats for cookies and juice, Pam took her usual chair right by the wall so that no one could sit beside her except for Corrine, but Ann Gillis dove into the seat instead. Pam stared at her.

"Hi, Pam!" said Ann. "I sat beside you because we're best friends."

Pam almost started laughing at Ann's presumption. From the corner of her eye she could see that Corrine was coming up behind Ann slowly. Pam felt excitement, nestling deep in her bowels.

"You're going to get it, Ann," she whispered.

Ann's smile widened doubtfully. "What?"

"I hate you, Ann," said Pam, evil and gleeful, bowels atingle. "I don't want to be your friend."

Ann looked astonished. Then she looked down at herself, and up again at Pam.

"Why?"

Corrine was standing directly behind Ann now, but she had no idea. Ann was stupid. Pam had to keep herself from bouncing up and down in her seat.

"Because..." said Pam. And at last she allowed herself to look directly up at Corrine, into her eyes, and Corrine was grinning back at her.

Before Ann could turn around Corrine had her lips pressed against her ear. "BECAUSE SHE ALREADY HAS A BEST FRIEND!!" she was screaming.

That was when they were four years old. That was when they were walking, talking babies. But it set the protocols, and they all had been operating accordingly ever since.

For example: Pam Cormorant and Corrine Fortune are best friends. They were the ones who decided that. They couldn't even remember when they decided it, they just remembered knowing it, always. Their mothers told them they met one Sunday afternoon at a church fair. Both had been wearing white tights and thought they were like twins. They went crawling around together underneath all the tables, blackening their knees. It must have been agreed upon then. They were scarcely two years old.

Even after figuring out they were not actually much alike, there was still no getting around it. Pam became fat and peripheral as Corrine grew indisputably more present. She was social and athletic and Pam was introverted and (that horrible, horrible term) bookish. There was no denying Pam was bookish. It wasn't just that she liked to read books, it was that she was *like* a book. Square. Flat. Loathed for whatever it was people imagined she contained. Certainly nothing fun, nothing exciting.

Corrine's hair plumped up and she developed what people called "a body." Apparently what Pam had developed was not considered a body. Guys started accompanying Corrine and Pam when they walked down Cosgrove Street to the store to buy Freezies. They were often stupid guys, or mean guys, or both, and they would make jokes about Pam, and Pam would try to make jokes in return, and Corrine would laugh like they were all having a good time.

But both knew there was no getting out of the deal. They were just going to have to adjust things a little bit. Pam became what she thought of as an afternoon friend. They were friends in the afternoons. They went over to each other's houses, and Corrine would tell Pam what she had done at night with her other friends. Pam would go to Corrine's basketball games and cheer for her, and afterwards they would sit in the bleachers together. At school they always met between classes, and in the classes they shared, they sat right beside each other, just like in kindergarten. Pam knew she was lucky, strolling around the halls with Corrine and Tracy Bezanson and Troy from Troy and Trina Wadden. So important and talked about were Corrine's all-day friends that people actually referred to them as the Three Ts. How could Pam ever have hoped to enter into such a pantheon? How without her bit part in this drama, the Corrine Fortune Story, otherwise known as life, the world?

Poor old Ann Gillis was locked in for life, after that, although you wouldn't have thought so to look at her back then. She seemed, at first, like she might have turned out like Corrine, or maybe Tracy. She had bouncing blondish ringlets and was dressed with great care, as though her mother—if not Ann herself—knew exactly what was at stake these first few days of sending her daughter out into the world. Spotless white tights.

But Ann didn't get it. Pam saw it in her face when she sat down in Corrine's chair, professing herself Pam's best friend, smiling and trusting. Ann didn't know not to be like that, that you had to be careful. *You're going to get it, Ann,* Pam had predicted. And ever since, Ann was the type to always be looking over her shoulder, jumping at shadows, speaking fast and then slow, angry and then afraid, as if she doubted every word coming out of her mouth but couldn't help herself.

I hate you, Ann. And Ann had looked down at herself, then, probably for the first time. Thinking: *Hated.*

For Pam, it was her first shame, like the apple for Eve. The sight of Ann gave her pangs, year after year. Ann peeing her pants in class: *My fault.* Ann going behind the train station with boys. Ann going through her punk rock phase when everyone else was listening to Top Forty. Shedding a sudden thirty pounds. Going Goth in grade nine, dating a twenty-eight-year-old from the Springdale Apartments who sold hash. Pam would peer at Ann from the golden aureole created by Corrine and the Three Ts. Skeletal with her dyed black hair and her old man's coat dragging in the dirt and cigarette butts. Pam would peer at Ann and read her mind.

Hated.

tOURNAMENT

THOUGH PRACTICALLY the only thing to do on the weekend was to head up to the rink and watch the kids play hockey, for several years after coming back from Toronto, Isadore managed to avoid it. He liked to tell the men in the tavern that once an individual has parked his derriere in the front rows of Maple Leaf Gardens while The Rocket sails one in as pretty as you please, the sight of a bunch of fourteen-year-olds falling on their asses every five minutes loses something in the offering. Some of the men agreed this was probably the case, but others argued that Isadore had it all wrong, that the team had some good god-damn players and there was no telling where one or two of them might end up. Often, these were men with sons and grandsons and nephews, which Isadore was well aware of.

When the games from Toronto came on the TV above the bar, Isadore would wander over to the pool tables to torment whoever was playing. Men would call from the bar, Where are you going, here's your beloved Leafs in your almighty sanctified Maple Leaf Gardens, right up there on the TV, you're going to miss it, and Isadore would call over his shoulder, Ach, boys. TV doesn't even come near to approaching it. Isadore didn't even look up when the men watching the game would shout and jump and raise their fists at whatever was going on. He wouldn't even come over to see when there was a fight.

When the games were on at the rink, and the tavern was deserted, Isadore would sit by himself at the bar with a newspaper, reading about boxing. Before crashing his truck, the tavern was almost his home. Leland MacPhedron was an old friend, and let Isadore work as a cook in the kitchen "on call"—which meant whenever he felt like it, or whenever he needed extra money. Sometimes months would go by, however, when Isadore showed up every day at ten A.M. and stayed until late, just like any other working man. But then he would go on a bender and disappear for a time, which Leland affected not to notice.

There was a period before his accident, however, when Isadore scarcely ever bothered taking off his cook's whites. He simply felt more like working than drinking during this time. Men took to calling him "Quincy," after some TV show about a doctor. It had something to do with how he would walk around in his apron, splattered with hamburger juice and grease.

Twenty years was a long time for someone like Isadore to deprive himself of hockey, but he did what he could to keep the need at bay. He snuck up to Halifax to see "grown-ups" play from time to time, and a couple of times even took the train up to Montreal to watch the Habs. The rest of the time he read about the games in the newspaper, because imagining them in his mind was preferable to the pain of television, squinting at some miserable box, knowing he had been there once, but he wasn't anymore.

Isadore disapproved of television in general—how it had crept into everybody's lives and taken over so completely in the past twenty or so years. Now it was as if people spoke in some kind of code. He hated when the men called him Quincy, because it meant nothing to him. They called Leland, the owner of both the tavern and restaurant, "Boss Hogg," after some other TV character, and this incensed Isadore to no end. If there were going to be jokes, he felt, everyone should be able to understand them, not just people who understood TV. He didn't own one himself, and didn't plan to. When his sister got one "for the kids," as she claimed, he told her it would make the children lazy and stupid and turn her and her daughter into sluts. Whenever he went over for dinner, the television was turned off and covered with a quilt. Marianne would put pictures and knickknacks on top of it to make it less obtrusive. Otherwise Isadore would bellow and break things.

He would sit in his sister's house some evenings and think about television and miss his father more than he usually did. Her house had been his father's house, and Emile had hated television as well. He had been a pious man and always knew right from wrong, and they would sit in the kitchen together when Isadore was young and drink tea so strong you could skate on it and bemoan the direction the world was going in. Isadore had always told himself he had returned home from Toronto to be with his father, and he was glad because the old man had only lived a few more years. But sometimes when Isadore was frying meat in the restaurant or walking home to his apartment in a snowstorm or sitting in his sister's kitchen by himself because her children had no respect for him, he wondered where he was supposed to get his sense of what was what without his father there to let him know.

He was complaining one night after dinner to Marianne and young Louise about what poor shape the world was in, and how the two of them were prime examples. He said when he was a youngster, the very kitchen they were sitting in was sparkling clean day in and day out, not a thing out of place. People took pride in their surroundings, he told them. Their mother had worked herself to death every day of her life and not once raised her voice in complaint, he said to Marianne. "Remember?" he asked his sister.

Marianne got up and started gathering dishes. "That's why she moved back to Cheticamp as soon as Daddy died. And do you hear me complaining?" she said. "When do I ever complain about anything?"

"Mamere never contradicts me either," Isadore added.

"Isadore, if you don't like how I keep house, you don't have to stay."

Of course they both knew that he did have to stay, for the time being.

"And she was never sullen," reflected Isadore. "If you ask me, the worst thing a woman can be these days is sullen. You see it everywhere. It's not attractive. If you think it's attractive, it's not." He eyed Louise at this point, who was as sullen a child as any. She never looked him in the eye, and it was just as well, because if the girl ever looked him in the eye with such a sullen face, he imagined he would have to smack it. Isadore despaired for his family, and he wished for the time when his father was alive. His mother had immediately moved back into her own parents' tiny house after he died, as if her sixty years of marriage were some kind of little vacation she was returning from. Isadore remembered his father being able to draw good will out of everyone around him. The kitchen was brighter then, Marianne's children were younger and laughed all the time, and Isadore didn't walk around feeling this blank weight like he was failing to keep everyone young and happy the way his father had been able to do. Like he couldn't stop the world from getting worse, the way his father always feared it would.

At that point, with the girl sullen and Marianne trying to annoy him with the clatter of plates, Guy came hobbling out of the bedroom in a Leafs jersey that Isadore had brought from Toronto years ago. The boy was attempting to balance himself in a new pair of Bauer skates, Isadore saw, with skate guards on them—just stalking around the living room as if he were a player in the locker room waiting for "O Canada" to start.

"What's with the skates?" shouted Isadore, because he had an irrational feeling of being made fun of. The boy glanced up in fear.

"They're new," said his mother.

"They're for hockey," said Guy simultaneously.

"I didn't think they were for doing figure eights out on the pond," said Isadore.

"Tell Isadore your news," Marianne urged the boy, who looked down at his teetering feet.

Isadore waited a couple of indulgent moments before shouting, "Well, what's the goddamn news?"

"He's been playing on the team in Big Harbour," said Marianne.

"I'm on the team," said the boy simultaneously.

Isadore took a good look at his nephew for the first time in years and saw he was actually a teenager. He was of a good height, a little skinny, but not a bad build overall. The only thing that concerned Isadore was his nephew's face. It was too young, so young it had kept Isadore from noticing the boy had even grown all these years. Soft and white with enormous, babylike eyes. It was not a player's face.

"We better get to work," he said.

The men teased him at first. "What to my wondering eyes do appear!" said Leland McPhedron the first time Isadore materialized in the bleachers, an enormous white blot among the dull mass of sweaters and toques. Leland actually broadcast these words over the radio and out into the rink, as he was announcing the game for the local station. Often he gave as much commentary on what was going on in the stands as on the ice, and since he was Leland, nobody said a word about it. Before the game, they always would turn on the loudspeaker and have Leland broadcast to the arena. He would crack wise for a few moments and generally keep the spectators in stitches. One of Leland's most famous jokes, Isadore remembered, was during the playoffs when, after solemnly introducing the players and asking everybody to rise for the National Anthem, Leland waited a couple of beats and, instead of turning on the recording, started to belt it out himself.

"If it isn't the man in white, ladies and gentlemen, our own Doctor Quincy, fresh from the morgue!" announced Leland as people were settling into their seats. "Well, you know we're in for some fine hockey tonight, lords and ladies, if jolly old Saint Isadore has lifted his twenty-year moratorium!"

A couple of people turned around to grin at him, but Isadore just sat and watched the ice, uncomfortable and euphoric at the same time. Saint Isadore was another of his nicknames, because of the white. He didn't mind it so much. A small bottle of rum was tucked in his jacket pocket and he held a cup of black coffee. Throughout the game, he took sips of coffee and replaced the sips with equal amounts of rum. His cup stayed full that way. Isadore took a sip and then replaced it and watched as the home team came out for some practice shots. The games had been going on for a while, which frustrated Isadore. It would have been better if he had gotten hold of Guy well in advance, before the imbecile coach, Dave Fifield, could teach him how to do everything wrong. Isadore scanned the rink for his nephew and couldn't identify him at first. They all had their helmets on already—Guy had said they weren't permitted anywhere near the ice without them—demonstrating to Isadore how completely out of whack Fifield's priorities were. Half the boys didn't even know how to hold their sticks from the look of them.

Isadore took another sip and then replaced it. The men on either side of him were engaged in the same sort of ritual—reaching quietly into jackets and back pockets. Taking off their gloves to uncap and then putting them back on again once they were done sipping. A man near the front shouted at a boy on the ice to hold his goddamn stick right, the other team would knock it the fuck out of his hands the moment they got out there. A little chill passed through Isadore, despite the warmth of his drink. Not once in the past fifteen years had he felt so at home. Not even in his father's house.

Guy, he realized, was the one who skated with his head down. He was not a bad skater, a beautiful skater, really, but he had a timid demeanour that could get him into trouble. Something about Guy was begging to be shoved into the boards. Isadore took a sip of his coffee, replaced it, and cleared his throat.

"Guy," he said. It felt strange, speaking the boy's name. Isadore had never called him anything but *petit*.

The kid hadn't heard him anyway. Isadore waited for him to skate around again, and then straightened up.

"Guy!" he bellowed.

Guy stopped skating and looked wildly around. One of his teammates bashed into him and the two boys went spinning on their asses.

When Guy came around the third time, he slowed down a little and raised his head. Isadore stood, huge and white.

"Guy!"

The boy's mouth went slack and he skated closer to the boards.

Close your mouth, Isadore wanted to say. With the wide eyes and open mouth, there was something about Guy's face that made Isadore want to reach down and cover it with his hands. Instead he yelled, "Keep your head up, uh?"

"Wha?" Guy yelled back, mouth going even wider.

"Keep your head up! Look where you're going!" Isadore wanted to tell him he looked like he was scared, the way he was skating, but he couldn't with the men on every side. It would have to wait until Isadore could get him alone.

Guy got the puck a couple of times during the game and Isadore felt the rush of excitement that was more familiar to him than his own hands. Both times, however, a quick little bastard from the other team was able to steal it right from underneath Guy's nose. Why? Because Guy refused to lift his eyes from the puck once he got it. He would not look up to see what was coming. The fury and frustration was familiar to Isadore as well, and just as unbearable as the surging hope, but at least, he thought, he was going to be able to do something about it. It was dawning on Isadore that this new experience of hockey could be the greatest of his life. For the first time since he had played as a teenager, he would have some measure of control over the outcome.

Isadore began staying home and having dinner with the family more often. He left Louise alone about her hair and how strange and slutty she was looking as she grew older, and complimented his sister on her cooking instead. At the table he told Guy what he was doing wrong on the ice and afterwards they put on their parkas and went out into the yard so Isadore could show Guy what he was talking about. Isadore began to notice that Guy's keeping his head down was not specific to hockey, but was characteristic of everything Guy did, so Isadore began a campaign to change it. At the dinner table, whenever he asked the boy a question and Guy would start to answer into his plate, Isadore would reach over and, with the heel of his hand, shove at the boy's forehead until Guy was looking him in the eye. Isadore instructed Marianne not to let him get away with it either, although Isadore didn't trust her to be firm. Eventually he started taking Guy with him on errands, or into the kitchen at the restaurant. Isadore would make Guy steak sandwiches with fried onions and insist he look straight at Isadore the whole time he ate. Isadore would tell him stories about Toronto and the games he saw, and he would inform Guy that if he didn't stop staring at that foolish box at his mother's house his eyes would go bad and he wouldn't even be able to see the puck in front of him, let alone what was going on around him, which he never noticed anyway because he wouldn't learn how to keep his goddamn head up.

Sometimes Isadore took Guy into the bar and showed him to Leland and the men. Isadore bought him a beer one time, but Guy wouldn't touch it, so Isadore told him he could just die of thirst if that was how he was going to be. Isadore thought Guy might feel guilty then and take a sip, but the boy just sat there, preparing to die of thirst. Normally when somebody snubbed Isadore's generosity, he would turn away and ignore him for the rest of his life, but he understood Guy was young and had a lot to learn, so he decided to give him a second chance.

"Got something against beer?" Isadore said after ten minutes of the silent treatment.

"I just don't drink," Guy replied imperiously.

Isadore snorted. "Oh, I see. How long ya been on the wagon?"

"Six years," the boy answered promptly.

"Ya do the twelve-step and whatnot?" Isadore teased, annoyed. "Give yourself over to a higher power and all that shit?"

Guy looked straight ahead, remembering to keep his chin up. "I just remember what happened last time," he said.

"Last time?" Isadore hooted.

Guy glanced at him quickly, and Isadore realized Guy expected him to know what he was talking about.

"What happened last time?" Isadore asked after a moment or two of debating whether he actually wanted to know.

"You got me drunk. You got me *sick*," said Guy, lowering his head involuntarily.

"When was this?" said Isadore.

"Six years ago," repeated Guy.

"Huh." Isadore hid his surprise. He scarcely had any recollection of interacting with his nephew at all before the past few months. Otherwise, his only vivid memory of Guy was a red baby in a long white gown christened *Guy Sebastien* and screaming from the water that had rolled into his eyes. Isadore was Guy's godfather. "How old would you have been then?"

"Ten," said Guy.

Isadore thought for a second. He knew Guy had had a birthday not long before Isadore crashed the truck and moved in. The boy was just old enough to drive.

"You probably drank it too fast," he finally said. "You probably didn't have anything to eat. You can't drink without something in your stomach to absorb it."

"Yeah, well, I just don't drink anymore," said Guy.

Realizing his nephew had let his chin sink into his chest for the last part of their conversation, Isadore got up off his stool and stood behind Guy, pushing his hands into either side of Guy's head and forcing him to look straight into the mirror behind the bar. From this perspective, Guy appeared to be growing out of Isadore's chest.

"I'm gonna get some kind of harness," said Isadore recklessly, tucking Guy's head under his armpit while he pretended to be trussing it. "And I'm gonna tie one end around your head, and I don't know *what* I'm gonna do with the other end. I'm gonna have to keep hold of it myself, I suppose, and give it a good goddamn yank every time that stalk of yours starts wilting."

They looked at themselves in the mirror. Guy reached to touch his own neck.

"You got the neck of a goddamn swan," Isadore remarked.

"I do not."

"You should be in the ballet," said Isadore.

Guy tried to sink his head between his shoulders again but Isadore wouldn't allow it. He grinned at his nephew in the mirror. Guy lowered his eyes instead.

"And I'm gonna get a couple of toothpicks for them eyes," Isadore added. "Leland!" he hollered down the bar. "Ya got any toothpicks around here?"

"In the drawer under the cash," Leland called.

So Guy looked up again.

During a game against Port Hull, Isadore became enraged after some big kid from the other team squashed one of Guy's teammates into the boards. The kid was like a big fat fist on skates, and the little guy melted into the ice as if his bones had been yanked from his body. A split second later, the other team scored. The ref hadn't seen the check and the home crowd rose to their feet in a single mass of outrage. Isadore's shouts were the loudest. He swore to rip the ref's limbs from his body the next time he found him alone. On the other side of the rink, a few parents from Port Hull clapped and whistled and pointed and laughed. Isadore felt cut, like a wound had been torn down the front of him and opened him up so the whole world could see. His sense of fair play was violated. The ref was blind. The fat kid would not be penalized.

"I know you!" Isadore screamed. "Freeman Day! Freeman Day! I seen you on the street!"

"He'll rip your legs off!" a man nearby rejoined.

"I'll rip your legs off!" Isadore agreed.

"Some none-too-saintly remarks coming from the home bleachers," Leland observed from his booth. "Freeman is looking somewhat unappreciative."

To Isadore's surprise and anticipation, the ref was skating directly towards him. He stopped in front of Isadore and the thick throng of supporters now around him and placed his hands on his hips. Isadore kept quiet, but couldn't wait to see what the prick would have to say.

"Listen now," said Freeman Day. "I don't need to hear this bullshit from you fellas."

The men erupted. Freeman was blind and retarded and he looked like a faggot standing there with his hands on his hips like some kind of goddamn faggot.

The ref pointed to center ice. "Those are your kids out there. What sort of example do you think you're setting with this kind of behavior?"

"What kind of fucking example are you setting?" demanded Isadore. "You can't even call a penalty! What the fuck kind of referee is that?"

"I don't need this," Freeman Day repeated, his long face pink from the cold, vapour clouds puffing out and disappearing with every word. "Now you fellas settle down or I'll have you kicked out of here."

Isadore laughed at him, even though fury was moving like worms through his bowels. The other men, about to surge with renewed outrage, instead took their cue from Isadore and laughed as well.

"I'd like to see it!" Isadore called as the ref skated off. "I'd like to meet the man who could do it! I don't think it's gonna be you!"

But it was good to be angry. It had struck Isadore more than once over the past month of hockey and Guy that maybe he hadn't really been alive in the last little while. It felt like that. Maybe not since his father died. Maybe not even since he returned from Toronto.

He pushed his way through the still-seething men, and leaned against the boards, towards the milling players, and he waited for Guy. The boy was used to Isadore's outstanding white presence at the games by now, and knew the sight of him at the boards meant to skate over and receive his instructions.

Isadore's chin jutted slightly because he was clenching his jaw, the tendons in his neck like fishermen's ropes. He shook his finger towards the big kid from the other team.

"Get him!"

"Wha?" said Guy.

"Close your mouth! Get that big bastard!"

"But," said Guy.

"That was your goddamn teammate! You go get him!"

"I'll get a penalty!"

"Fuck the penalty! This is hockey!" Isadore hollered, marveling at the child from the depths of his fury.

But Guy appeared to get it then; something came into his eyes. The words, perhaps because they were in combination with the outlandish anger, made sudden sense. Guy skated away, and ploughed into the fat boy, lowering his head at the last possible moment. The crowd on Isadore's side of the rink rose again as one, this time exploding with cheers and shouts. The people from Port Hull were on their feet as well, pointing and red-faced. Isadore watched his nephew carefully, trying to keep the pure bliss of the moment at bay and retain a degree of detachment. He wanted to see how Guy fought. He had taken the fat kid by surprise, from behind, which had worked to his advantage. Managed to get him down and on top of him. The boy was wailing away and the surprised Port Hull player could do little but try and fend him off. It was wonderful—them on top, Port Hull on the bottom. Isadore's nephew defending the honor of the town.

Freeman Day grappled with Guy from behind until finally the boy turned around and flailed at him as well, knocking Day's helmet askew. Isadore whooped, and the crowd behind echoed him. Guy had to be dragged to the box by the ref and Dave Fifield. Everyone on Isadore's side of the rink was shouting the boy's name like heaven-crazed fundamentalists calling on their Lord and Savior.

Instead of going home after the game, Isadore took Guy over to Leland's bar and bought him French fries and one Coke after another and let the boy play pool. Although Isadore didn't care for the game himself, he stood there holding a stick while Guy took shots so nobody would bother them about monopolizing the table. Men asked if they could buy Guy beers and stood talking to Isadore about him.

"Not a bad hockey player," they remarked.

"He'll be good if he can learn to keep his head up."

"Short fuse," they chuckled.

"Oh, you don't wanna fuck with him," Isadore assured them. "He'll go off on ya like *that*. Boom."

"He's quiet," someone observed.

Isadore looked at Guy and saw that he was quiet. He wondered if he should approve of it or not.

"It's the quiet ones ya gotta look out for," Isadore said experimentally. A few men grunted as if to agree.

"What the hell do you do with yourself half the time anyway?" he demanded of the boy on the drive home. Guy sat in the passenger's seat looking apprehensive because Isadore had insisted on doing the driving. He craned his long neck every few minutes to see if Mounties were following behind. "Do you play any other sports or what?"

"Soccer, in the summer," said Guy.

"Fuck soccer," said Isadore. "Baseball."

"There's no team."

Isadore almost veered the truck into the ditch. "No team! Well, we'll goddamn start a team."

Guy sat staring into the dark for a few moments. "All right," he said eventually.

"When I was your age," said Isadore. "I played hockey. I played baseball. I boxed."

"You boxed?" repeated Guy.

"You're goddamn right I boxed. Had a heavy bag set up in the shed. Almost went professional when I was in Toronto."

Guy sat silently for a few more moments, making Isadore impatient.

"Really?" he said at last.

"What do you mean, really?" Isadore exploded. "You think I'm full of shit?"

"No," said Guy.

"How about a shot to the jaw, would that convince you?"

Isadore made as if to do it, and Guy cringed. Isadore shoved him.

"Don't wince, *petit*. Don't ever wince. You gotta think, if I'm gonna get hit I'm gonna get hit."

They drove, the truck weaving back and forth over the yellow line. "Those were wild times," Isadore said after a while. "Not much older than you." He reached between his legs for his bottle and managed to open it up and take a sip without swerving much farther onto either side. He thought about boxing at the Trinity Club in Toronto and the men he met there, and some of the things he had learned. Suddenly he felt a little pissed off.

"You don't have a whore of a lot to say for yourself, do ya?" he complained to Guy.

Guy strained to see in the dark, trying to figure out where they were, how far from his mother's house. "I'm not very talkative," he admitted. He said this rather by rote, as if it had been told to Guy and he wasn't even sure he agreed.

"Yah, well, maybe that's a good thing and maybe it isn't," said Isadore. "Sometimes ya gotta speak up for yourself."

"I know," said Guy.

"People don't tend to put up with that kind of bullshit for too long," warned Isadore. "You think you're the only one who ever had any ideas, who ever thought maybe he should keep things to himself. I could be quiet too, if I wanted to. You used to hardly ever hear a peep out of me. But I learned the hard way . . ." He trailed off, peering at the road.

Guy waited a little while and then asked, "Learned what?"

Isadore's eyebrows came together like he was surprised and annoyed that Guy was still in the truck with him.

"I don't know!" he shouted, and drove awhile. "The bastards would like to forget you exist, if you let them," he finally added.

nORMAL

GUY LEARNED as much about "the bastards" as he did about hockey during the season he spent with Isadore. "The bastards" were one of the small number of things his uncle talked to him about that rang true. Although Isadore never came right out and explained it, in his view it seemed there were three kinds of people. The first kind were normal people—those of whom Isadore didn't particularly disapprove. They included Leland MacPhedron, for example, and Isadore's own father. The second kind of people were crazy people. Isadore could not really say he disapproved of them, because they simply didn't count. These were people like the environmentalist who lived in Point Tupper and was always campaigning to have the mill shut down. There was no point bothering with such people. Guy had observed that his sister Louise was slowly inching into this category. Isadore grew less and less interested in her the more mysterious her ways became to him. At first the only way he could think of defining her clothes and hair and makeup was slutty, but it soon became obvious that Louise was not exactly trying to make herself attractive. Sometimes she would whiten her face, fill in the hollows around her eyes with black, and go to school looking like a panda bear. And since he had no understanding of what else she could possibly be trying to achieve in making herself up this way, it seemed to Isadore that Louise was simply becoming a crazy person. Crazy people didn't bother Isadore, because he assumed they were just too stupid to behave normally.

Then there were the bastards, by far the largest category. Guy was not certain where he himself fit in, but he knew his mother often hovered around bastard status when she didn't do what Isadore told her she should. Buying a TV, for example, was an act of bastard insurgency, especially when Isadore had been so vocally against it. Marrying Kenzie, Guy's father—a confirmed bastard, reportedly—had been bad, but getting divorced was worse, seeing as how she was "supposed to be a Catholic," as Isadore often pointed out.

The one thing Guy really wanted to hear about from Isadore was Toronto, but whenever the subject came up, Isadore got angry and shut it down again. It was strange, because Toronto came up so often. For Isadore, talking about this subject was like picking a sore until it bled and then getting angry at the sore and slapping a Band-Aid over it until he could pick it again. Toronto came up and then was shut down so often because, according to Isadore, it was a veritable hotbed of bastards. He intimated that Toronto was the place where he learned everything he knew about bastards. But for Guy all this meant was frustrating and tantalizing glimpses into an important world where Isadore had briefly—to hear him tell it anyway—prevailed. When he was only a few years older than Guy, Isadore had up and left. At eighteen the world was his and he had known it. But no sooner was Guy allowed to envisage this young-man glory than it was yanked away from him. Isadore would become too irate and dissolve into anti-Ontario epithets. Clearly he pined for the city and believed it was in his blood and was hurt, for some reason, by its memory. Even Guy could see this was the pain of betrayal. Right there was the defining characteristic of a true bastard in Isadore's mind. One who had betrayed.

Preoccupied with bastards, the uncle and nephew wove in silence through the dark the rest of the way home.

When the two came in from the porch, they found Marianne scurrying to arrange knickknacks on top of the camouflaged television. Guy guessed she had been absorbed in the *Academy Performance* or something when they drove up. Tea was simmering on the stove as it always was, and Isadore, almost dozing with a mug between his massive hands, thudded onto the couch and faced the blanketed box.

In Guy's imagination a scenario took shape: *The mug goes flying into the quilt, the tea soaks everything, the porcelain shatters the screen, and no more cartoons or sports or anything else.* Isadore was in precisely the mood: drunk, at the point when he would either explode or pass out. The whole family had been expecting it since the television came into their home, after Marianne had won big at bingo. They had been fatalistically

67

unanimous about what they wanted to buy with the winnings, knowing all the while it was simply a matter of time before Isadore came and took it from them. Now the time had come.

Isadore took a sip of tea as Guy and his mother watched. It was just the sort of quiet, nonchalant gesture he would make before unleashing hell on them. Even hammered, Isadore had something of the theater in him.

But the uncle settled even deeper into the couch. The tight, invisible ropes around Guy and his mother loosened as they saw Isadore relax. The moment had passed. He would sleep. Isadore took another sip of tea and closed his eyes. The muscles in Guy's shoulders seemed almost to sigh.

Just as Marianne was turning around to go to the kitchen, however, and Guy was moving toward the bathroom, Isadore made a noise.

"Ooooooch," he said. He lifted a hand from his mug and waved it in the direction of the TV-shaped quilt.

"What, Isadore?" said Marianne.

"Ooooooch," repeated Isadore.

An interminable stretch of seconds elapsed as Isadore brought the mug to his lips for one last sloppy draught. "Let the boy watch his shows," he finally rumbled. "Played a good game tonight."

Guy looked at his mother. It was after midnight and he wanted to go to bed. She shrugged.

"Go on!" Isadore barked, his eyes closed.

So Guy tiptoed to the set, lifted the quilt like a bridal veil, and turned it on, careful to keep the volume low.

WINNER

ALISON FIRST saw Isadore Aucoin in a monastery, in the spring of 1977, sitting around a table with his brother alcoholics, bridge tricks in front of them, no one playing. Everyone listening to Aucoin instead.

He was telling them a story about a Canadian boxer everybody knew. A black man they all admired in the odd, detached way white men admired black athletes, seeing them as pure physicality in some ways, sheer man.

If their prejudices against black men could ever be articulated, wrote Alison, *the noise would sound like this: They are deep us. They are more us than we are. They are unthinkable, therefore. But sometimes one is great. That is certainly mostly us. That is deep us on display. Only then can it be celebrated.*

Alison suffered through two weeks of thoughts like this rising to the surface of his consciousness. He prayed to God, because that was what being in the monastery was for, that and drying out. But mostly, it seemed to him, God. Not drinking was more incidental to being in the monastery. He didn't like it. He was an agnostic on his weak days, an atheist the rest of the time, and he didn't know why whenever he wanted to get sober, people felt it necessary to cram religion down his gullet in lieu of booze. He had imagined starting his own chapter of AA a few years back. Triple A: Atheist Alcoholics Anonymous. He would have been lynched. At one of his first meetings, he had leaned over and whispered this sacrilege into the ear of a hip-looking woman wearing jeans and big earrings. She turned to him with a face straight out of *Body Snatchers*. Please direct any inquiries to the Higher Power, it said. And then her neat brown eyebrows came together and she seemed to possess all the righteous authority of the Trinity itself.

"What exactly are you doing here?" she had said to him.

Ring, resonate.

But he prayed now, he prayed anyway, because, again, he was in a monastery. There were brother-confessors on all sides of him. There was an altar a few feet away from his room. Why waste the opportunity? Besides, he felt weak. He didn't have the faith to disbelieve anymore. He was dried out.

Why do they call it drying out, it doesn't sound like a good thing. You picture a man on his back in the desert, his body all sucked in like there's a vacuum at his center.

Nice image. Except for vacuum, which made one think *vacuum cleaner,* and a vacuum cleaner at the center of a man's soul was not a particularly elegant image after all. Vacuum, like a black hole. Maybe a black hole at his center. Melodramatic, but better than a vacuum cleaner. Alison wrote that down, he wrote it in his "journal" along with the deep-us thing. The word "journal" always appeared to him in quotation marks now. He used to take it very seriously, his "journal." So seriously it was an embarrassment to him now. He would write in it, and his "wife" would read it. He would write about her and leave it out where she would find it. She would read it after he left the house, and sit around crying. He would come home and yell at her for reading it. They would have what he liked to define in his twenty-eight-year-old's brain as a "wonderful row." He had read that somewhere, something about a "wonderful row," and he wanted to have one too. So he made sure he did, with his "journal" and his "wife." Then he would have an excuse to go to a bar and complain to the other men there about his "row." Sometimes it was a "terrific row" or a "fabulous row," sometimes with his "better half." He always referred to her in complimentary terms: my better half, my one and only, my heart's desire, my heart's blood. That last one was a stealer from some British novel he'd been impressed with at the time. He used it sparingly, only in company he knew would never recognize it. Such as he was in now, but he couldn't very well go on about having a "terrific row" with his "heart's blood" to the good old *by's* up here in detox.

It was usually around this point in his glaringly lucid thought process, when he had sat for too long staring at the bleeding saints in the chapel or the flickering TV in the common room, when Alison would start to hate himself. He heard his own thoughts and hated them. The kinds of things he thought when he was sober. Contemplation of the perfect social occasion for tossing off some stolen literary quip. Alcoholism was better. How was that for going against the prescribed dogma? Benedictine brethren, I am a better man when drunk. I don't think this line of bullshit. I am deeper me.

He had seen Isadore Aucoin stalking around the monastery as if sent by the pope himself to straighten the place out. At first Alison assumed he was a repairman or something—he had that workman's arrogance that announced: Stand aside. I am the only man in the world who can fix your furnace. But once he figured out Aucoin was there to dry out with the rest of them, Alison avoided him. The man was Bully Incarnate. Big and loud. Hairy, too. His hair had not been cut in a while, and he had lots of it. In spite of Aucoin's obvious conservatism, he had the look of a declining rock star—a menacing, uncombed Elvis.

Aucoin whistled Hank Williams tunes up and down the halls, and he didn't seem to mind being sober. He would goose the monks through their robes, whenever one happened by, which the monks had no idea how to respond to. "There's just something about an ass in a dress," Alison heard Aucoin observing one night at supper. "An ass in a dress wants grabbing. I don't care whose it is!" At which point Aucoin almost threw up from laughing, and the other men joined him. If he had risen from his seat and started doing the highland fling around the table, they probably would have joined him too. Had Alison made such a statement—*Why yes, yes! I also have a proclivity for fondling the asses of God's ordained*—he would have found himself tossed from the window by dessert.

It was the completely arbitrary charisma of a large and therefore unselfconsciously confident man. Alison could only resent it.

And in the common room, the other men sat rapt, their cards turned down on the table or resting against their chests. Aucoin meanwhile waved his own hand around, showing his hearts and spades to everyone.

He was telling a story about boxing. The art of hitting and being hit. Alison had nothing against the sport—he enjoyed it as much as anyone—but it all seemed a little too apropos for someone like Aucoin. It was a little too on the nose. Great big scary man who has a penchant for, and is particularly good at, hitting other men. Cliché. But none of the other man knew or cared that it was cliché, they thought it was great. People clung to their clichés like sooky blankets in this part of the world.

Aucoin said he used to work out at the Trinity boxing club in Toronto every day, and men were always getting one look at him and wanting to take a poke. Well, one day in walks the champ—in town for a fight. And he's looking for a sparring partner, someone he can keep up with. So he sees Aucoin over at the speed bag, and sends his trainer over, one Jackie James. American fella, from down South. Has one of those black accents from down there. Oh, but he's dressed to the nines: charcoal suit, double-breasted vest. Aucoin went on for some time about the suit, to Alison's surprise. The men at the table—lobster fishermen and pulp cutters and drug store managers and fish plant workers and coal miners—their interest did not flag for one moment. Aucoin was a born storyteller.

So this fella comes sauntering up to Aucoin with his cufflinks and his alligator shoes and says: Look heah. Aucoin was attempting the accent now. It wasn't ridiculous. Look heah. My boy wants you to come over and go a few rounds with him.

Aucoin looked around at his audience with wide eyes, imitating his young self. "Well, I says, no goddamn way am I gonna get in there with your boy!" The men smiled at his frank cowardice.

"I says, I seen what that guy can do in the ring, and no thank you to that! So the man himself, he's standing by the ring and he sees me shaking my head back and forth. Just: No way. So now he's heading my way and I'm thinking, Well, Jesus Christ."

"What'd he say?" somebody asked. Aucoin switched characters suddenly, now a championship boxer. He spread his hands out and smiled easily, comfortably. It was a smile such as no one at the table had ever seen on a face familiar to them. The look of a winner.

"He said," said Aucoin, "Problems?"

The men sat back. They loved it. One word.

"Problems?" repeated Isadore, before turning back into a nervous young hick. "I said, you're goddamn right there's some problems, this guy wants me to get in the ring with you and you'll take my goddamn head off!"

Then Aucoin was loose again, the champ: "He says, No, no, I won't hit you, man, I just need a moving target. Well, I says, all right, and in I went, sparring with the champ. And I'll tell you boys something. He hit me once. On the shoulder. Felt like it had been tore clean off."

Some of the men shook their heads, impressed and willing themselves to believe the end of the story had been every bit as good as its buildup. Alison picked up a magazine. Too bad, he was thinking. He had us.

"So the trainer Jackie James comes up to me afterwards," Aucoin continued. Alison looked up with the other men, about to go back to their cards. They had forgotten about the exotic trainer with the slick name. "Look heah, he says. You ain't bad. But every time you go to throw a right, you doing this—" Aucoin jerked his right shoulder to demonstrate to the men what he did. "It's a giveaway, he told me, champ always knew when that right was coming. Oh, I says, well I don't know what I can do about that, I don't even know I'm doin it! Well, says Jackie James. I know what you can do about that. You just come over heah. So he leads me over to the heavy bag."

Aucoin pushed himself away from the table and stood, placing himself in a boxer's stance.

The men put down their cards again.

"Now, he tells me, jab left a couple of times, then throw a right. So, I," Aucoin jabbed for them. "Now I go to throw the right, before I can even get it out there, this crazy bastard brings his hand down on me like this—Pow!" It was an enormous karate chop. Aucoin fixed a look of surprise and outrage onto his face and Alison found himself smiling at it.

"I said, What the hell! Do it again, he says, go on. So I—" He pantomimed the performance a second time. "And again—

Pow! What in Jesus name are you trying to do to me, I said? Just keep going, he tells me. Well, he's the man, I figure, he's the fella who looks after the champ, so who am I to question? Well by God, boys, we stood there for pretty near an hour doing the same thing over and over. Jab, jab—pow! Jesus! Jab, jab—pow! Ouch! Goddammit!"

At this point Aucoin stopped to check out the audience and make sure just the right amount of suspense was in the air.

"So later on I'm in the showers and he calls to me, how's that feel?" Aucoin rubbed his right shoulder, playing irritated. "I still didn't know what the hell he'd been trying to prove. Well, I'll tell you, I says. I don't think I'm gonna be able to lift my goddamn arm for work in the morning.

"That may be so, he says. But you'll never jerk that shoulder in the ring again."

The men sat and blinked while Aucoin returned to his chair and tucked himself back into the table with them. He wiggled his ass briefly to get comfortable while everybody waited for the epilogue. He picked up his cards, glanced at them, and finally tapped his hairy skull with a finger. "See," he explained. "He wasn't workin on my body at all that whole time. He was workin on my mind."

"Ah!" went the men. Delight. Revelation.

My goodness, thought Alison. It's a parable.

dEFENSE

THE TOWN became a carnival of violence and the hockey rink was the main attraction, like a big tent pitched in its center. Leland offered absurd drink specials throughout the playoffs. Pitchers of rum—he never specified what brand—for $10 on Thursdays, $1.50 bar shots on Saturdays. People came and nearly killed each other every night. At four in the morning Mounties peeled them from the dance floor and the parking lot.

A fierce rivalry had sprung up between Big Harbour and Port Hull, and Isadore bragged it was entirely thanks to him and his careful coaching. Since the last game where Guy attacked the fat kid, the weekend dances in the area had become battlegrounds. With the playoffs, it only accelerated. Carloads of boys from Port Hull trawled one community hall after another, looking for players from Big Harbour, or else anyone wearing a Giants jacket. Big Harbour boys, in turn, drove through Port Hull at midnight, blasting Lynryd Skynrd and hurling bottles at storefronts and mailboxes. It all began with Guy's fight. Each community was trashed by the youth of the other every weekend leading up to the big game. Soon Leland stopped advertising drink specials on the sign outside his tavern and replaced them with slogans, such as PORT HULL MARTYRS! (the team was actually called the Saints). At first the teenagers tried rearranging Leland's letters into obscenities in response, but after a while they simply removed the sign and somehow managed to get it up onto the roof of the high school, where they proceeded to push it into the parking lot below. Then, having had so much success without being detected, the boys headed back to Leland's and broke a few windows for good measure.

Guy took it all in. He noticed how everybody pretended to mind, how everybody seemed to be bubbling with outrage, but nobody did anything to quell it. Even Leland MacPhedron, who had served as an MLA in the provincial government and had political connections and clout untold, didn't bother calling the cops about his sign or his windows. Instead, it was rumoured, he spoke to his two boys. The MacPhedron twins weren't on the hockey team, but he employed them to bounce and tend bar. They were the ones he complained to about his sign. Then he gave them the following Saturday off to do as they saw fit.

Inside the D'escousse community hall, everybody from his school was dancing in two parallel lines. Guy's mother had only started allowing him to hitch rides to the dances last year, before they got the truck, and he had been surprised to see the older kids dancing all lined up. On television, nobody danced like that. On *Happy Days,* guys sometimes grabbed hold of girls by the waist and swung them around. Guy hadn't been expecting *that* exactly, but he hadn't been expecting the two straight lines from one end of the hall to the other either. Why didn't they fill up the dance floor, he wanted to ask someone, like adults did at weddings? He was embarrassed for his peers in a way. The advent of television had intensified his embarrassment about his life in general. *Why do we all have to be such fucking freaks,* he wanted to exclaim when he first saw everybody dancing that way. Real human beings would laugh if they came here and saw us.

But he got more used to it and found it didn't bother him as much over time. He wanted to dance as well. He wanted to go over to a girl and lead her to the ends of the two lines and have her take her place across from him. But practically the only girls allowed to attend these dances in the middle of nowhere were seniors, and there was of course no way he could talk to an older girl from D'escousse High. He had called Corinne Fortune three times that week about the D'escousse dance. He had wanted to tell her he would come and pick her up if she wanted to go, it wouldn't be a problem. And even though she hadn't stayed on the phone long enough to talk to him about it, Guy kept looking around the hall, peering at the doorway every time someone new arrived, thinking she might have changed her mind at the last minute and come with some friends.

After a while he wandered outside to smoke cigarettes under the yellow spotlight of a hydro pole, where some guys he knew were gathered. Some of them passed around booze. Nobody ever bothered Guy about not drinking, so impressed were they to hear that he had "given it up a few years back."

Doug Forchu was describing how he had "played with" a girl last year in the very spot where they were standing, under the very same yellow light of the very same hydro pole. He kept saying he "played with" her, and would describe it to them in no other terms. It was infuriating in one way, but on the other hand, the way Doug said "played with" had such a smutty air it satisfied Guy's imagination to a degree. But Guy kept trying to get Doug to explain exactly what it was he had played with on the girl. He just wanted to hear Doug say it, but Doug wouldn't. And who, for that matter, was the girl? Was it someone they knew? Jimmy Joe Coffin made as if to punch Doug in the nuts out of frustration, but Doug danced out of the way, ludicrously graceful. A guy who had been approaching them from somewhere beyond the yellow pool of light stepped into Doug's spot across from Guy at the same instant and punched Guy in the nuts for real. The other boys stood dazed as Guy dropped to his knees. A second later he fell onto his side. The new guy—who wore a Saints hockey jacket, whom everybody now recognized as the bulky defenseman responsible for crumpling so many Giants—stepped forward and aimed a kick at Guy's middle. Doug Forchu, with his acrobat's reflexes, shoved the fat kid off balance just before the foot could connect.

"What the fuck?" Guy could hear Doug shouting across a roaring ocean of pain.

"Fight!" someone else hollered, farther away, in ecstasy. Guy could hear the hall rapidly emptying itself. He could imagine the two neat, straight lines dissolving into a single chaotic stampede.

"Get up, dickhead," somebody said, so Guy reached for the wall he had been leaning against and worked his way up.

If I'm gonna get hit, he found himself thinking, *I'm gonna get hit.*

That was it, Marianne told him a few hours later. Guy would either quit the team or else she would kill him herself just to get it over with quickly.

"Because I can't stand this, Guy," she said, snuffling as she rinsed blood out of his hair. "I have a bad heart and this is not the sort of thing I can stand to see. You can't just start coming home like this every day."

"I didn't have anything to *do* with it," Guy complained. "I couldn't *help* it."

Isadore was there on the couch, watching everything in silence, his arms folded over his stomach like Buddha. He had passed out earlier and woke up without a word once Guy came in. He kept uncharacteristically silent while Marianne shrieked and tried to keep herself from slapping her beaten-up child. Isadore let her fuss into the night, and even made a fresh pot of tea for them all. But when Marianne insisted for the second time that Guy quit the hockey team, Isadore grunted at her not to be dumb.

"Don't be so dumb," he said. Marianne stared at him. "He's not a little girl," he added.

"I don't care," Marianne said.

"None of this is your concern," said Isadore. "You just fix him up. This one's no mama's boy, uh? I have to tell you, *petit*, I was worried about you for a while there, with that father of yours."

"Don't say things about his father," snapped Marianne.

"Nosiree, we don't have to worry about this one, I can see that much for myself. Uh, *petit?*" Then Isadore winked, the first time Guy had ever seen him wink, the first time Guy had ever seen him full of pleasure in that house. Marianne must have seen the pleasure too. A plaster statue of Saint Anne stood on the windowsill above the sink. Marianne strode over and grabbed it like a pack of smokes, heading off to her bedroom.

Isadore pulled a chair beside his nephew and leaned forward. "Tell me now," he said to Guy.

Early the following morning, his uncle hauled Guy out of bed and told him to go outside and clean out the shed.

"Come get me when you're finished," Isadore said, attempting to fit his own bodily expanse into the warm little cove that Guy had left on the mattress. Guy watched as his uncle pulled the *Star Wars* sheets up to meet his grizzled chin.

"Go," he yelled with his eyes closed, hairy face weirdly cradled against that of Chewbacca the Wookie.

Guy hauled everything out and dumped it on the frost-stiffened grass beside the shed. He did not bother opening the rotten boxes and fishing around inside for anybody's memories.

He used to play in the shed as a kid and went through everything back then, when it was all meaningless and safe. He knew his father's stuff was somewhere in the heap. There were books on fly-fishing, and shirts, and photographs. His mother's wedding things were packed away somewhere as well. Everybody in the house knew the stuff packed in the shed was far from protected, piled in the cardboard boxes. It was just an old henhouse, it leaked. Pictures would be fuzzed with mold, clothes would be stiff from getting soaked in the winter and then drying up in the summer. When Guy picked up the boxes, he was careful to reach around to the bottom. He did not want anything spewing open at his feet.

Once everything was cleared out, he didn't bother actually cleaning the place. He was too lazy and he didn't think Isadore would care. Guy went inside and drank orangeade from a pitcher in the fridge. Louise was at the table, not eating or smoking or drinking tea. Just there at the table, fidgeting like a squirrel.

"What was that all about?" she said.

"What?"

"The thing I've been watching you do all morning."

"Isadore said to clean out the shed," said Guy.

"Did he say to dump everything in the yard like that?"

"No."

"What will Ma say?"

"Ma will probably have a shit fit," Guy said. "Not much I can do about it."

"No," agreed Louise.

"I'm supposeta go wake him up now," said Guy.

Louise looked around, wondering what to do with herself. She got up and went to another part of the house.

Twenty minutes later Isadore went into Louise's room, where she was not, and hauled her mattress off the bed. Guy stood in her doorway as Isadore brushed the blanket and sheets away like crumbs and carried the mattress under his arm to the shed. From the living room, where she sat with a magazine closed on her lap, Louise watched her bed float off down the hall, the look on her face like she was trying to remember something significant.

Isadore placed Louise's mattress upright on the ageless filth of the shed floor. Together, he and Guy managed to roll it up and bind it with rope. "This will have to do until we get you a heavy bag," he said to Guy. Isadore spent the rest of the day making Guy punch the mattress, sometimes standing behind it and moving it around. Then Isadore would lean it against the wall and show Guy how to punch properly. In slow motion, he aimed a jab at Guy's jaw, tucking his arm into his chest and then twisting forward until it connected with the curve of his nephew's face. Then he did it fast a few times, knuckles dabbing at Guy's cheek. Guy could feel the air around them rushing to get out of Isadore's way.

The word "patient" was not a word that came to mind when people thought of Isadore, and yet hours and days were lost in this manner—perfecting the trajectory of a single punch. Guy was surprised to learn how very little anger had to do with punching someone. He was surprised to learn this from Isadore.

Sometimes they forgot to have supper. Marianne would not disturb them. Once she did, and Isadore had a fit. He said, If you want this little pecker to come running home with a broken neck one day, just say so now. I'll toss this goddamn mattress out the window and leave him at the mercy of the world.

THE GAME

ALL I KNOW is I had the puck. It was mine.

I had checked a guy, fast and merciless like Isadore taught me, and it was mine. I could feel him crumple between the boards and my shoulder. He went "Ahh!" in my ear. And then I was headed straight for the net, not a soul between me and the goalie. He saw me coming and stood there in his mask and his pads like a startled lobster, and I just took one look at the way he jerked into position and knew: *It's going in.*

It would have been my first goal of the season. For the first time since I started, it occurred to me to wonder if Corinne Fortune came to the games.

The hand came out of nowhere. It yanked me practically off my skates by the scruff of my neck. I remember I felt *little* then, light as a puppy. And I thought, in all seriousness, *Maybe this is just a dream.*

And then this woman's face was closer to mine than any woman's except my mother's has ever been.

"You *fuck!*" it spat.

The woman's hair was insane, a huge amber halo, identical in colour to her coat.

But her hair was not her hair at all, it was actually a fur hat. She was swaddled in gold fur from head to toe. She had gold earrings the shape of flattened dice in her ears. She was yanking at the back of my jersey. She was strangling me and screaming in my face.

"Who do you think you are, you little bastard? That was *Scott!* That was my *Scott* you hit!"

That's when I realized I was on the Port Hull side of the rink. There were Port Hull people on all sides of me, laughing mostly, although some of them had ravenous looks on their faces exactly like hers.

Her face was red and then there was a whistle screeching.

"—You're choking the boy." Freeman Day.

"I don't give a *fuck!* You give him a penalty! You're blind!"

And I felt hands on my shoulders, hands around my waist. The guys on my team yanking at me, shoving at the lady, shouting. Above everything I could hear an echoing, booming laughter like God's. It took me a long time to figure out it was actually Leland MacPhedron up in the broadcast booth, laughing his ass off.

Then I was free. The lady's hands became unstuck and Freeman Day was steering me across the rink.

"Are you all right, boy?"

I held my neck and nodded. All around me the rink echoed with noise like a crammed, crazy henhouse.

"Are you going to be all right?"

Was I all right to play was what he meant, and I felt bad all of a sudden for the game where I got into a fight and whacked at Freeman, almost knocking his helmet off. I just felt incredibly bad about it for some reason. And then I clenched in horror, because I knew I was going to cry.

Dave Fifield came out of nowhere and took me by the shoulders. He looked into my face, and looked away fast

"Listen here, Boucher," he said loudly. "You just come sit it right down over here."

He steered me over to the bench. My skates just went in the direction he pushed.

"You just take a breather for a while, okay? Okay, son?" He was shouting. "Crazy bitch."

Here's the truth. Not even Isadore has ever scared me that badly.

The coach positioned himself on the bench between me and the other players. A couple of seconds later, I felt his arm land across my shoulders.

He squeezed once, hard and quick. "You woulda made that shot," he said. "You were in the clear." I knew I would have made it. I shuddered and the coach squeezed again, holding me still. "There," he said. "You're good now." Then he took away his arm and clapped his hands three times—as loud, it seemed like, as he could.

"Jessop!" Dave Fifield yelled. "Get out there! Day! Keep

the goddamn monkeys in their pen next time for fuck's sake!"

Freeman skated past, wearing his bad-smell expression that drove so many people up the wall. I watched him drift back over to the Port Hull side of the rink, thinking to myself that someone like Corinne Fortune would never be a hockey fan. She wouldn't come to a place with French fry and ketchup shoeprints all over the floor, where you could hear drunks throwing up in the men's room no matter where you were standing in the building. She wouldn't come to a place where guys cleared their noses onto the ice, where people screamed and spat at each other and parents knocked their kids' heads together—as if for luck—if their team was losing badly enough. She probably liked figure skating or something. Gymnastics.

I kept my head down for a while. I listened to Leland MacPhedron yammering up in the broadcast booth and yanked off my gloves so I could wipe my face.

"Oh, the natives are restless, ladies and gentlemen, make no mistake about that. Tempers are running high. What's this, now? Oh my Lord Jesus Christ, hockey fans, it would appear the white menace is on the move."

I looked up just in time to see a massive white blob detach itself from our side of the bleachers and make its way to the opposite side.

Overhead, Leland's voice said, "The member is crossing the floor!" Which meant God only knew what but didn't sound good. I could see the furry woman in her gold hat protruding from the center of the Port Hull parents.

"Now I'm sure jolly old Saint Isadore just wants to have a friendly chat." And then, from out of nowhere, "The Good Old Hockey Game" by Stomping Tom started to play. It was like Leland figured such a happy, friendly song would calm everyone right down.

The whole rink was dead quiet as Isadore made his way over to the Port Hull side, but everyone started laughing again when he arrived in front of them, just like they'd been laughing when that woman had me by the throat. He was just so massive, and his face was a bright pink globe floating above his cook's whites. His arms were flying all over the place, hands clenched into fists, and the little group of Port Hullers seemed to move as one farther down the bleachers every time Isadore took another step towards them in his rage. Leland was wetting himself up there in the booth.

From a distance, it was comical. It really did look funny from far away. I would never have guessed. I never saw it from a distance before.

"I told her I'd strap her to the front of the goddamn Zamboni and drive it through the wall the next time she pulled that kind of shit," he tells them now. Men's laughter fills the tavern, low and thick. He waits for it to die down and adds, "I meant it too."

We're sitting side by side in Leland's bar, surrounded by admirers. They keep making us tell it over and over again. I spat, "You *fuck!*" in a high-pitched voice, and they nearly died.

We keep everyone in an uproar for most of the evening, but when the mirth finally wears itself out, Leland wipes his eyes and stands in front of us for a moment looking from Isadore's face to mine, and then back.

"The two of you," he goes. "Faces like you're at your mother's wake. Two peas in a goddamn pod, you are."

That's when the thought occurs to me: I have no sense of humour. Nothing's been funny since I turned thirteen. The things that used to make me laugh as a kid are stupid to me now.

But it's never occurred to me that maybe Isadore doesn't have a sense of humour either, that it might actually be something I inherited from him. He laughs at stuff—but never at himself, or anything he's ever done, or anything that's happened to him. Maybe it's that distance thing, like at the rink. It's funny if it's far away.

It's never occurred to me to think about Isadore in these terms before at all. I've always thought of him like the weather—something unpredictable, unavoidable, to be endlessly put up with. I glance up at the mirror behind the bar and see the two of us side by side. He's always telling me how my eyes are too big and wide and stupid-looking, like a little baby's, but how about this: we have the same eyes, really. His are just more bloodshot and hidden under fat.

And that's when I experience what feels like a very grown-up thought.

Jesus fuck is what I think.

Before the night is over, we even end up pissing side by side. I didn't want it to happen, believe me. I didn't want to stand at a urinal with my dick out in front of Isadore and have Isadore say Christ knows what. But there's no getting around it. I get up from the bar and then Isadore rises, grunting, at almost exactly the same moment. He takes advantage of the fact that we're heading in the same direction and lets himself sort of fall on top of me when he loses his balance. It's like trying to hold up a fucking steer.

"Synchronized piss-clocks on the two of us, wha?" he mutters cheerfully into my ear. Like it makes him happy, this little coincidence, like it proves once and for all we're really on the same wavelength.

Dick, is all that I have in my head. What the other guys on the team call *prick* and what my mother used to call my ding-ding.

He doesn't even look at my dick, however. To my relief, he's in such a good mood that Isadore merely sings a little tune, as if to encourage his urine. He's having some trouble getting started, I can't help but notice, and he isn't the only one. Isadore shifts a little and then farts.

"That end works," he remarks, bobbing his head towards me.

This makes me smirk, and finally I'm able to go. I manage to finish up before Isadore even gets started. I wash my hands and leave him singing at the urinal.

And somehow I just know I won't play anymore.

h o u s e

AT AROUND the same time Pam's father stops buttoning his cuffs, his accent begins to return. He starts saying *me* for *my*. Every word that starts with a vowel now has an *h* before it. He grew up deep in the backwoods of Cape Breton and has relatives who live there still and look like something out of the movie *Deliverance,* but they pooled their money when he was eighteen and sent him to school with the hope that he would become a priest like seven of his uncles and three of his great-uncles. He stayed just long enough to have his accent ridiculed out of him, then used his homogenized speech and his half-assed education to get himself a good position at the mill. Then he married Mrs. Cormorant before Pam could pop out and embarrass everyone. The relatives couldn't say much, and since Mr. Cormorant had been to university, they knew they had no place trying to tell him anything anymore. He had a job and a house in town with a dishwasher and a piano, so what did they have to complain about. They called him up from time to time to ask him for advice.

Proper ting, he goes around saying now. He has dropped his *th*'s. He never went around speaking of proper things when he was sober. What are we having for supper? Sausage. Proper ting. Where's me TV listing? By your feet. Proper ting. He has gone back to speaking accented and old-fashioned like his relatives. When Pam was little, it seemed the most important thing for him to be, in order to be considered good at being a man, was undistinguished. So he spoke like he was from Ontario, dressed like men have been dressing for decades—white shirt, black shoes. Tie. Went about his business.

His second cousin Ronald would visit about once a month and bring them holy water and religious medals and trinkets from the shrine to Saint Anne in Port Hull to keep them safe. Ronald was not used to other people and he stuttered and answered questions like it was painful to him. He lived in a trailer and shot the animals who strolled across his yard and brought the butchered carcasses to his relatives and neighbors, just as his own father used to do. People used to love it whenever his father did this, and Ronald thought it was still the best thing you could do for a neighbour. He didn't realize that now they had the Co-op and Sobeys for their meat, and not as many people liked eating fresh-killed deer and rabbit anymore. Still, he'd visit the Cormorants regularly, stuttering greetings, slapping deersteak on the counter along with a two-litre pop bottle filled with holy water from the stream at Port Hull. Then he would sit for an hour in the armchair having polite conversation with Mr. Cormorant. It seemed very uncomfortable for Ronald, sitting there clutching the ends of his armrests, flinching whenever Pam or her mother trundled into the room, but he did it every month all the same. He always directed the same one comment at Pam.

"You. You. You. Are getting to be a big. Big. Big. Girl."

One fragrant spring evening this accented and unbuttoned new version of Mr. Cormorant relates to his daughter Pamela his belief her ass is fat. He speaks this from the floor, where he has fallen into blissful slumber hours before, lulled by the afternoon soap operas. *I was willing to give you the benefit of the doubt,* the television was saying, *until your mother fired that gun at Chelsea!* And then, *Your ass is fat.* Pam's gargantuan treads must have shaken him awake, mirrors breaking, pictures falling from the walls. She hadn't known he was there. The disembodied accusations startled her, as though the furniture were finally speaking its mind, and she jumped. It was the Lord's own intervention the floor did not give way.

"Why-eee," he says now. "Why-ee?" He talks strangely, as a drunk. Not just the returning dialect, but everything now has two syllables. "Why-eee muh-est you-ou be-ee so-oh fah-at?"

The floorboards creak agreement. Yeah, why? Pam stands as the trembling house settles around her. She is used to the house telling her she is fat—the stairs, the wordless furniture, the rattling windows. But he. He would merely eye her over eggs in the morning, dabbing his lips, sipping his coffee. A manager, he delivered his edicts to her before heading off to work. *To not be late for breakfast every morning, you must get more sleep.*

Can't sleep.

Well. You know what would help with that.

I know, I know.

Exercise, that's what'll knock you out at night.

And she used to despise these roundabout jibes, and the evenings, when it pained him to see her stretched out on the couch when she could be in the fresh air moving around, getting some exercise, out of his field of vision for an hour or two.

But at least he had never just come out and said it before. Now he shifts forward and balances momentarily on all fours before straightening up onto his knees like an altar boy.

"Pam-el-a," he prays, "What do-o you-ou do-o? What do-o you-ou do-o with your day-ees?"

"I," says Pam, "am going to be in a play." That is something. Mrs. K., the English teacher, has already cast it for next year. Pam has a starring role.

He shakes his head and pulls himself up onto the couch like it is Everest.

Something about the way he shakes his head gets Pam praying herself. Hello, God, yes, quickly. There is no need to have this happen now, is there? I don't need to have this happen now. I don't need it thrown in my face right now. I was laughing today. I know it is true and how it is and I have to face it sooner or later but I don't want to right now. Make it stop, make him sleep. I am still young. This is my parents' house. I should feel good and safe awhile yet.

"You're innn a play-ee," he repeats. Suddenly he gags. Of course he gags because he has been drinking all day, for no other reason than that. "God," he spits. Yes, God, thinks Pam. Where has my mother gotten to anyway?

"I have to tell you something," says her father, raising his head, suddenly articulate. "I don't think you're going to make it. I just don't see it happening for you."

What does that mean? What does that mean?

It means, dictates the swaying house, *everything you've ever suspected.*

"I," begins Pam.

Lookit this, Pam's crying. Look, we made her cry!

The father, balancing on the couch, attempts to cross his legs like he is behind the desk at the office, like he is the one doing the firing for a change. "Daughter," he says, "I'm sorry to have to tell you this." He can't maintain the managerial posture. His head begins to bob, his speech falters. "For someone like you . . ." Oh, but he is going to get it out. He's not stopping now, it's like picking an unripened scab.

" . . . there is . . ." Here it comes, Pam, are you ready? It's finally going to be articulated, no going back now, the walls around her contract. " . . . very . . . little."

Well, sighs the house, giving way.

LUCK

GUY OBSERVED how little time it took since the car accident for Isadore to start ignoring the restrictions the judge had placed on his life. In fact, Isadore had done nothing about the main edict, which was not to drink. He'd found it impossible to take seriously from day one. And soon the no-driving rule was out the window as well—the inevitable moment arrived when he wanted to go somewhere and Guy was not around but the truck was. What recourse did he have, Isadore complained to everybody, indignant. A man had to get around, he said. Later, if he stayed late at the tavern, he went to his apartment, not to Marianne's as he was supposed to. Soon he even forgot about "basic household maintenance," and things went back to the way they had been. The one aspect of the judge's ruling that Isadore deigned to retain was his right to come and go in their house as he pleased.

Except now he said he was finished with them. With Guy nowhere to be found on the ice during the second-to-last game of the playoffs, Isadore left the rink and drove to the house where he found the whole family gathered around the television set in an act of near blasphemy. He went to the shed and hauled Louise's mattress back inside and threw it down in front of them, knocking knickknacks and framed photographs onto their sides. Then he went to the porch where Guy had stacked the boxes. One by one he carried them back into the shed and emptied them out onto the floor. They heard him doing this, but none of them went to look. The family stayed put until he was finished.

"I'm shut of you crew," he announced when he returned. "I've had it with these betrayals. I'm sick of giving giving giving to this godforsaken family and not ever getting a goddamn thing back. I just thank the Lord Jesus Christ Emile isn't here to see this. He would look upon you," Isadore claimed, "and despair."

And then he left them alone.

"It's *good* you quit," Marianne insisted a pulsebeat after the truck had lurched off down the road. None of them looked at each other.

"I was sure that was it for the TV," said Louise, letting out her breath.

They didn't see Isadore for quite a while, though he was heard to have gotten into a good bit of trouble during that time. His alcoholism was in full flower, and word was Leland had banished him from working in the kitchen again. Still, Isadore continued to virtually live at the tavern, but then word got out that he had shoved one of Leland's sons one Wednesday night at closing, at which point Leland exiled him from the bar altogether. Last Guy and his family had heard, Isadore was blazing around the island in the company of Alison Mason, who had probably finished marking exams and was up for anything.

In the midst of it all, nobody except Guy had any idea that his sister was married. It added to his worry and apprehension. He was finding it unbearable, trying to keep the secret from his mother. A month ago, Louise had quietly graduated from high school, and seeing as she didn't make a fuss about it, nobody else did. Then, when Marianne suggested a party for her eighteenth birthday, Louise stuck her tongue out as far as it would go and ran to her room to hide behind her panda face. She did not want to know about her birthday, she said when Guy came to look for her, and closed her eyes so that her makeup made it look like there were two gaping, empty sockets in her head. She told him she could not stand to think about time passing. She had graduated, and soon she would turn eighteen. Her life, she said, was over.

So one weekend not long after graduation, Louise had married her boyfriend of six months, a twenty-two-year-old scallop farmer named Dan C. McQuarrie. Otherwise nothing changed. She told no one but Guy, and made it clear to Dan C. that she had no interest in living with him until he could find them a house, or at least an apartment, of their own. Currently, Dan C. rented a room a few miles away, in the home of the man he worked for in Isle Madame. He was from Glace Bay, but moved farther down the island because he wanted to get away from the mines and the steel plant. Dan C. had, Louise said, an uncle who'd been blown up alongside a coke oven, and his grandfather had been crushed underground in the mines. Secretly, however, Louise hoped they could move back there some time. She had always wanted to go away, she said, just not too far.

The family kept themselves tuned into the uncle's activities, meanwhile, like fishermen to the weather reports. Still, the night Isadore came back, Guy couldn't suppress a wave of fury at himself—and at Louise and his mother as well. They had somehow let themselves be lulled. They had relaxed, to a degree. Guy knew, because he could feel the muscles in the back of his neck clench into a small fist at the sound of his uncle's bootsteps echoing from the porch. And the moment he felt it, he wondered how he could ever have been so stupid as to let the little fist unclench in the first place.

"I'm back," Isadore informed his sister's family. "I'll be fucked if I'm gonna give up on you crew."

They were sitting around the table eating dinner. Only moments before, Guy had suggested they eat in front of the television, but Marianne said no, tonight was a special occasion and she didn't want to get into such habits in the first place. So the TV sat draped in the quilt as it always was when not in use. Though Isadore had stopped coming around, they covered it up out of habit, and the three shared a simultaneous, wordless gratitude for this circumstance the moment Isadore came barrelling into the kitchen, drunker than they'd seen him in ages.

He plunked down heavily beside Guy and put his arm around him even more heavily. A second later, Alison Mason stumbled in from the porch.

"Oh," said Mason, sitting down on the floor. "Pardon." His jacket was on inside out.

Isadore was resting his entire upper body weight on Guy's lean shoulders—or so it seemed to Guy. His spine quavered.

"You little prick," breathed Isadore into his ear.

"I will call the police," said Marianne.

"How's that young one with the crap around her eyes, uh? You keeping her satisfied?"

Louise stood.

"You sit the fuck down!" Isadore bellowed without looking up, and she did. Guy jerked under his arm, so Isadore put the other one around him. If someone had taken a picture of them then, it might have appeared a particularly affectionate moment between uncle and nephew, godfather and godson.

"The three of you, uh? Jesus Christ, you can't sit still for a minute. Won't even stay in the same goddamn room with me. I'm gonna straighten this place out once and for all." He gripped Guy tighter and shook him a little. "And it all starts right here— with this little faggot."

"Now Isadore," murmured Alison Mason, who was struggling to get to his feet—ass in the air, balancing on his toes and fingertips like a man doing yoga.

"Ever tell your girlfriend about that old man of yours? Me and him went off to the monastery to dry out the one time—damned if he ever came back! He liked it better up there with the boys!"

"I'm calling the police now," said Marianne, not moving from her seat.

"I'm worried about you, *petit*," said Isadore, looking around theatrically at Marianne and Louise as if to make sure they weren't within earshot. "Livin' out here with the women. Givin' up the hockey. This house needs a man and I'm afraid you ain't up to the job."

Guy began to thrash in Isadore's arms, his face going pink.

Isadore laughed. "There we go! He's off, by God!" And held him still for a while, just to show he could.

Isadore was arrested five hours later, not because Marianne had called the police, but because, they later learned, he took off into the night with Alison Mason and drove his truck into a convenience store, having meant to pull alongside it and buy cigarettes. He'd left the family once all the dishes were broken. He had flipped Guy's dinner plate onto the floor and then, as an afterthought, done the same to Louise's. For some reason, this was what got Marianne out of her chair.

"Do you know what that was?" she shrieked. "That was your mother's good china!"

Isadore looked down at the mess of potato and plate he'd created.

"Wha?"

"Mamere! The big family man comes here and then he ruins the family heirlooms."

Isadore swayed in the middle of their kitchen, seeming to teeter on a moment of clarity.

"Why," he finally muttered. "Why you usin' the good china for Christ's sake?"

"Because," said Marianne, holding her heart as she did at such moments, "it's your niece's birthday. She's eighteen. And isn't this *nice*?"

Isadore turned to look at Louise, but she had managed to disappear this time. Guy heard her lock the door to her room, preparing to defend her reclaimed mattress, maybe.

Isadore swayed a moment longer, and Guy clutched the table in front of him. This was the deciding moment, he knew. Isadore would retreat, shamefaced. Or else he would not. Or else he would gather up his outrage and indignation for one final onslaught.

Alison Mason made a sloppy attempt to hold him back, and ended up slipping in the potatoes as Isadore tossed the remaining pieces of the Aucoin family china about the kitchen. The whole time, he gave Marianne to understand that this activity was all her doing—it was her fault their family had sunk to what it had. She was raising her children without the proper respect, he said. He was the only male influence in their lives and she thwarted and undermined him at every turn. Made him look foolish. Made him feel unwelcome. Turned his own flesh and blood against him.

Once his point was made, Isadore crossed the kitchen to help Alison Mason to his feet, china crunching beneath his boots. "And that is what hurts the most," Isadore concluded, still panting. "Unwelcome in the goddamn house I grew up in. In my father's *own home*."

Marianne sat cross-legged under the table. "My heart can't take this," she said behind her hands.

"Oh, your heart's fine," scoffed Isadore, sobered, it seemed, and revitalized. Like Guy's grandfather, Isadore had refused to acknowledge Marianne's heart problem since the day it was diagnosed before Guy was born. When Emile died, they learned she had inherited it from him. A doctor later told them it was amazing the old man had lived the life he did, and for so long. As he cut hay into the evening season upon season and drove horses and dug rocks from the field and smoked one cigarette after another and never even sat down to drink his tea half the time—the whole while his deficient heart had been rattling along like a desperate, half-assed engine.

"You think you got heart problems," Isadore added on his way out the door, pulling a stupefied Alison Mason by the wrist. Isadore looked around the razed kitchen with a face of mourning, as if he'd just arrived and was disappointed to see things in such a mess.

"If anyone's got heart problems around here," Isadore proclaimed, "it's me."

He blew his nephew a ragged kiss before he left.

Louise hadn't wanted a cake in the first place, but her mother had baked one anyway, and had been so excited about it she made her daughter blow out the candles before they even started dinner that night. Marianne had wanted to begin the meal on a festive note.

"Eighteen!" she'd announced.

"My youth is gone," Louise had stated when the cake was placed before her.

"Oh my good dear sweet Jesus Lord," Marianne had exhaled.

She'd told Louise to make a wish and then had put the cake aside for later. Without even giving it a thought, she'd happened to put the aluminum cover over the cake, hiding it as if on instinct. After Isadore was gone, it seemed like holy providence Louise's cake had not been ruined, and for a short moment it seemed to Guy as if his mother had completely forgotten about her broken plates and wrecked kitchen. Marianne was simply thrilled to find the cake intact.

"This is our lucky day!" she called to her children, who had left the room.

Guy could hear everything she was doing out there. She cleaned the broken china up and cut a piece for everyone, but when Guy yelled he didn't want any, and Louise wouldn't even answer from behind her bedroom door, Marianne said they could both go to hell. She would eat it herself, she told them. He could hear her now. She sat alone at the table with a big slice, bashing her fork against the plate every time she went to take another mouthful.

She must have shoveled two pieces into herself before putting the fork down and struggling with a nauseated burp. Guy could hear that too. He imagined he could hear her swallowing it.

"All right," she spoke, because Guy's mother knew as well as he did how the acoustics of the house she'd grown up in worked. She knew he and Louise had been sitting in their rooms listening to the noise of her eating and bashing for the past twenty minutes.

"All right," she said again, like someone was sitting there arguing with her and she was getting tired of it. "There's a waiting list for the new housing outside town," she said. "You have to have a low income."

Guy sat up on his bed and listened hard—waiting for this statement to be retracted or embellished. He heard nothing for a while but the decrepit clicking noises the old house always made, as if it had bones. As if some endlessly knitting grandmother were stored away in a secret room somewhere. Above his head, the Canadian flag could be heard flopping around on the roof. Finally there was something else. He recognized his mother's miniature laughter beneath it all.

"See?" she called after a while. "Lucky."

the BEARDED LADY

SEE: SHE IS PRETTY. Corinne is fourteen, and the transformation is astounding. An aunt dies—an old aunt, her mother's aunt. They head deep into the island to attend the wake, where ancient relatives stand holding their rosaries, dressed in suits from the fifties and before, shiny knees on them. And relatives closer to her age, in pants and dresses from the Kmart, which, she has come to learn, is near unspeakable. The point is, they all see her. They see her and are amazed.

Didn't you grow up overnight?

Didn't you become a pretty young woman?

Dear God, how you've grown.

See that. She is wearing a decent dress, her mother's, because none of her own dresses look right on her anymore. It hits her all at once, on this one day, at her great-aunt's wake.

There is a man there, not a relative, a friend of one of the hick cousins. He gets drunk along with everybody else. He wants her to go somewhere with him. He wants to get to know her. He has tight, red curls and near-green skin and she thinks he is awful, but she is as thrilled as she is embarrassed. She's standing there with a glass of wine, dark purple mother's-dress. She imagines herself, and understands, she sees, she gets it. But has no idea how to deal with it.

Maybe I can call you up.

I live . . . with my parents.

Yah, so do I. But we could go out some time. Go for a drink. Can I get you some more wine, by the way?

She bursts out laughing. She's not good at this at all yet.

I . . . I . . .

You've had enough?

He is a huge nerd, she thinks. He is a grown-up nerd. Normally he wouldn't try for someone like me. But he sees I'm not good at it yet. I don't have my wits about me yet. What to do? Do grown-up nerds really count as nerds at all? Grown men? Grown men are important no matter what. They count in a way that boys don't. She gathers herself up in her mind.

I'll tell you what, big boy. You give me your phone number, and I'll think about it.

But, no. She's not quite there yet. She makes a decision, gulps back her wine and beams at him.

He takes a step back because no grown woman would smile at a grown man like that. Something is out of whack.

She puts her hands over her mouth for a second and doubles over. He looks around.

Do you want to know a secret? she giggles.

Only she and her mother had to go to the wake. The men stayed at home. When the two return, the mother and daughter take off their coats in the hall. Her father and brother look up from the TV to admire them in their good clothes and makeup.

Well, wasn't this one the belle of the ball, her mom remarks.

The belle of the wake, she corrects. She walks back and forth in front of her father and brother to demonstrate. It unnerves her father the way she plays these days, but at the same time he's interested to hear the mother's story.

Oh my, hasn't your daughter grown lovely? Mother, mimicking the wake-goers. Camilla Chafe, she just couldn't stop talking about it. She's growing up to be such a beauty! Said we should enter her as a princess in the festival this summer.

The father doesn't care to watch his daughter flouncing back and forth, but he's pleased by the news.

Well, there ya go, Corrie, you're a regular debutante.

Some guy wanted me to take off with him. Wanted my phone number. Wanted. But she can't brag about this to him. She follows Howard to his room instead.

It's just tits, says Howard. It's all big tits. You can have a face like Dad, guys don't care. So whoopee, you got tits.

Oh, don't pretend it doesn't bother you. I could be going out with a twenty-five-year-old tomorrow if I wanted. Because I . . . I am a wooooman.

She yanks his flannel bathrobe from the hook and begins to shimmy around the room, waving it around like a feather boa.

Stop being retarded.

She likes to piss off Howard. Howard was once her world. Howard taught her everything she knows about life. So she resents Howard a great deal in some ways.

Wooooman, she sings like Helen Reddy. She wraps the flannel boa around her neck.

Men desire me, she confides to her brother. Men at wakes, with dead people lying three feet away from them.

You're fuckin sick.

I'm siiiiick, she sings, sashaying from his room. I'm a siiick woooooooman . . .

Give me my robe!

Noooooo . . .!

Dad!

Everybody please shut up up there, calls the father. He has dealt this way with their disputes since life began. It was easier, he always said, than trying to figure out who was right and who was wrong—who hit who first. Just tell them to both shut up. Keep telling them to shut up and sooner or later they'll just shut up and the house will have peace.

The next day, the fallout. There are pamphlets on her bed when she gets home from school. She's seen them before, out front at the church and in the doctor's office. On the cover: *How Do I know if it's Really Love?* Inside: When you're over 21 and are married. Cover: *Sexually Transmitted Diseases: A Matter of Life and Death.* Inside: . . . but mostly death. Cover: *One Mistake is All it Takes.* Inside . . . more of same.

She gets in a car with a strange man—it's hilarious. She didn't mean to. She was on her way to school, and she was late. He leaned out the window and said hi. She thought she must know him from somewhere; he spoke to her like he did. He looked familiar. It is a small town and everybody knows everybody. She gets in beside him expecting, *So how's your dad doing these days with the business, your brother still playing the basketball, sorry to hear about your great-aunt.* But nothing like that, no mention of her family at all. Only her. He only wants to talk about her. Except for the guy at the wake, it is the first such grown-up she's encountered.

Where's she off to? She is off to school, just over the hill. How's she doing today? She's doing good, but she's going to get in trouble, because she's late for first period. Why not just skip the first period? Why not come for a drive? Well, she'd like to, you know, but she can't really skip school, she'd get into trouble.

She looks at him. He looks back and smiles. So what's your name?

What is her name? He doesn't know her name? He doesn't know her? She doesn't know him. She points ahead.

The school is just up over the hill, past the lights, she says.

Yep, no problem. Sure you won't come for a drive instead?

Yes. Thank you, though. And thanks very much for the drive.

No problem, he tells her again. There is a rotary he has to go into in order to let her off by the doors. There is another road going off towards the highway before they get to the rotary, however. But he drives into the rotary. He drives right up to the school doors.

Well, maybe I'll see you around again sometime, when you don't have anywhere to go in particular.

Yes! Maybe!

She is giddy all day. She tells her friends during free period. Pam wants her to go to the principal or tell a teacher or something.

Are you kidding? They'll think I'm an idiot! My parents will never let me leave the house again!

She feels they are almost at that point as it is, and she hasn't even done anything.

Never talk to strangers, never get in cars with strangers, never go for rides with strangers.

But say you can't sleep. Say you leave the house in the middle of the night. It's a summer night, so you can walk in shorts and a T-shirt. Say you walk all around town, deep into every little corner. You know this town like the inside of your brain. You've ridden your bike in and out of everyone's driveway. You've played war in the woods, tag in the graveyards. You've wound your way along the railroad tracks, right out past the causeway to swim where the water isn't as polluted. The point is, the town is all around and everywhere, there is nowhere you could go you haven't been before. And say there is a car. Say there is a car slowly coming towards you. Say there is a long black car. Inside is someone special and new. He sees you, walking around in the middle of the night, and instantly can tell you're special too, that you are meant for him. Say he's like a rock star or a vampire. Say he is desire.

Wouldn't it be okay then?

Or else: say you are bad. You walk around at night because you're bad. What kind of girl walks around in the middle of the night? What is she looking for? She is looking for one thing, obviously, and that's what she's going to get. Because that's what the men in cars are for, they have a purpose, they are the punishers, they are the ones who wait for you to step out of line and then they snatch you up. Because you're bad, and that's the kind of thing you can expect.

She stalks up and down in Howard's room. Why are you always bothering me, he wants to know. Why are you always in here?

She stops pacing and points her finger at him. Why are *you* always bothering *me*?

I'm not bothering you.

You don't even give a shit about me anymore.

What makes you think I ever did?

He is just being a mean bastard big brother.

Why don't you explain things to me anymore? she demands.

He leans back in his desk chair, smiling. Oh, sorry. I thought you already knew everything. I thought you didn't need me to explain things.

She's miffed because she did say that. Only moments ago, when she first stormed into his room. She kicks his chair. It has wheels, so she can't kick it out from under him, as she'd like to. She moves to kick it again.

Dad!

Please shut up, now, calls the dad.

Howard smiles. Dad! he yells again. Not because he's mad. He just wants to get rid of her and knows how.

Enough! yells the father. Go to your separate corners! Another favourite expression of his, valued for its referee-like impartiality.

Downstairs on the piano is a picture of her and Howard. He is wearing a T-shirt that says SURE I'M PERFECT. He picked it out himself when he was ten. She remembers him wearing that T-shirt. She remembers believing it. She sits beside him in the picture, far from perfect and knowing it, because he has told her. She has a big gut and chipmunk cheeks, not to mention buck teeth. She is fat, like the relatives, like her chubby friend at school. She is a hideous freak. He would vow he was going to sell her to the circus where she would be the star attraction with the goat boy and the bearded lady. She had nightmares. She dreamt of being in a cage with the bearded lady, straw on the floor. She never dreamt about the goat boy, it was the bearded lady who was truly hideous in her imagination. The bearded lady was huge, and towered over her. She dressed in clothes out of *Little House on the Prairie,* hair in a ratty bun, and a thick, curly, miserable beard, long and matted. Corinne would think she was alone in the dark cage and she'd pray the bearded lady wouldn't come. But she always came, and she always wanted to make her eat. The bearded lady tried to feed her horrible food, the same food that was used to feed the circus animals. Rotten meat and wormy, shitty straw.

Get thee behind me, Satan is something she has learned you are supposed to say when you are tempted by evil. She is not so much tempted by evil as she is curious about evil. Is it the same thing? She wants to check it out a little.

And what is evil and how is evil? Fruits are evil, dictates Howard. Homos. And whores are evil. But nobody has actually come out and said *evil*. There's no need. There's no need, the words seethe with it all on their own. Is evil the man in the car or is evil the girl at night? Is it both? Is it only both together?

Evil becomes her favourite word. She says it at school. She takes a bite of someone's Vachon cake. "Mmmmmmm. E-vil!"

She sits across from Howard in the living room and cups her hands around her mouth in the middle of one of his favourite shows: "Frooooot!"

He stares at her.

Frooooot! she lows, cowlike.

Stop it, he says.

She tells all her friends that they are whores. Hi, whore. Give me that, you whore. Pass me a pencil, please, whore. Everyone imitates her after a while.

She goes to church and decides to become a religious fanatic. She thinks about Jesus on the cross, and God in his heaven. She decides it is her mission to figure out exactly what God wants. Then she can tell everyone.

Did Jesus pee, she remembers wondering as a kid. Did Jesus *poo*? It was important. It was like a mystic, ancient riddle that only some mythical character could solve. Like the Sphinx would ask people.

She abandons fanaticism after a while because it is not sat-isfying. She remembers religious fanatics from the Bible. The whole point is to be empty. The whole point is to be in a con-stant state of dissatisfaction. The whole point is to be deprived of what you cannot live without. It's no good to her.

She gathers her friends together in the study area above the library. Listen, she whispers. I'm starting to think it's all a pile of bullshit.

The friends all look at each other and then, gradually, admit the same.

And that's it for God. She's feeling powerful now. It's been growing in her for a while, this wiggling, bucking seahorse inside, tapping its nose against her spine.

She necks at parties. Necking. Necking is weird. Everybody just necks with everybody. It doesn't really have anything to do with who you like and who you don't. It's just like trying every-body out—taking them for a test drive.

Somebody breathes in her ear, You got any condoms? They are locked in the bathroom, in the dark, and nobody can see or get in. She screams laughter anyway, like they're on stage.

I necked at the party, she tells Howard, who's watching some kind of rock concert when she gets home. No lights are on but the television's. It is Neil Young, singing: *My my, hey hey*. Howard is playing air guitar along with him, doesn't even stop to hear her speak.

Yep. She sits down in her chair across from him. Did some necking. I got to touch a guy's wang dang doodle.

Howard throws down his invisible guitar.

Oh—*gah!* he says, like he can't even finish the word *God*. What makes you think I give a shit about this stuff?

I just thought you'd take a brotherly interest.

You're going to get knocked up if you're not careful.

I just said I touched it. I didn't, you know, *touch* it.

She leans forward, but is frustrated to see Howard settling back, having collected himself already.

Like, with my vagina, she adds hopefully.

He points the remote and turns the volume up.

Vagina, she says again. Apparently that's the proper, scientific term for . . .

Quit it.

For . . .

Quit.

For . . . !

Her voice going up, up, up in suspense.

Howard stretches in his chair, yawns.

She decides to give up. Her mood crashes. It's been like that: she floats and falls, floats and falls. Some days she feels like God, or at least, a pretty decent rival. Head throbbing with wisdom and insight, like she could approach people on the street and tell them exactly what their hopes and fears were and not to worry about them because everything would be okay. Like she could reach into the minds of strangers and present them with the diamonds she withdraws. Howard made that go away, however. Often Howard, but sometimes other things as well.

In school, Mrs. Waycott teaches a special ed class. The retarded boys and girls keep mostly to their one classroom, but sometimes they trundle down to the pool for swimming lessons, or to the cafeteria for lunch. White, mostly smiling. Once a boy from special ed ran up and said he'd like to marry her. All her friends were around, and she promised him she would, once she went to university and got a good job as a movie star's assistant or something. Mrs. Waycott gathered the boy back to her, and Corinne's friends all went: Awww. That was so sweet.

But her mood was gone, had crashed as the simple boy went away, waving. She hadn't liked having him close to her, and suspected she was an awful person for it. He had looked at her with love. He kept trying to hug her.

She is fifteen. She is friends with everyone in school. She is popular. Boys have told her, and each other, that she is a cocktease, but nobody really holds it against her. She gets asked out, and goes out, and necks, and fools around a bit, but she doesn't get like her girl friends. She doesn't pick one boy and suture herself to him, in her mind if not in reality, for dear life. She goes to parties and just has fun. All the boys she knows are her friends. She can't imagine love.

Although she *pretends* to imagine love, like her friends do. She pretends to pant over the "hot guys." The hot guys in school, the hot guys in movies, the hot guys on TV. About a guy at school whose bones everybody wants to jump she claims, Oh, I'd like to jump his bones. And somebody says: Why don't you go for it? You could have him in a minute. And she floats on that power momentarily but then has to figure out how to make her friends forget she ever said anything and leave her alone.

So she tells them, Listen. You can't, can't, can't tell this to anyone. Remember that guy in the car? I saw him again. I was walking to the mall on the weekend and he drove by. We went for pizza. He plays guitar. He's from Halifax. He's twenty . . . three.

The friends gawk and shake their heads in slow motion. No. The pervert?

Yeah, but the thing is, he wasn't a pervert at all. He turned out to be a really nice guy. We drive around on the weekends. We go to Antigonish to see movies. But we're going to have to sneak around until I'm eighteen or my parents would kill me. So you can't tell anyone or else I'm dead.

It doesn't matter if some of them don't believe her. It's mostly for her, at first, this story. The guy in the car and the guy in the story have very little in common. The guy in the car was not in his twenties. He had black hair parted in the middle, sweeping off to the sides and a thin little moustache which was vaguely ridiculous. His car was not long or dark, but a Ford hatchback. She forgets about this guy and replaces him without even being aware that she's doing it. She doesn't know exactly whom she replaces him with. She can't find a face. But he is twenty-three and plays guitar. He has a band, but also a day job. She can't be bothered deciding what the day job is. He is not from around here, that is the main thing.

What does he do to her? He doesn't do anything to her. He does something, but she can't picture it. She pictures them eating pizza together, watching movies. She pictures herself getting into the car. She pictures them sitting together, apart. She gets excited and tormented, yet she knows it's not much of a fantasy at all. Still it makes her happy. It's all she needs. The only problem is convincing her friends of details she hasn't convinced herself of yet.

And his name? Is? Brian. Perfect name. It could belong to nearly anybody.

She thinks about Brian until she feels she has him perfected. He is just about real to her. She talks about him all the time, like any girl would about her boyfriend. Brian hates it when she wears makeup. But he likes her in skirts. He insists she wait for him to open the car door to let her out. He is an old-fashioned kind of guy. He wants a big wedding, one day. He can't wait to meet her family, once she has turned eighteen. He still has a stuffed toy beaver that was given to him by his godmother when he was a baby. It sits on a shelf along with all his track and field trophies. It is so sweet! She talks about Brian to her friends, assaulting them with details, until they have no choice but to believe in him. When she feels this, when they are sidling up to her in the halls, poking her sides and cooing, *How's Briiii-an?* on a regular basis, she knows she is ready. She's ready to take Brian to Howard.

Because if she can get it past Howard, the story will go on. She will finally be able to figure out Brian's face, for one thing. She'll be able to do things with him. As usual, however, everything first depends on Howard—what he thinks, what he says, what he does. Only it depends on her as well, a little, this time.

Howard went away to university last year, and then came back for a summer to work at the fish plant where he shucked clams and came home smelling of sea-rot every night. It was strange, for Howard. He had never been the kind of boy who stank. In the evenings he would mess around noisily in the shed. He said he was cleaning it. On weekends he was still in the shed, lifting weights and listening to the stereo. In August he told them he wasn't going back to university. He was going to live in the shed. He kept his job at the fish plant, but in October the shed got too cold so he moved his weights and stereo back into his old room, and he lived there still. Nobody had asked Howard any questions. Howard had been the most capable one in the family since the day he could talk, and it didn't make sense to start questioning him now. The unspoken family policy had always been: trust Howard. He was fixing their parents' car and doing their taxes by the time he was four-teen. He knew what he was doing.

They used to let him baby-sit alone when she was seven and he was twelve. Sometimes he would feel like playing the teacher and explain wonders to her. He was slow and patient with her kid's brain, digging out books with illustrations, set-ting up his chemistry set to do experiments, letting her partici-pate every step of the way, letting her learn. An entire afternoon would be dedicated to demonstrating one simple principle of physics, unearthing the tiniest puzzle-piece of the universe. She would go to bed with her mind throwing sparks.

But that got rare. More often he was restless and bored. Trapped together in the house, he'd dig out the chemistry set to terrify her. He unfurled his collection of small, sharp tools—scalpels and scissors and picks—kept elegantly rolled in a scrap of green velvet. He'd pick up one tool after the other and let it glint as he spoke. She cried and peed, one time. They cleaned it up together, him rapidly explaining how volcanoes came to be.

At best she held some kind of interest for him then.

Boys are calling on the phone, and it works in her favour that they sound so much alike. Voices uniformly broken, deep, choked with hormonal trauma. Voices of men, words of boys. One from out of town calls and calls. She stays on for hours, listing off her favourite this, her all-time-most-hated that, talking for as long as they both can stand it. All so she can swish downstairs in her nightgown and have the family make remarks.

Her father says she is like Scarlett O'Hara, so one night they rent the movie. And it's true!

That woman displays all the classic traits of a sociopath, Howard remarks a few minutes into it.

Her parents turn to scrutinize.

Fiddle de-dee, she assures them.

The one from out of town doesn't know her well enough to understand. He doesn't understand how she is, like the guys in her own school. He keeps calling. He wants to take her out and do the kind of things that she would only do with Brian. It is almost regrettable her friends have already seen him at the dance—otherwise he could *be* Brian. He could come to get her after school, could sit in the parking lot, waiting in his truck. There he is, you guys, gotta run! No, don't come with me, he's shy. I mean, he is a cradle robber, he's not exactly looking for attention! Bye! I'll tell you all about it tomorrow! Bye! I'll call you!

But everybody's seen him already, and they know he's not Brian. And she knows he's not Brian.

He continues to misunderstand, and finally she actually has to tell *him* about Brian. When she hears the words come out of her mouth, a joy rushes through her and she grins like an idiot, like a girl in love. She is speaking of Brian to a stranger. She is making him more and more real. And not only does the guy believe it, but he's jealous. It's thrilling.

He calls again. I'm sorry I got angry with you like that.

It's all right. I'm sorry too.

I wanted to hit you. I had to take off, because I thought I was going to hit you.

She sits up, and looks around her room. She cranes her neck to see down the hall.

Really?

Yeah, I was gonna fuckin hit you.

She wills herself to believe it. She wills herself to picture it. She wills herself to imagine a future scenario where someone will have to come and save her from the jealous boy from out of town.

But she can't. There is a cold spot in her imagination, a dead place that won't be warmed up no matter how crazily the rest of her mind bubbles and seethes. It infuriates her as it smirks, *This poor little Frenchman wouldn't hurt a fly.* There is a forlorn whirring in her mind as her mood sputters and gets ready to plummet.

I have to go, she says quickly. Don't call again, okay?

I didn't mean to scare you! He shouts this, like he knows she's putting the receiver down.

The cold spot speaks up, defying her, because she'd like to be scared. She'd like to sit on her bed and tremble into her nightie like a girl in a horror movie.

Poor dumb bastard it takes more than a thing like you.

If she could just apply her fingers to her temples and massage that voice right out of her brain, like a blackhead from a pore.

When the dead place takes over, grows tentacles and wiggles them about, she can only sit around and cry. The whole while, the cold mind saying, Stop crying, stupid cunt. Pointless. Useless. Dumb girl. Stop. Don't bother. Not interested. Quit. Stop. Her mother comes and rubs her back. Her father makes her hot toddies until she nods into phlegmy slumber. It's nerves, her mother confides to her father over her head. They talk like she's not there and she isn't. It's hard at this age, explains her mother. Her father walks around with the look of a man choking on his powerlessness. Is it a boy? Is it school? He can't think of what else it might be, so he asks the same two questions, reworded, reformulated, over and over again.

You don't understand, her mother hisses. It's never any one thing at this age.

Was a boy *mean* to you? her father pleads. Is it physics? I know you have a hard time with physics. We can get you a tutor.

She stays home from school a couple of days and her best friend from childhood brings homework and sits on the end of her bed. Corinne is not crying anymore, and feels a bit stronger. She looks at the ceiling and forces herself back into the fantasy.

The French guy, she tells her friend, grinding out the words with effort. Is nuts.

The innocent eyes of her childhood friend go wide. Why?

He's calling. He's like, threatening me and stuff.

Oh my God, you should tell somebody.

I've. Told. Brian.

She bites her lip and sobs quickly, because the cold spot is still rampant, speaking its mind. You know what? it inquires. You are so sad.

Her good friend rubs her leg. It'll be all right. Brian will take care of him.

I know but it's—she hiccups grief—it's *scary*.

The friend crawls farther up on the bed to give her a hug. The two used to sleep together in this bed as children, having belching contests into the dawn. She roots around in her brain for that old love. She knows it's not there, but she roots around anyway, out of duty and nostalgia.

The cold spot remarks, If you were a well and someone dropped a penny into you, they could listen forever and never hear a sound. Lucky for you, nobody is listening very carefully.

Her friend has to leave, and Corinne lies in the dark thinking she'll never get up again. And then light pours in from the doorway.

He stands there. Listen. He clears his throat, because the word came out in a rasp. Listen, he says again. What's the story with this guy?

She pulls herself up onto the pillows. What guy?

Pam told me there was some guy.

He came to her room. He stood up from his chair and walked up the stairs and opened the door just to talk to her. She blows her nose.

It's nobody.

She said he's talking shit to you or something.

It's nothing. It's just a lot of crap.

Well. He looks around her dark room with obvious discomfort. Well, like, tell him about me or something, okay? Tell him I'm a football player or a wrestler or something if he calls again.

Yah.

Seriously. If he calls again, I'll get on the phone.

Okay.

I'll even go look for him or something if he keeps calling.

You will?

Yah. Now . . . cheer up, all right? Jesus.

He shuts the door.

She throws back the covers, opens the curtains. Sun.

Her friends are enthralled with the story of her life—everyone in school knows it. There is Brian. There is the guy from outside town. She describes dangerous weekends when these two come together. Brian takes her to a dance out in Isle Madame—they can only go to dances out in the sticks, lest word get back to her parents—and there he is, the French guy. Jealous and hulking.

He tries to get her alone, the guy from out of town. He waits for Brian to go to the can, and grabs her by the shoulder. He tries to get her to dance, to come outside, to sit in his truck. She tells him she is waiting for her boyfriend, and looks around.

He kept grabbing me, she tells her friends.

Brian comes running up and pushes him. The other guy pushes back, and the crowd instantly shapes itself into a circle around them. She has been to enough dances to know the dynamic of violence, and she describes it to a T. There is no reason not to believe it happened. Everyone has seen the same thing play out almost every weekend of their lives.

They fight. Brian wins, but sprains his wrist. The bad guy hulks away, bleeding, cursing them both, calling her a bitch.

She hesitates before this next part, looking around to make sure she's got everybody's full attention.

He said, *You'll pay for this, you bitch*.

Pam jumps up like she's in court. That's a threat! she declares. That's a threat, you could call the police!

Yeah, brilliant. And have them arrest Brian for statutory rape?

Pam sits down again. I think you'd have to be fourteen for it to be statutory rape.

I can't risk it. That's the point, he *knows* he's got this on us. He *knows* Brian's twenty-three. He knows he could get me into shit at the drop of a hat, and then me and Brian would never see each other again. He's holding it over our heads.

The friend ducks her head, ashamed to have presumed so much. That she could ever hope to counsel a life so dangerous and different from her own.

I piss my pants every time the phone rings, Corinne continues, grateful to Pam for spurring her imagination in this way.

She practices cringing when the phone rings. Usually it's nobody but sometimes, sometimes, it's the guy from out of town. She doesn't run to her room like she typically would if she knew it was for her. She makes a point of picking it up in the living room now, where the television is. One night it works.

Hello?

Hi, he says. I'm sorry I was a dick. I just want to see you again.

No, she gulps, and clatters the phone back into its cradle. Sighs, sitting down.

On the couch, Howard shifts, keeping his eyes on the set.

After a moment: Was that that asshole?

Uh. Yah.

He sits up and shuffles his cushions around for a moment or two.

Well, fuck, I told you to let me know.

Sorry. I don't think he'll call again.

What's his name?

She pulls a knitted afghan up around her knees. Don't tell the folks.

I'm not gonna, just tell me his name, so I'll know.

But, she wants to say, you never go out. You never see anybody. You never do anything.

What difference does it make? she says.

Finally he looks at her. She pulls the afghan up higher.

I'm just saying. If he calls again, I can say, I know your name. I know who you are. I know where you live.

I can tell him all that—you don't have to.

He gets to his feet, Howard does. A sudden, deliberate movement. She breathes deep into the afghan, smelling old tea.

Will you let me— He stops. He starts again.

I can do this for you. This is one thing I can do.

Even though he's stopped looking at her, she realizes this is the first time in ages she's had his full attention. With a rush of gratitude, she understands this is the moment to ask. It might not come again. The big question. The question that is basically her.

Howard? What is it with guys? What is the matter with them, anyway?

He looks at her again as he speaks, a long time for him and her.

I don't want to talk to you, he says with diamondlike enunciation. I don't want to have a discussion with you. I am telling you something. Give me the phone next time. And tell me his name.

She is so tired that she does. She is so wrung out from their little chat that she starts to cry.

Why does everybody treat me like a fucking freak?

But he hasn't hung around for that.

Things her father used to do:

Sit her on his knee. For hours.

Tickle her.

Arm wrestle.

Take her everywhere he went.

Ride her on his shoulders.

Call her Princess. Kitten. Lovey-dovey. Best girl.

Tell her she was good.

Often she suspected she wasn't, even then. Sometimes she would sit in the church for almost an hour after mass was over, hoping to clean herself out. But then she'd go home, and her father would tell her she was, without her even asking him about it. Like he knew what was in her brain. He would clean her out with just a word or two. Good girl. *Best.*

But these days her suspicions about herself are just left to grow and grow unchecked. If she goes to church, pamphlets are placed there, in the foyer, specifically for the likes of her to find.

So she doesn't go to church anymore and her father stomps and raves about it even though he doesn't go very often himself. He doesn't *need* it as much as she does now, he insists.

What is that supposed to mean?

Your moral sense isn't developed yet.

Her mother stands by, shaking her head at the father like he's a child twirling scissors in one hand.

Corinne sucks in her breath, holds it for a moment, and then blows out the words from her diaphragm:

You think I am a slut.

He takes a step back. Dear! I.

A big fat slut, she persists, almost gleeful.

The father shakes his head as if the mother's gesture was contagious, and Corinne can see every thought in that round, salty gourd of his all of a sudden: How dare you. How can you. Well, I. That kind of language. I just think. There's no need. I think you. I don't want you to. And then the little window in his brain pulls its curtains, like someone has been caught coming out of the bathtub within.

Howard, he says now.

She blinks at her father. She puts her hands against her face because they seem to have become cold. She presses them against her eyes.

Yes? What about Howard?

Howard! He's calling him. She puts her cold hands on her hips. Let him call Howard, then. Let him call and call and call.

Howard! he shouts. Will you talk to this girl!

Please shut up out there, Howard titters from the next room. Separate corners, you two.

The father looks at the mother, jaw a-dangle, as if to say: What exactly are these creatures we have made together?

As the weather warms, she sees Howard contemplate the shed. He moves the weights back in for good, but carries the stereo back and forth because the shed leaks.

You are going to electrocute yourself in there, their mother says.

Corinne tries to joke with him: Don't leave me alone in the house with these maniacs, she says. God knows what they'll do to me. She doesn't even look up to see if he smirks, which he almost certainly doesn't. And she's not smirking either. She's not much of a joker these days.

But then, where there is supposed to be Howard's silence, there instead comes words.

What's that supposed to mean?

She looks up and he's angry.

What?

What's that alone in the house bullshit?

I was just kidding.

I don't fucking appreciate it.

I said I was kidding! God, they say I'm the moody one.

Howard looks surprised, and then pissed off again. I have

to get out of this house, he says. She hates him for it.

Go back to university, then.

That's more like it. That's the reaction she is used to. Silence, and the going away.

She has been fighting with Brian. With a new cynicism she informs her friends that they are "past the honeymoon phase." He is impatient with her youth. He wants to meet her family. He wants to proclaim their love from the rooftops, but she won't let him. She can't.

I tell him, just a little bit longer, just a little bit longer. He doesn't want to wait. He's talking about starting a *family* already, can you believe it? I mean, I haven't even gotten away from my own goddamn family yet.

There's such a big age difference, her friends point out.

She gazes into the distance like a soap star. Maybe it's insurmountable, she sighs.

And, jealous! Who would have thought that someone as sweet as Brian would have a jealous side? But it's awful, he's like a different person. He thinks she must be doing something to encourage the guy from out of town, because the guy keeps calling. She thought she was only being honest, telling him about the guy calling, but now it's made Brian suspicious.

So much for honesty, she grimaces. Her friends are in awe of her soaring maturity, which they equate with romantic disillusionment. They feel inadequate for not even having experienced the honeymoon phase yet.

She takes Pam aside to tell her the rest.

And he's getting weird with sex.

Pam swallows.

It's like, violent.

No, says Pam. She doesn't say it the way her other friends would, gasping with scandal. She says it like pain.

Well, rough. Like, domination.

Stop.

Stop? She's surprised to receive an order.

Stop seeing him. He doesn't have the right. It's illegal for him to do things you don't want.

Pam is always talking about things being legal and illegal. Justice. Pam will be a lawyer one day. She believes that good people endeavour to behave within these imaginary boundaries. She cannot believe that some people don't even know about them, that some don't even care.

I just want things to go back to the way they were, Corinne sighs, trying to lighten things up.

But they won't, her friend states, and a beetle of anger begins to scuttle up Corinne's spine.

What do you mean they won't?

They just don't. Things don't go back to normal after something like that. They can't. They either stay weird, or they get worse.

Why? Corinne whispers, like the two of them are under the covers of her bed again, six years old.

Memory, says Pam.

You can forget about the past! She smiles brightly.

No you can't, says Pam. Not if one person hurts another.

I read that people can't remember pain.

But they remember being afraid. That's what they can't forget. People can't have a relationship after something like that.

Pam is speaking from books now. They have been studying terrorism in their modern world problems class. Despite scattered complaints from a handful of parents, they have spent the past month learning about torture and post-traumatic stress disorder and the Stockholm syndrome. They learned about the UN Declaration of Human Rights. Pam, as usual, has been paying closer attention than Corinne has. Pam has been studying up on it outside class, for a project or something.

Corinne stands with sudden contempt at this realization.

Pam? Really? You have no idea what you're talking about. We're in *love*. She thumps the word *love* down in front of her friend like a trump card in a game of auction.

Abused women get symptoms of post-traumatic stress, Pam insists. Just like men coming home from a war.

They are hiding up in the study area above the library, skipping class together. She begged Pam to skip with her, she was so upset over Brian. Corinne needed to talk. Now she lies down on the floor and kicks her legs and shrieks laughter at Pam. Before Corinne can impress upon her friend how incredibly stupid she is, how mind-bogglingly naive, the librarian appears from downstairs and orders them away.

If you would just see me, he says. If you would just come let me buy you a pop.

It's really late.

I'm just around the corner. I'm just down at MacIssac's.

Just come for a sec.

Everybody's in bed. *I'm* in bed!

They won't know you're gone.

She hears a click. She can't believe he would just hang up on her. That he could be that sure of himself. For a moment, she's impressed. She considers throwing on her clothes, venturing out, if only to tell him to piss off once and for all. If only to see what he will do once they are alone.

But then his voice again. Are you still there?

She sits with her mouth open.

Hello? he calls.

Yes—are you?

He breathes a laugh into the phone. Well, yeah.

More clicks, but from downstairs. The click of the television being turned off. The front door clicks open, then closed. The screen door wheezes shut on its spring a moment after.

I think, she says, I should go now. And you should go. I think you should go home.

I can't. I got no truck. I hitchhiked down. I have good news, ya know.

Hitchhike back.

But she can tell he is encouraged, he is cheering up, because she hasn't spoken to him this long, or this gently, in a while.

Meet me, he coos, gaining confidence. *Meeeeeet meeeeee.*

She stuffs herself and the phone beneath a pillow in order to scream *fuck off* without waking her parents. She unplugs the phone, turns off the lights in an irrational effort to hear things better. Outside, there is nothing but the summer-sound of wind

moving through thick poplar leaves. The noise is like a million
whispered clicks, an insect tide.

ReTREAT

LELAND COULD not help feeling he was partially at fault. If he had not exiled Isadore, he thought, the lunatic would not have been driving all over the place looking for booze. So Leland stepped in and spoke to the Mounties upon word of the accident, and the next day Isadore found himself locked up in detox as opposed to a jail cell, even though—he later complained to Leland—there didn't seem to be great deal of difference as far as he was concerned. A judge had already decreed he was not to be let out for seven days, after which Isadore was ordered to seek counselling. At his old friend's suggestion, therefore, Isadore returned to the only place he knew that offered counseling—the monastery's AA retreat, where he had first encountered Alison Mason and countless other drinking buddies including Leland himself and Marianne's ex-husband.

SUMMER

boys

ONLY TWO BOYS from the 1980 honours graduating class still lived in town, and everyone talked about and speculated upon them for different reasons. "Honours" was a way of saying "college-bound" in their school. The courses offered that were not honours were called "doobie" by the students. But officially, there was honours math and then there was just math. The school administrators seemed to think that by not identifying the doobie math class as such, the students wouldn't notice the distinction.

Doobie courses were understood to be for kids too thick to take chemistry and physics. These were classes like oceanography and industrial arts. Such classes were filled almost entirely with boys, shit-disturbers. Those boys were the doobies. The men who taught these courses were uniformly overweight, and angry much of the time. Girls were never considered doobies—the closest equivalent was slut.

Howard Fortune and Hugh Gillis had never taken any doobie courses. Neither of them was a shit-disturber. But these similarities only scratched the surface, and they were considered to be exactly alike in the eyes of some people. They had both been sports stars—Hugh in almost everything and Howard in basketball and swimming. They had both been on the honour roll. Girls talked about them in the same tones they discussed musicians and TV stars. Howard was better-looking, but Hugh was more laid back and friendly.

People assumed, for these reasons, that the boys were good friends and had been all through high school.

The truth was they had an instinctual dislike of each other and had barely exchanged a word since grade seven. But if anyone had ever asked Hugh about Howard, Hugh would have said he was a good guy, but that he, Hugh, couldn't say he knew him all that well. Hugh always got the impression that Howard, in contrast, thought Hugh was just a jock from a well-off family who got everything handed to him on a silver platter. In his turn, Hugh might have replied that Howard was kind of an asshole. Howard had no interest in putting people at ease. If someone said something stupid in his presence, Howard would roll his sharp, grey eyes, and sometimes even call the person down. Because Howard was big and handsome and smart, there was scarcely anyone who could stand against this kind of thing. And somewhere deep inside himself, Hugh considered this sort of behaviour an abuse of power—the kind of power Hugh knew he possessed as well and tried to be responsible about.

Since they had graduated, the two stuck out in town like thumbs on a foot. Howard especially, because he had never been as integrated into the community as Hugh. Hugh had startled everyone by not leaving town to go to school. He kept his many doobie friends—all of whom started jobs at the mill and elsewhere around town the week after graduation—and took the exotic, new computer courses being offered at the vocational school, while his honours friends were packing trunks for university. He didn't want to leave, he said. "I like it here," he told people when they stopped him at the drug store or at the tavern. So people worshipped Hugh. They were grateful to him for continuing to grace the town, even though his parents were upset at first. It seemed to them—and they were not far wrong—that Hugh simply didn't want to end his routine of partying every weekend with his buddies, the same friends he'd had for years. He merely wanted his life to stay the same.

But Howard's reappearance in town was abrupt and perplexing. He went away to school as was expected, came back for the summer to work, also expected, but then neglected to disappear into the outside world again like so many of his classmates. People saw him putting gas in his parents' car midweek in mid-September, and scratched their heads. He kept a low profile for much of the year, so the community was slow to comprehend.

When people finally figured out Howard was there to stay, they decided the appropriate response was contempt—or more benevolently, pity. And they were thrilled to pity someone like Howard Fortune, who had the whole world waiting for him and upon whom his parents had pinned so many hopes.

But Howard's return made Hugh itchy. He finally figured out why one Saturday afternoon at his nephew's pee-wee hockey game. One of the guys Hugh was with, Mackie Pettipas, spotted Howard Fortune's little sister in the crowd and remarked, inoffensively enough, on how hot she was in her Calvin Klein jeans, so new and tight and blue they appeared almost wet against her legs. Hugh glanced over at the girl and agreed absently, more interested in the game, but it brought the subject around to Howard himself. He half listened to his friends discussing Howard for a moment or two when something about their tone and the nature of the discussion pierced his awareness.

"You guys," he said, turning to them, "are being fuckin catty, you know that? You sound like a bunch of women." Everybody shut up and watched the game after that, but Hugh was still digesting their conversation, and realized at last why the topic of Howard Fortune bothered him. Howard appeared to be doing poorly for the first time in his life, and people were taking pleasure in it. Howard had never hung around with "the boys"—as Hugh thought of his doobie friends—and "the boys" were the only people their age left around town. Anyone Howard might have considered a friend was now in university—which was of course where Howard himself should have been.

Hugh realized it fell on him to see how Howard Fortune was getting on.

Calling Howard Fortune out of the blue to say hello was simply not an option, however. Hugh's plan was to wait around for the next time he bumped into Howard at the liquor store, or somewhere, and take advantage of the occasion.

Five weeks went by before they met in the post office. Howard was licking stamps at a counter and affixing them to three large, crammed manila envelopes.

Hugh experienced a nervous jolt of adrenaline from having the opportunity he'd been waiting for arrive so unexpectedly. He used it to launch himself towards Howard before he could lose his nerve. But the closer Hugh got, the more aware he became that he just didn't like the guy. Howard stood there licking stamps like he was the only man in the post office, or the world.

"Hey, man," said Hugh.

Howard moved his head, closed his eyes, and when he opened them they were looking at Hugh—two steady, shining dimes.

Hugh thought, Fuck me.

"How's it going, Howard?" he pushed on.

Howard did the slow-blink thing a couple more times before his lip twitched and his face relaxed an infinitesimal degree.

"Hey," he echoed. "Good. What have you been up to?"

"Ah, you know, dicking around. Partying, mostly. Taking some courses up at the voc."

Howard leaned against the counter. Both made gestures of profound relaxation and ease.

"How's that going?" said Howard.

"Good." Hugh put his hands in his pockets and had to stop himself from whistling. "Seen you around," he remarked.

"Yeah," agreed Howard.

"You home for the winter?"

"Pretty much," said Howard, reaching protectively for his oversize envelopes.

Fuck don't worry man I won't ask, thought Hugh. He made himself smile, aware that he would have to convey enough good will for both of them if the conversation was going to be endured.

"Well, right on, we'll have to get together for a beer sometime," Hugh said.

Howard performed a couple more of his slow blinks and Hugh felt that if the guy had sat down in front of a mirror to devise the most alienating facial gesture imaginable, he could not have come up with anything more effective.

"Yeah," Howard answered once he was finished blinking.

"No, seriously, I mean it, man, we'll head out to the tavern some weekend," Hugh said.

"Sure," said Howard. He turned to his envelopes.

"Well, all right," said Hugh, nearly yelling. "I'll give you a call this weekend sometime."

"This weekend?" repeated Howard.

"Why the fuck not?" Hugh exclaimed.

Howard finally smiled like a human being. In his discomfort, Hugh had come across as wildly enthusiastic, and it seemed to have disarmed Howard somewhat.

I am going to have to go home and lie down after this, Hugh thought, grinning back at Howard like a lunatic.

But Hugh strolled out of the post office feeling something solid and certain about himself for the first time in all his happy, unremarkable years: that he, Hugh Gillis, was one hell of a good guy. Knowing this, he felt weirdly grateful and well disposed toward Howard Fortune, dickhead that he was—and knowing *that* made him feel pretty good about the world in general.

The problem was Howard wouldn't come. Howard had actually no intention of going out with Hugh for a beer. He had been lying to Hugh, it turned out. Howard had tricked him. This notion made Hugh, who was a competitor at heart, doubly determined to become friends.

"You bastard!" Hugh called from his car. Howard was returning from a run near the mill road, and Hugh had slowed down alongside of him. Howard jerked around at the accusation and stumbled, almost taking a nose dive into the gravel.

"Jesus Christ!" he said, righting himself and flashing his grey eyes at Hugh.

"I been calling and calling—you're never around. What are you getting up to?"

"I haven't been around," replied Howard.

"Yah—I got that much. Listen, that looks like a hell of a lot of work. You wanna hop in and I'll drive you wherever you're headed?"

Howard ran, staring straight ahead. A car moved past Hugh's sedan and honked its irritation, but Hugh kept trailing Howard until Howard was forced to acknowledge him.

"I'm almost done," Howard yelled, jerking his head towards the car to be better heard. "I'm gonna sprint the rest of the way."

Hugh pulled a little farther ahead so he could meet Howard's eyes, clouded from fatigue as they were and not as sharp as usual. He extended his entire arm across the front seat in order to point dramatically at Howard.

"You're fuckin coming out with me, mister."

"I just haven't been around," protested Howard.

"Yah, well. My feelings are gonna be hurt if you don't get off your ass."

"Give me a call—" Howard began.

"No way! Meet me up there Wednesday." There was no question Hugh was talking about the tavern. "No. I'll come pick you up after supper."

"Wednesday?" repeated Howard.

"Welfare Wednesday, man, best day of the week. All the fuckin freaks come out to play."

With that Hugh sped away, engine roaring, aware of what a magnificent figure he cut. He squealed the sedan's tires when he hit the turnoff into town, showing off and drunk on the sense of his own boundless power. A twenty-year-old wildman.

The first thing Hugh noticed was the difference in the way they were dressed. More accurately, he noticed how Howard was dressed.

Why, why, why is this guy not in university? he thought. Howard was wearing a dark green wool sweater and khaki pants with pleats. Hugh wore a hockey jersey over a T-shirt and jeans. They both wore sneakers. Howard looked as if he were wearing after-shave, but Hugh took a big whiff and could only smell his own, Brut, which he'd been splashing all over himself since grade eight.

"You look good, man," said Hugh, half teasing.

"Thanks," Howard snorted.

"But, you know, if you're looking to get laid I gotta warn ya—Welfare Wednesday, the pickings are pretty slim."

Howard snorted again in response.

Not an easy guy to like, reflected Hugh. He crammed a tape into the stereo and with the volume at full blast, roared up the hill. It was perhaps a three-minute drive to the tavern, so they didn't need to talk. Hugh's tape was titled *Drinkin' Tunes,* and George Thoroughgood and the Destroyers sang "One Bourbon, One Scotch, and One Beer." The song finished the moment they pulled into the parking lot, which made Hugh feel pretty cool, as if he had arranged things that way. But when they climbed out of the car, the silence between the two boys reasserted itself.

Howard broke it for a change. "Nice car," he said.

Hugh stood looking at it. "Yeah. My dad's. Kinda gay."

"No way," argued Howard mildly.

"Well, you know, it's a family fuckin car. I wanna get a Trans-Am or something once I'm gainfully employed." He grinned, more at the idea of being gainfully employed than the idea of owning a Trans-Am. Howard gave him a look that conveyed precisely nothing. Hugh found he was dying to go inside. There would be more music to drown out his discomfort, and beer to rekindle his sputtering mood.

Nobody looked surprised to see Howard and Hugh enter the tavern in each other's company, even though this was the first time in their lives they had arrived anywhere together. They paused at the bar to procure a pitcher from Duncan MacPhedron before moving to find a table. Although many people hailed Hugh, he didn't move to sit with any of them. Hugh's practice was to pick out a table all his own and let people come to him—which they always did. It was still early, so they found a good table overlooking the stage. A local band comprising a couple of high school guys would be playing later. They referred to themselves as the "house band" and though Leland MacPhedron had given them no so such indication, he let them continue to think they were, since they were good boys and he knew their parents. The band was called Karnage. Leland usually paid them with three free pitchers of beer.

"They're not bad," Hugh remarked of Karnage. "Do a kickass version of 'Sweet Home Alabama.'"

"Gerald Newhook and Wayne Meisner?" said Howard. He refused to refer to them as Karnage.

"Seriously—just you wait. Really gets people out on the floor."

Howard sipped his beer. The first pitcher went fast.

After Howard offered to go get the second pitcher, guys swarmed Hugh's table, simply to get caught up with him and reassure themselves of their places in his awareness. They reminded him of softball games, asked if he would be at the boxing club that weekend, told quick, funny stories about what had happened to them or mutual friends the past week. When Howard returned they tried to swarm off again, but Hugh reached out and caught Mackie Pettipas by the sleeve.

"What's your hurry, asshole? Pull up a chair."

Mackie reached behind and literally pulled up a chair, lifting a leg with astonishing grace in order to perch himself on it backwards.

"Check out Baryshnikov," Hugh remarked to Howard as the latter sat down again.

Howard said hello to Mackie, and Hugh instantly began to regret having invited him to sit down. Practically the sole thing Mackie knew about Howard was what the network of gossip had relayed about him—he had screwed up somehow at university and was stuck shucking clams at the plant in Donnell Cove.

"So," began Mackie, wanting to know the same thing everyone in town wanted to know. "What ya still hanging around this pisshole for?"

Hugh slammed his fist down on the table. "Pettipas, you fuckin busybody!" he exclaimed, grinning.

"I'm talkin to the guy," protested Mackie.

"Well, you can talk to him and mind your own fuckin business at the same time, can't you?"

"Jesus," said Mackie. But facing a figure so talked about and speculated upon was a rare opportunity, and Mackie was reluctant to back off. "I'm just wonderin why a fella with straight A's and a basketball scholarship would end up sitting here."

"Having a drink with a scumball like yourself?" finished Hugh.

"That's right," said Mackie, removing his eyeglasses to polish them on the frayed edge of his shirt.

They both looked at Howard. Hugh knew he should say something else, something that would shut Mackie up completely, but his own curiosity had gotten the better of him for the moment.

Howard leaned back and stretched. He spread his arms out completely and yawned at them, and while yawning said, "Who could leave all this?"

Hugh laughed. "There now," he said.

Mackie frowned, looking insulted. He placed his hands on the back of his turned-around chair and pushed himself to his feet, announcing he was off to get a beer and would be back in a bit. Hugh nodded and waved as if dismissing him.

By about ten o'clock, the evening was growing wild, as Hugh had predicted. Presently Mackie appeared on the dance floor, jumping up and down to Karnage beside a middle-aged woman who had taken off her blouse and was shimmying around in her black support bra. Old men who had been there since the afternoon scraping away at instant-win lottery tickets now rose as of a single mind to stagger back and forth across the bar, hollering at people and apparitions alike. One collapsed on top of Howard, and Hugh moved to pull the drunk off him. The old bum laughed and put his arm around Hugh and said something completely incomprehensible. Hugh pretended to agree with him, signalling to Robbie MacPhedron the whole while.

"Gah. Smelled like piss," said Howard with an expression of revulsion that seemed at home on his angular features. Hugh responded to the look with pleasure; it was the first time in the entire evening Howard seemed to have let his guard down. For a moment Howard's eyes had lost their protectiveness—a trait that reminded Hugh of a shark's second eyelid, which he remembered hearing about on a TV documentary. Hugh and Howard had downed four pitchers together at this point, and were halfway through another.

"Get a load of that babe," said Hugh, inclining his head towards the dance floor, where the woman in the bra had mounted a nearby table and was shaking her fists in the air to a ZZ Top cover.

He looked over and Howard was actually grinning—but in an odd, closed-mouth sort of way. Hugh took it as encouragement. "Imagine trying to fuck that," he said recklessly.

Howard shifted his gaze towards Hugh.

"No thanks," said Howard, still smiling in his queasy manner. But his eyes retained their unsettling depths. Hugh realized he was feeling excited. There was something about Howard's new openness that charged the air, making Hugh feel anything could happen.

"Maybe if you put a bag over her head," Hugh prompted.

"Put a bag over her whole fuckin body," drawled Howard. "And punch out a hole."

"Punch out a hole," repeated Hugh. "Jesus H."

Howard swivelled his head towards the dance floor, and then back to look at Hugh and with an almost audible *fwap,* the opaque eyelids came down and the smile returned to a smirk. Hugh gulped his beer, relieved and disappointed at once.

By midnight, Gerald Newhook, who was perhaps the only person in town interested in punk rock and who had long since finished his three free pitchers, insisted on playing "Anarchy for the UK," which was the last thing the Welfare Wednesday crowd needed or wanted to hear. When someone threw a beer bottle at him, Gerald was clearly delighted and spat into the audience in response, causing Robbie MacPhedron to mount the stage and cuff him in the head. The microphone picked up his voice—*We don't spit on our customers here, dickweed*— and the giddy, maddened crowd screamed laughter and rained beer down on them both. Robbie grabbed the microphone and yelled at everyone like an angry parent to settle the hell down or he would get the cops to clear out the place once and for all. For the most part, they did, but then Len Bird started break dancing, igniting a combination of fury and glee in everyone, and Mackie Pettipas somehow got hold of a cardboard box from behind the bar, placed it on his head, and lit it on fire with his lighter. Robbie and Duncan chased him all around the bar as people howled and shouted and threw more drinks until finally they tackled Mackie, stomped out the box, and literally tossed him out the front door. He banged on it for twenty minutes, infuriated and swearing to make them all pay.

Robbie, who was a good friend of Hugh's, paused at their table during a lull. He sat down without saying hello and put his head in his hands.

"How're those computer courses going?" he inquired from behind his arms.

Hugh laughed. "Wave of the future, man. It's not too late to sign up."

Robbie shook his head and pulled briefly at his bristly hair.

Then he looked up and smiled. "I wouldn't give this up for all the world." He turned to Howard abruptly and stuck out his hand. "How you doing, man."

Howard shook it. "Good."

Hugh realized with little surprise that Robbie was drunk himself.

"Hear you're up at the fish plant," said Robbie.

"Yeah," said Howard.

"Taking a year off school?" said Robbie.

"Yeah," said Howard. "Make some money."

There you go, thought Hugh. That's perfectly reasonable. Maybe the folks aren't doing so well. School's expensive. He was a little envious of Robbie for getting the entire story with such a meager line of inquiry. Then again, Robbie had present-ed Howard with the simplest of explanations, and Howard only had to agree to it to bring the subject to a close.

Robbie sighed and sat back, taking in the tavern. The fren-zied mood had peaked, and people were entering into a sloppy phase. Karnage had stopped playing and now Marvin Gaye blared from the sound system. Some attempted to dance to it, groping each other and coming close to falling over. A couple of people slept on their tables.

"I gotta clear all these assholes out pretty soon," mourned Robbie.

"Good luck, man," said Hugh.

Mackie Pettipas sidled up to their table and sat down. Robbie swung his head to stare at him, his mouth dangling open.

"How the fuck did you get back in here?"

"Listen," said Mackie, eyeglasses slightly fogged. "I just wanted to apologize for my behaviour."

"Oh well, good," said Robbie sarcastically. "You're lucky your head's not a fuckin piece of charcoal."

"I know," admitted Mackie with much humility, as though he were crouched in the confessional.

Robbie started to laugh and reached out to cuff Mackie in the same slight, fatherly way he had cuffed Gerald Newhook. Mackie leaned into it.

"For Christ's sake you're one sad bastard, Pettipas," said Robbie, and the table cracked up.

Robbie rose, grinning and shaking his head, to get them all a complimentary pitcher of draft. He pointed at Mackie. "But you have to sit here watching them two drink it. That'll be your punishment."

Hugh glanced over, making eye contact with Howard, who had been laughing as well. It took, what, ten jeezly pitchers of draft, Hugh thought, but the asshole is coming around. He was starting to feel like a regular boy scout.

Except something happened in the parking lot. Hugh walked ahead of Howard and Mackie and was fumbling with the keys to his father's sedan when something made him look up just in time to see Howard's arm reach spasmodically towards Mackie and, in a half-punching, half-slapping motion, knock the glasses off his face. The gesture was so sudden and aggressive that Mackie instinctively snapped his fists to attention and began bouncing wildly around, half blind, like an overwound mechanical toy.

"I'll-fuckin-kill-ya," Mackie kept repeating in drunken astonishment. He thrashed his head myopically and whirled his fists. "I'll-fuckin-kill-ya-I'll-fuckin-kill-ya." Hugh rushed over but staggered, and Mackie lashed out at him as he bore down.

"Don't fuckin swing at me, you asshole!" Hugh yelled, feeling the breeze of the failed punch touch his face. "I'll put you through the wall!"

"I'll fuckin kill the both a yas!" exclaimed Mackie.

Hugh looked up at Howard, whose face was white and eyes were bottomless. "What is this?"

Howard's lips shook and then parted. He croaked at Mackie, "You watch your mouth."

"You watch *your* mouth!" Mackie screamed hysterically. "I'll fuckin kill ya next time I'll fuckin kill ya won't see me comin 'cause I'll fuckin kill ya."

"What'd he say?" Hugh yelled on top of this.

The colour suddenly shot back into Howard's cheeks and he stepped forward and shoved Mackie across the parking lot and onto his ass.

"He can't *see*," Hugh tried to tell him.

Howard took a couple more steps towards where Mackie was feeling around for his glasses and shouted something. It was the first time Hugh had heard him raise his voice, and he disliked the way it sounded—primitive and soulless.

Howard had shouted: *Don't you talk about my sister.*

Hugh remembered Mackie slavering over Howard's sister at the hockey game. "You asshole, Pettipas," he said with contempt. He came and faced Howard—a little off to the side to indicate that he was there to hold him back if necessary—but looked over his shoulder at Mackie. "You better get the fuck out of here."

"I didn't say a goddamn thing about his sister!"

Hugh heard Howard swallow.

"I said get out of here!' Hugh warned.

Robbie MacPhedron came outside at this point wanting to know what the fuss was, appearing to hope it was something interesting.

"Fuckin Pettipas making an ass of himself again," Hugh told him.

"Pettipas!" Robbie shouted. "I knew I shouldn'ta let you back in. You are fuckin banned, man! You're going on the list."

"I didn't say a goddamn thing about his sister!" Mackie repeated. He remained on his hands and knees scrambling for his glasses.

"You're banned for a month, man!" said Robbie with relish. "I better not see your face around here for the month of September, or you're out for the year," he decreed.

Hugh picked up Mackie's glasses and threw them at him. They bounced against his chest and clattered to the pavement. Mackie grabbed them and got to his knees, adjusting them clumsily onto his face. But scrambling around on the concrete for so long had taken much of the fight out of him.

"This is bullshit," he protested, focussing in on the other three. "I only said I knew her. I only said I seen her one time."

"Get out of here," said Robbie.

"Hughie," Mackie said, getting to his feet.

"Go home, you stupid bastard," said Hugh. He and Robbie stood on either side of Howard, who was taller than they and shaking, slightly. A moment or two after Mackie stumbled off, Howard lurched to the back of the building and threw up. Robbie ran inside and got a bottle of Coke, which he gave Hugh to give to Howard when he was finished. Robbie and Hugh shook hands, patted shoulders, said good night, and Robbie went back inside to roust the remaining drunks and lock up.

In Hugh's car, Howard waved the Coke away and rubbed his face. "Fuck, I'm wasted."

"Yeah," agreed Hugh, whose sudden, overwhelming urge was to go to sleep. He put the key in the ignition and started up the car. Howard murmured something.

"What, man?" said Hugh, looking over at him. Howard's eyes were closed and his dark lashes lay against the arch of his cheeks. The light coming in from the tavern's yellow sign fell across his features and he looked, at that moment, like an old-time matinee idol.

"I said," repeated Howard, deadpan, "thanks for a great night, man."

Hugh started laughing, and was scarcely able to back out of the parking lot. *I made a friend,* he was thinking.

sHED

THE PLAN is to start grade eleven bulging from head to toe with muscles.

I bought this huge canvas duffel bag at the Frenchy's store for fifty cents and filled it with sand that I gathered from the beach. It took me weeks to bring up enough sand, and a lot of it leaked from the zipper when I tried to stand the bag upright. So I duct-taped the zipper and any other holes to get rid of the leaks, and then the only problem was figuring out how to harness the bag so I could suspend it from the roof of the shed. That took a while too. And once I figured out a harness, I had to get Rene Cormier to come over and help me hoist the bag off the ground. It was amazingly heavy. You wouldn't believe how much work this was.

"Where'dja get the sand?" Rene wants to know.

"Down the beach."

"Whynja call me to help you bring up the sand?" goes Rene. Rene is so dozy he thinks it would have been fun, carrying all that sand. I can't tell him I wouldn't have called him at all if I thought I could get away with it. There was no way I was letting anybody else in on my home gym. Once the bag was filled with sand, though, I realized my mother and Louise would be of no use whatsoever in helping me set it up. They're like birds, those two. They eat like birds, they flutter around like birds—just out of reach. That's how birds protect themselves.

And I keep wanting to say to Rene: *I am moving. I am leaving here at the end of the summer. Sorry Rene, but I won't be from around here and you will. You'll be from here, and I will be from Big Harbour and that will be that.*

But I don't want to make him feel bad. Rene knows I'm moving, but he doesn't know I think of him as being a part of it all. It isn't Rene's fault, but he just *is*—part of the school, the house, the Canadian flag tied to the weather vane—the supreme and utter retardation of my existence which mostly takes the form of Isadore. Rene is part of my retard-life. I want it over and done with, and that means So Long, Rene, and everything else in the story. I can't wait.

What needs to happen now is for Corinne Fortune to get a look at me and know—because she will. She will know. They can tell just by looking at you, this is one thing I've learned. I'll be big, and I'll be different. I'm already different, just knowing we're getting out of here. Soon I'm going to go to town and tell her, and she'll see with her own eyes. I've tried calling, but it's not the same. It doesn't work. She needs proof. She has to see.

You're not from around here . . .?
Well yes as a matter of fact it so happens I am thank you
very much.

I've been thinking about my body, how I can change it. All the
women on my mother's side of the family are minuscule. But a
lot of the men are big—although Isadore, according to family
mythology, has been the biggest so far. Mamere used to say
Isadore must be a direct descendant of Jean de l'Ours, the boy
from the fairy story who was so big and strong his parents had
to make him leave home before he hurt someone.

But I take after my father where size is concerned, I can
only assume. He was of average build, apparently—at least he
looks it in the wedding picture. My minuscule mother hovers
somewhere around his armpits. Average build is how they
sometimes describe criminals on TV cop shows. Average build,
medium build. TV, of course, is a completely different language. In real life, if you're of average build, no one comments
on it at all.

Isadore once told me Scotsmen were mostly big fuckers and
Frenchmen were mostly little fuckers (except when it came to
the Aucoin freaks) and that I was "lucky enough"—this was
pure irony—to be the offspring of the two combined. Kenzie
Boucher is my medium-size father—another thing Isadore
makes fun of, my father's name: *scotchie-frenchie.* So I, like
him, turned out exactly average. In between.

"Because you are lukewarm," Isadore once remarked, "I
will spew thee out of my mouth. That don't sound too goddamn

pleasant, now, do it?" And then he laughed, spewing spit as if to demonstrate.

This all took place back in the early, slushy spring when we spent days upon days together, jabbing and hooking and aiming uppercuts at Louise's mattress in the shed. Isadore would shuffle around behind it, trying to make it move the way a heavy bag would. I have to be honest: he taught me tons. How to stand, how to hold my fists. Not to put my thumb inside—little things like that. And big things. How to breathe, even. He said he was going to write up a training regiment for me, just like the one they gave him at the Trinity Club in Toronto. That would come in pretty handy now.

It is fucking crazy of me to miss Isadore, but the problem is I'm in the shed, where we spent the entire spring together. And I'm thinking about fighting and *getting big*. It's Isadore territory—whether I like it or not I can't get away from him. I think that's a sign of something bad in myself. It's like when I look at girls in magazines, or sometimes school, and want to be awful to them in ways I can't think too long about.

There was this girl who liked me back in grade eight. She followed me around until finally we went together into the wooded paths behind the playground. I never thought she was pretty, or even nice. She was one of those girls who never spoke to anybody, and was regularly tormented in little ways by one and all, and nobody really cared what might have been going on in her head. But she made it clear that she liked me—I could just tell. And somehow, without saying even a handful of words, I went into the woods with her that day knowing that she would do *anything*. We stood behind the trees and I asked her what she would do, point blank.

Name it, she had said, so I named it and she went: *Yup*.

And then I named something else, and she said: *Yup*. And I kept naming the most terrible things, I spoke every terrible thing I had in my head—all from magazines and Isadore. I got imaginative.

And she said *Yup*. She kept saying *Yup* to all of it.

I told her to turn around and count to ten and then I ran deeper into the woods to be alone and get rid of it. I hadn't even touched her. Never looked at her again after that.

It is a sickness, that's what I think: to miss a crazy man, to want to be mean to a girl. It's all of a piece.

Somehow, the answer is *getting big*. There are entire articles dedicated to *getting big* in the boxing magazines I found thrown around the shed. My mother said they belonged to Isadore when he was my age—like Isadore needed to worry about getting big. The magazines all showed men with very short hair, in tight trunks, inflated fists held in front of their faces. The guys on the cover didn't look particularly well built to me, but some of the stuff inside was still pretty interesting, and so I went into town to find some magazines from this century. Some of them were really good. Some weren't even necessarily about boxing. Some were about nothing *but* getting big. I bought one, stole a couple. When I have money, I'm going to buy a set of weights at Canadian Tire.

In the meantime, I yank on the rope with poor old Rene Retard, thinking one way I could work out would be to hoist the duffel bag up and down on the beam every day—if only I can get to the point where I'm strong enough to lift the goddamn thing by myself. That way, whenever I wanted to use the bag, I'd be forced to raise and fasten it. It's smart. And maybe I could fashion another harness of some kind to help me work different muscles.

Or I could just bring up more sand, and fill more bags. Bags of different shapes and sizes. This of course would take forever, and just as I got everything figured out, I'd have to move into town. But I could come back, if Louise was still here. Louise is married, apparently. She blows my mind, that one. It never occurs to her to do anything except exactly what she wants. She hasn't told my mother yet, but when Louise does, she says she's going to ask if she can stay in the house with Dan C. I do not want to be anywhere near this place when that particular conversation occurs.

Just when I've got everything figured out for my home gym, the beam on which me and Rene are attempting to raise the bag gives out this creaky, haunted-house groan and then splits in half, raining most of the shed roof down on our heads. It's a good thing we heard the groan, or we might have been really dinged and Rene would end up brain-damaged and I'd feel eternally guilty for having called him Rene Retard his whole life. Luckily I yelled "Look out!" and we both took off at the last second. This event should have come as no surprise to me whatsoever. The shed has been standing in the same spot since the turn of the century. I kick the beam and see that the wood inside has the consistency of clay.

"Aw, fuck," is Rene's comment. He'd been excited about the prospect of wailing away on the bag once it was up and "being like the guy in *Rocky*." I had to tell him that "the guy in *Rocky*" *was* Rocky.

"We'll just have to fix it," I say, looking up at the empty blue sky.

"We coulda been killed," whispers Rene.

I tell him not to be a pussy. Here is something remarkable: I'm smiling. I'm not pissed off about the shed roof caving in at all, even after all that work. Already I'm thinking about what I can do now, how I can change things. Maybe I'll just leave the roof the way it is, clear out the debris and simply put up one strong beam across the frame of the shed that can hold the weight of the duffel bag. It'll be an outdoor gym.

It feels like a sign. I have never believed in that kind of shit, but really—that's what it feels like. This happiness surges though me because I almost got killed by a shed, and I don't know how else to explain it. It's like the shed has spoken, and it's said that it is tired of being Isadore's. It's tired of the cardboard boxes, of serving as a storehouse for us to stuff all of our unwanted memories into. It's tired of me. That is, it's tired of me being a useless, medium-size kid with a sickness inside. So it tried to kill me. I can't say that I blame it either. I am actually grateful.

I say to Rene, "That was *cool*." I don't know how else to express what I'm thinking, the thing about the sign. I somehow feel great about seeing something destroyed, to be honest.

UnSEEN

SHE HAS a life. She does things with her days, nobody can say otherwise. The season has a title, in Pam's mind, and this title reads The Summer of Staying Away. She is very busy, living up to this title. The Christmas play, for example. Mrs. K. sent them home with their scripts for the summer, telling them to start memorizing. Next year will be the drama club's first official outing, and therefore a big deal. It's got to be Shakespeare. And it's got to be good, otherwise Mrs. K.'s meager funding will go right back into hockey gear and cheerleading uniforms where the good Lord intended it to be.

You would think the imperative to be memorizing page-long speeches would leave Pam housebound all summer, but in fact you would be wrong. It is The Summer of Staying Away, and she hops out of bed at the crack of dawn, a new purpose spurring her days. The purpose of Staying Away. The purpose of getting out of the house early and coming home late and beholding his face and listening to him speak for the absolute minimum amount of time possible.

Off to the waterfront to see the sun rise above the frothy squalour of the strait—to watch its rays illuminate the purple clouds of gunk that are cheerfully and steadily belched heavenward from the pulp mill day and night, bullying and crowding the real clouds out of existence. A Big Harbour morning. Use these quiet, stinky moments to go over the biggest speeches, the worst speeches, the love speeches, the ones she can picture herself speaking trippingly on the tongue in no possible imagined future.

> You see me, Lord Bassanio, where I stand
> such as I am.

> Ugh.

> Though for myself alone
> I would not be ambitious in my wish
> To wish myself much better, yet for you
> I would be trebled twenty times myself.

Mrs. K. is of course an insane person to put them all through this. Pam can hear the hoots already. *Pam Cormorant—get her down from there, the stage'll never hold!* Ha, guffaw.

And wasn't it the same, sad Mrs. K. who wanted to hold a talent show the year before? Pallid nerdlings emerged from basements and attics all across town, oboes in hand. It was their night to shine, and shine they did. Pam appeared at the piano by request of Mrs. K., bashed out a panicked Minuet in D, and got the hell out of there before the boys in the front row could get a clear shot with whatever organic matter they were able to produce.

However, it was Ann Gillis who stole the show. She topped them all—the oboe players, the grade nine girls who did a Scottish hornpipe, the judo demonstration.

With her access to Corinne and the Three T's, Pam has some idea how mainstream opinion about Ann shapes itself. The problem is Ann refuses to make herself unseen. She is clearly a freak, clearly a slut, clearly a loser, all of which dictates she should go into hiding until graduation. When people want to ridicule her, they seek her out, hold her up, shake her a few times, and then put her away—where she would be expected to remain, grateful. But Ann takes herself out, holds herself up.

The night of the talent show, like any slut, like every slut, she was asking for it. She took the stage in a black dress and sang "The Rose." People rolled in the aisles. Boys in the front and back rows searched themselves frantically for the most disgusting things they could think of to throw. Condoms rained down to no great effect, until somebody had the bright idea of blowing one up. Then another. It was a beach party. Teachers flew from their seats. Ann sang. Her accompanist was a tape recording, so there was no missing a beat. The principal hopped around in the wings until the final, endless note:

in the spring . . . becomes

the roooooossssse

which Ann apparently had no interest in shortening. The noise of the auditorium was a noise Pam replayed inside her brain frequently afterwards. It was a noise like the inside of a sick stomach, she thought. Like in the hockey arena during playoffs, when the score is tied, and there's five seconds left on the clock, and everyone is so sure it's going to go into overtime, they're not even paying attention. And practically by accident, the other team knocks the puck into the home team's net. It's a noise like the sound they make then. Disbelief and fury.

Why doesn't she shut up? Pam remembers thinking in her safe, dark spot behind the curtain. She remembers that now, sitting outside with her Shakespeare, the train tracks on one side of her, the stinking water on the other. Pam now believes she was not thinking that at all, that night. *Why doesn't she shut up?* It was everyone else, thinking their one thought so hard, it had forced itself into Pam's brain.

They do that, she considers.

Now she and Ann are in the play together. Mrs. K. has appointed them "study buddies" over the summer, because their characters spend so much time together. Their characters, it would appear, are best friends, even though one is supposed to be the servant of the other. Ann is Nerissa to Pam's Portia.

They meet at the library, because nobody goes there in the summer. Pam doesn't want to practice at her house and Ann doesn't want to at hers. When the weather gets nice, and they've got their dialogue down, they walk around in the sunshine together. Ann inquires how she likes Falconbridge, or the young Scottish lord, or the duke of Saxony's nephew, and Pam gets her responses mixed up. They laugh together, at Pam. Ann smokes cigarettes, chain-smokes them really, and one day it occurs to her to share. In this way, Ann provides Pam with a second diversion to make use of in her Summer of Staying Away campaign. She has the play, and now she has cigarettes. She embraces smoking like religion, because she likes the philosophy behind it. Or, at least, the philosophy Ann seems to represent, characterized by a clear contempt for her precious young health, her already wasted body, the so-called flower of her youth. Inviting eye-bags and yellow teeth. An early embrace of cronehood.

But mostly, because smoking is an excuse to go away, to leave the room. She likes how it gives her something to do in the evenings besides kicking around the rubble of the fallen-down house. She tells her parents—or, more accurately, her mother—that she is going for a walk. And it's true—she does walk.

Of course priority number one in the Summer of Staying Away is the same as what priority number one has always been. Pam's best friend, Corinne. Corinne has problems and needs ministering to, and Pam has never been more willing or able. She throws herself into their afternoons together. They meet at the Kentucky Fried for onion rings. Sometimes one or two T's will be in tow, but for the most part, Corinne's days are gifts to Pam.

"They don't get it," complains Corinne about the T's. "Like, they think it's funny about Brian and all that, they think it's all a big joke. They think it's great some guy is so nuts about me he's violent. Two guys really," she tosses out. "And Troy's just jealous. You're the only one who takes it seriously."

Pam takes it seriously all right. Brian gives her nightmares.

"If just that French guy'd leave me alone, Brian wouldn't be so jealous."

Guys are frightening in Corinne's world. Pam knows of guys' indifference and contempt, but not of this. How benign her experience seems beside her friend's, where the men and boys, even when they're beautiful-looking, even when in love, are mean and crazy half the time. As described by Corinne, male attention is like a funhouse—full of weird mirrors and grabby hands and hairy things that pop up out of nowhere to say *boo*. But then you come out, heart pounding and semi-suffocated, take a deep breath to calm yourself, and duck inside again. Because after all, it's a funhouse. After all, you're having fun.

Love, Corinne is saying. Pam has said, "It's not the French guy's fault Brian's gotten so possessive and jealous. He would have been like that anyway. He would be like that no matter what, you're just finding it out now."

The difference, points out Corinne, is love. "Yah," she says, "but Brian loves me. Like I know he loves me. The other guy hates me. He's hated me ever since I turned him down. He just wants to hurt me now."

"Well," says Pam, "they both want to hurt you."

"That is true," agrees Corinne, nodding her head, deep in thought. "Everyone wants to hurt me. But one of them loves me and that is the difference."

"There doesn't appear to be a difference," remarks Pam, more to herself. She remembers the French guy—the guy named Guy—standing in the parking lot, holding out his Coke, and can't imagine him full of hate and hurt. She has never met Brian, on the other hand, but envisages him with horns. The one inescapable fact is that Pam understands nothing about any of this so her impressions are basically invalid.

"The difference is *love*," Corinne repeats, like Pam is thick. And Pam can only assume Corinne knows what she is talking about.

aMERICA

ON TELEVISION, he learns about America. The States, everyone around him has always called it, but in America, he learns, they just call it America.

This is Canada, he remembers complaining to his mother their very first night with the TV.

Yes, said his mother.

But they just talk about America, he said.

The story is set in America, said his mother. It's made in America.

He watched some more, feeling upset.

But we sort of live in America too, his mother added after a little while. He turned around.

We're part of North America, she said.

He watched some more, feeling better.

He learns how people from America talk to each other. There is no uncertainty. They know whom they love and whom they hate. Bad people are ugly. Men are one way, women another. Dogs are men's best friends, diamonds are girls'. There are lots of mothers and fathers and brothers and sisters and boyfriends and girlfriends. There are lots of friends. There aren't very many uncles or cousins or aunts. But he has more of those than he does of the others.

He learns the language of television, what he believes must be the language of America. A boy and a girl Fall in Love the moment they see each other. Or else they hate each other for a while, first. One or the other. Members of families pretend not to like one another, everybody knows this, but Come Through for Each Other in the End.

People, in general, get along. Those who don't get along with other people are simply evil, and certain to be vanquished at the end of the hour. Violence is something that occurs suddenly, all at once, and only when called for. Violence, when called for, is huge and all-annihilating. Things are always better, afterwards. The world takes on gentle hues of great beauty, enduring peace.

But that's not how it is in real life.

Violence arrives like a natural phenomenon—so arbitrary it could only be from nature, like an undertow at Port Hull beach sucking children out of sight, water wings and all, before parents can look up from picnic baskets. Like a freak storm, or a lunatic uncle. It comes just when you imagine something else is going to come.

Violence steps up behind you when you've got a girl's face in your head and it's summer and night and warm and the only thing in your nose is the thick, fuzzy smell of dandelions and cut grass, bleeding green into the air.

The warmest of nights lolling beside the pay phone outside MacIssac's Confectionery, smoking the first perfect cigarette from a freshly bought pack, Diet Coke in the other hand. Cold, unopened, for her, when she comes.

He heard her say something before she hung up the phone, it was muffled, it sounded like *enough,* but he knows she is coming this time. It's in the air, the night is too warm, the air is too blessed and green for her not to come.

He's looking in one direction, and violence comes out of the other, asks him where he's from, asks him if he is French, asks, *Are you the little French fuck?* and doesn't wait for an answer.

FaLL

tHE CORMORANT WALK

HUNTING SEASON, and sure enough an offering of moose comes to the fallen-down house. Ronald's visits begin to occur with such frequency one could almost surmise he has learned of Pam's Summer of Staying Away and decided to answer with an Autumn of Coming to Visit. One night he brings an entire side of moose, already butchered and wrapped up in pink, waxy paper. He hauls it into the kitchen in a duffel bag, his work boots untied and splayed open at the ankles as he always wears them, wood chips sticking to his flannel jacket, looking like some kind of ancient, agrarian Santa Claus.

"This is too much moose," Pam's mother demurs as he unloads one pink package after another onto the counter.

"Can't have too much moose," Ronald avows, with no stutter.

Pam has just arrived from her nightly smoking exercise. Today Ann Gillis announced she was quitting the play, this scarcely a month into rehearsals. She said she could no longer abide its flagrant anti-Semitic overtones. Mrs. K. waved her pink arms and shook her chubby blonde bun around, but there was no talking to Ann. The English teacher went home that night looking defeated, and Pam surprised herself with how afraid she was the show might not go on. She needed the play. She needed something big and near impossible to occupy her time and thoughts.

There he sits, she sees when she comes in from the porch, from her spot behind Ronald and the growing pink pile of moose. Her father is nodding in the armchair usually favoured by his cousin when he visits. Pam's father never used to sit there until recently, having woken up on the floor one time too many after hours of dozing on the couch. He likes the sturdiness the armchair provides, the way it holds you upright and in place even when your bones and muscles have long since gone to goo.

What will happen now? worries Pam, grit in her lungs, smoke clinging to her tongue, a low-key kind of panic settling within the depths of her chest. Where is Ronald supposed to sit? She can't imagine him nestled into a corner of the couch. All is chaos. Fathers in armchairs and houses in ruins and moose in pieces on counters on the emptiest of nights.

"Boy!" Ronald calls into the living room suddenly. "Moose, here." Pam watches her father's head bob slightly, like some celestial puppet master has jerked a finger.

Faintly: *Proper ting.*

"You must bring some of this down to Della," Mrs. Cormorant suggests. "At least half."

"Ach. Della's got alls she can stomach."

"We've nowhere to put it."

"Deep freeze." There is no fooling Ronald.

"Did you shoot this moose?" Pam asks from behind him, and Ronald jumps a foot.

"You," he says. "You. You."

Are getting big big big.

But that is all Ronald says.

He turns back to her mother. "Cook er with coffee."

"With coffee?"

"Dump a cup of coffee onto er. Cream, sugar, the whole bit. She'll come out like filet min gon."

Pam and her mother look at each other. Ronald has not stuttered once and they have never heard him giving instructions to anyone before. He puts his hands in his pockets and gazes into the living room where Bill continues to bob.

"Maybe you could do us up a couple right now?" Ronald ventures.

"Now?" repeats Mrs. Cormorant. It is nine-thirty at night.

"Good for the blood." At the word *blood,* the tip of Ronald's nose, so hooked it almost meets his upper lip, goes red. He rubs it quickly as if he can feel this happening. Ronald pulls a piece of cloth from the turned-up cuff of his jacket and blows before delivering his final edict.

"And maybe make a whole pot a that there coffee."

Then he walks his bow-legged walk—what Pam's mother

has long dubbed the "Cormorant walk"—into their living room and sits down on the couch across from Pam's father. Ronald doesn't appear to feel strange or uncomfortable about sitting there. In fact, he looks like he can handle it.

WELCOME

MOSTLY THERE IS a smell. It smells *new* in the school. And, if possible, *sunny*. But I could be imagining this. I've never been in a building so full of sun.

On the first day a huge banner that reads WELCOME STUDENTS hangs from the overhead walkway. There're shitloads of students. Apparently two schools in the county have been shut down this year, one from River Bourgeois, one from the reserve. The River Bourgeois kids seem happy to be here. The reserve kids don't. The only people I know in the entire building are Corinne Fortune, her friend Pam, and a handful of guys from the hockey team. They wanted to kill me after I quit in the middle of the playoffs, but now seem to have forgotten all about it. I am a blank now. I am not from around here. I could be from New York City.

The town kids think I am from River Bourgeois. The River Bourgeois kids think I am from town. The reserve kids couldn't give less of a shit.

I watch the reserve kids. They stay together and appear pissed off. In some of the classes, the teachers will call their names and they won't answer. It's hilarious.

"Arnold Googoo?"

Silence.

"Is Arnold Googoo here?"

Everyone will turn to look at the only Indian kid in the class until the teacher has no choice but to inquire.

"Are you Mr. Googoo?"

Kid stares. Teacher sighs.

"Would you be Arnold by any chance?"

"No."

"What's your name, please?"

"Arnold Googoo."

The reserve guys kill me.

I am a ghost in the maze of bright hallways. The guys who wanted to kill me before don't even recognize me now that I'm among them. Corinne Fortune's near-white blue eyes move across me like I'm one in a row of lockers. I don't push to talk to her anymore, but I can't help but try and make eye contact. She won't, though. Pam says hi. We walk past each other.

"Hi, Guy."

"Hi, Pam."

It is like we are members of a secret society. The club for those who don't exist.

I think that it is good.

The town now seems like just an extension of the school. I go home to the apartment at lunch. My mother wants me to go to the house and eat with her and the kids she looks after, but I won't. I won't acknowledge those kids. My mother may belong to them, but I don't have to. I am enjoying this state of not belonging to anything. No one claims me with their eyes. No one calls me Frog or Gorf-boy like they used to when I came to town, because I live here now and they don't recognize me.

I used to think town would be the answer to all our problems, but it's not like that, exactly. One day and all of a sudden I had everything I wanted. My mother, her job, the apartment, the school, the mall. The absence of Isadore. And her. A fifteen-minute walk away.

And then I got the crap beaten out of me, worse than ever in my life. Even the guy from the dance last spring wasn't that bad. At least I knew what it was about, and was able to hold my own. It was about hockey, so it made sense. But this: without warning, without reason. The worst thing about it was how surprised I was, and the meaninglessness of all that pain. I couldn't make sense of it. I got to my hands and knees a while later and opened my eyes and saw blood, plopping fast from the middle of my face. I never told my mother what exactly happened and I never will. I'm never going to tell anyone.

It was the same day she announced she'd finally secured the apartment outside town, and the people she worked for were giving her an advance so she could pay first and last months' rent. We'd move at the end of the month, she said. We would get away from Isadore, and his truck, and have our own decent, normal life. I left the house to hitch to Big Harbour five seconds later—before Louise could make her own announcement, the one she'd been saving all summer. All I wanted to do was hitchhike in—truckless, free—and tell Corinne Fortune face to face so she could see I was finally going to live there, that I belonged there, like she did.

When I got home that night, my mother shrieked and clutched at herself and said she was going to lie down on the floor and die from the things her children did to her. I didn't even feel sorry. I said through my shredded mouth, *This is that stupid fucking town you want to go to so much,* as if I never had wanted such a thing. *This is what happens there,* I said. *I'm gonna get fucking killed one of these days and whose fault is it gonna be?* But I didn't mean to imply it was her fault even though it sounded that way and made her cry. I genuinely wanted to know whose it was.

Maybe getting beaten up by that guy was like an initiation, a purgatory I had to go through in order to achieve this invisibility. Things are very quiet now, and maybe will stay that way. Since moving to town, I have learned who he is. I saw his graduation photo on the wall by the office—*Grads, 1980.* Howard Fortune. He looks just like her. Same pale eyes.

I see him sometimes. I saw him at Shopper's Drug Mart buying gum, chips, and orange pop like a little kid. If I wanted to, I could have stood directly behind him with my magazine. I could have rolled it up and tapped him on the head.

I can't help but think he wouldn't even feel it. I could scream in his face. I'd scream, "Ow! That fuckin hurt!" He wouldn't blink. I'd try to push him and my arms would go through.

At night, me and my mother watch TV. The phone doesn't ring, unless Louise is calling to complain about Dan C. On those occasions, my mother puts the shit to Louise. I can hear her in the kitchen. The kitchen and the living room are practically one—it reminds me of a sit-com where the two rooms are right beside each other and the characters go into the next room to talk even though the other people are only a few feet away from them. The people talking pretend that the others can't hear and the others pretend that they can't hear too. Sometimes TV is just like life.

"Well, you're the big married lady now," I hear my mother saying. She's furious about that, still. "You're the one who went off and got married, so what do you need me for?"

I hear my sister's voice like a hornet on the other end.

"You're *married*," my mother repeats. She says that every time Louise calls with a problem. She is mad at Louise for deciding to be an adult so soon, so she refuses to let her be a child again, even for a moment. It must be an awful feeling for my sister.

The first thing my mother did when she found out Louise got married was call up Mamere and send a letter to Isadore in the monastery. I couldn't believe she would willfully interrupt our peace and invite him back into our lives like that. I'd told her not to. She had looked around the kitchen, blinking like a stunned bird. "It's marriage," she stuttered. "It's *family*. I have to." As if someone had pushed a button on her labeled: *Family*. Even with me standing there yelling at her, she wrote out a little card to Isadore, like he was this grand old uncle we all loved and whose blessing we wanted.

Isadore wrote back.

Dear Sister, it started, like we were in another era.

I was concerned to hear your news about Louise. If she has been knocked up, I will rip the Scotsman's head off for him. The rest of Isadore's letter was nothing like Isadore. Actually it was and it wasn't. It was yet another crazy contradiction that made my head hurt. It was a beautiful letter.

> *I recognize that I have not always been a good brother to you or a good godfather to your son and I plan to take responsibility for myself and my actions, and for you, when I return.*

I yelled at my mother *I told you so* after we read it together. "He was up in that monastery again," I complained. "He might have just decided to stay there."

"He wouldn't stay," my mother said. "Isadore can't stand that place."

"Well, he goes there enough."

"He goes there," said my mother, "because he thinks it cleans him out. Men are stupid about monasteries. They think there is something about being only with men that makes them pure and clean. Then they get out and they stop being pure and clean and they blame us for it," she said. "They figure it must be all *our* fault, and so they treat us—" My mother stopped, searching her English. "Like disease."

I looked at my mother.

"I hate that place myself," she added, rising from the table to find her cigarettes.

In her note, my mother told Isadore that Louise and Dan C. were living in the house, and that we were in an apartment in town. I raged at her for telling him where we were. She argued he wouldn't find us, because our address was General Delivery.

"He'll just get it out of Louise," I said.

"He won't go see Louise. Louise makes him nervous."

That was actually true. He doesn't understand Louise.

"He'll get it out of Mamere," I said.

My mother looked glum. "But if we went to Timbuktu, he would get it from Mamere," she said. She sighed, like this was our fate. Like if we really went to Timbuktu he'd show up sooner or later, in a parka with a quart of Hermit's under his arm, all set to raise shit.

Since the letter, I worry all the time. I don't want him coming to my peaceful autumn town where I am no one and laying claim to us again. Gouging his flag into my family like an American landing on the moon.

On certain days in October, on particular streets, like the one where my mother works, the trees rain prickly chestnuts that split open and lie on the street like oysters with shiny brown pearls inside. I love new chestnuts—I love opening them up and carrying the brown beads around in my pockets. I know it's a kid's thing to do. The little kids in town run into the doctor's yard after school and bash and shake the trees until the ground is bumpy with them. Then they scoop the chestnuts up into their sweaters and run home to do God knows what.

October in Big Harbour. On certain days the water is actually purple and the trees are just lunacy. If we still had the truck, my mother and I could drive into the countryside and take in all the crazy colour—we could go out to the house, but my mother doesn't want to meet Dan C. And the truck has been impounded. I doubt Isadore will ever have a license again.

And now that it's begun, there is no not thinking about Isadore anymore. There is no more drifting down the streets thinking of chestnuts and colour.

I start running in the mornings. There is a boxing club down on Cosgrove Street above the train station. They have a heavy bag, two speed bags, ropes, weights.

GaSP

CORINNE FORTUNE has a new catchword. She fixes an entirely phony expression of amazement on her face beforehand. That's how people know it's coming: *Gasp*. Pam is annoyed by it because Pam is annoyed by everything on this particular evening.

She considers the Christmas play a disaster, and will not hear any different. People congratulate her and she nearly spits on them. The play was a joke. Portia was not likeable or believable. Portia was fat. When Portia waddled across the stage explaining how the quality of mercy is not strained, the boys in the front row bounced up and down in their seats going, *Whoa! Whoa!*

And frankly Ricky Estabrooks was not a convincing Shylock. He was too sweet. People couldn't get a real hate on for him, as they were supposed to. At the reception afterwards, Somebody asks Mrs. K. why she didn't get Ricky a big nose to wear or something. Mrs. K. blinks rapidly, holding with both hands the cameo she always wears at her throat, longing to go home and drink gin.

"You were wonderful, Pam," Mrs. K. says.

"Thanks," says Pam.

The last person she wants to see at this point is Corinne, but one of the first people to come running up to her at the reception is Corinne. She stops a couple of feet away from Pam and positions herself in an exaggerated stance of awe and admiration.

"Gasp," she says. "The woman of the hour. The big actress. I'm so proud of you!"

"Thanks," says Pam.

"Let's go celebrate," says Corinne. "Troy's got a bottle of sangria."

Pam wants to drink the bottle of sangria the moment she hears of its existence. She doesn't even know what sangria is.

"Troy?" she says. The only catch is she doesn't want to drink it with Troy. If Troy had not been onstage gaining extra credit as a Magnifico, he would have been one of the boys in the front row.

Corinne leans in. "You're right," she whispers. "Fuck Troy. Let me just get the bottle off him and we'll take off!" Corinne covers her mouth as if she's gasping at her own audacity and flounces away. Pam is surprised Corinne would be willing to dump Troy in order to drink with her. They have never drunk together before, except for one time at a dance when Pam made a puking fool of herself in a failed effort to join the ranks of Corinne's all-day friends—Pam's first and last experiment with alcohol.

Despite the catastrophe of the play, it seems there is some kind of aura hovering about Pam. She has been onstage. For a moment, the entire school had no choice but to look at her, to listen to her. It was different than when Ann sang at the talent show, because unlike Ann, Pam had been in disguise. She was allowed to be up there preaching justice and mercy because she was acting, she was costumed, she was hiding herself. She did not insist upon herself alone, the way Ann had done. So Pam didn't get the condom balloons or the outraged shouts. Just a handful of assholes in the front row who were eventually rousted by the principal. Otherwise, they had watched, they had listened. Corinne wants to drink a bottle of sangria with her, not Troy. Troy being a mere Magnifico.

Ann comes up and slips a cigarette into Pam's palm.

"Take it—you deserve it."

"Thanks."

"Jesus—that was some kind of clusterfuck."

"Do you think?" says Pam. Now she's not so sure.

"Oh my God, when Ricky dropped the knife and then Jerry picked it up and gave it back to him! I nearly pissed my pants."

Jerry Boudreau had played Antonio. It was him Ricky should have been menacing with the knife.

"Still—the audience laughed."

"Oh, for fuck's sake," says Ann.

"I mean it *is* a comedy," argues Pam.

"It's a comedy all right," agrees Ann. "This whole town's a comedy. Listen to all the laughter."

They stand together, like they're actually listening. Ann looks as if she wants her cigarette back.

Corinne returns, jacket bulging. "Gasp," she says. Her new expression is at the height of its usage. She seems to say it by way of greeting Ann. "I can't believe you dropped out of the play," Corinne enthuses. "You would have been so good, Ann."

"I would have been better than whatshername, anyway," Ann agrees.

Perhaps Ann is not the martyr to art and social equality Pam once imagined her to be. Maybe Ann thought she had power, for a moment there. Maybe she thought she had so much power that to remove herself from the play would have brought it tumbling down like the proverbial card-house. Maybe she is pissed off that it hasn't.

Corinne bobs her bushy eyebrows. "Well—Pam's the starlet tonight."

On some level Pam knows this softness she's feeling, this syrupy glow, is not real and will not last. But knowing it doesn't seem to make much of a difference. She has only ever been the center of attention when people were serenading her with *Fatty fatty two by four; Pammie, Pammie, size-a Miami; Pam, Pam, flakes-a ham.* She never imagined being the center of attention could feel like this. One time the dentist gave her Valium and it felt like this. She asked him to pull some more of her teeth while he was at it.

She thinks about the sangria and senses it will make her feel this way as well, that it will buttress the ridiculous, temporary bubble of well-being and allow her to bob around inside of it for much of the evening.

Epiphany, then, standing in the auditorium foyer between Ann and Corinne. This is *why*. This is what it's *for*. This particular choo-choo train she now identifies as the Bill Cormorant Express.

Meanwhile, Ann makes herself gone. She blinks out of existence sullenly, like an unappreciated apparition, entirely unlike her usual self. Who knew she had such abilities? thinks Pam. Pam could have made her an honorary fat girl.

Out of guilt and stubborn perversity, Pam denies herself the sangria. She takes one sip and watches Corinne drink the rest of it. Pam lets her good-will glow fade to embers, and allows reality to reassert itself like a fat gut that's been held in all day. She sits listening to Corinne talk about Corinne, as much an afternoon friend as ever there was.

The Dr. Cormorant within, meanwhile, is taking assiduous notes on the aftereffects of her unprecedented moment-in-the-sun. What happens once this goofy, humiliating joy has worn off? The subject "crashes," it would appear. The subject swings from euphoria to melancholy, bitterness even. The subject feels stupid for having let that warm little light get inside like that, for letting down her guard. *Made ya look. Dirty crook.* Even now, despite herself, the subject finds herself wanting it back, and hates herself for it. A betrayed little Shylock whirls around within, with Ricky Estabrooks' baby-blue eyes and a KICK ME HARD sign taped to his back. Because of Pam and her stupid hope, he can't even be a Jew anymore. She's betrayed the true faith. Corinne has made her look.

"Gasp," Corinne is saying. "I'm so toasted. You have to have some of this, Pam, because soon I'm going to be puking up my shoes."

"No, I can't," says Pam, but Corinne doesn't hear her because she just continues talking about whatever she had been talking about before pausing to gasp and editorialize about how drunk she is becoming. They are down in the deserted smoking area, because it is sheltered and the outside door is often unlocked, so they can sneak into the foyer to warm up if necessary. Every year Mr. Forbrigger, the physics teacher, lectures them about how easy it is to die if you drink outdoors in the winter and every year the kids rush outdoors to get drunk like children going tobogganing. Indeed some of them get drunk and do go tobogganing.

There is a party tonight, and Corinne wants to get as much of the sangria as possible into her and go to it. She keeps telling Pam the party's been going on for hours, but that Corinne had opted to see Pam's play instead. It is not a high school party. Some guy who lives in one of the Springdale apartments down the street is having it. One of those lost boys in post–high school limbo, reveling in his sudden popularity as a guy with his own apartment, old enough to go to the liquor store.

"I'll probably go home," says Pam.

"Oh, you have to come with me!" Corinne exclaims. "I'll feel like a loser if I show up by myself."

"I'll walk you there," says Pam. Corinne nods, and doesn't argue further.

It starts to snow on them, fluffy snow, glowing orange from the light mounted above the doorway.

"Ho, ho, ho," remarks Corinne. There's silence. Then she sighs and slouches against the wall. "Oh, sex," she says.

"Sex?"

"I miss Brian," says Corinne. She has not talked about Brian in months. It got Pam so upset she had to stop. The subject had once been a source of endless concern to Pam.

"It's hard to go back to . . . you know . . . *high school* . . . after Brian," says Corinne, and Pam realizes she is using the term "high school" as a euphemism. Before Pam can reply, Corinne jerks up straight and sloshes some of the wine on her jacket. "Oh my God!" she yells, forgetting to even say *Gasp*. "Everywhere I look now, I see that French guy. I can't believe he's going to school here. It's like I'm being stalked."

Pam feels cold and annoyed. She rubs herself thinking, Isn't flab *good* for anything? Shouldn't there at least be some *use* to it? What about all they learned in grade five social studies about the Northern Peoples and their insulating layers of fat? What about whales and big blubbery sea lions? Shouldn't she possess the ability to paddle comfortably around beneath ice floes, catching fish in her mouth? She realizes the snow has soaked through her boots. She hasn't had the benefit of the sangria to keep these irritants at bay.

"Oh, Corinne," says Pam, stomping her feet. "That's foolishness." She says it like her drunken father, with his unhindered accent: *fooh*-lishness.

There's silence, so Pam looks up. Her friend is staring at her. Pam wonders if she's ever contradicted this person in all their sixteen years as playmates.

The hairy eyebrows pinch themselves together. "I'm *serious*. He gives me the creeps."

Pam's big toes are without feeling now. "Maybe you just feel guilty," she says, looking down at them.

"For what?"

"For treating him," says Pam, a glow inside returning, but this time a different kind of glow, "like a piece of shit."

More silence. Pam looks up. Corinne must have been waiting for her to look up, because the moment she does, Corinne bursts into tears.

"You don't know anything," she sputters. "How can you talk to me that way?"

"I'm sorry." Pam really is. She reaches over and pats Corrine frantically, as if to put her out. Corinne wriggles around, like the pats are insulting to her.

"You don't know!" Corinne repeats. "Everything I've been through! Everyone is after me."

"No one is after you, Corinne."

"*Everyone* is after me," she insists, her voice getting thick from the surge of mucus. Corinne sobs for a while as Pam pats away in horror, and then Corinne does something that scares the hell out of Pam. Corinne starts running towards the woods. She runs a few feet and falls like a shot deer. She lies face down in the new snow. Pam can hear high, buzzing, snow-muffled noises. Corinne starts bashing at the ground with her mitten-fists. A wind comes up and the snow that had been wandering down from the sky now spirals around Pam's head. The surreality of the moment is such that Pam feels it could be flakes of her sanity spinning around in the orange light, loosened from her skull. She runs over to where Corinne is bashing, and then just stands there.

"Corinne!"

Rolls over in the snow, face red and soaked.

"I think I need to kill myself."

Pam starts laughing from the fear. "You're so drunk."

"He hurt me so much," says Corinne.

Pam stoops to gather up her friend. They go into the foyer, because she—Pam—suddenly can't stop shivering. Corinne, on the other hand, has to take off her jacket, she's so hot. They huddle across from each other with what's left of the sangria on the floor between them.

christmas

dROP

LELAND WAS sitting at the bar when they entered the tavern that night, and didn't immediately notice Isadore and Alison when they arrived to mark the occasion of Isadore's return from the monastery. Leland sat conferring with a waitress, patrons on either side of him, vying for his attention. He was holding court, Isadore remarked to Alison, like an English lord. Apparently the tavern staff had had their Christmas party earlier in the evening, which was why Leland was present, eating from a bowl of potato chips left over from the festivities. The staff was a bit gassed up from the punch and eggnog they had drunk, and the waitresses were sporting fuzzy little Santa Claus hats with white pompoms that glowed like beacons as they moved from table to table. Leland had installed strange lights in the last little while, under which everything emitted an eerie glow. Isadore complained about them.

"Boss Hogg's got the place lit up like a goddamn Christmas cathouse."

"Disco lights or something," ventured Alison.

"My Christ, yes, he's got a real disco fucking crowd gathered tonight, don't he?" Isadore surely possessed the vaguest of notions what the term *disco* entailed but he was right in the observation that, by and large, the patrons of the tavern were not a disco crowd. Alison tittered as they settled at their table, gazing around at surroundings by this time more familiar to him than the house he grew up in.

"So—we're taking it easy tonight, yes? No hard stuff."

"Oh for Christ's sake, Mason, it's Christmas."

"Right—that's why we're here. But we have to look out for each other. No one goes overboard."

They had been drinking for the past three hours at Alison's house. Sherry. Alison used to have sherry every year at Christmas, and it made him depressed to think of going without it. Isadore said he shouldn't have to and brought him two bottles late that afternoon, tied together with a gold bow. Alison had become a little weepy at his friend's thoughtfulness, and put on some Christmas carols, and they drank the bottles together and talked about the old days before they had met. Alison told Isadore about Christmas with his family, which had always been a nervous, overorchestrated affair, and later with his wife, who had left him not long after he'd spent an entire December 25th at her parents' home, shuddering in bed with alcohol poisoning.

Isadore talked about his father, how he and his father would go into the woods together to choose a tree Christmas

Eve day and no sooner, though the rest of the family clamoured for them to get a tree earlier. But no: that was their own little tradition. The two of them together in the woods on December 24, by themselves. Sometimes they would bring the shotgun and shoot a rabbit to take home. Isadore knew Alison loved to hear such stories because they had so little to do with his own experience of the world. It was like a fairy tale to him. Alison's memories of his family were nothing like this. He remembered the tense table settings, his father insisting on reading Charles Dickens every year. How pained and embarrassed Alison eventually became at how contrived and desperately middle class everything always had to be. Isadore liked the idea of his own life and world as a fairy tale in contrast with the cold, urban, inauthentic America that Alison bemoaned. When Isadore spoke about his past he always played this aspect up, and as a result he and Alison both enjoyed his stories very much.

But they'd swapped as many stories as they could that afternoon, and Isadore became restless. The only place to go was the tavern. They climbed into the Honda, Alison behind the wheel, and made a pact to drink nothing but beer, Christmas or no.

"These lights are killing my eyes," Isadore said to Alison. "I don't know how anyone stands it."

Alison nodded, looking around for a waitress. He caught the attention of one of the girls in the Santa Claus hats, and she came over with a pitcher. Isadore complained to her about the lights.

"Don't talk to me, talk to the big guy," she said, tossing her head towards Leland.

"You tell the big guy he's got this place looking like a two-bit whorehouse," said Isadore to the girl, emphasizing the word *whore* to make her uncomfortable. She made change for them and went away.

"Girls are *hard,* these days," Isadore observed, watching her go. "I hate a girl who's hard."

Alison used to wonder what Isadore meant by this, but by now had heard it enough times to work out a rough definition. *Hard* meant just that, when applied to women or girls. Impervious, impermeable. Watertight.

The two drank their first pitcher, and Leland appeared at their table with another, sat down and wished them a Merry Christmas. Alison was immediately aware of Leland's transparent dislike of him. He didn't know what he had done to offend Leland in particular—the only thing Alison could fathom was that Leland was jealous of his friendship with Isadore. Such a petty schoolyard rivalry Alison couldn't help but be amused by, and the schoolboy within him couldn't help but feel a little triumphant. He kept quiet as Leland and Isadore conversed, however. He always did. They had in common a world and a past that Alison knew he could never partake of.

"Glad to see you, boy," Leland was saying. "I was hoping you'd drop by. Where have you been keeping yourself all this time? When are you coming up to the house?"

"Oh Jesus, Leland, you know what the holidays are like. I've been run off my feet all month."

Alison sat in awe at this exchange. Isadore had been in the monastery all month and Leland was perfectly aware of that fact.

"Well, in case you haven't noticed," continued Leland, "it's almost Christmas. Having our annual whoop-up over at the house—you should come by. We're putting a temporary skating rink out back. Bring Marianne and her boy, God knows when I've seen them last. Dory would love to get all caught up."

"Well, I'm not making any promises."

"Well, you never do!" Leland complained. "I'd say it's about time you started. Of course you're welcome to drop by yourself, Mr. Mason."

Alison tried to smile graciously. Leland had issued the invitation with the pleasure of someone yanking a tapeworm from his bowels.

"Still teaching at the high school out your way?" Leland inquired of him.

"Yes I am," replied Alison.

Leland nodded, duty accomplished, and turned back to Isadore.

"Well, you know we'd love to have you. And you know you're welcome any time, Christmas or otherwise," Leland was saying.

Isadore squinted pointedly around at the bar. "These lights you've put in are a real slut of a thing," he remarked.

"You don't care for them? Young Rob tells me they're the latest trend. All the clubs got them up in Halifax now."

"I think they can stay up in Halifax."

"Maybe you're right," Leland agreed. "Anything white starts to glow. Hard on the eyes. The kids tell me it's 'cool,' but I'm not a hundred percent convinced."

Leland was rising, waving to someone who had come in. He touched Isadore on the shoulder. "I'll be back," he said. "Gotta make the rounds."

"The old bastard needs to quit listening to them thick-headed boys of his," Isadore confided to Alison when Leland was out of earshot. "Not a brain between them."

Alison smiled but Isadore didn't, causing Alison some apprehension. He had drunk enough times with Isadore to know a bad night in the making. But he didn't know how to derail it. He typically hoped, cracked wise, complimented Isadore from time to time, and paid for drinks. It had worked once or twice, but it didn't always or even usually.

The night wore on and people got drunk. The bar had filled with kids, Alison noticed, college kids home for Christmas, young people with the physical constitutions to get wildly, boisterously hammered. Even the girls were doing shooters, flopping about the dance floor with full mugs of beer. Some of the regulars, like Isadore, were resentful of the crush of young ones, but for the most part the atmosphere was one of excitement and novelty. Most men and women who spent their lives in the tavern looking at nothing but the walls and one another for much of the year were revitalized by the presence of the university crowd. But a few looked annoyed, as if they felt impinged upon.

Alison was doubly intoxicated by the presence of so many young women. As a teacher, he had studied to just turn himself off in the classroom; otherwise the tide of blossoming bodies and gales of female hormones could have driven him to distraction.

He had trained himself to think of even the most poised and mature of them as creatures from another planet. But he didn't have to do that here, he realized. Although he supposed there did exist the awkward threat of coming across old students.

"Look at those girls," said Isadore abruptly, as if he were reading Alison's mind. He gestured to a table of six or so, who sat with a tray of shooters in the middle of their group and were chanting *Blow job, blow job, blow job!* in unison. After the third *blow job,* they would each smash back a shot.

Alison was discomfited until he figured out that blow job had to be the name of the drink. He conveyed this realization to Isadore, but the look of repugnance remained fixed on Isadore's face.

"This," he told Alison, "is how you judge a society's downfall. Right fuckin here it is, before us. You look at the women. You can tell by the women. Fall of the Roman Empire."

Alison wondered if it could be true. He believed Isadore to be essentially conservative, inevitable considering his upbringing, but he also had an instinctive feeling that—also because of his upbringing—Isadore was right about most things. Isadore simply struck Alison as being more tuned in than he was, as having a more fundamental, primal connection to the world around him.

"Fucking whores," Isadore spoke abruptly.

A voice spoke up in Alison as well. *Maybe,* it said, *maybe you are wrong about Isadore. Maybe Isadore is nothing but an ugly-minded, dirt-ignorant hick and you have been kidding yourself all along.* This voice had spoken up before, but Alison refused to give it credence. It reminded him of his parents and all their hypocritical, half-assed snobbery. He couldn't be wrong about Isadore, because Isadore had somehow evolved into Alison's single ethical foothold in the world.

"Will you look who I found!" Leland hollered into Alison's ear, having come up behind him.

Alison turned around, expecting to see someone wonderful and fascinating as indicated by Leland's tone, but the individual he beheld was a short man in his forties with dark eyes, lank black hair, and a drooping moustache. He was every bit a local, and clearly of Acadian descent. Alison had taught school in the tiny village that was Isadore's home for so long, he knew the physical type on sight. The little man was almost a caricature.

Alison looked at Isadore to get an idea who this personage might be, but Isadore merely squinted. The fellow stuck out his small hand. "Isadore! God love you!"

Isadore took his time reacting to the hand. A liquored hostility emanated from him. There's no way he's just been drinking beer, Alison reflected. He's got a flask on him somewhere.

"It's Sampson!" Leland yelled with impatience. Alison wanted to giggle at this oxymoronic moniker. "Sampson Roach!" Oh my God, thought Alison, taking a sip of beer.

The meanness suddenly left Isadore's face as if his mother had wiped it with a rag. He formed the word *Sam* with his lips before he was able to speak.

"Look at you!" he finally hollered.

Isadore grabbed Sampson's hand and held it tight, as if he didn't know what else to do with the little guy. Alison thought the astonished look on Isadore's face was not exactly one of pleasure. It was more the old cliché: *like he's seen a ghost.*

Sampson was smiling and wincing a little under Isadore's hand. "Allo!" he said.

"Allo yourself, you bastard!"

Sitting, listening, sipping his beer, gazing at the young women at the other table who were busy bringing society to its knees, Alison gradually got the story of Isadore and Sampson. It seemed they had worked together on construction jobs. Sampson had been an ironworker, like Isadore. They did a few jobs together in the Sydney area, after Isadore had returned from Toronto. Alison had heard much regarding Isadore's time in Toronto, but very little about the kind of work Isadore did once he got home. Alison always got the impression Isadore had worked odd jobs. "Jack of all trades," Isadore would confide with a wink, as if he were describing something naughty in essence. But Alison could scarcely remember a story about ironworking at all, which was strange, considering the number of evenings he had spent in Isadore's company being regaled.

Alison listened to them talk about spud wrenches and guy-derricks. He heard how Sampson had caught "ten shades of shit" for "riding the ball" up to a beam. At some point Alison realized that most of the memories they were discussing had taken place more than fifty feet above ground. He tried to pay closer attention after this, but didn't suceed. His mind felt lazy from the beer. His eyes kept wandering to the blow-job girls, having so much fun together. Their hangovers would be unspeakable the next day, but they looked as though they didn't have enough practice getting drunk to be concerned about it. He admired their blind ease and high spirits. He wondered what it would be like to belong to a group of friends in that way, to move together and laugh together and talk all at once as if sharing a single brain. For the first time in his company, Alison momentarily shed his anthropological interest in Isadore Aucoin and let his mind wander. He wondered what it would be like to be a twenty-year-old girl in this day and age. He wondered what it would be like to be a normal human being with a group of friends, existing in the world without fear or reflection. Without a hall of mirrors in your mind, echoing apprehension and ricocheting every moment of self-doubt you've ever had back in your face with ten times the original force.

One of the blow-job girls, wearing a pink sweater with an argyle pattern down the front, disengaged herself from the table and headed towards the bar. Alison had begun to embroider a fantasy about gently colliding with her on his way to get a drink when his attention was pulled back to Isadore and Sampson. Isadore was speaking in that low-voiced way he had whenever things were about to boil over—like a dog working himself into a slow fury. Also like a dog, the hair on Alison's body shot to attention. He watched it bristle on his hands at the sound of Isadore's voice.

"I thought you were dead," Sampson was saying, a happy, oblivious look of remembrance on his face. Obviously this man hadn't seen or spoken to Isadore in ages, otherwise he would have been backing out the tavern doors at this point. "We all did."

"Well, I wasn't."

Alison looked around for Leland, who had dispatched himself almost immediately after bringing Sampson over to their table.

"It's like you were made of metal, my son."

"Bullshit, Sam,"

"Holy snappin' arseholes, I just watched you tumbling to the earth. The strength pretty near left my legs. Good thing it didn't, though, or I woulda been following you the whole way down."

Alison made a mistake at this point. "You fell?" he inquired.

Sampson turned to Alison with quick eagerness. "In or around sixty feet."

Alison looked from one man to the next. Isadore was gazing in the direction of the dance floor. "No."

"I'm tellin ya," said Sampson, filled with glee.

"He could never have lived."

"He was whappin' himself on girders all the way down."

"No!" said Alison again.

The disbelief was just what Sampson was waiting for. He launched into the entire story, detailing how one day on the job, as Isadore unhooked a beam from the crane and settled it into place, the hook snagged his glove, hoisting him off the beam where he was working and dangling him sixty feet above the ground. "Like a piece of live bait at the end of the Lord's own fishing line," embellished Sampson. "Until the glove tore, that is," he added.

"Stop!" said Alison.

"See, he forgot to put the slit down his gauntlet, didnja, Isadore? You gotta put a slit in the back of yer gauntlet, otherwise you'll get caught. The two of us were always gettin in trouble with the safety manager, ridin the ball, runnin around up there without our harnesses. You wouldn't get away with that today."

Despite himself and his own good sense about Isadore's mood, Alison wanted Sampson to shut up about the gauntlet and describe the fall in detail.

"There's no way he could have lived," Alison insisted again.

"I'm tellin ya—the beams broke his fall. Slowed him down just enough."

"But sixty feet!"

"It's a long drop, I'll give you that." Sampson was chuckling with satisfaction and Alison got the distinct impression he told this story to every person he came across. It boggled the mind, and yet was so surreally in keeping with Alison's image of Isadore as some kind of primal force—a mythical, working-class superhero. Alison dared look over at him for some kind of confirmation, but Isadore continued to stare off into the crowd.

"So he . . ." Alison wasn't even sure he wanted an answer to this next question. "Just got up and walked away?"

"Jesus, no!" exclaimed Sampson to his relief. "Good Christ, the man's not . . . God. Laid up for a good while, weren't ya, Isadore?"

"Well, that was pretty much it for my back," Isadore finally rumbled, as if waking from a doze.

"You hurt your back?"

"On the goddamn disability ever since," Isadore said, as if he resented the income.

Alison thought it was strange he hadn't heard about this before. But it made perfect sense—why else would such a prime physical specimen as Isadore Aucoin, a self-described jack-of-all-trades not be caught dead, in all the time Alison knew him, doing physical labour?

Isadore wrenched himself to his feet to go to the washroom, and Alison saw how his legs wobbled as he moved from the table.

A noisy song started to play, and the blow-job girls whooped when they heard the first few chords and rushed at the dance floor. "I don't think he likes talking about it," Alison shouted over the music to Sampson.

"Well, it was a hell of a thing," Sampson agreed cheerfully. The man had no idea what was in the air around him.

A moment later, Alison watched Isadore emerge from the bathroom. Alison was entirely sober all at once and could hear his own pulse pumping away under the sound of music and the crowd. He watched Isadore roughly push his way through the dancers, towards their table. Alison watched a local stumble and turn with quick offense. The local was too drunk and thug-like to be intimidated right away by Isadore's size. Alison saw the stupid rube snap his mouth open and closed a couple of times, almost imagined he could hear the words—*Watch it!* They happened to be standing a few feet away from Leland's vintage jukebox, and Isadore pulled the man towards it and cracked its façade with the fellow's skull.

It might not have been so bad if it weren't for the blood. The ruckus might have simply been absorbed by the crowd as just another typical tavern altercation. It was getting late in the evening, and the time was about right for men to start shoving at each other. But the man Isadore had chosen was a bleeder. Alison thought his nose had probably been mashed. Blood spewed everywhere. The front of Leland's jukebox glowed crimson. Women screamed. And the sight of Isadore looming over this poor bloodied fellow, looking ready to do the same thing to anyone else who approached him, did not help his case.

"Oh my dear heavens!" remarked Sampson Roach, before stealing off to the men's room.

The young MacPhedrons were on top of Isadore, and then more men piled on for good measure. Alison stood and the next moment Leland was in his face.

"You take him out of here!"

"I," said Alison. He was at a loss because tears were squeezing from the corners of Leland's eyes.

"Don't you have a brain in that head of yours! Why in God's name would you bring him here?"

Alison gasped and laughed all at once. "Who *brings* Isadore anywhere?"

"Well, what the Christ is the matter with you? I thought you were supposed to be smart!"

I don't know what would have given you that idea, Alison started to say.

"He needs taking care of! That boy needs a *keeper,* he doesn't need some goddamn"—Leland flailed for the word—

"*minion* chauffeuring him from place to place and holding up his coat tails! Jesus Christ!"

Alison tried to look dignified. *Minion*. The shouting knot of men had managed to wrestle Isadore into the foyer and appeared to be stuck there. Leland glanced over.

"What I should do is call the Mounties."

"Oh God, Leland, don't."

"He needs help!" Leland swiped at his eyes. "He's going to kill somebody. If not himself. How do I help the son of a bitch?"

"I'll take him home," Alison promised. "I'll take him to his mother."

"Well it's time you did *something*." Leland was glaring at him, but Alison could see hope behind his skepticism. Leland wouldn't call the cops. He would tell his sons to let go of Isadore. He would put his faith in Alison and let them drive away, free and clear and drunk.

Because he's kidding himself, thought Alison with fierce clarity and a sudden, magnificent surge of self-disgust. I'm just the chauffeur after all.

He left the tavern with the knowledge that he was walking into a good couple of days—maybe as much as a month—of black booze oblivion. And as he approached the deranged god who was now leaning against the Honda with his hands in his pockets—whistling, not a scratch on him—Alison certainly welcomed it.

WeIGHT

PAM CORMORANT went to Ann Gillis in search of counsel on the subject of justice. Pam didn't want to tell Ann anything at first, approaching in the guise of intellectual inquiry. Pam went to Ann's house for the first time in her life and knocked on the door. Hugh answered, wearing only a pair of sweatpants, which thrilled Pam vaguely, embarrassingly. It seemed so unoriginal to be a teenage girl excited about Hugh Gillis with no shirt on. Hugh smiled at Pam the way he smiled at everybody—an expression that said he was too busy thinking good things about himself to bother thinking bad things about other people—and wandered away from the door hollering upstairs for Ann.

It was a Thursday, three-fifteen in the afternoon, in the middle of their Christmas vacation. Ann came downstairs wearing striped pyjamas, and regarded Pam in a businesslike manner. "Yes?"

"What is justice?" said Pam.

Ann made her wait out on the step until she put on some clothes. It was sunny, the temperature hovering just above zero. The really rotten weather would come in the next few months.

"I mean," said Pam once they were on the street, maneuvering their way through slush puddles, "where is justice?"

"You sound weird," noticed Ann.

"Say you want justice," began Pam.

"You've lost weight—"

Pam was too preoccupied to laugh at this. "Where would you go to find it?"

They trudged in silence.

"Where are we going anyway?" said Ann.

"We're just walking around," Pam told her.

"Peripatetic," Ann remarked, and Pam was silent because she thought Ann had said *Very pathetic*.

"This is all very Socratic," Ann persisted.

"So what does Socrates say about justice?" Pam forced herself to ask, feeling bad and angry at being called pathetic.

"I don't think he has anything to say about where it *is*, exactly. Where you would get it."

"The obvious answer is the police," answered Pam before Ann had finished speaking. She wrapped her arms around herself.

That was when Ann stopped walking, and would not get going again until Pam told her everything. As she spoke, Pam thought she could almost feel the world speeding up; the town's pulse quickening.

I'M NOT FROM
AROUND HERE, AM I?

"HEY MAN," Hugh said. "I heard about your sister."

They were in Hugh's basement watching television and listening to the stereo at the same time. For most of the night they had been indulging in lazy, beer-tinged conversation about people they knew around town, and the fact that there were almost no "women"—as they had taken to calling females their own age—left in the area. The only thing to do, they joked, was to trawl the high schools like a couple of dirty old men. After they laughed a little and sat in comfortable silence for a moment or two, Hugh—who had been in torment for much of the evening—felt the time was right to bring the topic to light.

He assumed that Howard would know what he knew. He had taken all the infinitesimal scraps of knowledge he possessed with respect to the life of Howard Fortune and woven them into what he felt was the most coherent explanation for the way that Howard was. Hugh figured Howard was such a sullen bastard because of what had happened to his sister (Hugh did not bother himself with questions of why Howard might have been such a sullen bastard throughout junior high and high school). Howard had returned from university last year, perhaps, to be with his family in this time of crisis. Howard had been so antisocial and broody the past year because of his sister. Howard longed for justice and hadn't gotten it. He freaked out on Mackie Pettipas, perhaps, because Mackie Pettipas knew, and had actually had the bile within him to say something about it to Howard that night. Howard's rage was eating him up from the inside out.

So Hugh simply leaned forward, the truth of these assumptions unquestioned in his mind, and fixed his friend with a somber, significant look. Howard smirked a little at the momentousness that had suddenly descended in the Gillis basement.

"Hey man," Hugh said. "I heard about your sister."

Howard put his beer on the table in slow motion. His smirk drooped. The shark lids, as Hugh had come to think of them, quavered for a second before snapping down.

"I'm here to tell you," added Hugh in a hurry. He had heard a guy on TV use the expression recently and had been impressed by the solemnity it conveyed. "I'm here to tell you, man," Hugh repeated, feeling uncertain because of the amount of beer he had consumed and because, he realized, this was probably one of the most serious things he had ever dealt with in his short life. "If you wanna get this guy . . . me and you will get this guy. Me and you, man."

Howard gazed through his shark lids at Hugh for what seemed like a full minute, and Hugh looked back at him steadily, determined not to become uncomfortable. He had come to the conclusion that Howard's off-putting way was simply that: just his way. A defense mechanism, maybe. For keeping the many assholes of the world at bay.

Hugh's nervousness got the better of him. "I'm here for you!" he came close to shouting.

Howard opened his mouth and tried to say something. But his voice got stuck, and nothing came out. He closed his mouth again. He cleared his throat and licked his lips. And then, of course, the slow-blink. One. Another.

"What," he said.

"What?" repeated Hugh.

"Guy," said Howard.

"What?" said Hugh.

"What guy?" said Howard.

Hugh's own mouth got wider and wider until it hung open. "You don't know?"

Howard simply stared at him. Hugh looked down at his hands for a moment, lazy mind turning in hesitant circles.

"We'll find out together," he said, looking up again. "French guy, the way I hear it."

Howard's muscles went slack. He leaned back and seemed to melt into the couch. He reached for his beer and drained it into his mouth.

"We don't have to talk about it," said Hugh. "Just know—"

"It's all right," interrupted Howard, speaking to the ceiling.

"I took care of him."

"You took care of him?"

Howard let the silence tick away until Hugh spoke again.

"Is the guy still walking around with his balls?" Hugh wanted to know.

Howard watched the ceiling a moment longer before raising his head to reply.

"Yes."

"Then you haven't taken care of him. This guy is shit. This guy shouldn't be allowed out in public. He's fuckin scum."

"Forget it," said Howard.

"I can't," said Hugh. "I got a fuckin sister too, man."

Howard shot to his feet. "Don't ever talk about this," he said.

Hugh spread his hands, offended. "I'm not gonna talk about this."

Howard ran his own hands through his hair and repeated the directive: *Don't talk about this*. But he said it with an air of futility, like he was torturing himself with the very pointlessness of the words.

BｒEAK

ALISON SWORE to have no more to do with Isadore, and planned on telling him so. But he hadn't expected to have to do it quite so soon—right in the middle of his week-long hangover. He was still immobilized on the couch with a two-litre bottle of no-name cola and an empty orange salad bowl for puking on the floor in front of him when Isadore arrived. Isadore knocked and then came in without waiting for a response, as was his habit, heading straight for the TV set in order to turn it off—also a habit. He was, Alison saw, lively and stupidly vital after the bender. Alison, on the other hand, could scarcely raise his head.

He never wanted to feel this way again. It was a familiar sentiment, he knew, a cliché even, but he felt it with every poisoned, dehydrated cell in his body—never again. It was Wednesday, the last day of classes before Christmas break. The phone had been ringing intermittently, its noise like a knitting needle jabbing through his ear hole into direct contact with the abused brain. He hadn't taken it off the hook; this was penance. He had woken up on the steps of the Catholic church in town on Monday—thank God not the morning before. Isadore nowhere in sight, perhaps dead. It seemed perfectly reasonable someone had died the day before, or maybe the day before that. Alison woke the way he always woke from blackouts: suffused with a pure, undistilled dread worse than any hangover. A certainty that the very worst had happened, and at some point within the next two-four hours it would spring itself on him in all its luxuriant horror, just before screaming *How could you not remember!* in his face.

He knew he had a few hours before the actual hangover caught up with him, at which point he would be incapacitated. He sprang to his feet. Anybody watching—and who knew, there was a whole squadron of houses lining the street above, all with lovely bay windows—would have been amazed at the vitality the corpse on the church steps had suddenly exhibited. It was chemicals, good old-fashioned chemicals driving him forward, as they had for so much of his life. Adrenaline in this instance. He stopped to glance at the huge, plastic manger scene he had spent the night curled up alongside, as if trying to derive warmth from the plastic cows and donkeys, or the Christ child's celestial glow. After all, it was Christ's own good grace the temperature had not dropped below zero that night. Alison crossed the church parking lot to the rectory, forcing himself not to think.

Even though he was trying not to think, when the priest himself answered the door Alison realized that he had been counting on a housekeeper. Some middle-aged, self-righteous old doll who cleaned bathrooms and did other people's laundry and had no time for any bullshit. If you could just call me a cab, ma'am, I'll be on my way. I don't need to come in, I don't want to bother you. Please. Just a cab. I know the number. Yes, look at me like I'm scum, that's fine. Loathing is good. I'm sure you don't want me on your step any longer than I want to be here. Could start vomiting, you never know. Not pleasant for either one of us. So. Please. A cab.

But it was the priest. Worse. The priest, it turned out, was Angus B., from the monastery, who had slept two rooms down. How in the hell are you supposed to have Alcoholics *Anonymous*, Alison thought with dim fury, in a part of the world where everybody is everybody else's first fucking cousin or third brother twice removed or sister's daughter's uncle's best friend's dog?

"Hullo, Al!" said Angus B., like he'd been expecting him over for coffee. "Happy holidays!"

Alison grinned. *Hi! Wanna be my sponsor?*

"Angus."

They looked each other over. Alison was flummoxed when he registered that Angus the priest was dressed only in a red velour bathrobe. In all his scarcely veiled girth, Angus B. had the air of a playboy, or some kind of decadent aristocrat, emerging perfumed and satiated from his harem. One of the priest's thick fingers was hooked into a delicate china teacup, but this incongruity only added to the overall impression of sordidness.

"I'm sorry to disturb you," said Alison. "In the middle of your tea," he added a second later.

"No," said Father Angus, in the abrupt, dismissive way many locals considered the height of courtesy. "Come in and have some."

He stepped aside and Alison noticed his pink, hairy bare feet.

"I can't," Alison yelped in a sudden, pleading tone. He looked at Angus steadily. "I need to get home. I was just wondering if you'd call me a cab, Angus. Father."

Father Angus puffed out his swollen, red-lined cheeks—a map of ruined blood vessels—and exhaled. The two alcoholics regarded each other with understanding.

"I could drive you," the priest offered. "It would only take me a minute to get dressed."

"No," said Alison, in precisely the way Angus had said the word a minute ago. This was the first time since his arrival here in the Canadian outback, as he used to think of it, that Alison found himself speaking the local tongue, as it were. He thoroughly understood, as he parroted it, the meaning behind that clipped, near brusque "no." The meaning was: *Don't concern yourself.* And: *Don't insult me by concerning yourself.*

The two men—one fat and one thin, one bathed and one dirty, one local and one from away—might have been from the same womb at that moment, they comprehended each other so completely.

So Angus B. called Alison M. a cab, passed him a twenty, and didn't insist he come inside to wait. Alison thanked the Lord—as was getting to be his habit now—for these tiniest of undeserved mercies that kept piling at his worthless feet.

He had the cab stop at a gas station along the way home and purchased five two-litre bottles of no-name cola. Sugar and caffeine was to be his first defense. The cab driver kept saying, the whole drive out of town, "I see ya made a night of 'er, eh, buddy? Really made a night of 'er, wha?" Like he was proud to be chauffeuring such a fellow home.

Isadore was saying something. He was always saying something.

"Need to hide out here for a bit."

"No," said Alison, without thinking. If he had been thinking, stone sober, in full possession of his faculties, he would have been too afraid.

Isadore laughed. "*No!*" he repeated. "Well, fuck you too!"

"I don't want you coming around here anymore, Isadore. I wanna get sober."

"How are ya supposed to get sober without me? I thought we were on the buddy system!" Isadore put on a look of genuine hurt, as if appalled their partnership could be so easily shrugged off.

"We're drinking buddies!" Alison shouted, holding his face with both hands.

"Just because we fell off the wagon a few times, don't blame me." Isadore picked up the cola bottle and examined it for backwash before taking a swig.

"We haven't been on the wagon since we left the monastery five years ago."

"That's what we got Boystown up there for," shrugged Isadore.

"We're alcoholics. We destroy everything we touch. We can never drink."

"Don't call *me* a fuckin alcoholic," said Isadore, without the typical threat in his voice. He was in good cheer overall, Alison saw—Isadore was, of course, drunk. "I'm not the alcoholic here. I'm not the one flat on his back." He raised a massive leg and poked Alison in the side with his foot. "You remember what they used to say up there in Boystown, don'tcha? An alcoholic's always looking for someone else to blame. That sounds like *you* to me. I'm just your friggin scapegoat, and I don't mind telling ya I got no interest in that bullshit." Isadore yawned and scratched his ass. "Well listen, let me borrow your car at least."

"I don't even know where it is."

"I have it."

"Oh." There was no point remarking upon the fact that Isadore was not supposed to be driving. "Then go right ahead."

"Much obliged," said Isadore.

"I don't *blame* you," said Alison. "I just can't be around you."

Isadore spread out his hands and cocked his head at heaven, wounded and innocent as Saint Sebastian. "Well, who invited ya?"

Alison closed his eyes to arrange his thoughts. "You should have been a politician," he whispered, "like Leland."

Sitting, Isadore's mood appeared to shift. "Don't mention that prick to me."

Alison smiled with thin horror, remembering the incident

at the tavern that had set their bender off. The smear of blood aglow across the front of Leland's jukebox.

Seeing him remember, Isadore railed, "I've been as true a friend as ever there could be—through thick and thin. I put up with all his bullshit and betrayals when no one else would. I'm the one he came to when he wasn't elected to town council in 'seventy-four." Isadore waved his hand as though the '74 election was merely the iceberg's tip when it came to what he had endured on Leland's behalf. "The problem is, some people don't understand the meaning of friendship. Some people have very convenient memories, and I think *you* know what I'm talking about, *M'sieur.*"

Alison knew exactly what Isadore was talking about—or at least, what it was he was attempting to do with his words. He was speaking a specialized language—Isadore Aucoin doublespeak—intended not so much to make sense as to convey his own magnanimousness in contrast to the feelings of guilt and unworthiness it instilled in his audience.

"Oh, I coulda been a politician all right. I coulda been a lot of things if I was born with Mac at the front of my name and a doctor for a father and a tartan diaper to soak up my piss and a set of golf clubs shoved up my ass."

Alison leaned back, content that he had not engaged in any particular atrocities in the lost forty-eight hours. The unpleasantness must have been all on Isadore's part, which of course was why he needed to "hide out." Alison wondered if Leland had gone ahead and called the Mounties on Isadore after all. If he hadn't, perhaps someone else had.

"You really could have," Alison said.

"I know I could have!" Isadore exclaimed, insulted by any notion it could be otherwise. "But it's a hell of a chore to try and do any good in this world, when the few people you think you can trust just go and turn on ya at the drop of a hat." He looked pointedly at Alison, who closed his eyes against a rising, weary anger.

What did I do to be included among the betrayers? Alison wondered. Said that he couldn't stay here. Said we can't drink together anymore. Said no to him just this once, for the first time in the five years we've known each other. No more the minion. Therefore, the enemy. What a blustering, lying, self-righteous, self-indulgent, tyrannical goddamn *baby* this man is.

Keeping his eyes closed, Alison spoke a truth that he would never have dared speak to Isadore in any other circumstance.

"Yes you could," he agreed. "You could have been anything you wanted. You're physically bigger than anyone I've ever met. You're stronger. You're healthy, in spite of your own best efforts. You're even good-looking, you know. You're probably the most charismatic man I've ever met."

"If you try and kiss me, you bastard, I'll put you through the wall," said Isadore slowly.

"You're articulate, when you want to be," Alison went on. "You're uncannily manipulative—which makes you a natural leader. You're perceptive. You're *intelligent,*"

Alison paused as they both chewed on this last observation.

"In short, Isadore," he finished, eyes still shut tight, "you're the ultimate specimen of manhood."

After a moment or so, Isadore attempted to chuckle. "I may kiss *you*." Alison opened his eyes and witnessed the man he had just been describing at a complete loss.

Isadore's face went through a number of transformations. There was a moment of sheer childlike glee at hearing what he had always believed about himself articulated so unequivocally. On its heels came grown-up suspicion: What was Alison after? What in hell was wrong with him, saying something like that? Then a weird nobility came over Isadore's features, and for a moment Alison thought he might stand up, take an elaborately humble bow, shake Alison's hand, and slip out the door without a word.

But the look was fleeting. It changed again to suspicion, dipped into anger, then took a nose dive and settled into perhaps the first honest expression Alison had ever beheld on that face. This was when he had to look away.

"Fuck you, Yankee man."

Alison smiled from nausea and reached for his salad bowl. It was after four and the shifting winter light coming in through the windows had sucked all the colour out of his walls and furniture. It was the hour of grey—the hour of lead, Emily Dickinson had said in a poem about being frozen, or feeling frozen—and, if he was not entirely missing the mark, being grateful for it. For Alison, this had always been the most depressing time of day. Silent and shadowed and colourless.

"Please turn a light on when you leave," he said to Isadore.

Isadore placed his hands on his knees and pushed himself to his feet. He took his time walking about the house, turning on every single lamp and light switch he came across, as well as the two radios, blender, record player, and, finally, the TV before he left. A few moments after the door slammed, Alison heard beneath the din a vague *pop* from the kitchen and realized Isadore had even put the toaster down.

Alison now had an enemy, a bad one, but he doubted this could do him any more harm than the friendship had. He stuck his head in the orange salad bowl aware that—yet again—he had gotten off easy. He was always getting off easy. After all, he'd seen Isadore bury his foot in another man's gut for having accidentally extinguished a cigarette in his unfinished beer. He'd seen what had happened two nights ago at the tavern. How many occasions had there been in Alison's life wherein by all rights he should have woken up crippled, bleeding, sodomized, who knew?

The mercies of even the past few hours let him understand: it was a message. One by one, the delicate persistence of these tiny amazing graces had finally managed to permeate his dulled consciousness. They spoke about this kind of thing up at the monastery all the time, irritating him to the bottom of his agnostic's soul. Charlton Heston in a fright wig. Bushes burning, clouds parting. But never was Alison able to fathom such subtlety, such uninsistence, such unspeakably tender, unspeakably undeserved *patience*. Brushing against his head like careful fingers, snowflakes of impossible fragility.

Forgiveness. Forgiven. Forgive . . .

Dropping like the gentle rains from heaven.

HE IS LIKE Santa Claus in reverse when he comes and takes our television. Rosy-cheeked, jolly, with a Merry Christmas for us both, and presents: a box of MacDonaldland cookies for me, and for my mother a large, plaster statue of Saint Anne, which happens to look as if it belongs in one of those church alcoves where exactly such statues are mounted. The saint is like a big plaster doll and my mother cradles it in her arms for a moment before placing it on the counter and following Isadore into the room where the TV sits. I've already positioned myself in front of it. Bing Crosby and David Bowie are on.

Peace on earth—can it be? David Bowie is singing.

"Now, *mon petit,*" goes Isadore in a fatherly tone. I stand in front of Bing and David and say nothing.

"Look how you've grown—doin some shoulder work, I see," he says, and then—almost like a punchline—moves me out of the way like another man might push aside a curtain. He picks up Bing Crosby and David Bowie and tucks them under his arm. "I only need to borrow it for a couple a nights. Mamere's is broken."

"Oh, Isadore it is *not!*" my mother shrieks, crying. The singing from the TV stops because the plug has come out of the wall. Sparks fly from the outlet.

"This place is a firetrap," Isadore observes. "Who's the landlord?"

And the only word I can manage to form is "Go."

"Well," says Isadore, "I can't stay. I just came by to say Merry Christmas, letcha know I was outta the monastery." He turns to me. "Look, son, I forgive you for the hockey. We can still box, uh? They got a club down the street."

"Fuck that," I say. Isadore arranges a look of drunken injury on his face.

I want to kill him. For saying these things to me. *You've grown. I forgive you.*

"Isadore you steal our TV don't ever come back," my mother speaks in a rush.

"I said I was borrowin it!"

"You don't even like TV!" I yell.

"I told you it's for Mamere! You people just gonna let an old woman sit with no TV over the holidays? And then you leave her there all alone, you don't even come for Christmas Eve!"

"Because we knew you'd be there!" I yell. I want to grab it from him and throw it to the ground myself, just so I can stop everything from being so inevitable all the time. At this point my mother comes over for some reason and touches my face. Her hand startles me, it feels so cool. Extremely Dry Skin.

"Some fuckin family this is!" Isadore says, wearing the expression of disgust he's always aiming at us. "The girl off knocked up by some greasy Scotsman—Jesus Christ, the cycle of life continues around here, uh?"

I start looking around for an object to pick up and hit him with. This is the sort of comment that could send my mother to bed for days, weeping from her strained nerves and bad heart. In the corner is a huge old rocking chair that the homemaker from social services brought us when we moved in, and I start calculating its weight and take a step towards it. But then my mother speaks.

"We are finished with you," she says. I look over and her hands aren't even anywhere near her heart.

Isadore has the TV tucked under his arm like a football. "Oh, you're finished with *me*," he says. "Good fuckin luck. I'm the only thing keeping this family together."

"No, you're not," says my mother. "You've been our ruin."

For a moment, I think Isadore is actually going to hurl the television like I imagined doing. "*Me!* he hollers. "I'm not the gay divorcee over here, am I?"

And suddenly I'm thinking, This is bad. I don't know what I was thinking before, but it's different now. There is something new going on, and my first instinct is to run from them both.

"You are the problem, Isadore," my mother says.

"The welfare mother tells me I'm the problem."

"Daddy died worrying about you."

"Now you just better shut the fuck up about Emile."

"He told me to always look out for you because your feelings were hurt so easily. *He's delicate,* Daddy always said about you, did you know that?"

"That's about the biggest crock of shit—"

"But I've *had* it Isadore, you're not a baby, you're not my baby brother anymore. I have my own babies to look after."

Isadore bends over and places the television set at his feet. He straightens again, taking forever, and put his hands on his hips, blinking and repositioning his massive jaw as though he might cry. "I can't believe you'd tell lies about my own father to me like this."

"The two of you are just the same!" my mother yells. "Neither of you could face the truth about anything! Daddy would have let me die of a heart attack if I hadn't gotten checked."

"He couldn't have known anything about that!"

"He did so know! That's why he didn't go to war! Mamere said—*both* of us, Isadore, both of us could've inherited this trouble and he didn't say a word our whole lives." She wipes her hands together. "So there's our lovely father," my mother says, seeming to shake the subject from her fingertips like dirt.

"It's a lie," states Isadore.

"You go ask Mamere, it's a lie," my mother challenges. "She can go on treating you like a baby if she wants. I'm done."

Isadore bends with dignity to retrieve the television.

"You take that TV, you don't come back. I wash my hands."

He gives her what my mother has always called his Lord Beaverbrook expression. I don't know who Lord Beaverbrook is supposed to have been, but she usually says it when Isadore is playing up the nobility thing. Isadore turns his wall-like back to us and heads for the door.

"And you don't talk to my son," she tells him.

He shoots her a look and turns the knob.

"You won't have us anymore," my mother warns.

When he's gone, I pace around the apartment, unable to burn up the adrenaline pumping through my blood. I feel this bizarre power, even though I just stood and did nothing the whole time my mother was putting the shit to Isadore. Most of all, I feel like flying from the apartment and seeking out the guy who beat me up at MacIssacs. I imagine leaping down on him from the top of a building, taking him by complete surprise, like a superhero.

"That was just like TV," I enthuse to my mother.

"We'll get a new one," she says, half listening.

I grab the oversize Saint Anne from the kitchen counter and put her on the TV stand. She gazes down at the carpet as though she's embarrassed. "Now we have our own shrine, at least," I say, freakishly cheerful.

My mother smiles at me and reaches for her heart. "I guess we better pray."

There is nothing for us to do but sit and talk. We make hot chocolate with cocoa even though there is Quik in the cupboard. My mother talks about my father, which she has scarcely ever done before. It's the apartment, I realize. There is something about the apartment that is good for us. The house has always been so thick with the past, it never even occurred to my mother to speak of it to me or Louise. It was simply there, present, all around us at every moment of every day. But now that we're free, and alone, my mother has finally remembered that I have no actual idea of anything that happened before I was born.

Kenzie Boucher was not a bastard, she tells me. He was simply weak, like Isadore. This takes me by surprise. I've always had this impression of my father as being the exact opposite of Isadore Aucoin. I don't know why.

But no, the first thing my mother tells me is that they were the same. They were afraid of life and couldn't face it, she says.

"Life," repeats my mother, when I ask what she means. "He was afraid of it. Life was me, and you and Louise and my bad heart. He was so scared, he had to hide," she tells me.

"He was scared of *me?*"

"Ah—" My mother waves her hand, gesturing to the world. "He was afraid of everything. First he hid in booze, then he hid in God. He thought he'd join the Benedictines for a while. Then he just hid. For good."

It's that simple, this enormous question mark that has always sat at the center of my life like some fat retarded guy speaking his own private language. It's a joke. *He was scared. He was like Isadore.* It is quite a bit like an insult.

eVEN

CROSSING THE CAUSEWAY into Auld Cove, Isadore compared himself to the Holy Mother of God. This was what it felt like to be Mary, he considered, on the eve of Christ's birth: knocking on doors, seeking shelter, a kind word, and being refused over and over again. First Leland—having vowed never to let Isadore through the tavern doors again. Then that draft-dodging son of a whore, Mason. And now Isadore's own family. No room at the inn.

In the back seat of Alison Mason's Honda, his sister's television sat wrapped in a car blanket—swaddling clothes. Isadore glanced over his shoulder to check on it periodically.

It was not the case that he had nowhere to go—he had his mother's house, all the way over to the northwest side of the island, in Cheticamp, and he did intend to get there at some point. But he was still irritated with her for having moved out of the Aucoin family home practically the moment Emile's spirit left his body, leaving the place to Marianne and her brood. Now that Louise and her Scotsman had claimed it, there was nowhere left that felt like his anymore. So on some level he wanted to punish his mother, though he knew she had probably made him supper after he called to say he was coming over. He'd made this call from a gas station down the road from Mason's place after the Yankee prick had "turfed him out"—as Isadore thought of it—without so much as a Happy Holidays. Turned Isadore away, and after he had gone to all the trouble a few days ago to stop at the liquor store, just moments after getting out of the monastery, and pick Mason up two nice bottles of sherry for Christmas. It just went to show. It went to show how ungrateful people could be, how quickly they forgot.

"By the way," it occurred to him to ask his mother before hanging up, "where's Marianne and the little fart holed up? I should stop by and see if they need help with the tree or whathaveyou."

And Mamere had probably lit candles, and had carols playing on the radio. It was after ten and the supper had certainly long gone cold. He imagined he would show up sometime around midnight, just as she was getting ready for bed. Isadore knew he would make her feel guilty for not having kept the supper warm. He was not consciously planning to do this—he just knew that he would. He was already gearing up for it, getting angry, preparing his wounded look, the things he would say.

But none of this could happen unless he showed up at his mother's house with a nice gift. Because certainly she would have a nice gift for him, probably more than one—she always did. None of Isadore's cruelties or accusations would work unless he had a present. He needed to be able to say, *And here I went to all this trouble to get you this nice* . . . whatever it was he was going to get her. He didn't know yet. Lauchie Puddicomb ran a pawn shop in Auld Cove and Isadore was headed back across the causeway to swap him the TV for something. Isadore had been to Lauchie's house earlier and bashed on the door and made Lauchie promise to let Isadore into the shop when he returned with the television.

He had spent the last week in various degrees of intoxication and was now at the point he liked best, where no matter how much he drank, his mood and state of mind didn't alter. Things stayed on an even keel. He was able to keep his mind on what needed to be done. It was a bit like being sober, except he had no reflective faculties. He could not have stopped to think about what he was doing even if he wanted to.

He knew he felt bad—it was just below the surface. But the even-keeled drunkenness kept the bad feelings at bay and kept his thoughts focussed on the easiest explanation for those feelings. He did not think, I feel bad because I am alone at Christmas; he thought, Everyone has betrayed me. *Everyone has betrayed me* was not the same sort of idea as *I have no one*. It made Isadore feel important. People betrayed generals and kings, saints and Jesus Christ.

He had been in bad cheer ever since leaving the monastery, and what set it off was a conversation with Leland the day he had gotten out. He had made straight for the tavern that afternoon, out of habit, and to announce his return to all his friends.

It was rare for Leland to be at the tavern these days, but on that particular afternoon he was sitting at the bar with his characteristic air—not so much one of proprietorship, but more that of a long-term patron. The two men shook hands, and Isadore was surprised by a sudden urge to put his arms around Leland and lift him right off the ground. He felt how strange it was for over a month to have passed without benefit of Leland's company.

"Jesus Christ, it's good to see you back here at the helm," Isadore kidded. "I'd thought you'd gone into early retirement!"

"Ach," Leland smiled. "We won't get any young ones in here a'tall if they see a couple of old bastards like you and me hanging around."

"Speak for yourself!" declared Isadore, pretending to be offended. "Some of us are just hitting our stride."

"I'm a grandfather," Leland remarked.

Isadore gaped. "The hell you are!"

"I'll have you know that it's the case."

"When?"

"Oh . . . little grandson not four months old."

"Who got married? One of the boys?"

Leland shrugged and smiled a little. "Ah well, that's not the way they do it these days, I s'pose. They don't bother with the formalities. Duncan hooked up with a young one from up Pubnico way. They're living together, but haven't made it official yet."

Isadore almost blushed on behalf of his friend. If it had been anyone but Leland's boy, he would've denounced such doings in no uncertain terms.

Instead Isadore strove to change the subject. "Well, congratulations, Grandpa. My young niece just got married herself," he contributed.

"Is that right? Little . . ."

"Louise!"

"Oh dear God, she must only be . . . what?"

"Oh, she's no more than eighteen . . . nineteen. The fella's a MacQuarrie, from up Sydney way."

"Nice fella?"

Isadore had no idea. "Oh, he's a good enough lad. They seem pretty happy. Living out at the house now."

"With Marianne?"

"No! Marianne's here in town, didn't you know?"

"Is that right?"

"She's working for a family down on Prince Street, so, you know, it's convenient for her."

"How's her young fella doing these days? You should bring him around again some time."

Isadore threw half truths on top of the outrage and pain that arose whenever he thought of Marianne and her crew. "Well, you know he quit the hockey." He placed his hands on his hips in a gesture of indulgent disapproval, a beer bottle jutting from underneath one of his fists. "Which was a bit of a disappointment to me because the kid was a hell of a skater. But what odds, as the Newfies say—you can't tell them anything at that age, they're just gonna do what they're gonna do. I'll tell *you* something though, by God, he's really filling out, last I seen him. He'll be bigger than me yet. Doing a little boxing . . ."

Isadore trailed off. Sadness was beginning to lick at his heels like an old, sick dog. He became aware of the beer in his hand and took a long swallow.

And even though Leland, with his politician's instincts, hadn't questioned further, somehow Isadore's mood had set like concrete. And the mood was bad. Later that night, after he and Mason had drunk all the sherry and returned to the tavern, Isadore remembered his conversation with Leland, and felt almost instant resentment because of it. He knew he would crack somebody's skull that night. He knew it the moment he stepped through the door.

He thought of what had been said about his father as *lies*. All he acknowledged was that his sister had aimed a barrage of lies about Emile at him to make him leave. Fine. She could lie all she wanted. Her words were false and slanderous, and for him this fit with the way the world seemed to be going in general. The family had betrayed the memory of Isadore's father just as they continued to betray Isadore. It struck him at this point as no more than the natural course of events.

DAWN

HOWARD DREAMED only of falling, and often. Even when he was just starting to drift off and his thoughts had been loosed from the fist of his waking mind. He would be walking, just walking in darkness across an endless expanse of concrete and he would trip. Nothing would be on either side of him. A pair of hands and arms would come out of the darkness and wrap themselves around him and hold his body immobile. And he would be paralyzed in every respect, without even the capacity to cry out. And then someone would start speaking very close to his ear. It took forever to break out of. And even then it was not like he had broken out of it, it was like he was let go. Like it was someone's idea of a game. He would suddenly be released and the next moment would rip himself from the bed, blankets flung across the room. He'd make his way to the living room couch, lie down when it felt safe, feel his chest reverberate, will his heart to slow.

This began happening every night as he tried to fall asleep. One morning his father found him on the couch, a bottle of Glen Fiddich normally kept away in a cupboard for guests empty on the coffee table beside him. His father shook him awake and told Howard that he himself had developed a problem with alcohol when he was Howard's age and if the same thing were taking shape now, Howard should tell him, and they would go to a meeting together. Howard sat up, blinked once, and seemed to shake any vestige of sleep from his curls. He covered up the ongoing pity he felt towards his father with his usual look of contempt.

I am having nightmares, he told his father. He knew they weren't exactly nightmares but had no idea how to describe what he'd been experiencing without sounding like he was losing his mind. He couldn't stand the idea of his father worrying about him, or wondering about him, or thinking that anything could be wrong with him at all. He knew that his father had lately been engaged in all of these activities. He wanted it to stop.

You are having nightmares, repeated his father, trying to determine how to slot this information.

I just can't get any sleep, Dad.

Convulsively, Howard's father reached over and felt his forehead.

Howard sighed. I'm not sick.

Well, you need your sleep, son. You'll put us in the poor house if you have to down a forty of scotch every night.

It wasn't even half full. We wouldn't be having this conversation if I drank the whole bottle.

I guess to God we wouldn't be.

His father smiled. It couldn't have been any later than six-thirty in the morning. The sun wasn't up. The house was so quiet they could hear the fridge humming in the kitchen. Howard could feel the longing coming off his father. Longing to talk, longing for Howard to explain things. Who are you, now that you have grown? You used to spend hours in the basement logging all your chemistry experiments in a notebook. What do you do now? Where do you go? Where are you exactly? His father lately peered at him as though through a snowy TV screen. Why are things the way they are now in this house?

He asked, What kind of nightmares?

They're always different, said Howard, the opposite of what was true. They were drearily the same: Say there was a big red plant called Awful growing deep in the rain forest. Say that scientists had harvested the plant by the thousands, crushing it to a pulp and distilling its juices into the highest possible potency. Like that. Like that has been injected into me.

It's a sensation more than anything, he added.

His father's blue eyes crinkled with concern, which Howard steeled himself against. He did not want it. He did not want the temptation to be eleven, to cry and shudder in the old man's lap. He felt resentful, thinking his father should know better than to offer this as an alternative, even tacitly. As a father, he should be shoving Howard upright, not encouraging him to lean.

The stairs creaked and his sister's bare feet appeared below the flannel curtain of her nightie. She made her way down the stairs with her eyes mostly closed, heading to the bathroom. When she reached the landing, she squinted at the two, grunting by way of commentary. Corinne was, in her mother's words, a bear in the early hours. She turned and staggered into an end table, causing the lamp to wobble briefly.

Careful, dear, murmured her father.

She made a peevish noise and lurched off down the hall like a pint-size Frankenstein.

You'd think it would have made a comical impression. You'd think they might have glanced at each other and shared a gentle laugh on so delicate a morning.

fREAK

RONALD COMES—he's been coming every other day. He brings them a tree, he puts up the outside lights. He buys two-litre bottles of pop from the drug store and lines them up in the storm porch to keep them cool. The fridge is now stuffed with woodland creatures—deer steak, rabbit, moose. Pam's mother cannot produce mincemeat fast enough. She's bringing tarts to all the neighbours.

Ronald calls into the living room to Mr. Cormorant, "Like a drink, boy?" like the host at a party. "We got everything you could want here for ya. We got orange, we got grape, we got lime."

Children's flavours. No cola or ginger ale. No mix.

Mr. Cormorant now makes no bones about the fact that he is an alcoholic. He has been going to meetings every week with Ronald, where he has been encouraged to come clean. He learned to admit, and then embrace his alcoholism, and now is letting it all hang out. It is frightening to Pam. He's wearing sweaters, jeans from Mark's Work Warehouse, not bothering to shave. Pam is used to her father as either a buttoned-up manager or a falling-down drunk, not this man, this sweater-clad monstrosity of candour.

"I want a little drink of *rum*," he singsongs from his chair in the next room. "And I want a little drink of *scotch*. And maybe a little shot of *whiskey* for my Irish ancestors."

"Oh, we all know what you *want*," rejoins Ronald, smiling. Ronald, for the first time she's ever witnessed, is in his element. Pam's mother confided that Ronald was something called a "career" alcoholic, but Pam had never known this because he had not touched alcohol since well before she was born. At first she could not imagine what this meant, having never seen him drunk. But now she understands, watching his competence with her father, his pockets stuffed with pamphlets from the program—he brought pamphlets for Pam, pamphlets for her mother. The book, the chips he carries around along with his religious medals. He is, indeed, a career alcoholic. It's his society, the one thing in the world he understands inside and out, and can partake of unselfconsciously. Ronald never once stutters when he speaks of "The Program." The culture of not drinking.

Ronald is there to serve, she perceives, as he bustles around, setting up the tree and performing all the other dadjobs. He is their humble salvation. She starts to trail him around the house, out to the back porch, helping him bring in wood. She's trying to find a way in. How to talk. How to talk to adults. How to talk to an adult like Ronald.

What she is thinking in her mind is that maybe Ronald is the male, grown-up equivalent of a fat friend, and she should be sitting at his feet.

"You help us," she remarks to him one day, in the hopelessly forced tone that always emerges when she wants to sound at ease.

Pam is making Ronald a pot of coffee. It is the one thing he asks that she and her mother do for him in return for all he is doing for them. *He doesn't know how to make filtered coffee, is another of Pam's mother's confidences. He always used to get me to mix him up Nescafé, but I gave him some of the real stuff one time and he loved it. He only has it when he's here.* It is a treat that Ronald associates with Pam's family, and so they keep a pot going all throughout Christmas. Pam has started drinking it too. It threads a low-grade hum of panic through her days.

Ronald looks up at her with his kicked-dog expression. He has been paring his nails with an ancient jackknife, the same one she's seen him use to slice chewing tobacco. The blade is crusty brown. Pam thinks of getting him a new one for Christmas, but realizes he'd never use it. He'd tuck it away in a drawer, perhaps, saving it for "good" like her mother did with family heirlooms.

Ronald lets his tobacco-stained parings tumble into a small pile on the kitchen counter.

"What, dear?" he says.

"You just help us," repeats Pam. "You're so nice." She looks away as Ronald's nose goes red. "I mean—there must be lots of other people you'd like to be with over Christmas."

"Who," says Ronald, blushing and stuttering while trying to sound cavalier. "Who. Who else would have me?" He tidily sweeps the nail parings off the counter and onto the floor.

Oh, listen, Pam wishes to say, impatient from caffeine and worry. I don't have time. I don't have time for us to smile shyly at each other across the counter. I need to know what to do. How to help someone in pain.

"I go where I'm needed," Ronald remarks. "I do what the good Lord put me here to do. I play my part."

"You play your part?" Pam repeats, heavy with dread.

"I do what the good Lord put me here to do," he says.

Did the good Lord make you a freak? Pam wants to yell. Just like he made me a fat freak? Is the good Lord perhaps a big freak himself? Why do the big drunk freak in the living room and the big beautiful freak up the street need looking after anyway, and why do freaks like us have to do it? Who decides all this?

Ronald notices Pam's clenched fists and folds his jackknife. "It's a duty," he adds.

What will happen when Mr. Cormorant is all better? What will happen when he's shaving and wearing shirts with buttons again, talking to Pam through her mother—*Doesn't the girl need some exercise? Hasn't the girl any better clothes than that?* Ronald will go, that's what will happen. He'll revert to the meat-foisting nuisance as far as they're all concerned, but basically he will be gone. Wherever he's needed. What will happen if he isn't needed somewhere else, though? This is what Pam wants to know. Will he retire to his trailer in the woods, languish on his bunk, drown in a stew of fingernail parings and tobacco juice until all the creatures of the forest gather to watch him decompose, the man who harvested their bodies to nourish his loved ones for so long?

This is how it looks to Pam. This is what happens to those who do what the good Lord put them here to do—those unlucky enough to know what it is. They're like disposable towels as far as the good Lord is concerned—celestial Kleenex. Pam has read up on the ancestors of Shylock. She knows the score. She knows precisely where the pious freaks end up. If not back with their locusts and wild honey, then worse.

Pam and Corinne are best friends again, all-day friends like before. They huddle together throughout the Christmas holidays, just as they used to. They go up to Corinne's room to exchange gifts on Christmas Day. They want to be alone, like lovers, like when they were little kids and they said they would marry each other.

Bath beads for Corinne. And different kinds of soap, shaped like tiny apples and hearts. She loves that stuff. Pam gets a bottle of Charlie perfume, and a little Christmas teddy bear with his arms wrapped tightly around it. He's hanging on to the Charlie for dear life.

"We are going to stink up the school," observes Pam. "They'll smell us coming a mile away."

Corinne cries, out of the blue. She has been a mess since the night of the play. She has been telling all her other friends she has the flu to explain why she hasn't been out with them over Christmas.

They get down to business. Pam and Corinne have spent the holidays conferring. Mr. and Mrs. Fortune have expressed a startling measure of delight at seeing Pam "after so long." Mrs. Fortune keeps asking her to stay for supper. Fred Fortune squeezed the breath out of her with a sudden hug when she arrived at the door. Pam can still smell him: wood smoke from the fireplace, wool, after-shave, and shortbread cookies.

"Have you said anything to your parents?"

"My parents will think I'm crazy. They already think I'm crazy."

"But you're . . ." How to put this. You're *going* crazy. "You're falling apart, you need to . . ."

"No, no, no," Corinne snuffles and wipes her eyes on her sleeve, arranging herself. "No, no, no, I just need time. This always happens, I just have to cry for a few days, but then I can get it together again."

Corinne becomes aware of the way Pam is looking at her and changes position. Pam must have a stunned, preoccupied sort of look on her face, like she's calculating a math problem. She's trying to determine how she could have gotten so wrong a person she's known her whole life. How long has Pam held the image of Corinne in her head as this sleek, perfect thing— as flawless and glossy and hard as a lacquered fingernail?

Guilt speaks through Pam. "I'm here for you."

Corinne continues to trickle, but bares her straight teeth in an appreciative sort of way.

"You could tell Howard," says Pam.

More teeth appear as Corinne clenches. "Howard's going *away*. He's *leaving* after Christmas. He's getting an *apartment* in fucking Donnell *Cove*."

Pam gawks. "Why?" Donnell Cove is only twenty minutes away, and a terrible place, celebrated for its lobster pound, fish plant, and its parish priest of twenty years, recently discovered to be a pederast.

"To be closer to the fucking *fish plant*," says Corinne.

The fish plant and Donnell Cove are two things that do not jibe with Pam's perception of Corinne's brother. Howard, in Pam's vision, is even glossier than his sister. Sharper and harder. More claw than painted fingernail. He belongs in a museum somewhere, not a production line wearing gut-stained overalls.

"Well, he'll still be around."

"No he won't," insists Corinne. "He hates me. He thinks I'm a slut."

"No he doesn't," says Pam. Having no siblings herself, she can't imagine such a thing would be true.

"He beat him up, you know," says Corinne, crouched on her knees and leaning forward.

"Who?" says Pam.

"Howard. Beat him up. The French guy. This summer."

"Had you *told* Howard?"

"No, but the French guy was calling all the time and Howard knew I didn't want to talk to him!" Corinne's red-rimmed eyes glitter, and a reluctant thrill creeps between Pam's shoulder blades. She imagines the two boys facing each other, squaring off. Light and dark, town and country, good and evil, prince and thug.

Corinne looks to be indulging in the same sort of reverie, minus Pam's embarrassment. The fact of the matter is, Pam was so in love with Howard as a little kid it sears her to even contemplate him now. Corinne used to let her into his room to feel around inside his underwear drawer.

"So clearly Howard doesn't hate you, then."

"Yeah. Anyway." Corinne shrugs, her eyes going dull like someone's pulled a plug.

"It'd be different if he didn't go to school here," Pam considers. "If you didn't have to see the guy every day."

"Well—" Corinne picks up a yellow bath bead and rolls it between her fingers. "We graduate in two years."

"We could get him expelled."

"I don't want anyone to find out!" Corinne yells. "I don't want to get in trouble!"

Pam puts her own hands over her mouth as if she's the one who's making all the noise.

"Just forget it, Pam." Corinne places the bath bead back in its box.

Pam slowly unclamps her hands. Whispers, "We can't just let it go."

"We can," says Corinne, sinking into a cold, after-tears indifference that Pam is getting familiar with. Corinne doesn't let herself be hugged or touched at this stage. "Everybody hates me anyways. My brother hates me. Brian hates me. My parents hate me. I don't have anyone."

"You have me," says Pam heroically.

Corinne somehow smiles and sobs at once.

The dream is that she can't find Ricky Estabrooks. There are only a few minutes to curtain and she's wandering around backstage, carrying his hat and a big rubber nose Mrs. K. wants him to wear so everyone will understand they have to hate him. Mrs. K. has told her: *The audience is fickle. If he isn't wearing his nose, they'll all go home.* In the dream, Pam understands fickle also means stupid. *What they really want to see are the costumes,* Mrs. K. says with resigned contempt. Pam's job is to find Ricky and make sure he's wearing his nose. But she can't find him. She walks around thinking *fickle,* finding everybody but Ricky. She comes across one useless Magnifico after another. She comes across Ann, who says, *Give it to me, I'll find him for you.* But Pam doesn't trust her. She thinks Ann might put it on herself, try to sneak back into the play, fake them all out.

It goes on and on and on, looking for Ricky. And when she finds him—*I was out having a smoke,* he tells her, even though Ricky doesn't smoke in real life—she looks down for the nose and now she can't find *that.* She wants to weep.

Oh well, says Ricky, peeking through the curtain. *The play's half over anyway.*

Is there anybody out there? Pam wants to know. There can't be, she's sure. They would have all gone home. She's ruined it for everyone.

CLOSE

PUDDICOMB'S NOW AND THEN was still dark when Isadore pulled into the driveway, and such a wave of indignation washed over him at the sight of the darkened neon OPEN sign, he could have ploughed Alison Mason's Honda directly through the display window.

"He told me he'd be open, and now he's closed," said Isadore out loud. "I go over there specifically to ask if he'll be open. He says, hell yes I'll be open. I go away, I come back. Is he open? No. Hell no. Why, hell no, he's not." Isadore continued to mutter as he hauled himself out of the car. To him there was something utterly emblematic about the situation

"I'm on my way out the door: All right, I'll see ya in a couple of hours then—you'll be open, now, won't ya? My God, yes, Isadore. You're goddamn right I'll be open, no question about it. May the good Lord strike me down if I'm not open.

May the angels fall from the sky this holy night." Lauchie's house was behind the store. Isadore strode around back, still muttering in disbelief.

The sky was trying to snow, but near-solid ice water shot down from it instead. Just as Isadore was crossing the causeway it had hit, splatting against the Honda's windshield. Disgusting weather. As the night wore on, the rain would freeze solid, encasing everything in ice. No one would be able to set foot out the door without breaking a hip. Isadore's breath plumed out in clouds as he spoke to himself. It was already well below zero, and he could feel the world around him hardening and growing slick.

As he passed Lauchie's window, Isadore noticed a crowd of people gathered around the dinner table inside. "Bit fuckin late for dinner, isn't it?" he muttered, heading to the back door.

He banged on it, jabbing at the doorbell simultaneously. "Puddicomb, you lying piece of shit!"

Isadore banged steadily until the door opened. Warmth and the smell of gravy enveloped him.

"Isadore," said Lauchie, looking pained. He was holding a greasy carving knife.

"Typical!" spat Isadore. "If this just isn't the most typical goddamn thing, I don't know what is! You said you'd be open."

"I said I'd be here. There's no need for this ruckus!"

"Well, clearly there is if ya figure you're gonna tell baldface lies to your customers on Christmas of all nights! Jesus Christ, Lauchie, I expected better of you."

A small child poked his head between the door and Lauchie's thigh. Slack-mouthed, he stared at Isadore.

Isadore put his hands on his hips and nodded at the kid. "Good day to *you*, sir," he said impatiently.

"Go on now, Ryan dear," shooed Lauchie, shifting the carving knife to his other hand.

The boy didn't look as if he were going anywhere. He goggled up at Isadore in frank wonder. Recognizing it, Isadore felt compelled to talk to him. "So?" he said. "What in hell's keeping that bastard Santa anyway? Didn't he bring you your presents yet?"

"No." The boy answered with earnest concern. "'Rampa says he might not come this year, he might be too tired."

Isadore met eyes with Lauchie, who looked as if he didn't know whether to smile or brandish the knife. "He did?" exclaimed Isadore. "Well, you listen here, I saw that lazy frigger over by the causeway checking that list of his. He says to me, Oh Christ, I don't know, Isadore, it's getting pretty late, I could freeze my balls off if I stay out much longer. Maybe I should just skip these next few houses, nobody important lives over Auld Cove way anyhow."

Ryan clutched at his grandfather's pant leg, panicked.

"Well, I said, listen here, Mr. Santa, I just happen to know a little fella over at the Puddicomb place—been good as gold all year the way his 'rampa tells it. You better haul ass over there, if you don't want me to kick it all the way back to the North Pole!"

"Is he gonna come?" asked Ryan.

"Jesus, yes, you should've seen him jump! He said he's just gotta pick up some feed for the reindeer, and he's on his way."

The boy looked around wildly for a moment, before ducking back into the house to herald the news to his family. Isadore grinned at Lauchie.

"Little fella don't know whether to shit or go blind," he observed.

"He's pretty excited," said Lauchie, looking worn out by the intensity of his grandson's youth and worry. Lauchie sighed. "What are we going to do with you, Isadore?"

"You're gonna get your ass in gear and open up the shop, first of all. Unless you want your own arse kicked just like that goddamn Santa Claus."

"I'll meet you in front," Lauchie said. "You're a hard one to figure, boy," he added, closing the door.

Isadore laughed and tramped back to the Honda. His mood had flipped like a pancake. Through the dining room window, he could see Lauchie explaining the situation to his family and guests.

Isadore had always liked children because children were consistently fascinated by him. They followed him around if they could. As he reached into the back seat for the television, Isadore had a sudden memory of Marianne's girl Louise calling him Friendly Giant when she was a toddler. She would run to him whenever Marianne and Kenzie were down for a visit, calling "Way up! Way up!" and holding out her arms wanting to be shuttled into the air. He used to think it was cute until Marianne told him *The Friendly Giant* was a show Louise watched on television.

He gathered the TV, still swaddled in the car blanket, and cuddled it against his body like the baby Jesus. He was thinking, *I will get them a better one after the holidays* when his foot hit a patch of ice and shot into the air, taking the rest of his body with it. The television left his grasp and flew off behind him and over his head like a bridal bouquet. It and Isadore landed at almost precisely the same moment, tube shattering as his spine hit the ground.

Everyone came out of the house to see.

gEE YOU WHY

HUGH THOUGHT the situation was a travesty. He had wanted to take care of it himself. He had images of himself and Howard Fortune prowling the streets every night until they came upon the guy. He had it all worked out in his head, what they would do. But the news leaked out, and soon the whole world of the town knew that something bad had been done to Howard Fortune's sister.

"This is *bullshit,*" he told Howard. "This just sends the guy into hiding. We'll never find him now."

"I know," said Howard.

In a way, Hugh blamed Howard. Hugh understood how hard the situation was for him, but Howard's slow-blink indifference had made Hugh wish to slap him. Howard couldn't get into it. Maybe he was in shock. At night, they'd sit in Hugh's basement. Hugh would make plans, and Howard would sit and drink.

"So what's the guy fuckin look like, man?"

"I don't know."

"Come on! You beat the shit out of the guy."

"Ugly," said Howard.

"No doubt. Can you give me a little more to work with here?"

"Just big and stupid," Howard shook his head. "Ugly. Ugly human being."

Hugh put his pencil down and took a drink. He had been taking notes. He picked his pencil back up again, and looked up at Howard like a secretary taking dictation.

"What's his name?"

Howard rubbed his face and then pulled at it with his hands. They were halfway through a two-four of beer.

"Come on! Don't tell me you don't remember!" Hugh was starting to feel he would have to torture Howard in some way to get it out of him when Howard smirked.

"Gee you why," he said.

"What?"

"Like guy," said Howard.

"Guy?"

"But French pronunciation. G-U-Y. *Guy.*"

"Like Guy LaFleur?"

"Yeah."

"Oh." Hugh massaged his head with both hands, pausing to stick the pencil behind one ear. "So where can we find him?"

"I don't think he's from here."

"So where? Louisdale? Isle Madame?"

"I don't know, man."

"Like," said Hugh, clenching his fists, physically grasping at his thoughts. "We have to get this guy. Don't you want to kick this guy's ass?"

"I want to do a lot worse than that," said Howard.

Hugh didn't believe him. Howard was flopped on the couch like a mannequin that had been pushed onto its side. He lay staring at the wall at a neon Molson Canadian sign, something Hugh had nicked from a Halifax bar one weekend when he was up with his hockey team. Hugh had turned off the television set so they could concentrate, but now Howard was just lying there staring at the beer ad. Hugh's patience was wearing thin.

"Your sister," he began, and immediately Howard sat up.

"People get over things," Howard said. "You know, bad things happen, all sorts of terrible things, but they get over them and life goes on, and everything is over with."

"Someone has to pay," insisted Hugh.

Finally Howard moved his eyes from the beer sign. "Why?"

"Because that's what's right," said Hugh. "Otherwise how could you live in this stupid world? Guys like that can't just be allowed to get away with shit, they can't. They have to pay."

Howard wiped his hands on his jeans and came to life. "So let's go make someone pay."

"Now you're talking," said Hugh, standing, feeling in his own jeans for the car keys.

"I don't care who," said Howard. "Anyone."

"Look, man, we'll find him," Hugh promised.

But they didn't. They placed what remained of the two-four between them in the front seat of Hugh's dad's car and drove around town and beyond, out to where the Frenchmen lived. They slowed down outside pool halls and storefronts, anywhere guys were gathered, staring people down whether they knew them or not. Hugh asked, "Anyone look familiar?" and Howard answered, "Could be any of them. Could be all of them. Let's fuckin kill them all." Hugh had to yell at him to focus. But by the end of the evening Hugh was so pumped full of boredom and thwarted violence that he was ready to punch a stranger too. They ended up turning around and driving back to a liquor store they'd already checked out. Some guys were loitering in the parking lot when Hugh and Howard had rolled past earlier, and called them fairies, yelling, "Don't be blowin' each other here, boys!" Howard had whiffed a beer bottle at them, and Hugh squealed away. Now the incident nagged at them both, and they wanted to go back.

The guys were still there. Howard and Hugh leapt from the car, and the three kids took off across the parking lot in the same moment. Whooping, Hugh hurled another beer bottle and caught one of them in the shoulder. The kid staggered, but kept going. They were small, Hugh saw now, high school age, and not worth more effort than that. But Howard had easily caught up with the smallest one, knocking the younger guy to the ground and kicking him hard in the gut. Howard strolled back to the car with the kid still writhing on the pavement behind him.

Later Hugh told Howard, "We do that every weekend from now on, sooner or later we're gonna find the guy." Hugh liked the idea of having this kind of purpose to his life, driving his days forward.

But no more than a week later, it was all over. The secret was out, everybody was talking about it, and everybody was looking for the guy. Hugh felt cheated. He took it out on his sister.

"You went and told everybody," he accused.

"I did not," said Ann. As a rule, Hugh believed almost nothing that came out of his sister's mouth, because she had told lies to him and his parents almost every day of her childhood. Outlandish, novelistic lies about being captured by gypsies or pirates or suchlike. One summer she hid in the woods overnight, sending the family into a panic. She appeared the next day and told them a witch had killed her and then brought her back to life, that now she was a zombie even though she looked the same and sounded the same. "The only difference is I have no soul," she reported. The story of the boy who cried wolf had been told and retold to Ann, with scant results. The only reason that Hugh believed the story about Howard Fortune's sister was because it had nothing to do with her. Ann didn't make up stories about anyone except herself.

"How would you like it if someone ran around telling all your secrets?" said Hugh.

"I didn't do it, fuck," said Ann. She punctuated all of her sentences with *fuck* when Howard annoyed her because she knew it drove him crazy.

"Don't fuckin curse!" he exploded, and Ann laughed her head off. He stood there with his arms folded. "Did you ever think about her family, that maybe they wanted to keep this private?"

"I didn't do it!" repeated Ann. "I don't care enough about Corinne Fortune to go around talking about her."

"Then who did?"

"It was Pam."

"Who?"

"Pam. It was Pam who told *me,* fuck."

"Stop it. Why did Pam?"

"Because Pam's her best friend."

"Oh." Hugh exhaled and sat down. "I guess she thought she was doing the right thing."

"Yes," agreed Ann. "That is what she thought."

1983

gAME SHOW

ONE THING a person can't do in a building made mostly of windows is hide. There is no way of lurking, to any extent. When Guy sees Pam is alone and Pam sees Guy looking at her, he has no choice but to just walk right up to her. There is no taking anybody by surprise in this school.

Pam is sitting at one of the free-period tables doing homework. It is their first day back after the New Year, and it's very bright inside the glass school because of sunshine glaring off the snow.

He says, "There's something going on."

Pam replies, "Fuck off, you fucking frog."

"That's not very nice," comments Guy after a moment. He is too stunned to state anything but this particular fact.

Pam seems to vibrate subtly. He thinks her eyes are bigger than they used to be. He thinks she has lost weight since last year.

He is standing in front of Pam because of what Ann Gillis said at lunchtime. As soon as the noon bell went that day he headed down to the smoking area. Hostility had rippled the air from the moment he walked through the school doors that morning. In the crowded, pre-first-period hall, somebody had brushed against him and whispered he was dead. It was unnerving. It wasn't one of the guys from the hockey team, or anyone he recognized. It was another total stranger. He didn't know yet that today was special. Today the nebulous rage that seemed to float over everyone's head in the glass school had finally been given a focus.

All he knew for the moment was that he wanted to get his cigarette in early before the smoking area filled with crowds of noisy guys who knew each other but not him. Ann was there too, had somehow managed to be the first to arrive. She looked surprised and went "Oh" when Guy showed up. He leaned against the opposite wall and didn't look at her. She was supposed to be weird. She was always alone; people called disgusting things to her from time to time, and she responded with nonsense. Once he heard a guy say, *Hey, why don't you wash down there once in a while, I could smell ya coming around the corner.* And Ann had said, *But where would I grow my corn and various legumes?* The guys had laughed because it proved to them she was slutty and fucked up. They could laugh at anyone for anything they said or did, when it came right down to it.

Guy and Ann smoked in silence for a while, and Guy became aware that Ann was just staring at him, even though he had been pointedly, and he thought politely, not looking at her.

You'd think she'd be grateful to be left alone for a change.
Finally he got annoyed and looked up.

She said, "You should really get out of here."

Guy felt nervous. It was like his subconscious had materialized in the person of Ann in order to finally and in no uncertain terms articulate the predominant instinct of his life.

"Where?" he inquired.

"Like, here," she gestured with her cigarette. "There's gonna be guys soon."

"I know there'll be guys."

"Well, they're gonna wanna kill you."

Guy looked around. It was unreasonable, and yet completely unsurprising. *I'm tired of everybody wanting to kill me,* he almost sighed out loud. *I'm bored of it.*

He got mad a second later. "What the fuck did *I* do?"

"Ask Pam," said Ann.

"Pam?"

"Yeah—you know Pam. Pam is the one," said Ann, "who makes things happen. Pam is a woman of action, unlike so many of us."

Guy heard voices in the stairwell, a thunder of work boots and sneakers. Hollered conversation. The sound of boys.

He got out of there.

"Listen," Pam says. "I hate you." And somehow being told this point-blank by a near-total stranger is worse than anything anyone has ever said or done to him. Guy looks down at himself as Pam leans forward to make her next point.

"You're going to get it, Guy."

Under the winter sun's glare, it is so cold the snow squeaks under his boots. His nostrils stick whenever he takes a breath. He feels a familiar surreality to being at liberty in the middle of the afternoon on a school day. People in cars roll past him glancing suspicion, and there's an overriding feeling of lethargy, maybe caused by the fact that everyone under the age of nineteen has been corralled for the day. He remembers this feeling of transgression, of being a vague sort of outlaw. It comes to him when a pulp truck goes moaning past. He remembers it from skipping school to see Corinne Fortune.

Town seemed like fucking Disneyland to him then. Back then it was spring. He had a truck. A girl had given him a picture for his wallet.

Waiting for him in the apartment lies Isadore, head and feet poking over either end of their couch, magazines and sports pages piled on the floor, a new TV donated in sympathy from Puddicomb's Now and Then prattling away for the invalid's entertainment. Big Saint Anne, as they had christened the statue, still managing to keep her eyes averted even from her new vantage point perched on top of the set. Guy has nowhere to go but home to Big Saint Anne and Isadore.

The uncle has been flat on his back since Christmas. He is not to move unless absolutely necessary. The hospital gave him a plastic bottle to pee in. Marianne said he could have her bedroom, but Isadore had insisted on the living room. He insisted on being positioned right in the middle of their lives. His pee bottle often sits on their living room floor alongside the teapot. Guy wonders if he will get them confused one of these days.

He arrives after an hour or so of wandering around in the cold, trying to figure out where else he might possibly go. There are people deployed to look out for kids skipping school at both the mall and the pool hall, or so legend has it. The boxing club does not open until four. He walks until his hands and toes are numb, until his nose is running and he can't even feel it, heading home only when it's agony to stay outside any longer.

Inside, Isadore is hollering at the game shows. The game shows have been a revelation to Isadore. He participates every step of the way. It is comical to see him playing along with *The Price Is Right*—he has no idea how much anything costs. They hold up a can of corn. Isadore screams, "Six fifty!"

"Spin!" he is yelling when Guy comes in. "Spin the fuckin wheel!"

Guy's numb hands begin to burn the moment he's inside. He sits down in the rocker social services brought them, the one he thought to heave at Isadore Christmas Eve. Guy and his mother were so jubilant that night, having exorcised the demon, they stayed up past midnight singing carols and even broke tradition and opened their Christmas-morning presents. Only to have the uncle dumped on their doorstep twelve hours later, the biggest, smelliest present of them all.

Isadore notices Guy and points at the television. "This asshole is going to lose everything he has, you mark my words. Look, he's not gonna spin, he's insane."

"Whatever happened to your truck?" asks Guy.

"It was impounded or something." A commercial comes on. "What in hell are you doing out of school?"

"Could we get it out?"

"Not much point, I couldn't drive it. Legally." Isadore winks.

"I could drive it."

"Then you can pay the fine, *petit*."

"How much would it be?"

"More than you got." Isadore glances at the television. He shifts under his blanket, grunting. "Thank Christ you're here. You empty this for me, son, uh?"

Guy thinks he must be talking about the piss bottle, but then spies it on the floor beside its teapot companion.

"Empty what?" says Guy. But he can see now. Isadore has removed a bedpan from underneath himself—pale, plastic hospital blue.

"Fuck that!"

Isadore rises comfortably to the anger. "Well, what in hell am I supposed to do, lie here in my own shit?"

You took a shit in our living room?

Guy screams this. Out loud or not, he isn't sure.

"I can't goddamn move!" Isadore roars. "I got nobody here to help me all day, what am I *supposed* to do?"

"I don't care what you do, I don't care where you shit," says Guy. "Just not here! Why do you have to always be here?" He notices spit flying from his own mouth again, just like on Christmas Eve. He knows it's no good, what he's feeling, he knows it, from experience, to be pointless. Isadore is already smirking at his nephew's reddening face.

"What you gonna do, you gonna cry?" inquires Isadore. "You gonna cry like with hockey? You gonna cry like I always make you cry? Look at me, I'm flat on my fucking back, and I can still make you cry."

Yes, as a matter of fact I think I will cry, thinks Guy, heading for his room. He isn't crying, though.

"Why don't you hit me, you hate me so much?" Isadore hollers after him. "Uh? Why don't you kick me in the gut? Go on, take a poke! I can't do nothing! It's the chance of a lifetime, *petit!*"

Guy dumps textbooks from his schoolbag and stuffs it with socks, underwear, and a change of clothes.

"Oh, isn't this dramatic," comments Isadore when Guy returns, yanking his jacket back on.

"Tell Ma I'm going to see Louise."

Isadore cradles the bedpan on the expanse of his chest.

"How about I throw this on the floor? Who's gonna have to clean it up, uh? Your poor mother, that's who."

Guy stands.

"But I suppose that's just fine with you, you got no problem, your poor mother has to clean up shit. That's just he way it goes around here, uh, your poor mother works her fingers to the bone cleaning up other people's shit all day, you go driving off in people's trucks, you couldn't *give* a shit."

Guy puts down his bag.

"Just like that goddamn Scotsman father of yours, uh, just up and leave when the going gets rough, and your poor mother has to clean up the shit that's left over."

The phone interrupts.

"One thing I never do, *petit*"—Isadore's voice accompanies Guy as he lurches into the kitchen—"I never *leave*. I don't abandon the people who need me, no matter what. A man doesn't leave. Not like you-know-who. He don't just *go 'way* whenever the spirit moves him."

And there is Marianne, crying on the other end.

"Oh Guy, what are you doing?" she asks, like she's been watching him the whole time from on high. *What* can *I do?* he is about to argue, but she keeps speaking in a rush, over the argument raging in his head, over Isadore's monologue in the background. "The police were to the school and they were *here*," is what he makes out.

"God knows I could've bummed around, seen the world, could've stayed in Toronto, made myself a fortune," Isadore is saying. "Might've started doing the boxing circuit, Christ knows what might have happened if I'd have just stayed put up there, trained, saved some money, done a little investing, bought some property. But fuck that, I says to myself, I got a family that needs me. Sometimes that has to come first. Dad sick with the heart—your poor mother about to be abandoned, with the two of you. Not even sometimes, goddammit, *all* the time, no matter what life might dangle in front of ya. There's more important things than material wealth, I'll have you know, and that's something you need to learn, *petit*." Guy wanders from the kitchen and sees that Isadore is holding out his bedpan. Like everything Guy could ever need to know resides within.

"You didn't know about Grampa's heart," Guy says, moving over to Big Saint Anne. "Nobody did."

"A son knows," insists Isadore.

"The police are looking for me," Guy confides to the oversize saint.

Isadore lies back and lets the bedpan balance on his chest again. "Well," he says after a moment. "I'm not one damn bit surprised."

However, he does look surprised when Guy takes the bedpan from him and disappears into the bathroom. After few moments, he returns. Just as absently as he took it, Guy hands the bedpan—emptied and pristine—back to his speechless uncle.

Town, he had been thinking standing there with Big Saint Anne. He was thinking *town* the way his mother had probably thought *men* from time to time, the way Isadore thought about practically everyone other than himself: *the bastards.* The problem. The moment Guy took the bedpan from Isadore, however, was the moment something else occurred to him: *No. Town is not the problem.*

Guy picks up his bag again and heads for the closet. "Tell Ma I'm going to see Louise," he repeats, seeming to pick up where they left off. "I'm taking your parka."

"Bullshit you're taking my parka."

Guy has pulled it out of the closet and holds the coat to his nose to see if it smells tolerable. He slips it on over his jacket, causing Isadore to hoot.

"You look like some kinda pygmy Eskimo in that thing!"

"It's cold out—you won't need it," says Guy.

"Adding thievery to your list of crimes. I knew this would happen. Ya know when it started? When you quit the hockey.

And didn't I say so at the time!"

"No," answers Guy. "You said I could go fuck myself was what you said at the time."

"Your poor mother," Isadore starts to proclaim, but stops when the door clicks shut. Or so it sounds to Guy.

OFFICIAL

FOUR PEOPLE had called the station to relate the details of what happened to Corinne Fortune—or at least what they claimed were the details. A couple sounded like kids, one claiming he wanted to remain "anonabus" but the other two were clearly adults. The first call was from Deedee Whinnot, who ran the school cafeteria. She told Constable MacLellan it was a shame such a thing could happen right under everyone's noses and the Mounties would just look the other way. MacLellan replied no similar complaints had been filed.

"*I'm* filing a complaint!" claimed Deedee.

"You can't file a complaint about something that's happened to someone else, Deedee. This is nothing but a rumour, as far as I'm concerned."

"Well, I just think it's a sin!" Deedee Whinnot lamented. "You want a complaint, well, I'm complaining, by God. I'm complaining about a police force that can't even protect our young girls!"

Constable MacLellan had grinned as he spoke to Deedee. She called the detachment regularly to complain about the various shady "goings-on" around town, such as her conviction that Cindy Burke—Deedee's unmarried educated neighbour and the town's only physiotherapist—was keeping a house of ill repute. But after the third phone call about the Fortune girl, MacLellan started taking notes just to see if any of the information jibed. Much of it did, although it was scant. It was Fred Fortune's daughter and it was some French boy from out of town. It had happened last winter some time. The fellow was just running around now, free to do the same to whomever else he liked. Something had to be done; each of the four people who called were in agreement.

The following Sunday, MacLellan gazed down the street from his upstairs window and saw Fred Fortune shovelling his driveway, face pink beneath his fur hat. The constable pulled on his coat, trudged down the sidewalk, ploughed through a snow bank to where Fred Fortune was shovelling, and told Fred about the rumours. MacLellan thought it was a father's right. He regretted having been so blunt almost immediately, however, because Fred Fortune dropped the shovel and clutched his chest.

"Jesus, Fred!"

"I'm all right," said Fred Fortune quickly. "I'm just *hurt* and sad." This odd statement came out in a rush. They went inside to drink a pot of tea together and speak to Corinne.

She was at the kitchen counter in her nightgown when they came in, and her father asked her to please go upstairs and change into some clothes and then come down again and talk to them when she was all set. She dashed from the room. MacLellan didn't even think she stopped to look at them.

"My wife is getting the groceries," said Fred, putting the kettle on the stove. The constable thought he sounded mournful relaying this information—like his wife not being there was another catastrophe thrown atop the heap.

Howard came in from outside, wearing only sweats, and sweating. "Hi," he said when he saw Constable MacLellan. Howard pulled his sweatshirt up over his face in order to wipe the perspiration from his eyes.

"Oh son," said Fred, with a heavy note of gratitude in his voice. "Can you stay, please, while we talk to your sister?"

"Yeah," said Howard, looking from one man to the next. "I gotta have a shower, though."

"Can you wait just a bit?"

"Yeah," said Howard again. "What's going on?"

"Have you heard any of these rumours? About your sister?"

"Rumours?" Howard looked to Constable MacLellan and barked a slight laugh.

"A number of people around town have been in touch with us about this," said Constable MacLellan. "I became concerned."

"Yeah, but they're rumours," said Howard.

"So you've heard them?" said his father. He was taking some cups down from the cupboard and fumbled them briefly. The porcelain chattered like teeth.

"Watch it, Dad." Howard took the cups and set them down on the stove beside the kettle.

"Why didn't you tell me, son?" Fred wanted to know. The men all sat down together at the table at that point, as if of a single mind.

"One," said Howard, "I don't know if it's true. Two, I thought if it was, I could find out and take care of it myself."

Howard's father smiled with vague pride. Howard smiled back at him.

"Only one person can tell us for sure," MacLellan pointed out. He wasn't smiling at Howard. He was thinking why the hell wouldn't the boy just ask his sister if he didn't know for sure.

Howard was apparently reading MacLellan's mind.

"I didn't want to freak Corinne out," he said.

Corinne appeared from the hallway and the three men looked up at her. She put her hands over her heart—almost precisely the same gesture her father had used a moment ago.

Hurt and sad, thought Constable MacLellan.

"Dear," said Mr. Fortune. "Sit down."

"No," said Corinne. She hovered in the doorway that separated the hall from the kitchen.

"Dear—" Mr. Fortune took a breath. "Has a boy been mean to you?" He looked relieved, somehow, to be asking this question.

Corinne blinked and shifted from one foot to the other like a nervous dog awaiting the next command.

"It's all right," said Howard. "Just tell them about the guy."

Corrine stared at him for a moment. "I don't want to get in trouble," she whispered. She glanced at Constable MacLellan, who still hadn't taken off his heavy woolen coat.

"You won't get in any trouble, dear," he assured her. "I'm not even here in an official capacity."

"You're not?"

"No."

The kitchen was quiet as Corinne stood apparently trying to determine whether or not this information made any difference to her. Constable MacLellan was aware of the authority implicit in his very presence. He hadn't taken off his police-issue coat because underneath he wore a work shirt and khakis. The coat helped consolidate that air of authority. One time, he had put on his uniform just to go and meet with a real estate agent about some property he was looking at buying.

"We just want to make sure this isn't something we should be looking into," MacLellan added. The reference to "we" was another of his tactics. But the constable would have been outraged if anyone had accused him of using tactics of intimidation with Corrine that day. To him it was like breathing, like the inevitability of his moustache, or timbre of his voice.

"Please, dear," said Fred Fortune. The kettle began to scream and he jumped up. Corinne looked at Howard again.

"Just *tell* them about the guy," he repeated.

"No," she said. "I don't even know what you guys are talking about." Her voice wobbled.

Constable MacLellan leaned back in his chair. "Dear," he said. "You see, if you're afraid of this fellow, we can lay charges. You won't see him again."

"Here's some nice tea for everybody," said Mr. Fortune,

placing the teapot on the center of the table. Howard leaned forward and picked it up again. He placed a hot pad underneath it before it could melt the plastic tablecloth. Fred picked up one of the cups and gestured to Constable MacLellan with it.

"Gordie?"

"Please, thank you, Fred."

"It's not steeped yet, Dad," said Howard, taking the teacup from his father and placing it in front of Constable MacLellan.

When the men returned their attention to Corinne, she was leaning against the doorframe.

"I don't know what you heard," she said. "This guy was just calling me all the time last summer. He was bugging me."

"What was his name?" said Constable MacLellan.

"Like, he didn't do anything," said Corinne.

"Then why have you been acting like such a freak all year?" Howard challenged his sister suddenly. She stood up straight and her composure seemed to drain away.

"Because I *am* a freak," she replied, tearing up. "I just am one. So, so screw you, Howard."

"Dear, don't talk like that," said Fred. "Come have a cup of tea."

"If you don't tell them, I will," Howard told her.

"Dear, I'm not here investigating anything officially," Constable MacLellan assured her again. "I just want to be able to put your father's mind at rest."

"But why can't *I* do that?" Corinne nearly shrieked. "I just told you he didn't do anything."

"Well, someone did something," Howard uttered with such

an air of command that his father nodded without knowing he was doing it. "And someone has to pay."

Corinne burst into tears. Everyone in the room had been expecting this at some point. She bolted up the stairs with her father's pleas and pity noises in her ears.

So Howard told Constable MacLellan the name, and Constable MacLellan, who happened to have his notebook in the pocket of his heavy coat, wrote it down.

When he couldn't find Guy at school the following Monday, MacLellan stopped in at the house where Marianne worked and said he would drive her home after work so they could both sit down and talk to Guy. She said that would be fine, but asked if he would not pick her up in his police cruiser because her employers would have returned home by that time. MacLellan promised not to, but forgot to go home at the end of the day and hop into his wife's station wagon as he had been planning. He only remembered the promise after he had pulled up into the driveway and seen Marianne's face.

"I'm sorry about this," he said as she climbed in. "It completely slipped my mind."

"Oh, it's all right," said Marianne, waving goodbye to the family, who stood watching behind their screen door.

He pulled away from the house and told her, "Now, I just want to stress one more time: this is not an official investigation by any stretch."

Marianne nodded, staring straight ahead and not bothering to question why Constable MacLellan had become involved with her life if this was the case. Or why he should be escorting her home, like they were two kids on a date.

"The girl's parents are worried," he explained. "They just wanna get this whole matter settled."

"Of course they do," said Marianne. "What is it . . ." She stopped to cough. "What is it they think Guy did?"

"Now now," went MacLellan, "that's what we'd like to hear from the young fella himself." They were approaching the apartment block where Marianne and Guy lived. "Now which building is it?" he asked.

Marianne pointed.

"My brother has been staying with us," she told Constable MacLellan in the hallway. "He had an accident over the holidays." When she opened the door the ponderous background music of some late-afternoon soap opera overwhelmed them. Isadore was asleep, cradling the empty bedpan under his arm like a stuffed toy. He woke the second Marianne shut off the television.

"Hey," he said.

"Isadore," said Marianne. "Is Guy here? This is Mr. MacLellan."

"Constable MacLellan," said the constable. "As this lad right here well knows!"

Isadore rubbed his eyes and attempted to maneuver himself into a sitting position. "Oh, Jesus save us," he said, clearly wrenched with pain.

"Careful now," said Marianne, cramming an extra pillow behind his head.

"Boy, you're in sorry shape," observed MacLellan. "And this is what you get, a fella your age indulging in such shenanigans over the holidays."

"Gordie Mac!" exclaimed Isadore. "I didn't recognize ya in the daylight!"

The two men laughed like old friends as Marianne hugged herself.

"Can I get you some tea?" she asked the constable.

"No, thank you, Mrs. Boucher."

"You can get *me* some tea," said Isadore, reaching down beside the couch for the pot. Marianne bent and grabbed it before he could extend the piss bottle to her, around which his hand had tightened.

MacLellan stood over Isadore, smiling and shaking his head indulgently. "So what happened? That little fella from Leland's place sic his buddies on ya?"

"You heard about that slight altercation, did you?"

"Jesus Christ, you're lucky I didn't come down there and pick you up. A couple of people made the call, I'll have you know. There's some say you shouldn't be out on the street."

"Ach," said Isadore, falling into MacLellan's Gaelic accent. "Boys will be boys."

MacLellan's shoulders jerked with amusement. "Some boy you are," he commented. "Good thing you got Leland following behind, sweeping up your tracks."

"Leland can sweep up me *shit*," said Isadore. "As far as I'm concerned."

"Don't tell me you got banned?"

"Forty years, I been behind that man. Supported him in the election. Hell, I campaigned for the ungrateful prick."

"Ach, you'll kiss and make up. You'll be cracking his patrons' skulls and destroying his property again in no time." Constable MacLellan put his hands on his hips and had a good laugh.

"Not anymore," said Isadore. "I've had it."

MacLellan had been watching as Marianne disappeared into one of the bedrooms before returning to put the kettle on.

"He's not here," she told him.

He put his hands on his hips and frowned.

"Now what kind of trouble has that little fart gotten himself into this time?" Isadore inquired in a loud voice.

"He's never been in trouble," said Marianne. "Except he got into some fights."

"Ah—that's how it always starts, isn't it?" Isadore mused. "Kids going around, having to prove how tough they are."

"Where do you suppose he's gotten to?" MacLellan asked Isadore, who he had determined was the family's voice of authority.

"Well, I tell ya," said Isadore. "He was here for a bit this afternoon, but he got that phone call from his ma and was off like a shot."

"Phone call?" repeated MacLellan, glancing at Marianne, who actually wrung her hands at his look.

"After you left this afternoon. I wanted to see if he was home."

"And he was?"

"Yes."

"I suppose I should have thought to have you call home when I was there," said MacLellan, but his look let Marianne know that he blamed her for deliberately not thinking of it for him.

Isadore shifted with impatience. "What in hell did the boy do?"

"He didn't do anything," said Marianne instinctively.

"Well, there's some concern that he bothered a girl."

"What girl? That girl from town, here? She's a slutty one."

"Oh, Isadore," said Marianne, looking ashamed.

"Is that right?" said MacLellan. "Who said that, now?"

"It's no secret. He told me about her. I seen a picture she gave him."

"She gave him a picture?" At last MacLellan sat down in a nearby rocker.

"Yes, she gave him a picture. With a love poem or some such thing written on the back. She was hardly an unwilling participant, whatever may have occurred, I can tell you that."

MacLellan looked at Marianne. "Did you know about this?"

"I remember he showed me a picture," said Marianne. "I didn't know it was the same girl."

"It's the kind of thing a boy don't like to discuss with his mother." Isadore winked at the constable, who smiled a little. "But *I* certainly got an earful from time to time."

"So they were . . ." MacLellan glanced at Marianne again. "*Sweethearts* for a time."

"Thick as thieves," confirmed Isadore.

"I remember he skipped school to come see her sometimes," said Marianne. "I caught him once and gave him hell."

The constable leaned forward in the rocker. The kettle was bubbling away and Marianne was standing perfectly still.

"I'll be honest with you," Constable MacLellan said, allowing himself to smile conspiratorially at the two. "This does a lot to put my mind at ease." Isadore folded his arms.

"But her poor father," the cop added, rolling his eyes as if to convey the universal torment young girls had been putting their fathers through since the beginning of time. "I certainly wouldn't mind getting a look at that picture she gave him. Maybe then we can put all this to rest."

"I'll have a talk with the boy," Isadore decreed.

"Did you happen to hear where he was going?"

"Didn't say. Off to see one of his friends, or some such thing."

MacLellan got to his feet. "Well, you'll give me a call when you see him next, won't you? It would be nice if we could put this all behind us. I'm sure the boy was just a little spooked when he heard a cop was poking around for him." MacLellan smiled again, but looked directly at Marianne.

"We'll certainly be in touch," said Marianne.

Constable MacLellan made his way over to Big Saint Anne on the television and patted her veiled head. "That's a nice-size Mary," he observed.

"It's Saint Anne," said Marianne. "You can tell because she has a book."

MacLellan peered into the saint's averted eyes, doubting. "Well," he concluded after a moment, "she's a big girl, whoever she is." He bent to shake Isadore's hand before he left. He told Isadore to take care of himself.

dONE

OUTSIDE IS HARD and bright. It neglects to cloud over, or snow. The screaming blue sky like an impenetrable dome. Pam has been drinking coffee like her addict father, giving herself diarrhea.

He sat her down over the holidays, Ronald at his shoulder like a priest and began, "Honey"—and wasn't that in itself a riot—"I know I've been neglecting my duties to you. I've been neglecting my obligations to you as a father. I haven't been a very good father these past few months. Maybe these past few years." This part must have been unrehearsed because a look of minor alarm crossed his face when he said it. He seemed to shake it off quickly, however. "I should have been spending more time with you. I should have paid more attention to you."

No, no, no, thought Pam, you're getting it wrong already.

"And from here on in I promise to try and do better. But in

the meantime, Pammie, I just want you to know how sorry I am for how things have been around here."

Pam kept expecting him to pull out the little AA book he'd taken to carrying around with him during this speech, just to make sure he was getting it right.

"And if there's anything I can do," he said, "to make things better, to help you in any way with your . . ."

Pam glared as he searched for a word.

"Doings" was what he eventually came up with. He smiled with relief. "I want you to please let me know. Because that's what I'm here for."

Pam crossed her arms. "There *is* something you can help me with."

The look of alarm returned and he craned his head towards Ronald for help. Ronald nodded towards Pam, and with hesitation, double-checking to make sure Ronald meant it, Pam's father turned back to her.

"There is?"

"No," said Pam, unfolding her arms. "Actually there isn't." She got up and walked away without waiting to hear any more.

She had come to the conclusion this recovery thing was alcoholism in disguise. Instead of liquor you drank coffee and got drunk on thinking about being an alcoholic, soused on self-pity.

She was hating hick cousin Ronald too, because he had left them shortly after that, feeling his work with the Cormorant family was complete now that Bill was sober, penitent, and committed to the AA philosophy. She rang in the New Year despising men and boys. When she encountered Guy Boucher the first day back at school she could have torn him up with her teeth.

Any good she had left in her went to Corinne, the only one in the world who deserved it. They called each other every day. They stayed on the phone for hours. They walked in the snow, made angels, looked at lights. Pam did not talk about her family—she never did. She encouraged Corinne to talk. Pam thought it would be good for her. Pam listened like no Fat Friend in the history of Fat Friends had ever listened. She gave way to what had always seemed her destiny.

Until a few days after New Year's, when Corinne called and screamed at her. She screamed, "What in fuck are you trying to do to me?"

"What?"

"You blabbed to everybody!'

Blabbed, thought Pam. They were six years old again.

Corinne said everyone in town was asking her about the French guy. Troy from Troy came up to her first. He said he would do whatever she wanted to the guy, she just had to name it and he would do it. Trina and Tracy and everyone in the world were calling to see if it was true.

"My parents know," she said. "My fucking *father* knows. The cops have been to my house."

"The cops!" Pam repeated. Cops weren't a real thing. Cops were a TV thing. Here there were Mounties with yellow stripes down the sides of their pants, who sold raffle tickets at the hockey rink and came to school to give safety demonstrations or warnings about the dangers of talking to strangers and throwing rocks.

"Gordie MacLellan from up the street says people are calling the station."

"I didn't think anyone would do that."

"Like, what were you thinking, blabbing it to everybody?"

Pam hadn't actually blabbed to everybody. She'd told three people including Ann Gillis, knowing it would amount to the same thing.

"Well," began Pam. She had to clear her throat. She realized she was getting ready to cry soon. Because Corinne was yelling at her. "Something had to be done."

"Done!" wailed Corinne. "You and fucking *done!* You're always talking about what has to be done, even when it's none of your business what has to be done! You had no right to do anything! You were just supposed to be my friend and help me, not go around *doing* stuff!"

Book of Helpful Fat Friend Conduct, chapter one: Never do stuff. Sit and eat and wait for your friend to have need of you. Read women's magazines. Keep abreast of the kind of problems your real-human-being friends may have at some point. Always be at the ready.

"But Corinne, it's wrong. It's wrong to just pretend it never happened. He could do it to someone else."

"He *won't* do it to someone else."

"How do you know?"

"Because I know him."

Pam stuttered for a moment, Ronald-like. "You. No you don't."

"*Yes I do,*" Corinne yelled. "It's *me*. It's not anyone else.

I'm the one. I'm the thing it happens to. I'm the freak."

"You're"—channelling Ronald now, overtaken by his blinking uncertainty—"You. You're not . . ."

"And now everybody knows it!"

This being the thrust of her complaint, apparently. Because she hung up right after saying it.

And now school, and now everything buzzes. Pam's head buzzes with caffeine and apprehension. To walk into the school without Corinne. To maneuver the corridors without Corinne. To attempt to exist without the halo, the certainty that she is, at least, Corinne Fortune's Best Friend, if nothing else, to anyone.

The play is over. Her hours at school are empty without the imperative to be reciting Portia in her head at every spare moment. Pam's too used to it, the pretend-lawyer inside her head. *Tarry, Jew.* It was her favourite scene: she still knows all the lines by heart. The love scenes are forgotten. They had been torturous—she ploughed through them and there was nothing Mrs. K. could do about it. It was the lawyer scene she put everything into.

She had told Ann she hated the play, but now she misses it. She had resented Corinne, resented the play, but without them time seems to have stopped. Her life has iced over. The French guy, the guy named Guy, even though Corinne pretends not to remember, is nowhere in sight. Pam told him to fuck off and he did. She banished him like a queen would.

Yet her days are full of a nameless, dreamlike guilt—the feeling that at some point between bells, when the corridors are stuffed and bustling with cranky post-holiday students out for blood, someone is going to turn and point her out. Someone whose face she can't make out will stand up and articulate exactly who she is and what she's done. Even though she doesn't know herself what this might be—there is someone out there who does, someone who keeps exact accounts, and that person's time, she feels, is almost upon her. Once exposed, Pam doesn't think she'd last a minute.

nOTHING

SO THEY FOUGHT and fought, Howard and Hugh, to take out their frustration. They got addicted to trawling the nighttime roads. The guys who hung around parking lots and storefronts on the weekend got to know Hugh's father's sedan on sight. Sometimes Rob MacPhedron came with them when he had an evening off. They chucked booze bottles, bashed mailboxes. They perfected the choreography of climbing out of the car at precisely the same time, unfurling their bodies, slamming their doors in unison for maximum intimidation effect.

Drinking and driving around the back roads every weekend in their alternating outrage and exhilaration, Howard and Hugh wove together a sort of mythology involving Guy Boucher. By now they both knew his name, but they called him That French Fuck. Mackie Pettipas was involved as well. Howard and Hugh determined between themselves that Mackie and That

French Fuck had to be friends. This explained Mackie's baiting Howard about his sister that first night Hugh and Howard went out together. Howard had never told Hugh exactly what Mackie had uttered, and Hugh respected this, assuming it was something too crass to repeat. But clearly Mackie knew what had gone on with Corinnne, was maybe even involved somehow.

Hugh had an idea what That French Fuck looked like in his head, partially informed by Howard's vague description of him as big and ugly, but mainly he was just a composite of every asshole Hugh had ever encountered. Without thinking about it, he assumed he would know the guy on sight. He didn't even bother consulting Howard now, as they rolled past the suspicious clutches of thuggery who congregated outside storefronts and dances. It was as if he expected some kind of malignant halo to be hovering above the guilty party's head, which would identify him. Hugh imagined that he and Howard would leap out of the car without exchanging a word and simply descend, simultaneously.

This was the fantasy that propelled Hugh's weekends.

In the meantime they "kept themselves limber," in Hugh's words, by picking fights with any random assholes they happened to come into contact with. Usually someone was willing to go every weekend, guys very much like Hugh and Howard, bored to the point of wrath.

Howard has told Hugh about Constable MacLellan coming to his house the previous Sunday, to interrogate them.

"You can tell he's not going to do anything," said Howard. "'Now this is strictly unofficial,' he keeps saying. Like, why are you even here, then, upsetting my sister and freaking out my dad? You should have *seen* my old man's face when he found out. From a stranger. From some busybody cop who lives up the street." Howard polished off his beer with a long pull and placed the empty bottle at his feet with the others.

Hugh punched the dashboard with the heel of his hand. "Cops are fuckin useless, man! I told you! Now they're going to be watching *us* to make sure we don't kill the guy, instead of the fuckin prick they should be watching! Jesus Christ!"

"It's not like there's anything I could have done about it," said Howard, because he heard the accusation in Hugh's tone. Hugh hadn't done a good job overall in disguising his opinion that if Howard had gotten off his ass and acted more quickly, he and Hugh could have shut the guy down by now.

"I wanted to get that guy from day one, man."

"I didn't?" said Howard.

"I'm just saying," said Hugh. "It sucks."

They drove in silence for a while, until Hugh, tired of it, jammed some AC/DC into the tape player.

When they came upon Mackie Pettipas, the two were feeling ill-disposed and almost on the verge of going home. Their initial mutual dislike, which for a time had been squelched by the shared excitement and crisis, kept trying to reassert itself. Drinking and fighting had kept it at bay, but the all-encompassing boredom of their days and nights was ever present, always threatening to overtake them in moments of quiet. The reality that, temperamentally, Hugh Gillis and Howard Fortune were never meant to be friends. Therefore, Hugh half sensed, there had to be as few moments of quiet between them as possible.

"It's fuckin Mackie!" Hugh hollered above the music, jabbing at the tape player's eject button to bring the noise to a halt. Hugh had spotted him drinking with some other guys in one of the dugouts at the baseball field

Howard sat upright and then lurched forward as Hugh jerked the car to a stop on the side of the road. Mackie had already disappeared into the woods, where the nature trails began. Hugh and Howard soared from the car, past Mackie's hollering drinking buddies in the dugout, and dove into the woods after him. In the summer, the trails were easy to maneuver even in the dark, but in winter the nights were pitch black and everything was nearly indistinguishable. Still, kids ventured in every weekend, deep into the bowels of the woods where they knew they wouldn't be caught, lit bonfires, and drank until they vomited. Hugh had done it himself almost every weekend of high school. It was miraculous nobody had died winding their drunken way back up from the fire pit in the middle of the night.

It looked as if Mackie was instinctively following the trail that had been stamped into the snow by kids heading back and forth from the fire pit. All that was left for Hugh and Howard to do was follow it as well, knowing there would be nowhere to go once Mackie arrived at the pit. Teenagers were huddled around the fire drinking out of paper bags like hobos. Mackie skidded behind a wall of guys and started to scream.

"You bastards stay the fuck away from me!"

Hugh simply slammed his way through the guy-wall and tackled Mackie. They tumbled in the snow like two big dogs playing.

In the firelight, Howard could make out Hugh struggling to get himself on top of Mackie, trying to pin him to the ground so he could start punching. The surrounding guys collected themselves, recircled, began to shout. Howard moved in to aim a kick, connecting with the ribs, and the crowd behind him made a betrayed sound, a sort of booing.

"Two against one!" someone shouted.

Howard turned around just as a liquor bottle caught him in the mouth. It didn't break, but it knocked him down. New snow puffed out all around him, like he'd collapsed onto a dusty old bed. Steam rose from his face, from the hot blood covering it.

Above him, white treetops. Cold stars. Millions.

Sounds of Mackie and Hugh grunting in unison like they were having sex. Guy-shouts, happy and enraged, like animal noises. Boots.

Jesus Christ, Darren, you trying to kill him? I think you fuckin killed him.

Boots. Close. Nothing.

You okay, man?

Howard lifted his head, taking his eyes off infinity. The guy, holding his hand out to him, winced.

Ooooh. Shit, man. Not pretty.

Dead, said Howard.

The guy moved closer. Didn't hear him. Tried to take his arm.

But Howard grabbed his instead and yanked, hoisting himself into a crouch at the same time, so their positions were reversed—mind full of empty white stars.

The circling congregation howled and cheered. Joined in, a moment later.

HE LET THE HONDA sit in the parking lot of Puddicomb's Now and Then well into the New Year. Alison didn't go anywhere over the holidays, saw almost no one. For Christmas dinner he enjoyed Chef Boy-ar-dee beef ravioli and a bag of sour cream and onion–flavoured chips. He went over the twelve steps during this cold, lucid period, while sheets of snow flapped in the screaming wind outside his house. Isadore Aucoin once told Alison that his property must have been owned by Scotsmen before him. "Scotsman's idea of landscaping," Isadore always remarked about a lawn bereft of trees or shrubs. Indeed Alison's house sat alone on the top of a small, bare hill completely unprotected, daring nature to do its worst.

Alison wrote letters to his wife and parents. He planned to buy stamps and mail them on the day he hitchhiked out to Auld Cove to retrieve his automobile.

The superintendent of schools had called after Christmas and asked if Alison would come in for a meeting before classes began. Alison thought about the hike to Auld Cove, the drive back, shaving his face, ironing a shirt—and knew he wasn't up to any of this. He trembled when he held a tea cup. Loud noises made him want to bury his face in his hands. So he told the superintendent to go ahead, that he didn't mind being fired over the phone. Smiled to himself at the frustration in the older man's voice—Wayne must have been gearing up for a real oration, a veritable shitstorm of reprimand, only to have it thwarted.

"Son, don't you give a damn? It doesn't have to come to this."

Alison knew it didn't. He'd been through it before. Probationary periods. Colleagues flaring their nostrils whenever he wandered into the teachers' lounge. Mandatory AA meetings. He was a high school teacher, after all, and burnout occurred in his profession with the regularity of national holidays. Alison knew the routine. They were going to give him a lecture, a leave of absence, and finally another chance. He didn't want it. He didn't even want to deal with the possibility. He hung up on the superintendent before compassion could trickle into the old man's voice, ooze from Alison's receiver, and feed into the self-pity that had been the milky center of Alison's being throughout his adult life.

But he knew the day had come to get his car when one morning, well after the sun had come up, he looked out the kitchen windows and saw the jagged icicles that stabbed the air beneath his roof dripping rapidly into nothing. A moment later, a small deer crossed his yard in search of food. Alison went to his fridge, but any fruits or vegetables he once kept had disintegrated into the bottom of his crisper. He had nothing to offer the deer. For the first time since the bender, he felt prompted to leave the house. He would buy apples, carrots, celery. He would buy some of those huge clumps of bird seed shaped like bells to hang in front of his kitchen and living room windows. Maybe he would go to Canadian Tire and buy a bird feeder for the middle of his yard. He could sit at his kitchen table and watch sparrows and swallows alight and take off again every long afternoon that was to come.

He put on work pants, a parka, wool socks, and winter boots. Dug out a toque and pair of gloves from his closet. It took a while for him to find everything—typically Alison drove everywhere and scarcely had need for outdoor gear.

Once outside he paused to admire the delicate pattern of deer tracks in the snow before trudging out to the highway. It was too warm for a toque and he yanked it off his head, a little disappointed. Out on the road, a shiftworker headed for the mill pulled over and offered him a lift almost immediately. It was that kind of day.

After Lauchie helped him scrape the remaining ice off the windshield and give the battery a jump, Alison went to the Co-op and bought fresh meat and vegetables. He was pleased to see he didn't need to go to Canadian Tire to find a bird feeder; the grocery store happened to have some in stock. In Big Harbour, it had gotten colder, definitely below freezing. Though the sun looked smaller here, it was just as bright.

"Beautiful day," the cashier remarked.

He went to put some gas in the car and get the oil checked. Bought some antifreeze while he was at it. He had to stop and turn around just as he was on his way out of town. He'd forgotten to send his letters. He headed back to the mall where there was a fat red mail box waiting to swallow them down and shit them out in America.

On the drive home, Alison spotted Isadore Aucoin plodding along the side of the road through the brown slush. For a moment, Alison thought he might be hallucinating with DTs; Isadore was distorted. He looked shrunken somehow, stooped, as though he had aged in the previous weeks. Alison had heard about his fall on the ice from Lauchie Puddicomb, who called to tell him about the car. Now Alison wondered just how serious the damage had been. Had Isadore hit his head? His arms dangled at his sides, almost flopping in time with his gait. As the car approached, already slowing down, Isadore turned and stuck out his thumb.

Except it was Guy. Alison didn't know if he was relieved, or even more unnerved than he would have been were it a shrunken, defeated Isadore trudging towards the Honda. Alison wasn't sure he liked Isadore's nephew. In class, he had been sarcastic and sullen—not an original attitude amongst local boys, but knowing him as he had outside of school made Alison wary. He'd eaten dinners and, he vaguely recalled, some breakfasts with Isadore's family more than once, in varying states of coherence. For the first time it occurred to Alison to wonder what this boy must think of him.

He stopped wondering when he saw the look on Guy's face once the kid had yanked open the passenger side door. Alison made himself smile anyway.

"Hello, Guy!" he greeted. "It's a beautiful day."

BLACK or SOMETHING

EVERYONE HAS always said that Alison Mason is an amazingly large fruit. I never bothered wondering if it was true or untrue, before now. It seems likely. But it seems just as likely people call him this because he is an English teacher and plays a Russian ukulele, reads poetry to us and makes us read it back to him out loud, telling us to feel the words in our mouths and then— I don't think he even knows he's doing it—makes as if his mouth is full of something. Back in my old school, it never failed to crack up the guys in the back row. But they could say that anyone was a fruit and did. They called me a fruit, Rene Retard, each other. Everyone's a fucking fruit at some point.

Alone in the car, though, I feel like asking him. I remember the morning I drove him to school, asking him if he was a draft dodger and a back-to-the-lander like every other American around here. It seems like centuries ago I asked him this. I can't imagine myself doing that now, just coming out with it to see what he would say. I was angry that morning. These days I'm too worn out to be angry, to ask questions.

"How's it going, Guy?" he wants to know. "How are you liking living in town?"

I laugh and laugh. He stares at the road, rolling his tongue around in his mouth like he's got some more poetry in there. Just when I'm starting to settle down I remember this poem he got us to study one semester. It started, *A narrow fellow, in the grass—* and then I'm pissing my pants all over again.

He's just sitting there, driving, smiling, waiting for me to finish laughing. Very polite. Isadore would have pucked me on the head at this point; my mother would have been holding her heart and feeling my forehead at the same time.

"That good, eh?" says Algernon.

He's trying to be funny. He doesn't seem insulted that I just sat there laughing at him for the last five minutes, which was really an asshole thing to do, when you think of it. I would never have done this around any grown-up but Algernon. It's strange, when you think how easy it is to have no respect for teachers. It's just impossible once you've seen them standing up there every day, bullying you, bribing you, practically crucifying themselves for your attention, your interest. Finally freaking out when they don't get it. Coming apart before your eyes. There are teachers who give themselves away like that, and teachers who don't. There was another teacher in my old school nobody fucked with for some reason—Mr. Marchand. He stood up there the first day of grade nine and wrote on the

board, *Thou shalt not drive the teacher crazy*. And then he pointed to it and said that this was the golden rule of his class. So
nobody drove him crazy. I don't know how it worked, but it did.
But Mason wasn't that kind of teacher. He was the other kind. I
remember the day he was so drunk and I made fun of him in
front of everybody. It was an easy thing to do, and made me feel
good for about five seconds. And then I realized I was like every
other asshole who had ever walked the earth, and tomorrow
some guy could be doing the same thing to me and I would be
sitting there wondering why life was so cruel and unfair.

So I get myself together and tell him I'm sorry.

"That's all right," he tells me. "Sounds like you needed to
get it out."

"Yeah."

"How's school?" he says.

"I'm dropping out," I tell him, having decided at that very
moment.

A mistake. I suddenly remember his cockeyed lectures at
our supper table and assume I'm in for another one.

He's just nodding, though. "Sorry to hear that," he says.

Algernon is stone cold sober, by God.

"Listen," he says. "Do you mind if I ask why?"

It occurs to me that this is a very nice way to put a question to somebody. I have a choice. I can just tell him yes or no,
either I don't mind or I do.

"No, I don't mind," I finally choose.

He smiles and checks his rearview mirror. "So, why are you
dropping out, Guy?"

I wish I hadn't said I didn't mind. I flop around in my seat a little.

"It's. Like. It's *killing* me," I tell him, hoping it doesn't sound as dramatic as I think it might.

He's nodding again, saying nothing, which I appreciate.

"It's a fucking war zone." I'm making no sense, I think. But just as I think this, Alison Mason comments.

"Yes. It is that."

"You know what I mean?"

"I do," he says. "I know what you mean."

Is that why you're this enormous alcoholic? I'm tempted to ask. It becomes clear to me. Of course that is why he is an enormous alcoholic. The real question is, why aren't I an enormous alcoholic? The older I get, the more it's like I'm in a hostile country, like Russia or something, and I don't even know it. They can tell I'm a foreigner by looking at me. They shoot first and ask questions later. Meanwhile, I don't even understand the language.

When Isadore gets pissed off, when he feels like he's been treated badly—which is practically all the time—he goes around with his hurt/pissed-off look and his hands palms out saying:

What am I, black or something?

Like if he *was* black, then maybe he could understand it. But I'm willing to bet he wouldn't. I don't. And I think that sitting in this car with Mason I have figured out why.

Because it's not supposed to make sense. It's supposed to do what laughing at Algernon Mason on his big drunken day did for me. Make you feel good about five stupid seconds out of a whole long life of suspecting yourself to be a dick.

He hasn't been bullshitting me, that much is obvious.

And just like that, I'm telling him everything—about Corinne, and getting beaten up, and Isadore using our couch as a bathroom, and people saying they hate me without explaining why. I'm spilling my guts to Alison Mason. This guy I don't respect, this guy I've seen asleep on my mother's kitchen floor, who has vomited in our toilet, this guy who reads poetry, tells you to feel the words in your mouth, who is best friends with someone like Isadore, this ridiculous alcoholic, a huge fucking fruit as far as anyone knows, a coward, someone not even from around here: American. I'm talking to him like I would talk out loud to myself, were I insane.

gIANT MACASKILLS

THAW

THE WEATHER got better and better. Snow melted, birds flitted around. People saw their lawns again—grey-yellow and flattened from the shock of winter. Corinne Fortune was not in school and nobody knew why.

"I know why," Ann Gillis claimed. People like Tracy and Trina said for her to shut up, that they weren't talking to her. In the smoking area, later, she confides to Pam, "It's like being Cassandra. People want to kill you when you know stuff." And she puffs away, waiting for Pam to beg her to tell.

What people did know was that Howard Fortune and Hugh Gillis had been charged with assault. Everybody knew, too, they had been out looking for the French guy and agreed it was disgusting that these two young men, who had taken it upon themselves to seek justice, were being punished for doing what the police could or would not. It was appalling. This would remain on their permanent records, and what would happen to the truly guilty party?

Scot-free, people said, spat. *And isn't that just always the way.* They didn't know who it was Hugh and Howard assaulted, but everyone knew in their hearts these were the kind of boys who did the right thing, no matter what the consequences.

Howard had to get stitches. His perfect mouth was now divided by a diagonal slash that started at his right nostril. Instead of two lips it looked like he had four. Pam knew, saw, because she had gone to see Corinne, before anybody knew that she was gone and Howard was in trouble. Pam knocked on the door, a penitent seeking absolution.

Sorry for doing stuff, she would say. Sorry for always wanting something done. I am heartily sorry for having offended thee, because you are so good. Please let me be your friend again before I disappear.

But Howard came to the door, and smiled hazily through the screen.

"Pam-bam, thank you ma'am," he recited. It was something he used to chant when they were kids. She hadn't known what it meant back then, never cared, was just thrilled to be ritualistically named by Corinne's older brother. *It was dirty,* she realized a few years later, sort of thrilled again. It was like her name had rhymed with *fuck.* Later, however, she came to understand that boys made everything dirty. It was their instinctive way of having fun, like turning sticks into firearms, making bullet noises, missile sounds, machine gun fire, exploding bombs. Every boy was born with an arsenal in his mouth.

"Hi," said Pam. "Your face."

"Yeah." He placed a finger across his lips, touching the scar. "Very macho." He nearly grinned then, something she could not remember having ever seen. "I'm flying on codeine," he explained, now poking at the scar. It went white underneath his finger, and then came back an angrier red when he took the finger away. It was mesmerizing.

"Were you"—brotherless Pam racked her brain for the kind of things boys did to hurt themselves—"playing hockey?"

"Got into a fight," he said, like it was something that happened all the time. Pam assumed that, therefore it must have been.

"I should see the other guy?" she tried to joke.

"No," said Howard. "I don't think you would want to."

And then she thought of Guy. The last time she saw him, he was looking down at his own body. *I hate you.* Then he had looked up at her again, in amazement, as if she had just shot him and he couldn't find the hole. Pam had kind of felt that way too—like an act of violence was shimmering between them, sudden and unreal. A second later she felt so powerful she had almost chased after him. But now he was gone, like Corinne.

Pam gazed up at Howard and was struck by how tall he was. She had been sitting when she spoke to Guy, and even then he hadn't seemed as tall. She couldn't think what to say to Howard at this point. So she just said, "I wouldn't?"

"Nope," answered Howard. "You're getting big, Pam,"

"Yeah," she agreed, blushing helpelessly. "I'm huge." She wondered why he didn't yell for Corinne, but didn't ask. She asked instead, without knowing she was going to, "Was it *him?*"

"I meant you're growing up," said Howard.

"Was it *him?*" Pam asked louder.

Howard's eyes shifted, darkened. "I forgot," he said. "You're the one who set the whole thing in motion."

"No I'm not." The denial came out of Pam fast and thoughtless, like the apostle Peter's.

"I remember," he said. "You were the one who first told me about the guy last spring when she was acting all weird. I should thank you."

Pam attempted to meet his eyes to see if he meant what he said. But he was gazing out towards the motionless strait, across which two oil tankers moved like the hands of a clock.

"The guy's dead, anyways" said Howard. "You don't have to worry."

"But not like, *dead,*" said Pam. Howard closed his eyes and looked at her when he opened them again.

"Were you worried?" he said. "Did you think he would hurt you?"

Pam laughed. "God, no!" It was like asking if Pam were worried about getting invited to the prom. Corinne had been right on that front: *She* was the one. Corinne was the freak. That particular breed of freak, anyway.

Howard kept smiling in his drugged, intimate way.

"Maybe you should have been," he told her. "Guys like that are sick."

She swallowed and smirked like a good sport, looking away. Nice one. Guess the joke's on me. Felt something slicing down her cheek.

"I didn't mean it that way."

She backed up, raising a mitten to her face.

Howard was looking at his pointing finger. Pam half expected him to blow on it, toy-gun style.

"Jesus, I'm sorry," he said. "Time to cut my nails."

On either side of the threshold, Pam and Howard shook themselves like animals coming out of hibernation.

Was Corinne home? She was not. Okay. Pam would give her a call later on. Good. Bye.

But Howard didn't tell Pam she would not be back later, either.

Ann leans against the bricks, puffing inscrutably away. She is not looking well these days: she does not look like a girl. She looks brittle and yellow and agelessly wise.

"Hey," Ann pipes up. "It's my birthday today."

The information acts as a kind of detonator for Pam, who has been standing, smoking, waiting patiently. "For God's sake," she erupts. "Are you going to tell me where she is, or what?"

Ann gives her a look of blank insult.

"Yes, I'll tell you. You just had to ask."

"Yeah? I don't have to do a dance or turn around three times?"

"You're kind of impatient," observes Ann. "To be honest, you're kind of mean these days. I thought we were friends."

Pam stops herself from saying *You did?* and says "Sorry" instead. One thing she doesn't want to be is mean. Mean is the worst thing to be. People are mean to Ricky Estabrooks, for example. Because he is sweet, underdeveloped, and guileless. Mean is easy. It is easy to yell at Ann, she is so weird. Everyone in school succumbs to it, teachers even. It would be easy to tell her she looks like shit, that she can't sing, or act, that she's not as goddamn smart as she thinks she is. Pam is tempted because she knows it would bother Ann to hear it: *You know, I do not think you are all that smart, really.* And the other power Pam realizes she still has: *I hate you, Ann. I don't want to be your friend.*

Pam still remembers the tingling in her bowels, back in nursery school. All of them crawling frantically over one another like piglets staking out a teat, gaining their footholds, establishing hierarchies.

"I'm sorry," Pam says. Ann sniffs, puffs. "Happy birthday," says Pam.

"Yeah."

Pam settles down to wait. There is no rushing attention-starved Ann. *But hurry before the boys come,* she wants to say.

"It might surprise you to know that I see a shrink," speaks Ann one leisurely inhalation later. Pam looks up to see if she should laugh. If Ann is serious.

"Apparently I'm troubled."

"Hm," says Pam.

"Every month, we go up to Halifax to see my shrink at the hospital. My mother tries to take me shopping afterwards, for a treat, to make it fun. But she won't buy the kind of stuff I like, and we always end up getting in a huge fight. I tell her, I want black. I want big stuff. Long, loose dresses, coats. Velvet, and satin. Old-man pants. I want to get my ears pieced three more times. I want big silver jewelry, not delicate gold chains, those little dabby earrings you can't even see. I want to buy records. She won't take me anywhere I want to go. So she takes me to Fairweather in the mall and I grab all the black turtlenecks and blazers and long skirts and take them into the dressing room; meanwhile she's throwing floral blouses over the door, thinking I'm going to slip up and try one on and, like, fall in love or something. Like, oh, it's a whole new me. And slips and stuff because she thinks I need to wear slips under everything like it is 1958. So I fire them back over the door at her, and she's like, *Dear!* And we have a big fight right there in the middle of the store and the salesgirls are looking and the people in the other dressing rooms can hear us. So we end up buying nothing and then we walk out to the station wagon across the parking lot in total silence and then we sit there in the station wagon and she says to me, Why do you do this every single time?"

Ann laughs like a dragon, smoke pouring out of her nostrils.

"It kills me," she says at last.

Pam nods. "It kills me too."

"So that is our ritual. That is our Pretending We Aren't Really Here to See Ann's Shrink ritual."

Pam nods again.

"You see, and I'm the one who's troubled."

"Yes," says Pam. "I see."

Ann slumps a little against her eternal brick wall. Boys, now, in the stairwell. *How about you suck me off while you're down there!* Clomp, stomp. *Fruit!* She glances up and smiles, like the guests she's invited have finally arrived.

"Anyway," says Ann. "Corinne's there in the hospital. I saw her in the psych ward."

Boys burst through the doors like high tide. *Hi, ladies!* George Matheson dragging Earl Meisner along in a headlock.

Pam gnashes, swallows, digests. "You can't blame her—I guess."

George proceeds into the slushy yard, flinging Earl Meisner's body back and forth by his head, trying see if he can snap the boy's spine in two. Tucked beneath George's armpit, Earl's head is like a blond, bulbous grape. It emits a high-pitched squeal of mirth.

"I can," says Ann. "I can blame her. She gets to stay. She gets to stay put, up there. She gets everything she wants, that one."

Pam leaves as she traditionally does at this point, once the guys arrive, when Ann is shaking out her second smoke and just getting comfortable. Pam is grateful for the guys this time, and their alienating clamour. This is the problem with people you feel sorry for. Guilty about. You can't be friends with them. You know they are always waiting for you, you who've showed them sympathy, waiting with their pain, holding it away from themselves, towards you, like something that stinks.

CaTCH

LELAND WAS a politician, and therefore a man of loyalty. When he was voted into office sixteen years ago, his friends got jobs. Their roads got paved. He made good on his promises, and then some. He fought hard for his constituents. He compared the premier of Nova Scotia to a used colostomy bag one day in the legislature, and the town rippled with glee for months afterwards. People slapped Leland's back when they ran into him at the Co-op, stuck newspaper articles about Leland on their refrigerators. There was a sense that Leland would do anything on their behalf. Every Christmas, he visited as many homes as he could, eating pie, cake, squares, biscuits, cookies, and drinking tea, coffee, rum, eggnog, vodka, and scotch. He staggered to his car at the end of these evenings, wondering when the heart attack would hit. One year he threw up and felt immediately better afterwards. He wished his guilt over the elaborate hospitality of his constituents didn't prevent him from shoving a finger down his throat after every such excursion.

This temperament was essentially the reason Leland could not stand the thought of Isadore Aucoin languishing friendless on Marianne's couch throughout New Year's and January. Leland felt he had banished Isadore from the only real home he'd had in the past twenty years. He ranted about it to his wife. She had been his sounding board for years and understood that his directing his soliloquies at her had nothing to do with soliciting her opinion. Dory would say things like, "Well, what do *you* think?" And "I know you don't really believe that."

"He's just such an *arse*," Leland complained to Dory. "The poor bastard has never been able to get his act together long enough to get anywhere in life."

"Well, he has a drinking problem," said Dory.

"But *I* have a drinking problem, everybody has a drinking problem, I'm still able to get my ass out the door to work in the morning. He's had the deck stacked against him since day one, that fella. He hasn't had the same advantages as you and I."

Dory nodded.

"But Jesus Christ, he doesn't realize he could *kill* someone! He's like a goddamn ape. He can't just be coming into my bar putting people through the jukebox!"

"No, he certainly can't," said Dory.

"He can't drink. That's the long and the short of it, the man cannot drink."

"That's right."

"But God Almighty, the man's been drinking for the past thirty years, he's not gonna stop now."

"No."

"What he needs is sympathy. What he needs is help. I'm the only friend he's got left and what do I do? Turf him out on his ear."

"Oh Leland," said Dory. "You've always done everything you could for Isadore."

"If I was any kind of friend, maybe I'd have him locked away."

"Oh Leland," said Dory again.

"But I can't do that," Leland sighed, sitting down on the bed. "I've known him too long."

Dory had been managing to peruse a copy of *Chatelaine* magazine the whole time Leland was rambling, but now she put it face down on her lap. "Well," she said to her husband, "what do *you* think?"

"I think my job is to be a friend—and that's all I can do."

"Mm-hm." Dory picked up her magazine again.

"But then sometimes I think the best thing I can do is forget about the stupid son of a bitch and let him drink himself to rot if that's what he wants to do."

Dory gave him a look and flipped some pages.

"I know you don't believe that," she said.

Soon after this conversation, Leland heard from Lauchie Puddicomb about the accident, and once again his friend's luck struck him as being, somehow, entirely his own fault. A reproach from God for not having been there to catch his friend the moment he slipped on the ice. Leland agonized into the New Year, even made a couple of stealthy phone calls to Marianne to check up on Isadore's progress.

"Well? How's the old fart shaping up?"

"He's up and moving around a little. But I think he likes being waited on."

"Oh, I'm sure he's in his element. You might wanna try spilling some hot tea on him in a couple of days, see if he jumps."

Tee-hee went Marianne, and Leland's heart chugged. Marianne was someone else he felt needed looking after. After her husband left, Leland offered to lend her money almost every time he saw her until finally Marianne asked him to stop. He took a breath.

"Now, Marianne dear, you must be having a hell of a time taking care of that oversize baby and with the young fella still in school and whathaveyou . . ."

"Leland—"

"It certainly can't be easy with—"

"Leland, it's okay, Isadore is still getting his disability pension. He's been off welfare for a while but we've reapplied. They've given us some emergency funds in the meantime."

Leland winced at the word *welfare*. He knew he had to come visit. He would bring presents.

"Well, you've got the old girl herself looking after you," Leland said, patting the head of Big Saint Anne. Isadore lolled on the couch as Marianne sat unpacking the gift basket Leland had brought.

"Oh look, Isadore. There's *Turtles*. Plum pudding. Gingerbread men!"

"Those are from Dory," said Leland.

"A little late for Christmas presents," Isadore remarked.

"Ah listen, boy, you know what it gets like for me around the holidays, making the rounds. If you had come to the Christmas party like I told you, you could've gotten your present then!"

"Well," said Isadore, "as you can see, I was in no shape for a party."

Though he knew Isadore hadn't hurt himself until a week or so after Leland's party, Leland nodded with sympathy.

"You're in sorry shape, that's for certain, but then what else is new. Hell of a spill, wha?"

"I've had worse," Isadore grunted.

"True enough," agreed Leland. *Ah, goddammit,* he thought, *your whole life has been one big spill, you foolish old shit.*

"Well, when you're back on your feet, you just wobble your sorry arse right back up to the tavern, and I'll pour you a free one. How does that sound now?"

What else had Leland to offer? The inside of his head was a swamp of impotence and conflict, feelings Isadore always evoked in him—the need to be of help struggling against the need to wrap his hands around his old friend's neck and squeeze. Leland looked to Marianne and she simply smiled at him—no look of warning or resentment. She seemed to want the same thing Leland did. Friendship. Peace on earth.

"Oh my," Isadore yawned after a moment. "Now, I seem to recall last time we had a visit up there, I was made to feel somewhat less than welcome."

Leland might have sat on the floor just then. That the man could just lounge there like some kind of maharaja, withholding his favour and good will. Demanding—what?—from Leland. An apology? For not letting the cretin run rampant in his bar?

"You son of a bitch!" Leland drawled, the words unfurling with slow incredulity. Out of the corner of his eye, he saw Marianne shift, and he glanced at her. She wasn't smiling anymore and her hands were like claws in her lap. Leland looked back at Isadore—who was smirking now—and started to laugh, shaking his head with disbelief. It was like the force of his anger had been filtered through the image of Marianne sitting there and came out thinned.

"*Jesus,* the balls on this one!" he exclaimed.

Isadore started to laugh as well, and Marianne too, with her heartbreaking *tee-hee.*

But now that everyone was friends again, Leland found himself anxious to leave, and nearly toppled Big Saint Anne in the process of yanking his coat on. In fact he was feeling vaguely sickened, much as if he were coming off another politic evening of shovelling cake and pie and squares down his gullet, smiling all the while, asking for more.

BiG

ISADORE WAS NOT the kind of drunk who needed to be drinking all the time. If someone, during his convalescence on Marianne's couch, had brought him a bottle of booze, he would have drunk it. But he never bothered anyone with such a request. He simply convalesced, getting stronger and healthier as the days went by.

After a few weeks on the couch he felt physically better than he had in years. It didn't occur to him that this had anything to do with his not drinking, even though it was precisely the same kind of vigour he experienced after a month of drying out in the monastery. He simply thought he felt pretty good. He found himself "in good cheer," and assumed it was because the pain in his back was finally dissipating.

He liked Marianne's apartment. He liked how she was gone all day, leaving him with the television, teapot, and Big

Saint Anne. Once he was moving around on his own, he enjoyed the ritual of making himself a pot of tea in the late morning, putting down toast, turning on his game shows. Isadore had come to realize that he had not given television a fair shake all these years. It was all about what time of day you watched. You had to pick and choose your shows, separate the gold from the garbage. He still thought the stuff they played in the evenings was nonsense, and would say so whenever Marianne settled in to watch after supper. But daytime television was good fun. He watched game shows voluptuously, throwing up his hands and howling with pleasure whenever a contestant lost everything.

He liked this time alone. Sometimes he would turn down the television and sing Johnnie Horton tunes, loud as he pleased. Everyone else in the building had gone to work.

The locks on his old apartment in town had been changed after he went to the monastery without bothering with the rent. It hadn't concerned him at the time, losing the apartment—he didn't even care about his things within. He had always felt that his real home was Marianne's place outside town. The only reason he hadn't been living there, he told himself, was his impatience with the way she and Kenzie's children comported themselves in his father's house. But in the back of his mind, he always felt there was the option to come and go as he pleased, and he always had.

By five-thirty at night, he was ready for Marianne to come home. She would head straight for the kitchen, clinging to the dregs of her energy, not allowing herself to relax before getting the supper on. Isadore would sit on the couch hollering inquiries and comments to her as she banged cupboards and pans. If Marianne had stopped at the store before coming home, Isadore would ask her who she ran into, and what did So-and-so have to say for himself these days? He would ask her about the family she worked for, the MacAskills, whom he assumed he didn't like. Isadore would find some way to mock or disparage everything she told him about them—even their last name. "MacAskills! Who do they think they are, a family of giants?" he once remarked. He was referring to the legendary Giant MacAskill, the seven-foot-nine Scotsman who had lived in the 1800s and whose massive wax likeness had graced the museum out by the causeway for years. Isadore had always thought this foolish, and often pestered Leland when he was the MLA to have the statue removed. The local freak show, Isadore called it. Isn't this a lovely image for the tourists to be carrying away with them, he had complained. Leland had assumed out loud that Isadore was just jealous of the one man on the island bigger than himself.

"They think they're big, do they?" he said of the MacAskills.

"No," Marianne would call wearily from the kitchen.

"The Giant MacAskills," Isadore had referred to them ever since. "How were the Giant MacAskills today?"

Isadore's health had improved a fair bit since Gordie MacLellan's visit. Something about dealing with a cop had vitalized Isadore, and the effects were lasting. His brain, sluggish from too much TV, had pricked up like animal ears at the sight of MacLellan standing in Marianne's living room, and his instinct for manipulation shifted into gear before Isadore even knew what the cop was after. Isadore had been happy to hear that his nephew was in trouble, and knew from the moment MacLellan started talking he would be able to deflate this trouble with a couple of well-placed yet casual remarks. Isadore knew Gordie would take him seriously, that the constable trusted and respected him. No matter what his reputation might have been, Isadore was a local boy and he and Gordie MacLellan had known each other for years.

But MacLellan hadn't known Isadore's nephew, and that was why he was going after him. When he saw Isadore, however, Guy fell into context. That alone had done a great deal to defuse the situation.

Which meant that the boy getting off the hook was entirely Isadore's doing. He had saved the day. He felt strong and in control again and his sister brought his meals out to him on a tray so that he could watch hockey and the news—well after he was capable of getting up and coming to the table.

MY BAD HEART

EVERYBODY THOUGHT Kenzie had left Marianne, but it never occurred to anyone that Marianne might have told him to go. Nobody asked, and Marianne never had any occasion to say one way or another. She thought it was funny, the assumptions people made. Had she told her parents or her brother the truth at the time, they would have thought she was lying or crazy. They believed, in varying degrees, that Kenzie had been a neglectful husband, sometimes sullen, often self-righteous, but they also knew he was educated and religious—pious even. In those days a religious husband who didn't drink was a great prize, one whose secondary faults could be readily overlooked. Marianne suspected that even Isadore, who professed to despise her husband almost from the day of their wedding, felt this on some level. So when Kenzie disappeared, people figured Marianne had been abandoned, like a child.

They felt sorry for her and brought her loaves and casseroles for many months.

Nobody knew what Kenzie was really like. Her family found him cold and distant, his conversation perfunctory. They assumed it was a consequence of his being so pious. Nobody knew Kenzie was in pain every second of the day. His words came out clipped because he was struggling against the opera within himself. To him a cold pot of tea was tragedy. The sound of his mother's cat-scratch brogue, the sight of his father's cracked, yellow hands—pure despair. But people commented that Kenzie walked like he had a stick up his arse. Isadore, upon meeting Kenzie: *That's what happens when they don't put fences around graveyards.* Only Marianne knew her husband was like a sturdy, unremarkable door pushed shut against a closetful of squalour and bogeymen. Around other people, however, he held everything in. He walked so straight and his eyes were so blank because Kenzie was full to bursting.

At dinner one evening before Marianne and Kenzie got married, Marianne's parents had talked about the terrible explosion at the mill, which had happened only days before. Men had been blown apart, and people in the area could talk about little else. Kenzie had lost two of his cousins in the blast, but he made no mention of them. Instead he remarked on the jobs the repairs would create, not to mention the many new vacancies.

Oh my, her mother had murmured over the dishes. Butter wouldn't melt in that one's mouth now, would it?

Marianne chided him on the way home for being heartless and he shrugged. Not caring about anything, caring too much. On the outside, he told her, it looks the same.

Around Marianne, however, he let it all out. It was not pleasant for her. *I had booze,* he would say, *I had God. But now I have you.*

Jumping Jesus Christ, Marianne remembers thinking to herself.

I don't get you drunk and I won't get you to heaven, she'd joke. But you could never joke around Kenzie, never, it was one of the things that drove Isadore up the wall.

You do both, Kenzie would say, head on her lap as he liked to lie for hours. She'd never liked it. Her legs would go to sleep and she would start to think of the leftover food drying on the supper dishes, beckoning flies.

Near the end, she just told him, I don't want to do this anymore. I don't want to be your pillow. I don't want to be the thing you use to hide. She wouldn't let him drowse in her lap, bury his head between her breasts, wouldn't tell him everything was going to be fine, wouldn't sing Acadian lullabies.

She started to say things like, I have a bad heart. If you don't get a steady job, your children will die. Your daughter will get scurvy. Your son's teeth will rot and fall out. How do you like them apples, mister?

And he started to go to the monastery again, like he was moving backwards in time. First he reverted into a recovering alcoholic. During this time, she would say to him, While you were away on retreat, I cleaned house for two women. They felt sorry for me. They gave me their children's old hand-me-downs for our kids to wear. How was the retreat? Did you have fun? How was God? Did you ask him where he's been?

And just before he left for good, he went back to drinking, awash in booze and God once more. He needed to hide from *her* now, he said. He would come home at three in the morning and complain she had betrayed him, and Marianne was so infuriated at this point in her life that had she been a man she would have rolled up her sleeves and beaten the hell out of him.

Instead she yelled and said terrible things. She knew how easy it was to torture Kenzie and indulged in it often. It was the only power she had, so she wielded it wantonly.

I thought, she would say, you were supposed to be a man.

What does that mean? he would plead with her. What is that supposed to *mean*?

It made her even angrier, because if neither of them knew, they were hopeless together.

It means be of some *use!* Be someone I can trust!

You don't trust me? he would say, flabbergasted.

He was like her father. He would prefer to disappear up his own ass than raise his head and let the world come at him full-on. They were cowards. They were useless when it came to real life. Her father had been gentle, kind, a nondrinker, a good provider, and he would have let his children die because he couldn't, even for a moment, face the thought of their being sick. He had rolled up into a ball and stuck his callused fingers into his hairy, old-man ears, hummed a little tune, and waited for someone to make the bad hearts go away.

I'm not going to make it all go away for you, she told Kenzie. So if that's what you want, you should go.

Contemplating her lump of a brother on the couch every time she came home, Marianne remembered how intimidated he had been by Kenzie, and still was, and she thought it was funny. Just as she thought it was funny that other men were intimidated by Isadore. Except, in spite of his generalized cowardice, Kenzie. Kenzie knew a kindred spirit when he saw one. He recognized a man propelled through life by fear. Isadore didn't. He was too vain. He couldn't imagine someone as extraordinary as himself having anything in common with anyone else.

Isadore had told her, after MacLellan left, that Guy went to see Louise. Marianne felt relieved but thwarted. He instinct was to call and talk to him, but she hadn't called Louise at the house since the girl ran off and got married. Marianne wasn't talking to her daughter, and she couldn't stand the thought of Louise picking up the phone and thinking Marianne had given in. Marianne had a point to prove: if Louise figured she could go ahead and get married without consulting or involving her mother, she could just try living her life that way for a while and see how she liked it.

So she waited for Guy to call. A few times she tried to talk Isadore into calling. Of course he wouldn't.

A couple of days later, Constable MacLellan phoned her at the MacAskills wanting to know if Guy had returned yet, and Marianne told him at once where Guy was. She was grateful to

MacLellan for calling, and asked if he would tell her son to come home. The cop's reiteration that his investigation was "strictly unofficial," combined with Isadore's boasting of the effect his own glowing character undoubtedly had on MacLellan's opinion, had calmed her a good deal. It had been a shock—a pure, full-body jolt—to have a Mountie show up at her place of work inquiring about her child. Her cuticles went to hell and she found inordinate amounts of her hair in the sink only a day later. She was surprised it didn't go white.

They never talked about what she said to Isadore about their father Christmas Eve, how she'd warned that Isadore wouldn't have them anymore. Isadore made it known that he forgave her. But he also made it known he was wounded, and would not necessarily forget. Here he was, he spoke in his language of tea bags, TV trays, and the Giant MacAskills, putting his ass on the line for that son of hers in spite of their having turned him out, *kicked* him out, on Christmas Eve. The very evening of the birth of Our Lord. Here Isadore was, despite all he had suffered, going to bat for her and her son. Here he was remembering, while all others had forgotten, the overriding importance of family. Living up to the convictions of their father, Emile, of which the rest of them continually fell short. Here Isadore was, when by all rights he should have left them to their dissipation long ago.

On the day Marianne finally decided to give in and call the house herself, to tell Guy to get his ass home and back to school before he lost too much of the year, Constable MacLellan called her first. He did not sound as reassuring as before.

"Mrs. Boucher," he said. "Now, I don't appreciate being lied to."

"No," said Marianne, like it was obvious. "I'm sorry," she added. The words came out sounding like an instinctive apology. She had meant it to be a question, asking him to elaborate.

"Now, you told me your young fella would be out Louisdale way."

"That's where he said he was going!"

"Well, I don't mind telling you, I took a ride out to the house the other day, and that girl of yours alleges she hasn't seen the boy."

Alleges. He was using police words with her.

"I have to say, for a good boy who hasn't done a darn thing wrong, I'm wondering why he's so hard to get ahold of."

"I haven't talked to him since he left," said Marianne. "I don't know." She put her hand over the receiver and sobbed, fast. A little MacAskill sat at the table across from her, dipping Oreo cookies into a glass of milk precisely like the child in a commercial he'd seen. But he stopped dunking and shoved the entire Oreo in his mouth when Marianne made this noise.

"I guess what I'm saying is," Constable MacLellan was saying, "I'm a little bit disappointed here. I was hoping you and your boy would be as interested in getting this here business cleared up as I am."

"But I don't know where he is," Marianne whispered.

"That's hard to believe," remarked MacLellan. "And if it's true, well, I think it's a little bit sad."

Marianne fought not to scream *cocksucker* into the phone, as a tight bud of fury suddenly blossomed in the middle of all that fear.

"Well, why don't you find him?" she snapped. "Because if he's not there, he's lost, because that's where he told Isadore he was going. So he could be hurt, or in trouble. Jesus Lord God, he's been gone for three days and you're worried about some slutty girl who led him on!"

MacLellan backed off. "Now, now, now. I'm sure the boy's fine."

"Well, where *is* he?"

"I'm sorry, Mrs. Boucher," said MacLellan, sounding sincere. "I thought that you would know."

Marianne hung up on the cop and called her daughter.

DeTACHMENT

MACLELLAN HELD his hand over the phone cradle for a moment and then picked it up again to get a dial tone. He dialed Isadore at Marianne's apartment, face pinkening, throbbing with insult.

"Hello, Gordie!" Greeted Isadore, and made a loud slurping noise in MacLellan's ear. "Just settling in with a cup of tea. Now what can I do for you today?"

"Be honest with me, Isadore. Where did that little fart of yours get to?'

"Little fart of mine?" repeated Isadore.

"Your nephew Guy."

Isadore could be heard taking another long slurp of tea. The sound made MacLellan feel both annoyed and thirsty.

"Why? Wasn't he out at the house?"

"No, he wasn't. And the girl says she hasn't seen him."

"Well, the girl's full of shit. He was off pulling his pony in the bathroom or some such thing,"

"I don't think," said MacLellan.

"Well, Gordie," Isadore said after a moment. "I'm afraid I'm stumped."

MacLellan made a noise of frustration, pushing air between his clenched teeth.

"I'm going to be honest with you, Isadore, I don't think it looks very good for him."

"Oh horseshit, Gordie," scoffed Isadore. "You're a sixteen-year-old boy and someone tells ya the cops are chasin' ya down? What do you do, wait around? He was probably carrying some of the hashish or whathaveyou, maybe ripped off a candy bar up at Shopper's the one time. He doesn't know what in hell he's supposed to have done, but who wants to get caught either way?"

"I suppose," MacLellan sighed after a moment.

Isadore took another long, almost conversational, slurp. "Ahh!" he punctuated. "Well, I guess I'll be talking to ya, then, Gordie."

Last they spoke, Isadore had MacLellan more or less convinced the whole thing was a rumour blown out of proportion. But the thing was, MacLellan wanted to put it to rest, and was getting frustrated. He had brought the matter to Fred Fortune, and now felt he owed it to Fred, as a friend, to clear the whole thing up. His plan had been to talk to everyone involved, thoroughly alleviate people's fears, and then see himself understood by the town as a man who would go the extra mile to address their anger and concern even when no one else was willing to do so. He had been annoyed to learn what Fred Fortune's son and his friend had attempted, and gave them a lecture in the police station that night. But he understood the impetus behind it.

The problem was, the thing was dragging on too long. He had planned to sit down with the boy, scare him slightly with talk of jail and I'll-be-keeping-my-eye-on-you. Then be on his way with one less shit-disturber to worry about in the future.

But the boy would not present himself. And the mother had been uncooperative from the very beginning. Her blatant fear of MacLellan and passive compliance made him a little contemptuous at first, but secure in the knowledge that Marianne was not someone he was going to have to worry about. On her word, however, he had used his lunch hour to drive out to their place in Louisdale, only to find himself on a wild goose chase. He felt made a fool of. So he had called Marianne on his coffee break, after grinding his teeth about it all afternoon, and given her shit.

And then he was made to feel bad about having giving her shit, when she shrieked down the phone at him all of a sudden, and hung up. He could not quite believe the woman had hung up on him. The whole thing was starting to make him feel sour and annoyed, somehow taken advantage of. *Unappreciated* was the word. What they didn't understand or care about, it seemed, was that he had been ready to forgive the bunch of them and let the matter go—right up to this point. He had told them over and over again: he just wanted to get the matter settled, for Christ's sake.

nO ONE

PEOPLE LIKED him better with his split mouth. They liked him better now that he had attacked a total stranger, drawn blood unprovoked, in the name of defending his sister. Men he barely recognized stopped him on the street to converse. Older men, mostly, not men his age. Of course there was hardly anyone his age left in town.

They said things like, "Nice work there, Howard, buddy." People older than him still said *buddy*. They didn't call each other *man* like Hugh and Howard. "I woulda done exactly the same thing in your shoes," they said.

Howard didn't particularly appreciate these men presuming to talk to him out of the blue, as if he had been appointed a member of their club without their asking if he wanted to be. They appeared surprised by Howard's surprise, when they spoke to him. They were incredulous when he did not want to go for a beer, meet up at the tavern later, play pool. They didn't believe it. They would say, "Some time in the next few days, then, wha? We'll be seeing you around."

But Howard still spoke and acted precisely the same way he always had. In the same manner that would have put these same men off a month ago, would've had them muttering *arsehole* to themselves as they continued on their way. Now, when Howard looked through them in the slow-blink way he had, they smiled warmly and looked through him in return. When he grunted a response, they heard something else. He belonged, whether he liked it or not.

He wanted to go.

His father asked him to put off the move to Donnell Cove. Howard said he couldn't, and his father got angry at him for the first time since Howard was perhaps eight. He blinked and looked down as his father ranted about what a difficult time this was for the family. Then Howard brought himself to look. He sat and watched his father like a movie. Howard was fascinated, in a way. His father's anger was irrational and impotent, he saw. His father was angry because everything was so confusing and no one would explain things to him. He made no sense as he yelled at Howard. He was like a very old man. Senile. Hollering at shadows, figments.

"This is a very difficult time, and you have no concern!" he said. "You can't always think about yourself, Howard. We are a family here. I know it's hard for a young man, and I know you need to feel that you're doing what you have to be doing, but goddammit! Where is your sister? What is she doing up at that hospital? She's not home, she's not here, she's not with her family where she's supposed to be. And that's why we need to stick together now. There are problems that every family goes through, and maybe we've been lucky up until now because we've always been so content. But you can't expect it to always be smooth sailing, Howard, the world does not work that way, unfortunately. You have to ride out the storm sometimes. You just have to take the punches as they come. And that's what we're doing, but we can't do it without you and that's what you need to understand. You're a young man, Howard, but you're not a boy anymore. You're a man now. It's important for people to know they can count on you. If people don't have that, then what do they have? If a family can't count on each other for support, who can they count on? Exactly no one, and that is the truth. These are confusing times. These are hurtful times for your mother. And think of your poor sister and how much she needs you. Think of what she must be going through, even though nobody knows, God knows I don't know, and maybe it wouldn't make sense if we did. But that's precisely what you have to be thinking about at this point. That's all that matters, Howard. I hope you see that. I hope you understand this above all else: nothing else matters. I am asking you to understand."

All Howard could see, hear, was his father begging, his father afraid. Howard's mother sat at the table following Fred around with her restless eyes, but otherwise still and silent as a plaster mannequin.

"Dad," Howard sighed, "the lease is signed. I've paid a deposit. It's only a twenty-minute drive."

Mr. Fortune kept his eyes on the kitchen floor, where they had been during much of his speech. He continued to move his lips even as his son was speaking, standing with his head down and hands held together at his back.

"Lease," he repeated without looking up. "Lease?"

"Yes, Dad," said Howard. "I've signed the lease. I can't get out of it now."

Mr. Fortune finally met his son's eyes. His lips stopped moving and then fell apart. He licked them.

"You say you've already signed the lease?"

"Yes," said Howard.

Mr. Fortune sat down beside his wife.

"Oh well," he said at last. "I suppose if you've signed the lease then there's not much you can do."

And he stood again and wandered from the room like a sleepwalker.

The plan was for Hugh to help with the move. Fred made a few half-ass gestures to be involved; he carried a rocking chair out of the attic and down to the basement and started to sand it so Howard "could have somewhere nice to sit." But when the day arrived for Howard to go, the old oak chair was still sitting in the basement with only part of the armrest sanded down.

In the middle of his last supper at home: "Oh! I haven't got that darn rocker ready for you yet!" Fred jumped up from his uneaten meal, ready to head to the basement and apparently finish two days' worth of work in a couple of hours.

"It's okay, Dad, sit down. I won't need it right away."

Sitting back down, slowly. "Won't you? But where will you sit?"

Howard swallowed his food, looking elsewhere as his traumatized father grew more doddering by the moment. Every cell in Howard's body spoke: *Go go go go*. This was a special meal his mother made for his last night home and to him it tasted like white.

"I'm taking the couch from the shed," Howard ground out.

"That old thing?"

"It's fine, Dad," Howard assured him. "It's fine."

Go.

"It really will be fine," said Howard with the assurance of one who has never been doubted. His parents nodded, like they nodded at everything he ever said.

BrIDGE

UNLIKE HOWARD, who was apparently Mr. Cool Fucking Cucumber, the idea of being charged with a crime was horrifying to Hugh, a Good Guy who, up until now, had had nothing to hinder him in life. Now he had a police record. It was not as if he planned to live in town forever. One day he might like to travel. One day he might like to go to the States, go to school, get a job, for shit's sake. Wouldn't this be attractive to potential employers. Here he was busting his ass to learn computers, living at home to save money, biding his time, waiting for the inevitable opportunities a young, smart, happy guy attracts. Though his future had always been fuzzy, Hugh had never doubted for a moment it was secured. Now there was a black mark on his formerly spotless persona, and Hugh felt transformed. He didn't feel as sure about the world. His parents had given him apocalyptic shit, not having the blind, unconditional regard for their son that the Fortunes apparently did. Hugh's father took away the car, and Hugh felt like an adolescent again. Gawky, uncertain, not as smart as he thought he was. Perhaps even a little thick. He blamed Howard.

He thought Howard was a fucking crazy man, truth be told.

But he had offered to help Howard move over a month ago, and the Good Guy in Hugh wouldn't let him back out of it. He fumed as they taped boxes, loaded furniture into the Fortunes' truck, with Mr. Fortune occasionally wandering out onto the front step to spit over the railing and offer them advice and encouragement. Howard, typically, took no notice of Hugh's uncharacteristic silence. He seemed perfectly comfortable with it, in fact, insofar as Howard seemed comfortable with anything. Once the truck was loaded up he offered Hugh a beer.

"No," Hugh grunted. "Let's just get this shit over to the new place."

"Good idea," Howard agreed. "We'll drink when we get there."

But Hugh was not the kind of guy who could sulk indefinitely, waiting for someone to notice and ask what was the matter. He exploded in the truck after Howard asked, "How's the ear?" Hugh's ear had swollen up like a cauliflower after the fight down in the trails, and he had been terrified it would stay that way, like sometimes happened to boxers.

"How's the ear?" he repeated. "Fuck, man, like you care."

"Are you implying I don't care about your ear?" said Howard. "That hurts me."

"Oh man. Fuck you, Howard."

Howard was behind the wheel, barreling across the causeway too fast. His split mouth twisted into a grim smirk. "What?"

"What," echoed Hugh. "Thanks to you, I'm fucked. You started a free-for-all at that goddamn fire pit, and now I'm going to jail."

Howard laughed. Hugh's voice had gone up pathetically at the word *jail,* and he sounded about ten years old.

"Nobody's going to jail. Nobody ever goes to jail."

"Yeah, well we spent a night in jail and that's enough for me, thanks."

"An hour," said Howard. "We spent one hour in jail. And then our daddies came and took us home."

"And now we've got a police record," Hugh spat.

"We're just two high-spirited boys, out fighting the good fight."

"Bullshit! We're not boys! We not being charged as youths! We were supposed to get *Mackie.* We were out for Mackie, and you turned it into a Jesus hockey fight!"

"They threw a bottle at me," Howard protested mildly.

Hugh had forgotten about that. He settled back into his seat. "Yeah, well—"

"*Yeah, well,*" Howard mocked in the voice of an imbecile.

Looking back on that day, the day Howard moved, Hugh remembered the sudden knowledge at that point of how much he actually despised Howard. He wasn't just mad at him anymore, he realized. He saw that he had been expecting the two of them to hash it out. This was the real reason he hadn't told

Howard to go fuck himself when he called to get help with the move. On some level, Hugh believed they would make up. He was pissed off, for sure, but essentially he understood that what was done was done and no level of pissiness at Howard was going to change that. So he imagined blowing off steam, Howard apologizing in a guy kind of way—maybe they wouldn't even see each other for a while. But after that he had been imagining looking back on it all five years from now and laughing together. Part of him knew getting the shit kicked out of you together was the kind of thing that made you friends for life. But that was never going to happen, he realized, barrelling across the causeway in Fred Fortune's truck. Because he wasn't going to keep on being friends with Howard Fortune. The guy was a prick and always had been, and Hugh could no longer stand the sight of him.

They unloaded the truck and said little, Hugh more thoughtful now than angry. They maneuvered the mildew-smelling stained couch up a flight of stairs and shoved it in a corner. They dumped everything else in the center of the living room and, sweating, cracked a beer each. Hugh sat on the couch, even though its cushions sat in a pile at his feet.

"Not bad, man," said Hugh, gazing around. He had no standards by which to judge, but was jealous of the apartment nonetheless. The freedom, the level of independence it represented. Howard, standing in the middle of his new greyish apartment, now struck Hugh as being infinitely more grown up than himself. Blood had poured from Howard's mouth in terrible amounts, through masses of paper towels and onto the floor of the police station, but he had gazed around, unconcerned. When Mr. Fortune came to pick him up, Howard had done all the comforting and calming down. Hugh, meanwhile, had to hold his hands on his lap to keep them from shaking.

Now Howard walked over to one blank wall and poked at a spot where the paint bulged out. "It should suit my purposes," he agreed.

Hugh watched him. In the unfamiliar surroundings, they might have been strangers. "I should get going," he said.

Howard dug in his pockets for the keys and tossed them to Hugh, who had agreed to return the truck to the Fortunes' so that Howard could stay and set up his place. Normally Hugh would want to stay, open another beer, offer to help, suggest they get a pizza, but he didn't and Howard didn't seem to notice. Did Howard ever notice anything, was Hugh's question. Did Howard even know that Hugh and others walked the earth.

"Thanks a lot," said Howard.

"Yeah," said Hugh.

"Hey," added Howard as Hugh started to leave. "I guess you should know." He grinned. "I can be an asshole sometimes."

Hugh flashed a wry, Howardesque smirk. "I do know that, Howard."

"Yeah, well, what I mean is," said Howard. "it's basically my fault." He looked over Hugh's shoulder at another grey, inexpertly painted wall. "All this bullshit," he added. "I mean, you should know that I'm the problem."

Hugh rolled his eyes, "Oh man—if I thought I could blame you for everything, believe me, I would."

Howard's shoulders drooped. Hugh could see him wanting to get the confession or apology or whatever the hell it was over with, being as contrary to his nature as it was.

"Seriously," said Hugh, "I was the one who went for Mackie first, I shouldn't've—"

"No," interrupted Howard, nearing impatience. "I'm not talking about Mackie, or the French guy. I'm the one. It's no one else."

Howard stopped talking and simply stuck out his hand. Hugh was too stunned by this gesture do anything but shake it and say goodbye.

He felt badly as he left. He didn't understand Howard, and realized he never had, but still he felt sorry for him. Hugh was soaked all of a sudden in the knowledge that Howard was alone. The fact that Howard seemed neither to know nor to care made it worse instead of better.

Driving, Hugh noticed, as he had been noticing since childhood, the little miracle of the water on one side of the bridge bashing and whirling in a winter frenzy while on the other side—the town side—it lapped in gentle ripples. Both sides, however, were storm-cloud grey, practically indistinguishable from the sky. February was a depressing time of year, thaw or no. It was the first time in Hugh's life he had deliberately given up a friend, he was thinking. But under this was an experience he knew but couldn't articulate. It was the first time a thing as dreadful and real as this compassion had brushed against him, and as a result, the nice world that had always seemed laid out for his pleasure was revealed as something else. A living and arbitrary thing, independent of Hugh's wishes or beliefs. Determined to make him doubt, to make him old.

aND FORGET

"HI-EEE! LONG time no speak! You'll never guess where I am—
I'm in Halifax! Sorry I haven't called. Did you think I ran away?
I almost did. I was going crazy, as you know. My parents thought
I needed a break. I'm at my aunt's! We've been shopping like
crazy, just doing nothing, it's been so great, Linda is my favourite
aunt. She got me drunk! She let me wear her clothes and makeup
and she snuck me into the Palace. I danced with all these guys
who thought I was twenty or something and we drank shooters
and Long Island iced tea. They said not to worry about school,
which is weird, but I'm trying not to. It's only been like a month,
I can catch up. Yeah! I'm coming back. So you'll help me, right?
Can I borrow your notes? For, like, everything—it's going to be
insane. But I've decided I'm just not going to worry about anything anymore. Life is too short. Life is too short. It's all about
having fun and feeling good and not dwelling on the past, that's

what I think. So, fuck everything. That is my new motto. Oh my Jesus fuck you'll never guess what. I saw Brian, remember Brian? It was totally weird. I was hanging out on Spring Garden drinking hot chocolate with my aunt. He looks *so hot*. There's no way I would get back together with him after the way he acted but oh my God. He's let his hair grow. It's like what's his name's now. The singer. What's his name in the Doors, the guy. Yeah! He's always reminded me of him to be honest. Did I ever mention that? I did talk to him, though, I admit it, I couldn't avoid it, because he saw me and just came right in—he didn't even care that my aunt was there or anything. You should've seen the look on her face. She shit her pants right there. She left us alone for a minute though to go to the bathroom—*that's* how cool she is. You're not going to believe this—he said he was sorry! Oh my God it was so sweet. He practically got down on his knees and apologized. I think he really meant it. He goes, Listen, I know I've hurt you. I ignored you and I was mean to you and I basically treated you like shit and I don't know why because the whole time, I loved you. I'm not saying I did it because I loved you, but the fact is I did it and I loved you and it wasn't right. And I still love you and I'm never going to hurt you again. Because you are the most special person in the world to me, you are the most special person period and you deserve to be treated with love and respect and kindness and you will be if you come back to me. I want to marry you and take care of you forever, forsaking all others. You are good and kind and should not be hurt. You should never be hurt, he said, and I will never hurt you again.

"Yeah. It was a pretty heartfelt speech. I was, like, *bawling*.

Nobody has ever *spoken* that way to me before, and at the end of it all I was thinking, Maybe I'm crazy. Maybe I should give him another chance. How often do you come across that kind of devotion? How many guys in the world are going to feel that way about you, this is what I'm wondering. Anyway, you know what he did? He sees my aunt coming and he just goes, You have my number, and he's gone, just like that. And I do have his number and all I can say is that it's mighty mighty tempting. But anyway, I can't think about all that right now, but as you can imagine I've been *dying* to talk to you. I don't know why I didn't call before now. Everything was just crazy.

"I just feel like forgiving and forgetting. I just want to forgive everybody for everything. Like, fuck that French guy. Whatever, who cares. What happened happened. I don't even *know* what happened. What comes around goes around and we'll all be punished for it one day, on some level of existence. In the meantime, live and let live. And let's just forget about everything that happened, everybody finding out and stuff, because I realized it's not my fault. None of it is my fault and I didn't do anything and I'm not a bad person because of it. I'm a good person, right? We're all good at heart. Everybody makes mistakes and things happen and people get mad or get hurt but then life goes on. And friendship goes on. Because nothing gets in the way of true friendship. True friendship can never die. Just like true love.

"Anyway, I can't wait to be home. We should go for fries and gravy when I get back, because I'm dying for fries and gravy. I've been craving it, all that fat and grease.

I know. It's pretty gross of me, isn't it."

MERCY

ONCE ISADORE was feeling mobile and somewhat recovered, he took to wandering around town like a big stiff stork, back and forth to the tavern to see Leland and his friends. He hadn't taken a drink in over a month—not because he didn't want to, but because the past few weeks of being the man of the house in Marianne's two-bedroom apartment had made him feel competent and superior, a feeling he wanted to maintain for a bit. He would hobble over to some of the regulars in the tavern during his first few days of being up and around, and shake his head like a disapproving grandfather.

"Jesus murphy, Archie, you're starting early, aintcha? What is it, is it even lunchtime yet? My Christ, man, things can't be that bad, can they?"

Sitting down with another man he might remark, "You know, I'm not saying I don't know how it is. I used to get into that stuff pretty heavy, and I'm not saying I still don't enjoy a hit from time to time. The fact is, however, that one of these days you're gonna look around and realize that life has passed you by. The world's forgotten all about you rotting away here in this godforsaken hole—no offense, eh, Leland, boy!—and it's gone on without you. And how are you gonna feel then, huh?"

"Saint Isadore walks among us once again," Leland quipped. Amongst themselves, the patrons said Leland was a fool to let Aucoin keep walking through his doors. They hunched over their beers and griped at God whenever they saw Isadore ambling towards their tables. They braced themselves for the bone-rattling slap on the back, the neck-wrenching headlock. Then they looked up and grinned and shook his oversize hand when he finally arrived.

It wasn't long before Isadore confided to one and all his family worries. His nephew being chased by the police for some kind of nonsense, his poor sister worried sick about it on top of working her fingers to the bone every day for this MacAskill crew, who wouldn't even let her off for lunch. People raised their head at the mention of Guy and filled in the holes in Isadore's narrative for him. The girl had been shipped off somewhere, they reported, and the immediate speculation arose that she was pregnant. The men gave each other knowing looks. That young Fortune one was always a bit spinny, someone remarked. And it needed to be faced, someone else added; there was never any proof of anything, now, was there?

Isadore was a bit disappointed, having assumed the whole town was essentially mobilized against his nephew. The situation had shifted in the new year, however. The shouts for blood had stilled and the phone calls to the RCMP detachment had tapered off. When people realized the police were doing nothing, it occurred to some that perhaps there was nothing to be done. Nobody really knew anything about this French guy anyway, or what he looked like. None of the men in the tavern had realized it was Isadore's nephew people were discussing until Isadore came in and told them so. And some people's sons and friends had been victims of Howard Fortune and Hugh Gillis's acts of vigilantism, and said these fellas were just looking for an excuse to crack skulls. Little sister's case of hysteria, or whatever it was, happened to be a very convenient excuse indeed.

Poor young Mackie Pettipas, someone said. Had anyone gotten a look at him lately? The two of them kicked his head in and they couldn't tell you why any more than he could.

"Well, I don't know about that, but I can tell you one thing," Isadore interrupted. "I was there at my nephew's baptism and I happen to be his goddamn godfather, and I can tell you right now these are not the kind of doings he would ever find himself involved with. I'll be goddamned if I hear anyone saying otherwise!"

Men nodded and remarked that no one was saying otherwise.

"Well, I just think it's a hell of a thing when some little—I won't say what, because I don't know the girl—but some little thing like that can just come out with some filthy story to alleviate her own sense of guilt or whathaveyou, and send my poor sister and her young fella into a tailspin!"

Now the men remembered Isadore's nephew more clearly: the young hockey player who had wailed on old Freeman Day the one time during the playoffs, much to everyone's delight. The lad who liked pool and wouldn't say boo to a goose. By God, Isadore was right. There was no way that boy was capable of such a thing. Where, they asked Isadore, was his nephew now?

"Well, Jesus Christ, where would you be with everyone out for your blood?" Isadore demanded. "He certainly won't be poking his face in here any time soon, now will he? Boy's even been missing school."

"This is ridiculous." Leland spoke from behind the bar where he was furiously squirting cleanser from a Windex bottle. "For Christ's sake, I'll call up the detachment, Isadore, put all this nonsense to rest once and for all. The boy can't be driven out of town like it's the goddamn nineteenth century with the lynch mobs and all the rest of it."

"That's good of you, Leland," said Isadore with so much nobility he imagined everyone in the bar knew he would refuse Leland's help. He could see the patrons looking at him now with grudging admiration, remembering, perhaps, that Isadore was one of them no matter what kind of shit he may have pulled in the past—a solid man whose life was no easier than anyone else's, yet who always seemed to have a good word and to be concerned with the things that really counted in life. Family, community, and loyalty above all.

"That's *awfully* good of you," Isadore emphasized. "But the fact of the matter is, Leland, this is something we have to work out on our own—as a family."

"If there's anything I can do," said Leland.

"Well," considered Isadore, "last I heard, he was holed up out at the house with his sister and her new husband. You can let me borrow your car so I can go and get the little fart—let him know the whole world's not against him."

Leland handed over the keys without hesitation. "You tell that boy he's welcome in my place any time," he advised Isadore. "And I'll be *fucked* if anyone lays a finger on him with my two young fellas here keeping watch."

Isadore felt stronger and more himself with each passing moment. That day, he wanted to celebrate. He had climbed out of bed in the morning feeling lucid and extroverted, and decided this was the day to see Alison Mason and let him know that Isadore forgave him. Once he had bullied an apology out of the hippie bastard for having so callously turned Isadore away at Christmas, they could let bygones be bygones and get back to the business of drinking. The time had come. The only question in Isadore's mind that morning was how he was going to get out to Scotsman's Paradise, as he called Mason's desolate half acre. The idea of walking and trying to catch rides with his back in the shape that it was would be out of the question.

But the universe—in the form of Leland—had provided. Just as it so often had in his younger days. Back then it seemed like God was always keeping one ear cocked for Isadore. He remembered the magic of that certainty, what a particularly young feeling it was. A feeling of youth. Everything came so easy, he had assumed that life—his life anyway—would always be as such.

It's that kind of day, Isadore reflected. When you feel assured that you have things, that you are a certain *way,* that the people in your life understand this about you—this way that you are—and that they love and admire you for it. The past couple of hours holding forth in the bar and the nodding attention of the men had reinforced this conviction in Isadore. Leland's readiness to help and eternal trust in him confirmed it.

Isadore's first stop in Leland's car was the liquor store. For the first time since the holidays, he got himself a forty— Captain Morgan spiced rum, which struck him as festive. He bought a small bottle of champagne for Marianne, to give her later, just to be nice. He bought sherry for Alison Mason.

THE RING

GUY WAS THINKING of a dream as he shoveled heavy, wet snow from the walkway. He was at the boxing club with his red-haired father. His father was standing in front of him with his hands up, like a trainer, red head bobbing away, encouraging Guy to punch. Guy punched as hard as he could, solid and satisfying punches that his father didn't mind. His father was pleased with the force. Good, good, he kept saying. Atta boy.

But other guys were getting impatient and wanted to spar with Guy and his father wouldn't let them. He's not ready yet, he called to the boys outside the ring. He's just getting limbered up here, you fellas wait your turn, all right? But Guy could see these guys were annoyed, they wanted to get in the ring. They were starting to think that maybe Guy's dad was an arsehole. Guy wanted to say something to his father about it, but they were having such a good time together for the first time in his life, he couldn't bring himself to spoil it. But guys were shouting things and their hostility was spreading itself around now, extending itself to Guy as well as his father. He glanced between the ropes and could see the guys muttering to each other, planning something.

Dad, he said. Kenzie. Maybe we should let them in.

You just ignore them, Kenzie said. You just keep on at me.

Guy was annoyed at that, the obliviousness of his father to the feelings of others. Was he trying to get him killed? He punched harder and harder and his father kept going, Good! Oh son, that's good! He was getting smaller as he said it. Some of the guys around the ring made pleased noises, cheering. Guy was getting rid of his father for them—the harder he hit, the smaller Kenzie got.

Good! squeaked Kenzie.

Guy was hit from behind. A familiar puck on the back of the head, like a casual swipe from a bear. He was so surprised he dropped the shovel.

"You goddamn little shit!" said Isadore. Surprised, angry. Jovial in a weird way. Instinctively Guy staggered over to the shovel and picked it up.

"Oh now, what are you going to do with that? Haven't you gotten yourself into enough trouble already? Jesus Christ, your mother and the whole town tearing their hair out over the likes of you and you here getting up to God knows what with that Yankee arsehole in there?"

Isadore reached out and somehow wiped the shovel from out of Guy's hand. But, Guy wanted to say, he is your best friend, I thought.

Alison Mason came running from the house, his boots undone. "Isadore," he called, tramping through the snow. "How've you been?" He huffed and puffed, trying to position himself in front of Guy. "How's the back?"

"How's your own fuckin back?" barked Isadore. "What in God's name have you two been getting up to out here in the middle of nowhere?"

Alison glanced at Guy, who was moving towards the shovel a second time.

"We're on the buddy system," he told Isadore.

"What fuckin buddy system?"

"Like in the program."

Isadore looked down at the two of them with deliberate repulsion.

"This little pussy's no drinker. *Petit,* I'm going to say this once, you go for that shovel again, you'll be swallowing it, uh?"

"Isadore, don't say that," pleaded Alison. "Guy's been through a lot these days, and I've been through a lot—though it's been my own damn fault. The upshot of the whole deal is, we're going to be buddying up for a while."

"Buddying up," repeated Isadore. "You mean fruitin it up, from what I can see. Well *goddamn de goddamn* as my old man used to say, turns out the apple doesn't fall too far from the tree after all now, does it?"

"You fucking shut your fat fucking mouth about my father!" Guy screamed over Alison's shoulder. Alison held his head and closed his eyes and the next moment he was lying on his side in the hard snow because Isadore had nudged him out of the way. The shovel made a noise then—one loud, metallic exclamation point.

He picked himself up out of the soggy, packed snow and wiped the blood from his eyes. He looked at it on his glove and blinked rapidly before bursting into violent, terrified tears. Guy witnessed this, head humming the same note the shovel had just rung out.

"You two are terrible people," Isadore stuttered, unable to stop looking down at his own blood. "And *you!*" to Guy. "To think of all I've *done!* To think of how much I've loved you!"

Alison, still on the ground, reached speechlessly for Isadore, who jerked away like he was expecting pain. Guy stood, his lips working like a fish's, the shovel quaking above his head.

"To think of all I would have given you *both!*" shrieked Isadore. "This is what I get! This is what I get for all my love!"

He gasped from the force of his despair and ran for Leland's car, slipping and staggering and bawling like a spooked child.

Guy saw into the future then, head still singing, the bunched muscles in his arms and shoulders gone to water as the shovel fell to the ground. The incident would hover in the minds of all three forever, almost as a shared religious experience. Something both awesome and awful. Never to quite be believed, discussed, or forgotten.

THE POINT

"THANK GOD," said Alison, serving Constable Gordie MacLellan coffee. He was not making tea, because Alison had never learned to make a pot of tea "the right way," according to his neighbours. You were supposed to boil it, you were never supposed to boil it; never use more than one bag, use one bag per person otherwise you may as well be serving piss. Quickly he gave up trying. "Thank God he made it out to you okay, I was afraid he might have a concussion. You know he still might. Please make sure he gets checked."

Guy was at the window the moment MacLellan had informed them that Isadore was sitting out in the cop car. He had, according to the Mountie, driven directly from Alison's place to MacLellan's home, interrupting his dinner. Standing at the stove, Alison watched Guy move the curtain slightly aside. Over Guy's shoulder Alison could make out the shape of MacLellan's car, looming in the driveway like a large, crouched animal.

"Oh, he's fine," muttered MacLellan. "Got a head like a wrecking ball, that one."

"He's certainly indestructible," Alison agreed. "I imagine you heard about his famous sixty-foot drop?"

"What sixty-foot drop?" said Guy, turning.

"He never told you?" marvelled Alison.

"Maybe you can tell that story a bit later, as I do need to be getting along," MacLellan said. The cop spoke abruptly to Alison, barely sparing him a glance. It was a demeanour Alison recognized. He had been openly disliked by enough of the local populace to know when he was being openly disliked.

"You had some questions, you said, for Guy," smiled Alison, sitting down with his coffee.

"Yes," MacLellan agreed, turning to Guy. The Mountie cleared his throat, reminding Alison of a student about to give a presentation. "Now I just want to emphasize that this is not an official investigation by any stretch."

"I don't understand," Alison interrupted.

"I beg your pardon?"

"I don't understand what that means. If it's not an official investigation, then what exactly is it?"

MacLellan turned around in his chair. "Well, now—Mr. Mason, is it?"

"Al."

"Oh yes, I understand your name is Alison. Well, what I'm getting at, sir, is there's been a great deal of concern around town about this boy."

"Concern."

"Yes, about himself and his relationship with a young lady, a certain young girl who is the daughter of a very good friend of mine."

"Is that right?"

"Yes, it *is* right. Now Guy, what might you have to say on this front?"

"I'm sorry," Alison interrupted again. "Excuse me. But I think this is inappropriate."

MacLellan fingered his moustache. "What's that, now?"

"Guy tells me you've been to his school. You've been to his mother's place of business, is that correct?"

"Well, if by place of business, you're talking about Cameron MacAskill's place, then yes, I have."

"That's where she works," said Guy, by the window.

"And you're telling me Guy hasn't been charged with anything?"

"Well, not as such," said MacLellan, drawing himself up. "That is to say, not yet, however, unless we—"

"And as a matter of fact he's not even *officially* being investigated for anything?"

MacLellan stood and turned back to Guy. "Son, aren't you even interested to hear what this is about? Wouldn't you like to clear your name?"

Guy blinked at him. "Did Corinne say something about me?"

"Like what, for example?" prompted MacLellan.

"Wait a minute," said Alison.

"Goddammit, pardon my French, Mr. Mason, but if you

don't mind, here . . ." MacLellan trailed off and turned back to Guy, supposing, perhaps, that his aggressive tone would be enough to startle Alison into silence.

"Constable MacLellan," said Alison, "do your superiors know you're here?"

MacLellan folded his arms and turned slowly back to Alison. "Mr. Mason," he enunciated. "you're from . . . where exactly? You're not a local fella, now, are you?"

"I am from New York State," said Alison.

"Well, isn't that nice. I did some hunting down that way in 'sixty-four. And how long might you have been living in this part of the world, I wonder?"

"I'm wondering what your point is."

"Here is my point," said MacLellan. "I have known Fred Fortune my whole life. And I have known Isadore Aucoin my whole life and this is my community. I don't know what it is to you, but this is where I was born." MacLellan stood there. Apparently this was all there was to his point. Alison put his coffee down on the table and stood also.

"Be that as it may," he said, concentrating on the linoleum floor. "I am not from around here, that's true, and I'm no lawyer either, but it strikes me that what you've been doing, and what you're attempting to do now, is illegal. So I don't think I am going to let you harass this boy any further." He looked up from the linoleum and smiled apologetically.

"Harass," MacLellan repeated, flushing.

"This is nonsense," Alison added. "This is absolute *non-sense,*" he said.

The word had been uttered and sat in front of them as squat and banal as the coffeepot. MacLellan frowned like a sleepwalker, like Alison had just snapped his fingers in front of his eyes.

It had been like watching TV, Guy told Alison later. Watching a movie, *The Academy Performance* or something, and being totally engrossed. For Constable MacLellan, it must have been like having someone walk into the middle of the movie, look into the camera and say, *This is just made up, you know, it's not real.* It's something you know all along, but when someone points it out, when they say it out loud you could just kill them.

go

HE WANTS to have a bath. The apartment isn't particularly well heated and after sitting for a while in front of the television he realizes his fingers have gone numb, that the February weather has managed to work its way inside him. He could get a baseboard heater from the shed at his father's house, but his phone is not hooked up yet. He would have to go across the street to the convenience store to call but doesn't feel like it. It's his first night there and he wants it to himself. So he gets in bed for a while to read, but feels like an old woman tucked in there. It occurs to him to have a bath.

He didn't notice how dirty the bathtub was when he first moved in. The previous tenants pulled the shower curtain over instead of bothering to clean it, and it worked. There is Howard, stuck with other people's filth. So he cleans the bathtub first. He gets out a can of Comet and scrubs until he even gets rid of the rust and hard water stains. He cleans the tiles while he is at it and the bathroom floor. It takes him over an hour, during which time he hums tunelessly, continuously, like a television channel that has gone off the air once the national anthem has played. When everything is immaculate, he turns on the hot water tap and stands watching it until steam fills the air. Then he turns it off again and puts in the plug. Turns it back on. Lets it run. He wants it like boiling oil.

To immerse himself is agony little by little. The process takes a good deal of time. Perspiration blooms on his forehead, runs down the scar across his mouth in a little river. His heart chugs from the shock of heat. Once in all the way, he raises a leg out of the water and it's pink like a boiled hot dog, steam rising from the flesh.

He gets used to it, sweat rolling down his bare chest, catching in his hair, tickling. He rubs at it to make the sensation go away, reaching for soap, a razor. He shaves the hair away. He doesn't have a lot of it to begin with. His chest smooth and immaculate as the porcelain tub now. He stares at how pristine. Shaves his belly, shaves over the taut gully of his navel, shaves his pubic hair, as much as he comfortably can.

He would like to go on to his legs but they strike him as being endless. He leans forward and turns on the hot water tap for more. Soaks a washcloth, which he uses to cover his face for a few moments.

He's still humming, he realizes, like the TV left on, white noise. The cloth vibrates on his face.

Shaves his face with great care. The kind of precision which

would strike anyone who knew him as being wholly characteristic. Pure Howard, they might say. *That is Howard all over.*
Does his eyebrows.

If he was thinking, he would be thinking, *Clean,* running
the blade up his arms.

If he was thinking, he would be thinking, *Just not think a
little more.*

SAINT

"I AM THE ONLY one who is *normal* in this godforsaken family," Isadore orated to his sister. "I am the only sane man in this entire town. Everyone else is goddamn crazy in the head, with my father gone. You're cheating on welfare and that girl's well on her way to the same status, getting knocked up at her age, and that son of yours may as well toddle his arse on over to the police station and hold out his hands for the cuffs because Jesus Christ I've never seen the like, I've never seen such lawlessness in all my born days. God knows I have tried to instill some kind of morality in that boy, some sense of right and wrong, but it's a damn sight hard to do when his own mother is cheering him on in all his doings. You protect him like a crippled pup when Jesus Christ he's going around forcing himself on innocent girls, getting in fights, and now he's doing God knows what up on that hill with that *faggot* from the States! It is time to take responsibility, Marianne. You know I don't like telling you your business, but my good Jesus Lord, wouldn't you say things have gotten a little out of control?"

Marianne was curled up in the rocker from social services, remembering a dream she had where Big Saint Anne lifted her eyes from the living room carpet one day and started talking; stating ideas and opinions—making plans. In nonchalant tones, the statue told Marianne she had always been able to speak, but just hadn't bothered. Saint Anne said she was waiting— watching and waiting for the time to be right. Marianne remembers she had replied, *Thank goodness. It's about time somebody started talking some sense around here.* She had tried to smile and seem impressed and appreciative but in reality Marianne was annoyed at the saint for having kept her mouth shut all this time.

Things have gotten out of hand, Isadore continued, and there was no way Marianne could deny it, and if she was any kind of mother she would listen to him once and for all. He gestured with his empty bottle of spiced rum. Inside, it still smelled of Christmas—nutmeg and ginger and cloves. He paused to sniff at it from time to time, and his face went slack with nostalgia at those moments.

"Emile," said Isadore, looking around like someone else has said it. "What would Emile say to see us all like this?"

"He would ask you to talk to me," said Marianne. "And me to talk to Ma and Ma to talk to you. And then he'd go into the TV room and have a little sleep."

Marianne watched her brother with the eyes of Big Saint

Anne, with all the bottomless compassion of an embarrassed saint. She watched him take offense, get angry, lurch to his feet and pace. She watched him stand there speaking pointlessly about their father, almost chanting, as if trying to invoke him in the flesh. She watched him rage about her son and touch the cut above his eye, and she saw his bottom lip begin to tremble like a child's. She stopped watching, thinking: This is why the saints all look away from us in church, why they can never meet your eye. It's mortifying, to feel so much pity.

Ma, I won't come back, Guy had told her when he called—scarcely ten minutes before Isadore erupted through her door. I'm not trying to be tough, or an asshole or anything, Guy said. I'm just saying to you now because it's true. And sorry I took off like that. I won't come back with him there, though. I never will. I'll stay with Mr. Mason or I'll move back with Louise or something. But that's my decision.

Oh fine, Marianne had answered, keeping her voice low and trying to exert her old authority. Her nose was running, but she didn't sniff, because she didn't want Guy to hear it. So you're just making all the decisions for us now, are you?

No, said Guy.

Well, it sure sounds that way, mister.

But I haven't, Guy argued. I haven't decided for you, I've decided for me.

"Family," Isadore was saying, like he always seemed to be saying. "If you don't have family, what in hell do you got?"

You have to decide for yourself, Guy had said.

SPRING

the INEVITABLE HEAT
DEATH OF THE UNIVERSE

THEY ARE teenage girls, doing the kind of things that teenage
girls have done forever. They write the names of singers and
actors all over their scribblers. They draw hearts. They pass
notes in class when they are bored. This was once the two best
friends' most cherished form of communication, Pam's in particular, especially once they were in high school and she had
only Corrine's notes and afternoons to sustain her. What Pam
used to like best about the notes was the intimacy. That the
pretty girl could be passing notes to anyone, but it was Pam she
had chosen to spread her pearls before.

Sweet mother of fuck, I'm bored!
What's the mitochondria again?
Troy's been drinking Jaegermeister in the boys' locker room all
through lunch!

k really good these days, are you dieting?

, in biology where a teacher known as Sid Vicious because
his hair and his overbite is droning about the Inevitable Heat
Death of the Universe.

Pam replies, *I'm smoking.*

Corinne unfolds the note and drops her jaw like a cartoon
character.

That's not a healthy way to lose weight!

Pam drums the desk with the eraser side of her pencil for a
couple of seconds, thinking about a reply. The blankest, most
meaningless, most nonlethal thing she can say. This is her only
consideration these days: to do no harm. Not to be smart or
funny or request someone's attention or beg for love. Just to
keep her fat mouth shut and not make pain. Another note lands
in the opposite corner of her desk. It is from Ann. It is not
unusual to get notes from Ann; she ships them out regularly to
anyone she considers a sympathizer.

It says, *Sid's not doing this topic justice.*

Pam pays attention to Sid. She is able to do pretty much
anything she wants in class as she always sits at the back and
never causes shit and, let us not forget, is also invisible.

She thinks that it is good.

"Everybody knows the first law of thermodynamics, which is
that energy can neither be created nor destroyed, but not too
many people know about the second law of thermodynamics."

Ann's note says: *Nobody wants to know!*

"The second law states that in a closed system entropy r
Entropy means chaos. The ultimate closed system, of co
the universe."

Ann's note says: *The universe has cancer.*

"Entropy can only increase."

Another note comes flying from Corrine: *Oh my god look outside.*

But Sid is just getting to what he says are the two profound implications of the second law of thermodynamics.

Corinne gets to sit near the back with Pam, because Corinne is good. Corinne gets to sit where she wants. *She gets everything she wants, that one.* Pam meets her eyes and flashes back to their being four years old, conspiring to scream into Ann's ear. Pam's best friend from childhood has thick eyebrows, pointy in the middle, shaped liked arrows or steeples. They were that thick even when they were children, which gave little Corinne a slightly monstrous appearance. Pam can remember Corinne attempting to shave them off when they were both eight, lathering up her forehead with Mennen shaving foam, moments before her mother came in and shrieked. But Corinne has grown into her eyebrows and now reminds everybody of the model Brooke Shields. She points them towards heaven now, and cuts her pale eyes at the window.

on the ground, Pam sees boys. Troy, a couple of ⬚ificoes from the play, and Ricky Estabrooks wear- ⬚ylock hat. It's like an impromptu, belated cast party.

⬚, that the universe will eventually die, wallowing in its ⬚n entropy—the heat death of the universe. Two, the universe ⬚annot have existed forever, or it would have reached its equilibrium end state an infinite time ago."

The boys are all probably drunk, but Ricky is the only one who really looks it. He looks like Charlie Chaplin, some kind of caricature, staggering in circles. Troy is doubled up and the mouths of the other boys are calling things, opening and closing.

"To put it another way: Just as the universe did not always exist, the universe will not always exist."

Take heart is the message that follows from Ann.

Ricky crashes into Troy, and ricochets face first into the school wall.

When he rebounds, it's like his face exploded. Pam can see Corinne's conscience get the better of her. Her guilty hand shoots into the air, signals to the stage manager.

Curtain, please. Bring it down.

ENOUGH

DAN C. ISN'T all that bad a guy. It's weird when I remember how sure I was he must be an asshole, without even having met him. I didn't even think it—I just felt it had to be a fact of life. My mother thought so too—she's still not convinced otherwise. She came when they invited us to dinner and announced she had only shown up to see me, managing to make us all feel bad at once. I got mad and told her she could see me all she wanted if she'd get a restraining order like Al said. That's when she cried and got Louise to drive her back to the apartment where Isadore was no doubt waiting to take her money and break her things and tell her how terrible a mother and sister and person she was.

I think both of us went home that night feeling guilty and crappy and blaming poor old Dan C. for the whole situation. He'd scarcely said a word the entire meal—just sat there blinking as we barked at each other, eating his food as fast as he possibly could.

nce the weather got nice, I started dropping by the
gain to plan out my home gym and he came out one
oon to see what I was up to. He said he'd been wonder-
what the duffel bag was doing in the corner all winter long.
e said he was afraid to look inside, he thought it might be a
oody. So I told him about me and Rene almost getting killed
when the roof caved in, and he laughed at us for yanking on the
old beam like that. He laughed at me, but not the way I'm used
to people laughing at me.

And then Dan C. totally got into the whole gym thing. I told
him about my idea for putting a new beam across the frame, and
he said he had a friend who worked at the sawmill and was getting free lumber for his buddies all the time. His "booh-dies,"
Dan C. pronounces it.

"Me booh-dy could probably get us enough to put on a
whole new roof," he told me.

I told him I wouldn't know how to build a roof, and Dan C.
said, "It's easy." And then he goes, "You know what would be
easier, d'ough?"—he's got a pretty thick accent. He also goes
around talking Gaelic all the time. He says *Eayus* instead of *Jesus*
when he curses. Isadore would lose his mind around Dan C.

"What would be easier?" I asked.

"Knockin the whole damn ting to the grount."

I looked at the shed and felt sorry for it. For one very short
moment.

"Then where would I work out?"

"*Eayus* God," goes Dan C. "We'd build you a better place
den dat!"

At first I thought he must be full of shit, b
went into the house and I had supper with him ar
and realized there was something wrong with the kit.
felt crowded, somehow. I looked around and coul
Louise smiling at me. Finally I figured it out—there were r
cupboards all along the wall coming in from the porch.
went over to check them out. On the outside, they smelled of
fresh white paint, but inside was the smell of trees. Lumber
so fresh, it might have been cut the day before. I stuck my
head inside and breathed.

Louise was saying, "Go look out back! Dan C.'s building a
patio this summer."

The smell made me think of her. The pulp trucks interrupting us that day I skipped off school to see her, their smell
of gas and sap. It seemed like every time I opened my mouth to
speak to her, a truck would belch at us from the highway.

I don't believe in signs, but maybe that was a sign. Al and
I have talked about this—I told him about the shed caving in
last spring, how perversely happy it made me feel. Al said he
believed it, that he believed in signs and maybe this was one. I
said, surprised, "So you believe in God?"

And he leaned back and answered, "Not necessarily."

And then we were off on one of our big philosophy talks.
I'm a brainiac these days. I've only been back at my old school
a couple of months and I'm already practically caught up. It
helps when you're living in the same house as your teacher. Al
convinced them to forget about midterm exams and just grade
me on the work I do this semester, but I still might have to go to

.ool. Al says there are worse things than summer employment, for example.

...ow we sit around talking philosophy after school. I go, ...v can you believe in signs, and not believe in God? Who's posed to be giving you the sign, then? The devil?"

And he goes, "Aren't there any other choices?"

Sometimes I find I have to lay down the law with Alison Mason, otherwise he'll set sail upon this unending ocean of bullshit, and just when you think he's getting to the point, you realize there actually isn't any point at all and he's just enjoying listening to himself. So I said, "No. Of course there aren't any other choices. What, you think it's like your fairy godmother or something?"

And Al, wiseass that he is, goes, "You talk as if the idea of a fairy godmother is ridiculous, while the idea of a fellow in red pyjamas with pointy horns and a pitchfork makes perfect sense."

"Answer," I said. "Do you believe in God or not? Yes or no?"

"You always want straight answers," he told me, stalling. "Straight means simple. And you know what simple means?"

"Yes," I said. "Retarded."

He looked surprised, and then started to laugh. He thinks it's funny, the way I call everything retarded. Whenever I mention "that retarded-guy book," he cracks up, but in a scandalized sort of way.

I couldn't help it, I was trying to be serious, but I started to laugh with him.

"I'd like a retarded answer, please," I said. "Yes or no."

"Then the retarded answer is no," he told me.

I sat there in one of Al's dusty armchairs, fee.
for a while.

"Do you see why that isn't enough?" he said.

I don't think I was ever in love with her or anything.

It was just that one great night I couldn't let go of, wi
we danced so many times and she didn't know who I was an
she said that I wasn't from around there like it was the best
thing a person could be. I couldn't get it out of my head. I never
wanted it out of my head.

aCKNOWLEDGEMENTS

FIRST, I should thank my family, and not just for all the usual reasons.

In particular I need to thank Britt Coady for acting as technical adviser on matters of boxing and small-town hockey leagues; my mother, Phyllis, for her knowledge of the Nova Scotia judicial system; and my father, James, for never failing to fire my imagination with his superior gift for storytelling.

Thanks to the good friends who let me borrow their homes to write in: Peter Tucker, Sara and Daniel O'Leary, Kim Goodliffe and Tim Carlson. Oh, I didn't forget.

A long overdue thank you to my tireless agent, Denise Bukowski. And thanks to everyone at Doubleday Canada for your faith and support these past few years. Thanks, especially, to Maya Mavjee.

God bless and keep the Canada Council for the Arts and

enter for the Arts. Also Heidi Pitlor, steadfast editor, you so much for everything.

nks to Elle Osborne for "Katy Cruel."

nanks to Christy Ann Conlin for reassurances about title, and so much else.

Thanks always to Charles Barbour.

NOTE: I have messed with Nova Scotia geography and land-marks. For example, there is a shrine to Saint Anne in Nova Scotia, but this shrine is not in Port Hull. There is no such place as Port Hull, that I know of. There is also no such place as Big Harbour, not as I've conceived of it. There do exist, however, such places as Monastery, Port Hastings, Louisdale, and Auld Cove. But not Donnell Cove. I've done this, and point it out, mainly so that no one can accuse me of getting my facts wrong. This is not a work of fact, but fiction. Any facts I might have gotten right I put down to pure luck.

LYNN COADY